Also by Jeremy Leven

CREATOR

SATAN
HIS PSYCHOTHERAPY
AND CURE BY THE UNFORTUNATE
DR. SEYMOUR KASSLER, J. S. P. S.

The Savior

AND
THE SINGING
MACHINE

The Savior

AND THE SINGING MACHINE

JEREMY LEVEN

iCREATOR PRESS · NEW YORK · 2019

The Savior And The Singing Machine
All Rights Reserved. © 2018 by Jeremy Leven

For more information or to book an event, please contact the iCreator Press Speakers Buerau at 1-212-496-8918 or visit our website at www.icreatorpress.com

No part of this book may be reproduced or transmitted in any form or by any means, graphic, electronic, or mechanical, incuding photocopying, recording, taping, or by any information storage or retreival system, without the permision in writing from the publisher.

This book is work of fiction. Any reference to historical events, real people, or real places are used fictitiously. Other names, characters, places, and events are products of the author's imagination, and any resemblance to actual events or places or persons, living or dead, is entirely coincidental.

No patent liability is assumed with respect to the use of the information contained herein. Although every precaution has been taken in the preparation of this book, the publisher and author assume no responsibility for errors or omissions. Neither is any liability assumed for damages resulting from the use of the information contained herein.

Cover design by Nena Miller
Published by iCreator Press

An imprint of Creator II LLC Publishing Division
151 West 86th Street, Suite 3D, New York, New York 10024

CIP data for this book is available from the Library of Congress.

ISBN: 978-0-9600353-2-8

ISBN: 978-0-9600353-0-4 (eBook)

For
Roberta Danza

This book is dedicated to
those who love and who believe.

"Faith is the assurance of things hoped for, the conviction of things not seen."
Hebrews 11:1

PART I

Pincus's God

CHAPTER 1

In the beginning was an ache — a deep-seated incurable ache that filled Max Pincus's bones with a pain so dreadful that Pincus thought he would never survive it. And the ache was with God — although the Almighty must have been confused in a most terrible way about how exactly Pincus's primal longing had been raised to such a spiritual level. And the ache was one single all-encompassing ache that incorporated all aches born of this earth and all realms beyond.

For Pincus, this ache required no simple remedy, for, among the large stock pot of items stewing in his brain, he saw the cure as an answer to all the mysteries of the cosmos, a salve for all ailments, an inoculation against all possible misfortune, the redemption of his soul, and the possibility of life everlasting in, what Pincus now called, "a better place." It would establish universal peace and harmony. It was a prayer to God. What Pincus's ache boiled down to was this.

Max Pincus wanted a woman so badly he thought he would die.

For Pincus, there was nothing sexual about the dull pain that throbbed in his bones. This female who filled every waking moment, every dream, was a specter — her face shown, but it had no features, and her being was a confabulation of every romantic moment Pincus had experienced or desired. It was a winter night he had spent with a college classmate, her hips swinging back and forth under his hand as they walked through the matted snow, her dark hair brushing his coat and his cheek, their arms around each other, caught in the web of youth. They kissed, their eyes ablaze, burning through the cold with possibilities.

It was a summer evening on the back porch with the elementary school teacher who had taken her first job in his town, rocking, her head resting against his, her legs spread on each side of him as she rode up and down until, at the moment of release, Pincus thought how good it felt to be alive and wondered whether life could ever be better than this.

And, then it was gone.

One night Pincus woke up and wanted to cry. His heart ached, and he prayed it would burst. His wife slept beside him, his two children in the next room, and Pincus knew for certain that he would never again feel the lightheaded delirium of being in love. That day he had celebrated his fiftieth birthday.

The next morning, a fine sunny morning at the very beginning of 1980, he stood in front of his bathroom mirror, shaving, and thinking that Eisenhower might not have been such a bad president after all. Adlai Stevenson had been the right thing to do. And, as a twelve year old rumbling through puberty much like a tank at Prokhorovka, Pincus had labored for Stevenson with a great sense of purpose, handing out leaflets to whomever would take them, not too young to be unaware that the destiny of his nation depended entirely on Adlai Stevenson becoming the next president.

Secretly, however, Pincus now, for the first time, admitted to himself that, deep in his heart, he envied those fellow twelve-year-old classmates with the pure uncluttered Weltanschauung to like Ike. And, it was this slogan, "I Like Ike," that had driven poor pubertal Pincus nearly crazy. Everywhere he looked, seventh graders walked through the halls of Thomas Jefferson Junior High with huge red, white, and blue buttons proclaiming "I Like Ike," and Pincus ate his heart out. Puberty and Adlai Stevenson both at the same time seemed terribly unfair.

Pincus had taken the inevitable defeat personally. It was as he suspected all along. Intelligence, vision, the ability to be articulate, would always come in last – to absolutely everything else. Pincus decided at this early point in his life that this provided clear evidence that he, himself, was doomed.

Now, here he was on the fateful morning that would forever alter his life, knotting his necktie with visions in his head of Richard Nixon, Gerald Ford, Jimmy Carter, and the inevitable soon-to-be new occupant of the White House, Ronald Reagan, and suddenly Pincus felt a great fondness for General Dwight David Eisenhower.

There had been, Pincus decided, something ultimately comforting about picking up *The New York Times* and finding on the front page a photograph of the Commander-in-Chief in golf cap and cardigan, teeing off next to Bob Hope, while Joe McCarthy crushed communism and the Communists crushed Hungary. Whatever else might transpire, American Life would prevail.

And so, as he slipped on his suit jacket at the age of fifty and looked in the mirror to confirm that everything was in its proper place, Pincus felt a great sense of liberation.

He should not have worked for Adlai Stevenson. That was a mistake. He had been innocently seduced by intelligence, sound ideas, and the well-spoken word.

Nor should he have gone to medical school. He should have been a poet or an artist.

He should never have had children, however much he loved them and no matter how untempered the joy was that he had found from them. They had made his life hell — bright, clever, amusing, well-liked, the envy of everyone who knew them, most of all, himself.

Then there was the matter of Becki, the suntanned coed he had married at the end of college. It was all clear to him now. Becki was to compensate for Eisenhower. He should have married for love.

And so, having now worked it all out in his head, Pincus adjusted. As a physician, he was no stranger to seeing people live with pain. Mind over matter. The value, he realized, of having a brain as well-developed as his was that it could explain away just about anything. Love, Pincus convinced himself, bore the same resemblance to marriage as hamburger did to a chateaubriand.

His wife, the former Becki Stone-Thomas and now Becki Stone-Thomas-Pincus — a conjunction of names that made Pincus feel that he had approached the altar with a relatively appealing young woman and walked away with a brokerage house — did not take long to grow weary of Pincus's chopped steak metaphor. It was not just being compared to a cow, or even ground meat, that bothered Pincus's wife. It was the accommodation that it implied.

"But I love hamburger!" Pincus would chase after her. "It's one of my favorite foods! You can't live on chateaubriand!"

"Go fuck yourself," Becki Stone-Thomas-Pincus would explain.

And yet, by the end of the day, or the week, or, on occasion, the month, they would make love with that passion born of the hope of renewal and change.

"Now isn't that better?" Pincus would say following their lovemaking.

"Much," Becki would respond.

And for just a moment, there in the dark, with the children asleep, with the katydids creaking out their song in the night, with his fingers laced in hers — they believed they were happy.

It was momentary. Their lives consisted always of what had been and what might be, but the present never seemed to exist. Time stopped the day they married.

For Pincus, a new time began. He soon convinced himself that because they seemed to enjoy each other's company well enough and had not divorced — claims that very few of their friends could make — *ceteris paribus*, he must be happily married.

Pincus took a certain pride in announcing this revelation whenever the opportunity presented itself.

"As a man who has been happily married for nearly twenty years …" Pincus liked to begin sentences to weeping colleagues sharing with him the details of their divorces, to his Sexually Transmitted Disease patients, and especially to the nubile young women students in loose skirts and tight blouses, who would sit across from him to interview for lab assistant jobs, the white crotches of their panties flashing briefly in the sunlight as they crossed and uncrossed their legs. "Yes, indeed, a happily married man...." It was reassuring to Pincus.

Then something happened.

Pincus was listening to his car radio on the way home from his lab and office at the University Medical School, when the disc jockey asked listeners to participate in a phone survey. The question was this:

"If you had it to do all over, would you marry your present spouse?"

It hit Pincus like a lightning bolt. For a reason he could not fathom, the question had never occurred to him — that there was a choice. That it could have been different. And this made him inconsolably depressed, not because it could have been different, or even that it could *not* have been different, but because he didn't know.

"Maybe this is it," he ruminated. Maybe Becki Stone-Thomas may be as good an alternative under the circumstances as any other, because, in the long run, this was all there was. He just didn't know.

Love, true love, real deep love, could, in the end, just be a fleeting aberration of adolescence. It was a dreadful thought. And for the first time, Pincus felt the ache.

It started in his gut and encircled his heart. It shot out fibers that hooked up with his brain. It sent collaterals down the inside of his bones and wound around his muscles, until the ache was so all-encompassing that small tears worked their way into Pincus's eyes as he fought off the pain.

For all of Pincus's life there had been a possibility. Somewhere there was love, eternal and pure, capable of making life totally worthwhile — not for him, but at least for some other lucky sonofabitch. And now there was the possibility that there was nothing. Could God really have done such a thing?

As tears welled in his eyes and the ache filled his body, Pincus knew that he could not live with this uncertainty. Nothing else mattered. He must find out.

He pulled the car over to the curb and took his briefcase out of the back seat. Then as a gesture of good faith, as a first step toward removing all worldly goods that might distract him from his pursuit and cloud his view, he gave the keys to his Mercedes to the first passer-by, a young man with a single gold hoop in his left ear, wished him well, and walked off to begin his search for perfect love.

CHAPTER 2

"You did what?" Becki Stone-Thomas-Pincus looked up from the sink where she was peeling onions under a tap of running water. She studied Pincus, who was sitting at the kitchen table, shoes off, feet resting on the table, drinking a beer.

"Faith comes from revelation. But revelation comes only to those who are prepared for it," Pincus took another long drink of his beer.

"You gave away our Mercedes?" Becki Stone-Thomas-Pincus asked, as she walked over and slid her husband's stockinged feet off the kitchen table, then went back to her onion.

"It was a worldly good that I felt would corrupt me on the path I am taking to revelation. It was also registered in my name."

Becki Stone-Thomas-Pincus turned from the sink and looked into her husband's vacant eyes.

"It was community property," she announced calmly, "and why are you drinking beer, Max? You don't drink beer."

"It's a grain. I am making a dietary transition to grains and grain derivatives. I must prepare my body to receive the light of perfection."

"Max, please, go get the Mercedes back," Becki tried a logical approach. "We paid a lot of money for that car. We're *still* paying a lot of money for that car. Be reasonable."

"I am following a greater authority. Authority demands of us faith and prepares us for reason. Reason, in turn, leads to perception and cognition. The Mercedes is inconsequential — *credo ut intelligam*."

"Forty-four thousand eight hundred dollars is not inconsequential!" Becki shouted, but, already a sudden pang of sympathy for this deranged man was striking at her. She sensed in her heart what was happening to poor Pincus, although she had no name for it, and she sat down on a white wooden kitchen chair across the table from her husband, and took a deep breath to calm her nerves.

"We need to talk, Max, dear," Becki said with all the compassion she could muster.

"I agree," said Pincus, popping the top from another bottle of beer. "I feel a need for absolute candor."

"Perhaps, this isn't a good time for anything absolute," Becki said patiently.

Pincus thought about this as he sucked the rim of the bottle in his hand.

"I have always felt that women are inferior to men," Pincus bared his soul.

"Please, Max."

"No, really," Pincus revealed the innermost workings of his psyche to his spouse. "I've never expressed it to you before, but there's nothing I can think of that a man isn't better at."

Becki studied Pincus's eyes. They were pools of sincerity.

"I've tried to say supportive things about your work over the years," Pincus continued, "but the truth is, Becki, that you've been doing half as good a job as a man might do in the same position. My heart has never been in it. It's all been a charade. Women are basically nest-builders. That's where they belong — in the nest."

Becki's eyes were slowly narrowing into two tiny epicanthic slits. She felt the compassion draining from her body as she saw the Max Pincus she had always suspected lurked beneath the layers of intensive indoctrination in the liberation of the sexes.

"You're a great cook," Pincus went on. "You're extremely nurturing to the children. The house always looks terrific."

"And sex?" Becki asked, but it was not a romantic inquiry.

"Exactly. Considering the limited nature of the female sex drive, you can be extremely sexy at times. But you need the time to take care of yourself."

Becki Stone-Thomas-Pincus looked at Pincus guzzling his beer in a state of total bliss and thought very hard, but not particularly long, before she responded.

"I would like a divorce, Max," she said.

"I can understand that," Max answered from the small private space he occupied on this planet where gravity no longer existed.

CHAPTER 3

Mrs. Burkhardt looked up at her fifty-year-old physician. She was in a state of shock.

"What do you mean, you don't know?" she asked in horror.

"Just what I said," Pincus answered calmly. "Your pains could be nothing at all. Or ... this could be the end. I run the tests, I examine as carefully as I can, but who really knows?..." Pincus shrugged his shoulders.

"I thought *you* would," said Mrs. Burkhardt. "Or at least someone with medical training ..."

"You'd think that, wouldn't you," Pincus agreed. "Doctors ..."

Mrs. Burkhardt looked at Pincus strangely and started to back slowly across the room.

"Doctors always think they have the right answers." Pincus went on. "Three-quarters of them I wouldn't let treat my dog, and the other quarter are so caught up in medical minutia, they over-treat you to death." But Pincus's mind wasn't really on what he was saying anymore. He was thinking about how easy it had been to leave Becki. Had the last twenty-six years ever existed, he wondered, and, if they had, what had been their purpose? Truth, revelation, certainty — what difficult things these were to attain in a world filled with marriages and a Mercedes.

Mrs. Burkhardt reached behind for her brassiere, keeping her eyes glued on Pincus.

"Mrs. Burkhardt, I feel I owe it to you — I feel I owe it to myself — to tell you how little I actually know."

"Don't do me any favors," Mrs. Burkhardt offered, but Pincus wasn't paying attention. With every word he spoke, Pincus could feel the fetters of his life loosening, falling to the ground, and dissolving to nothing. He felt as though he could float to the ceiling like a smiling rabbi in a Chagall painting.

"Someday you will need help, you sonofabitch," she said, resolutely snapping her brassiere to emphasize the great weight of her words, "and you will get crap, that's what you will get — pure, useless crap. And then you will see how it feels," and Mrs. Burkhardt stepped into her panties with such vigor that her foot caught in the leg-hole with a loud ripping sound, totally destroying the garment.

Mrs. Burkhardt looked down in dismay at the rag in her hands, and then over at Pincus, who was sailing lightly over a blue Chagall moon.

CHAPTER 4

Pincus's two offspring, Phillip, age nineteen, and Anne, age eighteen, sat in chairs in their father's office, waiting patiently for him to announce the reason they were there. Their summer break from college had just begun, and they were already tanned, most likely from standing at outdoor ceremonies, receiving the usual array of awards they seemed to garner wherever they went, Pincus concluded as he studied them.

As previously noted, Pincus's children tended to make him a little crazy. In addition to being good-looking, clever, amusing, loving, and well-liked, they had both worked for the election of Ronald Reagan, and Pincus suspected that this might have been a major determining factor in why Ronald Reagan was soon to be his next president. All these thoughts swept through Pincus's already overburdened brain as he regarded his offspring.

"I have summoned you here today," Pincus began in a manner reminiscent of King Lear, "to provide you with instructions before I depart."

"Where're you going, Dad?" Anne asked politely.

"It's not clear," Pincus answered.

"Well," Phillip offered, "I'm sure that wherever it is, this must be very important to you."

"And whatever you need ..." Anne smiled helpfully.

The generous support from his children was making Pincus nauseated.

"Your mother is okay?" he asked with concern.

"Oh, yes," Anne replied. "She's great."

"Great?" Pincus cleared his throat.

"I mean — considering ..." Anne hurried to soften the blow.

"I think we've all understood how difficult things have been for you —" Phillip spoke to his father, " — how hard a time you've had — fitting in...."

"You have?... I have?..." Pincus's voice broke slightly.

"From a 'comfortable' standpoint," Anne explained.

"Fitting into what?..."

"Well, kind of like — the family...." Anne answered.

"My family?... I've had trouble fitting into my own family..." Pincus was having difficulty dealing with the concept.

"Maybe 'fitting in' isn't expressing it well," and Anne looked over at Phillip for help.

"Comfort," Phillip returned to his original formulation. "But it's really not important. We've always felt that you went out of your way to become a part of us."

"What 'us'? I'm not 'us'? Who's 'us'?" Pincus jerked his head back and forth between his son and his daughter.

"Anne, me, and Mom," Phillip answered straight-forwardly. "I mean, there's no question that you've been doing your damnedest."

"No question," Anne seconded. "Absolutely none."

"Shit," Pincus commented.

"What was it you wanted to instruct us in?" Anne asked sweetly.

"I'm not sure anymore," Pincus mumbled.

"Life?..." Phillip offered. He hated to see his father so disappointed.

"Termites," Pincus said with an intensity his children had never seen before. "Termites!" Pincus banged his fist on the desk.

"They can spray —" Anne smiled reassuringly.

"Like termites gnawing away at the foundation of a house," Pincus said, "things, little things, tiny little things, undermine your life. Oh, your visions are so grand — grand, grand visions — turned to sawdust by — everything...."

Anne and Phillip sneaked glances at each other from the corners of their eyes, being careful to keep their heads stationary, riveted on their father.

"Love ... Is there love? Do you think there is love?" Pincus turned to a new subject.

Anne and Phillip felt a need to exercise caution.

"I think ... there *could* be...." Anne said carefully.

Pincus thought this over. Then he spoke to his children with a burning intensity.

"How? With all the damn termites?! Can you be in love on the way to the dry cleaners? What about when they destroy your best suit? Or you need a new carburetor — the third one in a year? Fever blisters? Clogged gutters? Telephone solicitors calling in the middle of the night?" Pincus squinted his eyes and let fly with a hiss and growl. "A Mercedes...."

Anne and Phillip stared at their father with a mixture of sadness and concern. The room was still. Pincus looked at his two offspring. His heart filled with a fondness for them that spilled over into his eyes, moistening them.

"I have a mission I must undertake," he told his children quietly. "I must search for a love so pure that the termites will not dare nibble at it — and life, and life —" and now Pincus's eyes filled so with tears that the two children he loved were only hazy pools fixed ahead of his vision like a distant mirage, " — a love so pure that life will cherish it."

And seeing Pincus so distraught, Anne and Phillip walked over and put their arms around their father, even though they had not the foggiest notion what he was talking about.

CHAPTER 5

For what seemed like many years now, although in fact it had been less than ten, Pincus had been conducting research in his laboratory at the medical school on the human brain. He had arrived at what he considered to be his *Three Significant Findings*. They broke down something like this:

Significant Finding Number One. Human beings have not one, but three distinct brains. The First Brain comprises the upper spinal cord, parts of the midbrain, diencephalon, and basal ganglia. He named this brain "The Pagan Brain." According to Pincus, it spent most of its time eating and having sexual intercourse.

The Second Brain comprised mainly the hippocampus, septal nuclei, mammillary bodies, fornix, and gyrus cingulum. Meaning no offense, Pincus named this "The Jewish Brain." It devoted itself to guilt and pain, joy and misery, laughing and weeping.

The Third Brain was comprised entirely of neo-cortex. It spent its time trying to determine what the other two brains were up to and attempting to control their lustful and comical activities. Pincus named this "The Christian Brain."

Significant Finding Number Two. The development of the human brain over one's lifetime is nothing more than the so-called *higher* centers inhibiting the so-called *lower* centers. Thus, the need for the powerful engines of lust and delight in order to keep intercourse and laughter alive or the brain would reach a state of total impotence.

Significant Finding Number Three. The most important structure in the human brain is the cerebellum, which Pincus described as a sensory-motor map of hell, projecting an iron-walled grid over what to do and feel to make certain that we stay on course. Unfortunately, Pincus claimed, it also restricts us to this grid, and so we are forever locked out from what lies beyond.

And Pincus postulated that, if we were ever to free ourselves from this anatomical prison, we would find worlds out there beyond our wildest dreams. More to the point, it was Pincus's contention that it was only by escaping the cerebellum that one could finally find God.

Those trained in the neurosciences, to whom Pincus was not at all shy about presenting his *Three Significant Findings*, raised what seemed to them to be the reasonable question of how exactly Pincus could, in the pursuit of God, or anyone or anything else for that matter, go out of his mind?

Pincus had an answer for this.

It was Pincus's position that each of us has, in fact, two distinct minds at work. We dream and are aware we are dreaming. We notice as we fall asleep that we are falling asleep, that we are passing from one state of consciousness to another, that we are both the sleeper and the spectator observing the sleeper going to sleep — two minds at work.

Pincus was convinced that there is a self, a consciousness, that exists independently of our bifold-brain and transcends it. And, if it exists without our brain, then it must exist without our body.

And it is here that Pincus made his great leap. This consciousness that exists without our brain is, Pincus claimed, our soul and, since it does not require a body, therefore lives forever. It is, in fact, immortal. And this could only mean one of two things to Pincus — either God exists, or *we* are God.

Of course, those who had the privilege of hearing Pincus's postulations had no little difficulty sorting all this into a coherent theory, especially how the initial three-brain Pagan-Jewish-Christian formulation had now been reduced to two brains, one of which might not actually exist as a brain at all, but as the soul. Pincus's response to this was what might be called, if one were to be kind about it, an endless loop. Pincus would explain once more from the beginning his *Three Significant Findings,* concluding with two brains, one being a transcendent entity observing the other and floating free, finally, into the heavens, wherein it would encounter God, if it was not God, itself. And so, those in the field of neuroscience soon learned not to ask for any further clarification.

In fact, for Pincus his transcendent brain was the road to nirvana. In fact, his colleagues had reached the conclusion that Pincus's transcendent brain had found the well-traveled path to schizophrenia.

Pincus was aware of the diagnosis, but he was not one easily to give up his beliefs. Pincus was searching for the escape hatch to — for lack of a better word — God. He believed it was somewhere around the thalamus.

For Pincus, it all made a strange kind of sense. The search for perfect love must also be the search for God, since, God is love — and both must be a function of his brain, that brain which was not his brain, the other brain which tended to drift off and observe his thinking, a higher brain that was striving to free itself from his mind and body and transport him — where? Pincus didn't know. But he was going to find out.

With this sort of formulation percolating in one or another of Pincus's brains, Pincus vowed to demonstrate to his esteemed colleagues that all but he were heading in the wrong direction.

"We're not exactly sure why," Norris Knowles spoke for the assembly of researchers sitting around the conference table staring at Pincus, "you chose as your conclusion the one experimental result that differed from several hundred other identical ones."

"You want to know why I chose the exception?" Pincus asked with an edge of defiance.

"That's it exactly," Knowles nodded.

"Because it happened," Pincus stated directly.

The dozen men and two women seated around the table moved

uncomfortably in their chairs, as though they were one long, multi-headed, serpent.

"But," Knowles continued to act as spokesperson for the group, "all the other results happened, too. And they all happened the same way. Every one of them was approximately minus 6.2. Doesn't it seem to you that the one result of plus 844.3 might be an anomaly?"

"No," Pincus answered. "It doesn't."

"Perhaps," Alice Beckerman suggested, "if you were to repeat the experiment and replicate the results?..."

"I might never get that result again," Pincus said.

"That's kind of our point," Knowles explained patiently.

Pincus looked around him at the serpent, heads fixed on him, patiently waiting to strike.

"Numbers," Pincus told the leviathan. "Is that what Truth is to you — numbers? If I can show you one man who can fly one time just by flapping his arms up and down, would you say that we can fly? Well, would you?..."

"You know someone who can fly by flapping his arms up and down?" Knowles asked with more than a passing interest.

"Suppose I could show you someone living without a heart or a brain or lungs, what would you say then?" Pincus asked confidently.

"Living well?" Knowles was trying to sort it all out.

"Married, kids, an active sex life, runs the marathon, an authority on Boolean algebra — just happens not to have a heart, lungs, or a brain," Pincus smiled smugly at Knowles, feeling he really had the man now.

"I guess I'd find it hard to believe."

"Yes, but would it be true? What about God? If I have seen God just once, then I can say He exists, don't you agree?" Pincus pressed on.

"You've seen God?" another head queried.

"Not me," Pincus answered.

"The man who runs the marathon with no insides?" asked another head.

"True Science," Pincus explained to the increasingly restless serpent, "is not what we think. Oh, no. Reason, logic — they're worthless. Our emotions must tell us which reasons are of value. Am I right or am I right? That's why I selected the exception. I liked it. It was fun. The other results were boring, unappealing, and, frankly, extremely repetitive. Ah, but this result — it wasn't even on the scale. It was absolutely extraordinary."

Heads bobbing, body swaying, slithering upon itself as one head consulted another, the serpent danced dangerously in front of Pincus.

"From now on," Pincus announced, "I suggest that we throw out logic! I know *I* am. Toss scientific method to the dogs! Pay no attention to levels of significance, probability, and correlations — who needs them anyway! Defy reason!"

The serpent focused silently, speculatively, on Pincus when he finished his plea.

"I wonder," Knowles hissed, his tongue licking at his lips, "if you could excuse us for just a few moments, Max?..."

And so it was decided that a man such a Pincus who did not especially believe in reason should probably not be doing brain research. At least at that particular medical school.

CHAPTER 6

All in all, the previous year, 1979, had not been a great year. The Shah of Iran had been overthrown and the Ayatollah Khomeini had appeared on the scene, making his mark not long after he arrived by taking 52 members of the U.S. Embassy as hostages. Saddam Hussein became president of Iraq. Soviet forces invaded Afghanistan. Closer to home, Three Mile Island had one of those bothersome nuclear meltdowns in Pennsylvania; the Skylab space station fell from the sky, scattering its parts across the Indian Ocean to Australia.

On a more personal front, when 1979 came to a fortunate end and 1980 commenced, Pincus was, for all intents and purposes, totally unaware of what was happening inside his own brain. He knew he was divorcing a woman for whom he had always had great respect and an abiding fondness. There was something faintly mysterious about this. He knew, as well, that he would soon be terminating his medical practice, and, of course, that he was a matter of hours from leaving his position at the medical school. He had, however, not a clue why all this was happening.

"My God, what have I done?" Pincus asked himself, standing by his lab bench at the medical school, filling culture dishes with a particular enzyme. But what might have been a rhetorical question became a tabulation.

"I have left my wife, or at least arranged a convenient parting. I have estranged my children, if they were ever more than strangers to me. I have ..." Pincus trailed off as a vision, a voice, specifically the voice of the Friar John Tauler, seeped into his brain, spreading over all other thoughts like a pink cloud.

Tauler told Pincus, "The well of life is love, and he who dwelleth not in love is dead."

Pincus could not have agreed more. He longed for a love, but not any love, a love at once so grand, so magnificent, so pure and transcendent, that it would suffuse him with a vitality that would awaken his spirit and transport him, body and soul, to the paradise of life fully realized.

Pincus knew this for certain: there was something to know and love that was more durable and greater than anything provided by the illusions of sense, that there was something else, some final satisfaction beyond the useless stream of sensation that bombarded his consciousness. He knew now that science did not hold the key to his sensory freedom. For that liberation, it was not enough to arouse his mind. His entire vitality must be aroused. Passion alone would suffice.

Pincus was convinced that it is the lover and the poet who, for just a moment, frees us from the earth and lifts the veil of Isis that science handles so ineptly, leaving only its dirty fingermarks behind. Pincus had no doubt in what remained of his mind that science was an illusion and all materialists would eventually be damned to hell.

What Pincus had learned, although it would be some time before he would become aware of it, was that man is his most magnificent when he sees in nature something beyond the phenomena and in himself something that transcends death. It was for this reason that Pincus had come to suspend all "natural" laws (along with his medical practice and his profession, which pretty much depended on them), setting aside the notion once and for all that science was real and religion, the soul, and God were not.

Pincus had decided to merge all his senses into the one sense, the only sense, that would apprehend all life and the universe and make final sense of it — love.

Pincus saw this love that awaited him as clear as day.

"I am all you have ever dreamed," she said to him. "You are everything I want."

A smile began on Pincus's lips as he continued to squirt small beads of enzyme from his pipette during his very last day in his laboratory. He imagined making love to the voice. His smile grew.

He looked down at the slices of brain material in dishes around him and imagined another day. He reached for a nearby pad and removed a pen from his lab coat.

This is what Pincus wrote:

"On that day, I will have grasped the single intuition given only to St. Thomas's angels, the entire workings of the mind. More than that," Pincus wrote slowly, forming each letter as perfectly as he could, "I will have been transported beyond my own neuroanatomy into another realm. I will be with the angels. I will be with God. I will have seen what lies on the other side of the molecules that limit my substance. I will be pure mind. I will be consciousness."

A light came into Pincus's eyes that illuminated his face.

"I will have escaped," he wrote.

PART II

The Thaumaturge

CHAPTER 1

All men have fallen in love with Aletheia, the daughter of Zeus, goddess of Truth, irresistibly alluring among those who cohabit with the gods of Olympus, but few have courted her with such unrelenting devotion as Max Pincus.

Having removed from his existence all those things that, to this point, had served only the single pragmatic purpose of making his life livable, Pincus would awaken in his new Manhattan apartment wondering whether mind could dominate matter.

In the shower, he would contemplate whether the universe had a purpose, and whether it contained order or only chaos.

He reserved for his ritual with the Waterpik the question of whether man can survive his own death. Tiny droplets spattering on his face and on the mirror before it, Pincus would stare into the mist and imagine his soul floating forever in eternity.

He wondered, as the morning news played on the bathroom radio, whether as a spiritual entity in the hereafter, he would continue to follow the exploits of the Boston Red Sox, and whether, given eternity, they could win a World Series. It was now 1980 and the year 2004 was an eternity in the future, if it existed at all for Pincus.

By the time Pincus had finished his first cup of coffee, he was determining whether, in the cosmic scheme, life held more importance than astronomy would lead us to believe, or, on the other hand, whether our emphasis on life on this earth was a result of arrogance and parochialism.

Having considered these issues by the time his breakfast was finished, Pincus now had the remainder of the day available for the question of God.

His laboratory no longer available to him, his medical practice ended, and his Mercedes gone, Pincus had to be content to probe the question of a Supreme Being and any possible divine Offspring while walking through a nearby park or sitting on one of its many wooden benches, defending himself against battalions of surprisingly well-organized pigeons.

Now, the search for God, Pincus concluded, was obviously an attempt to find the ultimate order that would give reality to his existence — to all mind and all matter. But — Pincus constructed his syllogism — mind and matter were nothing more than aspects of consciousness. And, because consciousness was a brain phenomenon, so then was God.

Now, brain phenomena (Pincus continued to build his logic while kicking at the gray birds pecking the tops of his shoes), were nothing more nor less than the conductivity of electrical impulses. But, while he could name the source of almost all other impulses, he was at a loss to explain what stimulated a neuron to conduct an impulse it would call "God."

Pincus was absolutely convinced that there had to be a neurophysiologic explanation for the Lord God Almighty that, because of years of racing to tax-deductible medical conferences throughout the islands of the Caribbean and the South Pacific, Pincus seemed to have missed.

As it turns out, this was not the first time Pincus had brought his unique intellect to bear on the great puzzles of human existence, particularly those of a religious nature, nor was it to be the last.

The very first time occurred during his second year in private practice, 1960, and involved a gentleman by the name of Gabriel Pantera, otherwise known as the Thaumaturge.

CHAPTER 2

Pincus grappled for the ringing telephone in the dark and placed it against his ear, one late wintry night in 1960.

"Dr. Pincus?" came the rasping voice of a man with a thick foreign accent of indeterminate origin.

Pincus pressed the telephone closer to his ear.

"What?" Pincus asked in his half-awake state.

"Dr. Pincus?" the voice repeated with some urgency.

Pincus looked over at the illuminated clock beside his bed. It was 3:16 a.m.

"Yes," Pincus tried to get his bearings in the dark. He had been dreaming about Ted Williams, who had been asking Pincus for batting tips.

"My daughter is not well. Can you see her?"

The words on the other end of the phone line were beginning to take shape in Pincus's head. The man had a sick child. Pincus was (just barely) a physician. While he had worked many nights as a resident, and had set up his office practice just over a year ago, this would be his very first call to go out into the darkness and practice his profession.

From the other room came the sound of little Anne crying to be fed. Becki Stone-Thomas-Pincus stirred beside Pincus, kicked off the covers, and headed to the door. As she stumbled into the hall, the light shined through her nightgown, outlining the curves of her body. Pincus watched the female form before him, lurching half-asleep toward the result of their frequent love-making, now screaming for nurturance, transfixed at the way her bottom pushed against her silk nightgown as she walked, at the way the light illuminated the delicious space between her legs. Pincus was a romantic.

"You hear me, Pincus?" the voice in the phone startled Pincus from his reverie.

"I wasn't able to, no," Pincus snapped out of it. "Our baby was crying."

"I don't think so."

"You don't think what?"

"That our baby is crying. She was. She's not anymore."

"*Our* baby was crying," Pincus explained.

"I'm sorry to hear that. Maybe it's a medical problem. Have you taken her temperature?"

There was a long silence. Pincus decided on a fresh approach.

"Who is this?" he asked.

"I am Pantera."

The name didn't ring a bell, but Pincus needed every patient he could get. It was worth a shot.

"What is the problem, Mr. Pantera?"

"Our daughter is suffering from consumption. She needs medical attention. Can you come over immediately?"

"Consumption?..." Pincus rolled the archaic medical term over his tongue.

"Exactly. Consumption."

"What is consuming her, Mr. Pantera?"

Becki walked into the room, cradling Anne in her arms, as the baby sucked on one of Becki's swollen breasts. She stopped at the strange turn in the phone conversation and raised her dark eyebrows.

"Can you come over and see her?" Pantera pleaded.

"What are her symptoms, Mr. Pantera?"

«Pains, Dr. Pincus. Terrible pains. And a bloating."

"You should probably take her to the emergency room. Where do you live? I'll tell you where the nearest hospital is."

"We are a religious family, Dr. Pincus. We cannot go to hospitals.

We are Anti-Synoptics."

This was a new sect for Pincus. "Anti-Synoptics?" he asked, trying not to sound judgmental.

"We doubt the first four gospels."

"You don't believe Matthew, Mark, and Luke?" Pincus asked. Becki sat down beside him on the bed, intrigued.

"No, why? Are they true?" Pantera inquired.

"What about John's gospel?" Pincus explored the scope of the situation.

"We believe in the secret gospel of Thomas, but we're not sure he wrote it, or if he existed."

"Thomas wrote a gospel?"

"He might have. We're not sure. If you come over and treat my daughter, who will surely be dead by the time this conversation ends, I will give you a pamphlet."

Pincus took Pantera's address, assured the worried man that he would be over shortly, and hung up. Then he turned to Becki.

"He doesn't believe in Matthew, Mark, Luke, or John," he informed his wife as he slipped on his trousers.

Becki nodded sympathetically. "It sounds terrible."

CHAPTER 3

There was a feeling of optimism in the air as 1960 came to a close, in spite of some anomalies regarding the Soviet Union shooting down one of our spy planes over its territory, and strangers starting to occupy lunch counters throughout the South and thereby coining the catchy phrase "sit-in," a fad that journalists almost unanimously declared would soon disappear like the Shmoo, the 1950s comic character who, when fried, came out chicken, when broiled, came out steak, and whose eyes made excellent buttons for suspenders.

On a more promising front, John Fitzgerald Kennedy had been elected president of the United States of America and eight years of Camelot lay ahead. The first weather satellite had been launched, along with the first spy satellite, and now we would know well in advance whether to make preparations for being destroyed by nature or incinerated by mankind.

Science also vaulted into previously unimagined territory with the invention of *Teflon*, and, not to be outdone on the non-sticking front, the pharmaceutical industry introduced the oral contraceptive.

Now the year had come to an end. It was December and snow had been falling heavily for several hours in the city. Busses had ceased to operate at this late hour, and the taxis wouldn't return until the weather improved. So Pincus started his long trek across the city on foot.

As he trudged ahead, the wind blew the thick flakes into a multitude of churning storms at Pincus's feet, sending icy particles up his trouser legs, numbing his calves. Pincus brushed his trousers with his gloved hands, wrapped a scarf over his face, and, physician's bag in hand, pushed into the bleak night, across a city frozen into silence.

By the time he had reached the thoroughfare that divides the city into eastern and western halves, the wind was blowing so ferociously that visibility for all but the shortest distances was impossible. Blinded by the storm, Pincus picked out the brightly lit top of a huge skyscraper as his guide. Pantera and his child lived in a small building near its base.

Finally, frozen to the bone, teeth chattering, matted with snow, Pincus reached the brick building with the address that Pantera had rasped plaintively into the phone. With enormous effort, Pincus pulled the heavy door against the wind and stepped, at last, into the sanctuary of the foyer.

In the dim light, Pincus examined the names beside the row of buzzers until he reached "Mr. and Mrs. Gabriel Pantera." He rang the bell.

"Yes?" a familiar voice inquired.

"Dr. Pincus."

"Who?"

"Pincus. Dr. Pincus."

Pincus squinted into the darkness to verify that he had pushed the correct button. He had.

"Yes?" the voice asked as though there had been no previous communication.

"Mr. Pantera?"

"Yes?"

"You called me to see your child. It's Dr. Pincus."

Pincus could hear voices whispering. Suddenly, through the glass-paneled door in front of him, Pincus could see another door open down the hall. A dark figure stuck his head outside the door, peered at Pincus for a moment, and then ducked back inside his apartment, shutting the door behind him.

"You're Pincus?" Pantera's voice came over the intercom.

"Yes, I am."

"You're very young."

"I am, yes. But I do good work. May I see your daughter now?"

Once again the apartment door opened, the figure stared at Pincus, and then disappeared behind the door.

"We're religious people, Dr. Pincus."

"I will examine your daughter with great piety."

Another whispered conference on the other end, and then, two figures — one male, one female — poked their heads from the doorway down the hall. They quickly slipped back inside. Pantera spoke over the intercom once more.

"Do you believe in the power of prayer, Pincus?"

Pincus stood in the cold, black vestibule and gave the question his earnest attention. It was a tricky question, especially when the questioner was an Anti-Synoptic, who either could or could not believe in the efficacy of appealing to God, or, even more likely, not be entirely certain. Pincus decided that honesty was the best policy.

"I believe that sometimes it can be helpful, yes," Pincus answered sincerely.

Another conference. Another inspection by Pantera and his wife from the end of the hall.

"Do you know any prayers?" Pantera asked.

"Only one that I can think of."

"What's that?"

"I believe in one God, the Father, the Almighty, maker of heaven and earth, of all that is, seen and unseen. I believe in one Lord, Jesus Christ, the only Son of God, eternally begotten of the Father, God from God, Light from Light, true God from true God, begotten not made, one being with the Father. Through Him all things were made. For us men and for our salvation, he came down from heaven: by the power of the Holy Spirit he became incarnate with the Virgin Mary, and was made man. For our sake he was crucified under Pontius Pilate; he suffered death and was buried. On the third day he rose again in accordance with the Scriptures; he ascended into heaven and is seated at the right hand of the Father. He will come again in glory to judge the living and the dead, and his kingdom will have no end. Amen."

"Amen," said Pantera.

The buzzer sounded on the door in front of Pincus and he was permitted to come in out of the cold.

CHAPTER 4

"You omitted the Holy Ghost," Pantera called down the hall as Pincus approached.

"I forgot," Pincus answered, attempting to make out the dark figure ahead of him.

"And the prophets, and one holy catholic and apostolic church, baptism, the forgiveness of sins, and the resurrection of the dead — did you forget them, too?" Pantera continued his interrogation.

"I suppose I did. I remember them now. I'm surprised that, as an Anti-Synoptic, you believe in the Nicene Creed."

Pantera said nothing.

"You do believe in the Nicene Creed?" Pincus asked.

"Not a word, why?" Pantera said.

Pincus wasn't sure what to do next. He stood at the door to the apartment and stared into Pantera's eyes, which were extraordinary — large dark spheres. And, as Pincus stood at the doorway, he could sense a second set of eyes — also dark, but gentle and warm — inspecting him from inside the apartment.

Finally, Pantera stepped aside, allowing Pincus to enter, and then quickly locked the door.

Pincus found himself in a small room with heavy Persian carpets and no furniture. Candles burned in niches and illuminated gold-leaf renderings of Christ that hung on the walls. Incense, burning in tiny brass pots, filled the chamber with a hazy smoke and pungent aroma.

Pantera was a large man and wore a long black garment, a furry cassock of some sort, closed at the waist by an ornate gold belt with a large buckle on which was inscribed the letter "S." His hands, clasped together just above the buckle, were thick and hairy. He had the broad shoulders of one who spent his days carrying loads back and forth. From the neck up there was only black hair — a rabbinical beard reaching to the middle of his chest, mixing with the thick curly hair that fell from his shoulders. Amid this mane, his dark eyes reflected like those of a cat.

A step behind Pantera, and partially obscured by him, was a woman of striking beauty — Mediterranean features, thin Roman nose, olive skin, dark brown hair, full lips, and coffee eyes. When her eyes met Pincus's, she averted them with a modesty from another century and stepped back into the darkness.

"Your daughter is in the other room?" Pincus was beginning to feel uncomfortable.

Pantera nodded. "I will wait here. Her mother, Annabelle, will go with you."

On cue, the woman stepped from the darkness and escorted Pincus through a doorway strung with beads, her light garments flowing behind her like lace wings.

The hall down which they proceeded was lined with candles and additional renderings of the Messiah.

"She is Rosalie," Annabelle Pantera informed Pincus when they reached the door to the daughter's bedroom.

"How long has she been ill?" Pincus asked, but Annabelle didn't answer. Instead, she rapped lightly on the door.

"Go away," a girl's voice demanded from the other side of the door.

Pincus was surprised by the adolescent quality of the voice.

"How old is your daughter?" he asked.

"Fifteen," Annabelle sighed, and then called back through the closed door. "Please open the door, Rosalie."

"No way," the girl answered defiantly.

"Dr. Pincus has come to see you, dear," Annabelle explained. "He's come all the way across town in the middle of a terrible storm."

"I don't care if he came from Bethlehem on a camel, I'm not unlocking the door."

"Then," Mrs. Pantera countered, "I will call your father, and he will change your hands into cloven hooves, which means that you will be unable to use the phone, dear."

Pincus looked at Annabelle and smiled at her caustic sense of humor. Annabelle showed no signs of amusement.

There was some fumbling on the other side of the door before it finally opened. The young girl who stood there was as blond and fair as her mother and father were dark. Her blue eyes were lively and intense, her face was round and lightly freckled, her body was full, and in contrast to her disposition, cherubic.

"Don't tell Daddy," she said to her mother.

"Let Dr. Pincus examine you," her mother responded noncommittally and escorted Rosalie back to her bed.

"I don't want you in here," Rosalie informed her mother.

Pincus waited in the silence that followed to see how this instruction would be handled.

"I'll wait outside the door until the doctor is finished. Call me if you need me."

It was not clear whether the offer was made to Rosalie or to Pincus, but Rosalie took it as being directed to her.

"I won't need you."

Annabelle looked at Rosalie, then at Pincus, nodded and withdrew from the room, leaving the door slightly ajar.

CHAPTER 5

Pincus claimed that he was not one to speculate upon the essence of the divinity, to concern himself with beliefs about angels, about the destiny of mankind, about the personality of the Supreme Being. He has insisted that his quest was always for one thing and one thing only — perfect love. And any consideration he might have given to the above can be understood only from that perspective. That She came into the picture is another story entirely, and was, he has said, never the result of some ontological or epistemological endeavor on his part.

This is, of course, absurd. Isaiah's belief that when the Messiah arrived, the eyes of the blind shall be opened, clearly did not take Max Pincus into account.

And, thus, when the door to Rosalie's room had partly closed, leaving a crack through which her mother's eyes could be seen riveted on the proceedings, Pincus found himself staring motionlessly at the young girl now lying on the bed awaiting his medical attention, and he found his spirit filling with a strange mix of emotions. He felt light-headed, infused with the kind of delight one experiences on encountering an object of exceptional beauty, as in a museum — a never-before-seen painting, an exquisite object from antiquity, a sculpture so life-like that one wants to converse with it.

At that moment, Pincus felt as though he were being transported someplace else, some place sunny and tropical, where birds sang and there was the sound of the sea all day and night. It made him smile.

Rosalie started to laugh, half the giggly girl, half the amused woman.

"Just look at you," Rosalie said, and Pincus, basking in the glow of his palm-treed paradise, looked at Rosalie in surprise, suddenly landing with a metaphorical thud in the real world, causing Rosalie to laugh even louder.

This was followed by the sound of Rosalie's mother on the other side of the door.

"That's enough, Rosalie!"

Rosalie stopped laughing so quickly that it startled Pincus out of his reverie.

"Yes, Mother," Rosalie answered.

Not entirely satisfied, Annabelle opened the door and stuck her head into the room.

"What kind of doctor *are* you?" Rosalie's mother demanded of Pincus, who stopped laughing and instantly adopted a more professional demeanor.

"A good one, I assure you," Pincus responded, but there was a touch of sadness in his voice at having lost the seashore.

"Then I suggest you drop the vaudeville and examine my daughter," she responded, and Rosalie's mother ducked back behind the not-quite-shut door.

Pincus, trying hard not to look at Rosalie, who already had a smile on her face that could easily have started everything up again, reached in his bag and took out his stethoscope.

"Where do you hurt, Rosalie?" he asked in his most professional voice.

"I don't hurt at all. I'm just pregnant. Daddy wants you to examine me so you can tell Mother that nobody's popped my cherry, and then maybe she'll calm down."

Pincus looked at Rosalie in stunned silence.

"Hymen? Cherry? It gets broken when you have sex?" Rosalie explained to her novice physician.

"And from a lot of other things — biking, gymnastics, a bad fall, horseback riding...."

"Do I look like I own a horse?"

"And even if it's not been broken, there are instances in which women, girls, have had intercourse and become pregnant with the hymen still intact. It's rare, but it can happen."

"Yeah, well, it didn't with me. I don't even have a boyfriend."

Rosalie flipped off the covers, yanked up her nightgown and spread her legs, revealing, in addition to her vulva, an abdomen distended by a fetus well into its sixth month.

"Can we get this over with, so my parents'll stop driving me crazy?"

Pincus stared motionless at the sight before him.

"You're pregnant," he said.

"I am? Golly, imagine my surprise."

"And your parents don't know it?"

"Of course they *know* it. That's not the problem. The problem is *how*."

"Rosalie, there's only one way that a woman becomes pregnant."

"Apparently not. Now, will you *puh-lease* examine my hymen?"

"I don't have the tools I need to examine you. And I'm not a gynecologist. I could feel with my hand and see whether it seems to me that your hymen hasn't been ruptured, but it wouldn't be definitive."

"Definitive enough. What do my parents know. Look, I'm not a gynecologist, either, but it seems to me that if you feel in me and you find a hymen that *seems* like it hasn't been broken, then it's probably *not* broken, and this'll be good enough for now. So, will you please do it."

There was a brief silence from Rosalie, followed again by "Please?"

It took a while, but it finally hit Pincus.

"Your father wants to prove to your mother that you're a virgin mother?" he said.

"I'm not a mother, yet, just pregnant," Rosalie answered, "and, honestly, I don't have a clue what my father wants or why he wants it.

All I know is that he's got some theory that he's been messing around with, and some weird glass contraption for trapping something or other, little souls I think, and now I'm having a baby, and, to tell you the truth, I *wish* it'd come from having sex with a boy, because there's something just not fair about missing the fun part, but I can tell you that it didn't come from having sex with anyone, and no angels appeared to announce anything to me, either, so now will you please do what you've got to do so we can get this thing over with, okay?"

Pincus reached in his medical bag, removed a pair of surgical gloves, and began pulling them on his hand.

"Bless you," Rosalie said.

"Have you ever had an internal exam before?" he asked.

"No, have you?"

"This is going to feel cold," Pincus responded, and gingerly inserted one finger, and then another inside Rosalie.

"You'll stop before you get to your elbow, won't you?" Rosalie asked.

"Actually, I'm stopping now," said Pincus, and he withdrew his hand, and removed his gloves.

Rosalie waited in silence for Pincus to say something, but he was silent. Finally she spoke in a whisper.

"Well?" she asked.

"As near as I can tell, your hymen has not been broken."

"Hallelujah," said Rosalie. And then she began to cry.

CHAPTER 6

Pincus sat across the kitchen table from Annabelle Pantera, trying to sort out the situation without success.

Could there be any meaning to this beyond an adolescent girl trying to make her parents believe that she had never had the sexual intercourse she obviously had had, and her father obliging her deceit in a bizarre attempt to convince his wife that her daughter was about to have a virgin birth?

Was there anything about these events that might suggest a referral for family counseling was in order? Was Rosalie the victim of child abuse of a form not yet defined? Certainly, someone claiming to be well on the way to a virgin birth might find psychotherapy beneficial.

And, then, suddenly, Pincus came to his senses, not regarding the need for the intervention of the Department of Child Welfare, which was more and more a certainty, but for his giving validity to Rosalie's claims of her virginity.

It has never been clear whether, during this encounter, Pincus was to any extent aware that, though still far in the future, he was taking the first steps on the road to his own salvation.

"Your daughter is pregnant," Pincus finally announced, as they sipped their cups of tea.

"Yes, I do know that," Annabelle responded. "I think the question is *how*, or, perhaps, even more important, by *whom*?"

"Well, yes, that *is* the question, of course," Pincus was quick to agree, "and I'm not sure I can help you with that. For that, we have gone beyond the realm of medical science. All I can offer at this point is that your daughter's hymen has not been broken."

"And do you have an explanation for this?"

"It's rare, but it is possible to become pregnant without the hymen being broken."

"So, then, your conclusion is that Rosalie has had sexual intercourse with someone?"

"That *is* the way women become pregnant."

"So I've heard. Are there any other conclusions you're considering?"

"Actually, I was kind of hoping that you might tell *me* what's going on here."

"My husband has an explanation."

Pincus looked over his steaming cup of tea with some interest.

"And what would that be?"

"That would be that Rosalie has been impregnated by the Divine Spirit — with not a small amount of help from him, he claims — and She is now within her."

"She? You know it's a girl?"

"Me, no. My husband, yes. He is absolutely certain that it's Her, that She is within Rosalie."

"She? Who is She?"

"For that, you should probably ask my husband, the Thaumaturge."

CHAPTER 7

Gabriel Pantera sat on the floor of the candle-lit room, legs crossed in a guru position, his back lightly touching the wall. Pincus, upon Pantera's instructions, had assumed the same position not far away, facing Pantera, still attempting to make sense of what was transpiring, and wondering whether such unusual events were more or less to be expected by a thirty-year-old physician just starting his own practice. He could not afford to be choosy, and, accordingly, he decided to focus on two goals: first, to assure that all medical and psychiatric issues were being treated, and second, to handle the situation in such a way that, upon his departure — something he very much hoped would be soon — the family would speak highly of him and his medical skills, leading others to avail themselves of his services.

As he sorted this out, facing the silent contemplative cross-legged Pantera, the sound of voices came from behind the closed door of Rosalie's room.

"It's okay, sweetheart. It's all going to be okay," Annabelle's voice could be heard saying.

"No, it's *not!*" Rosalie responded loudly. "I can't *believe* that my own *father* has done this to me! My own *father*! If he needed to grow some divine spirit, couldn't he have done it in a glass *dish* in his lab or something? Or used the womb of someone else, not his very own *daughter*! What am I going to do with a *baby*?!"

"We'll find someone very nice to adopt Her, Rosalie. Or we'll find a good foster home."

"You're going to put *The Messiah* up for *adoption*? You don't put

The Messiah up for *adoption*, Mother! For chrissakes! Do you have any idea what'll happen to you, to *all* of us, if we put *The Messiah* in foster care?!"

The word "Messiah" rang in Pincus's head like the Zygmunt Bell of the Wawel Cathedral in Krakow, recently determined to weigh 18 metric tons. And, as is customary, it rang in Pincus's head each and every time Rosalie said the word "Messiah."

And then there was silence and Pantera, the Thaumaturge, spoke.

"She'll get over it."

"Mr. Pantera, I'd like to suggest two things," Pincus began. "First, I'd recommend that your daughter see an obstetrician; I can give you some names if you wish. And, second, I'd also recommend that your family see a therapist to deal with some of the issues here."

"What issues might those be, Dr. Pincus?"

"Well, obviously, you're all a little upset about Rosalie's pregnancy."

"I'm not upset. I'm delighted."

"Okay, Rosalie and her mother, then."

"As I said, they'll get over it. Once She's born, they'll be happy as angels dancing on the summit of Sinai."

"Your wife mentioned that you knew that Rosalie's baby would be a girl. Has she had an amniocentesis?"

Pantera shook his head. "Not that I know of, why?"

"Well, then how do you know that the baby will be a girl?"

"Because it's Her."

"Her who?"

"Her who is all things seen and unseen. Her for whom all men long. Her who is being and unbeing. Her who is the answer to all questions, the order of all that is, was, or will be. Her who is the lover and the beloved."

"She is God?"

"No, not *God*. *Beyond* God. She is the God of Abraham, Isaac, and Jacob; and the God of the Father, the Son, and the Holy Spirit; and the God of the Muslims, and the Hindus, and the Bedouins of the desert, of the tribes of the Amazon, of the natives of Africa. She is Who all men seek, everywhere, and forever. She is the Mother of all Gods. And I heard She's not bad looking, either. A real knock-out."

Pincus decided it would be unproductive to follow Pantera's notion of the drop-dead gorgeous Mother of all Gods and elected to move on.

"What about the well-being of the mother of the Mother of all Gods?"

"Who's that?"

"Your daughter."

"No, no. Rosalie is just a conduit for expressing Her will, in this case, Her appearance on earth."

"I don't understand, Mr. Pantera. If She's such a powerful God, the God of all Gods, then why does She need a conduit? Surely, She has the wherewithal to appear fully-grown and skip all the steps in between."

"Because that's not the way things work. You want to appear as a human being on earth, you need to be born. *Surely*, you must have encountered that somewhere in your medical training."

There was a moment of silence, the stillness broken only by the plaintive sound from the other room of Rosalie's sobs and her mother's comforting "there-theres."

"How does your wife feel about all this, Mr. Pantera?"

"My wife?"

"Yes, the mother of the mother of the Mother of all Gods."

"It doesn't work like that. She's not Her grandmother, if that's what you're saying."

Pincus studied the dark eyes of the Thaumaturge.

"Why not?"

"Because she's not Her grandmother, that's why. Nor am I Her grandfather. If it went like that, then my wife's mother would be Her great-grandmother, and Her great-grandmother's mother would be

Her great-great grandmother, and there'd be all these uncles, and aunts, and cousins, and nephews, and nieces, and, before you know it, we'd all be related to Her in some way or other. No, that wouldn't work at all. How'd you like to wake up one morning and discover that you were the Messiah's brother-in-law? No, this is the way it has to be. Rosalie is simply a vehicle for Her appearance — not really Her mother, although it's probably best to maintain that for appearance's sake, I would think."

Pantera nodded, satisfied he had resolved all open issues. He picked up a pipe that lay beside him on the floor, placed it in his mouth, then snapped his fingers. Fire spouted instantly from his hand and lit the tobacco. He puffed several times to make certain the tobacco was well-lit, then closed his hand, and the fire disappeared.

"Very good," Pincus admired Pantera's prestidigitation. "So. You're a magician."

"Thaumaturge," Pantera corrected. "There's a difference."

"Thaumaturge?"

"Do you believe, Dr. Pincus, that a supra-sensible world exists, one that is amenable to the labors of both physics and philosophy, something beyond what we call the 'real' world that we experience through the illusionary manifestations we call 'sense'?"

Pincus was lost after the first few words. The still faint bell-ringing in his head was now replaced with a buzzing, as though Pantera's voice was an insect that had lost its way in Pincus's ear.

"I'm not sure I understand what you mean?" was the best Pincus could manage.

"Do you believe in an unseen but, nevertheless, experienced world? A spiritual world? Something beyond our senses that is important, and real, and intimately connected to our lives? That this world exists just as certainly as the world in which we live each day?"

"I'm not sure."

"Not sure you believe in it or that it exists?"

"Aren't they the same? Don't you have to accept that something beyond us exists before you can believe in it?"

"Not necessarily. But that's another issue entirely."

"And if it's beyond our senses, how would we 'experience' it, or even know it was there?" Pincus pointed out.

"Exactly. But we do," the Thaumaturge smiled, as though he had just won a major victory.

"You were saying that you are not a magician," Pincus thought it best to try another door.

"I'm not. Magic is nothing more than the scientific temperament trying to extend its powers into the supra-sensible world. It works toward enlarging the sphere on which the human can work — as when I produce fire from my hand. Magic does abnormal things, but it doesn't actually go anywhere.

"Mysticism, on the other hand, is a movement of the heart, of the spirit, of the innermost sanctuary of personal being. With it we experience what we cannot with our senses.

"Mysticism penetrates the reality that lies beyond the veil. It establishes communication between the spirit of man, entangled in a material world, and the only true 'reality' — the Absolute.

"At a certain point, the harmony between us, between our minds and 'things' becomes so complete that it produces actual emotions within us. '*Oh beauty, so old and so new, too late I have loved thee.*'"

Pantera smiled at Pincus.

"Augustine. This is what he knew. We only experience what life has given us when the Beautiful becomes Sublime. *She* is the Beautiful *and* the Sublime."

Throughout all this, the buzzing in Pincus's brain continued, growing ever more a din the longer Pantera talked. For Pincus had not the slightest notion about what Pantera was talking, certainly not the details, but not even the general arena in which his words belonged. As far as Pincus saw it, he was 30, comfortably married to an attractive woman with whom he felt a certain compatibility and, if not the profound love of a sublime nature, certainly, a productive and lucrative career ahead of him practicing the art of healing.

So Pincus returned to his original question.

"Then you are a mystic?"

"Thaumaturge, Dr. Pincus. Try not to over-simplify things. What I do is an act of love, of surrender, of supreme perception. It is a deep-seated desire of the soul towards its source."

"Toward *Her*?"

"Yes, She is the Source."

Pincus latched on quickly to the opening Pantera had presented him.

"Yes, well, this brings up an interesting question. Might I ask, Mr. Pantera, how exactly, in your view, She, the Source, became implanted in your daughter?"

"You certainly may. Come with me."

CHAPTER 8

Pantera unlocked a door with a large skeleton key that hung from a chain around his neck, pushed opened the door, and beckoned Pincus to enter.

Pincus found himself in a laboratory not unlike the ones that he had encountered at his medical school, not unlike the one in which he would one day work. Glass apparatus were attached to metal stands on the workbench. Petri dishes stood near microscopes. There was a centrifuge in one corner, a mass spectrometer in another. Pincus was impressed. The cost of this equipment, even if obtained secondhand, had to run into hundreds of thousands of dollars.

"Donated," Pantera said, as if he had read Pincus's mind.

"What exactly is it that you do, Mr. Pantera?" Pincus asked.

Pantera gestured at the laboratory before him.

"This is what I do, Dr. Pincus."

"I mean for a living, to support your family."

Pantera smiled, amused already at what he was to say.

"I depend on the generosity of others," he answered.

"I see," Pincus nodded. "And is it with this equipment that Rosalie has become pregnant?"

"Well, not exactly. It is with this *equipment* that I have learned in what manner I could induce her to bring forth a child who would be Her. Do you know Virgil, Dr. Pincus?"

Pincus shook his head that he did not.

"*Ore omnes versae in Zephyros stant rupibus altis, exceptantque leves auras; et saepe sine ullis conjugiis vento gravidae (mirabile dictu) saxa per et scopulos et depressas convalles diffugiunt...."*

Pincus shrugged. "Latin?"

Pantera nodded.

"I never learned Latin."

"*The mares to cliffs of rugged rocks repair, and, with wide nostrils, snuff the western air: when (wondrous to relate), the parent wind, without the stallion, propagates the kind.*"

"Virgil believed that mares could conceive with no stallion being involved, simply by sniffing the west wind?" Pincus wanted to make certain he had gotten the full drift of Virgil's words.

"Exactly. It was very common in his time for mares to become pregnant in such a manner, with no coition, simply by turning to face the west wind."

"You're telling me that your daughter became pregnant like one of Virgil's horses, by facing the west wind?" Pincus asked.

"I'm telling you that sexual intercourse is not always essential to conception. Hippocrates informs us that his mother frequently told him that she had had no intercourse with his father for nearly two years before his birth, but that she found herself strangely influenced one evening as she was walking in a garden."

"No doubt by some gentleman who was nearby."

Pantera did not react to Pincus's remark.

"An oracle foretold that Acrisius would have his throat cut by his grandson, and so he locked up his only daughter in a tower and had her guarded night and day, so that it was impossible for anyone to get near her, except, of course, the wind. Still, she gave birth to Perseus, who dispatched Acrisius in short order by slashing his throat."

Pincus studied Pantera carefully, attempting to judge by inspection alone, just how disturbed this Thaumaturge was and whether he, Pincus, had a duty as a physician to have Rosalie removed immediately and placed in a healthier environment.

"Where does the soul originate, Dr. Pincus? Is it in the sperm, or in the egg, or in the conjunction of the two, and, whatever the case, where *exactly* does it reside? Have you come upon it during your medical training? Or do you believe that the soul doesn't exist at all?"

Pincus had no answer.

"In the air, Dr. Pincus. The soul floats in the air, all around us, tiny, unseen, until it is inhaled by the mother where it infuses with the fetus and shapes its character. But prior to that, it is pure soul, pure being, the spirit of which we all partake.

"I have captured this, here in my lab, tiny animalcula, and I have looked at them with wonder, even, on occasion, turning romantic as I wondered which would become a hero, a criminal, a lecher, a patriot, a legislator, or even a monarch. What I did not know is that if taken in, in the manner of Virgil's mares, and given a hot bed on which to expand themselves, they would grow too large to be confined, much like seeds in a cucumber frame, and could, without the presence of egg or sperm, give rise to life itself, and this life, this pure life uncorrupted by human characteristics, would then have to be, of necessity, Her. Because, Dr. Pincus, She is pure soul. There is nothing purer. And that is what I have captured from the west wind."

Pincus was finally convinced of Pantera's insanity.

"You have seen these animalcula?" Pincus pursued his diagnosis.

"I have, indeed."

"And what do they look like, Mr. Pantera?"

"Well, at first, they appeared to be nothing more than wriggling silkworms. But, as I peered more closely through my microscope, I could see tiny little legs and arms, flailing about, anxious for their receptacle, to reach their final destination. Man is truly, in fact, made in Her image."

Pincus started pacing, trying to determine the appropriate course of action. Pantera had more to say.

"Think, if you will, Dr. Pincus, what a wonderful discovery I have made. How many girls, how many women, have over the centuries, in one culture or another, had their reputations unfairly soiled, been wrongly censured for adultery or premarital intercourse, when they have done nothing but breathe the west wind? And think how many of us have, solely for the purpose of having children, entered into matrimony, an arrangement often agreed to be, if not immediately then in due time, intolerable, completely inconsistent with the continued experience of pleasure, destructive of freedom, and leading inevitably to whoring, divorcing, even poisoning, just to break loose from the fetters and escape from a fate worse than Egyptian bondage. With my discovery, I believe I very well might have saved all of mankind, and it is my intention, once I have documented all the details in a way that will satisfy even the most skeptical minds of science and government, to apply for a patent."

"I would like to ask once more, just to be completely certain," Pincus said, "how *exactly* has your daughter become pregnant, Mr. Pantera?"

"*Exactly* — I have taken the hermetically sealed beaker you see over there, and to which I would advise that you not get too close, as I cannot guarantee what might happen if you were to take a deep breath, and I placed it under Rosalie's nose at a time when she believed she was suffering from nasal congestion and the wind was coming from the west. I then asked her to breathe deeply — which, obviously, she has done."

CHAPTER 9

Pincus wrote on his prescription pad the name of an obstetrician in clear well-formed letters, and then added the name of a psychiatrist. He handed the paper to Pantera.

"If these don't suit you, I'm sure they'd be happy to recommend others in their fields."

Then Pincus had a thought and wrote everything out a second time on another slip of paper and handed it to Pantera's wife, as he was not confident that Pantera would follow through, but suspected he might have better luck with Rosalie's mother.

"It's important that you see these doctors," Pincus said.

"So I surmised when you wrote out the second slip for my wife," Pantera responded.

Pincus decided not to react to Pantera's sarcasm and simply dropped the prescription pad back into his bag and snapped it shut.

"If there's anything further, don't hesitate to call," Pincus offered. "But it's best to call my office number. If I'm not available, they'll know where to reach me or someone who's covering for me."

"I found you fine at home," Pantera smiled.

"Yes, I know," Pincus said and started toward the front door, accompanied by Pantera.

"You said on the phone that you are an Anti-Synoptic," Pincus said as he walked down the hallway, past the icons of Christ, candles still burning.

"Yes, that's correct."

"Meaning that you don't accept the gospels of Matthew, Mark,

Luke, and John."

"Yes."

"Might I ask why?"

"Well, let's see. Putting aside for the moment that all that is written in the gospels about Jesus can be reduced to a span of three weeks of his life, nativity excluded, leaving a few details of the life of the Son of God curiously lacking, the Matthew gospel could not possibly have been written by Matthew because it is based almost entirely on Mark. But Matthew knew Jesus firsthand and traveled extensively with him. It's absurd to think that he would base his gospel on the writing of someone who knew Christ not even half as well.

"Regarding the story of the nativity, there was no such worldwide census under Augustus. There was, indeed, a census of Judea, Samaria, and Idumea, the territories ruled by Herod's son, Archelaus, until the Romans exiled him to Gaul and annexed his lands in 6 C.E. Quirinius, imperial legate for Syria in 6 to 7 C.E. would have been in charge of that census. But that was ten years after the death of Herod. In addition, we know from census and taxation decrees in Roman Egypt that individuals were registered where they were living and working. They had to return *there*, if they were elsewhere. The idea of everybody going back to their ancestral homes, like Bethlehem, for registration and then returning to their present homes would have been a bureaucratic nightmare. What was important then, as now, was to get you registered where you could be taxed.

"The nativity is a charming story, as are all of the gospels, but they are pure fiction, a creation of the apostles' imagination, providing in the case of the nativity, for example, a way of getting Jesus's parents to Bethlehem for his birth, a birth, by the way that Matthew says was conveyed to Mary's husband, Joseph, in a dream, while Luke says it was announced directly to Mary by the Angel Gabriel. The Bethlehem birth, like the virginal conception, is linked to Old Testament prophecy, explicitly by Matthew and implicitly by Luke, because the scripture said that the Messiah would be descended from David and come from Bethlehem, the village where David lived.

"Jesus could not possibly have been born at the time of Herod or in Bethlehem. Nor, just for the record, could he have been directly descended from David, as Luke claims with a genealogy vastly different from Matthew's, and still be an immaculate conception from God.

"In the gospels, Jesus is reported to have gone through Sidon on his way to Tyre and then on to the Sea of Galilee. Unfortunately, Sidon is in the opposite direction, and there was, in fact, no road from Sidon to the Sea of Galilee in the first century A.D., only one from Tyre.

"Tell me when you want me to stop, Dr. Pincus, because I have a lot more to say on this matter."

Pincus nodded toward the icons of Christ on the walls.

"But then you don't believe in Christ?"

"Of course, I believe in Christ. How can you not believe in Christ? He was a Jewish troublemaker, and, believe me, as a Jew, I have known some Jewish troublemakers in my day, and the Messiah could out-do them all. But how can you not believe in a rascal like that from a poor family of no significance when the results are the *Passions* of Bach, the *Pietà* of Michelangelo, Leonardo's *Last Supper*, and the Cathedral of *Notre-Dame*. A *nudnik* like Christ would *have* to be the Son of God to inspire such works for over two thousand years, don't you think?"

Pincus had no response and soon found himself out in the snow-covered streets of Manhattan, where the snow had now stopped.

Pincus had much to think about as he moved forward, his feet crunching the snow, surprised that there was no sound of snowplows and snow blowers, just a stillness that put him unexpectedly at peace with the world.

He ran over in his mind the events of the past few hours, which had not, in fact, ended with Pantera's discourse on the invalidity of the gospels. At the door, Pantera had made Pincus an offer.

"At the apex of your spirit is a little door, so high up that only by hard climbing can you reach it," Pantera had told him, as Pincus was putting on his coat and wrapping his scarf around his neck. "I can guide you, but first you must trust your deep instincts, your latent powers.

"The two eyes cannot both perform their work at once," Pantera explained to Pincus, contrary to some notions Pincus had been taught in medical school. "If the soul sees with the right eye, then the left eye must refrain from working. Similarly, if the left eye is considering outward things, engaged with time and creatures, then the right eye is hindered from working. No man can serve two masters. Think about it, Dr. Pincus. It is not too late for you. You know where to find me." And, at this, Pantera shut the door.

Now Pincus, closing first one eye and then the other as he walked, imagined the tiny door at the top of his being, a gold ladder of great length extending up to it, with, at the top, beside the door, a window through which he could look out and see — well, Pincus didn't know what. A great Something. A spectacular Somewhere. Perhaps, someday he would find out, as it was not an altogether unappealing concept that there was something beyond him, something glorious. But for now, Pincus saw no reason, in the midst of starting a practice and a family and keeping a marriage going, to pursue it any further.

And so Pincus said nothing to Becki when he finally returned to their apartment. He undressed and climbed into bed. Becki stirred but didn't awaken, and Pincus went to sleep, knowing he would be getting up in two hours.

The next day, over dinner, Becki finally asked what had happened. Pincus, who had a tendency to go into details far beyond what anyone listening desired to know, was surprisingly circumspect.

"Their daughter was pregnant. I checked her out and she seemed fine. I referred them to an obstetrician," he told Becki.

"How pregnant do you think she was?"

"Five, six months, maybe."

"You'd think they'd know."

"Yes, you would," Pincus answered, as he imagined the tiny window, way up high, to which he had now added sky blue shutters that lightly flapped open and shut in the breeze.

PART III

Rosalie

CHAPTER 1

Pincus rarely thought of Pantera, the Thaumaturge, after that night. It all seemed out of a wintry dream.

Strangest of all to Pincus, now that he was divorced, his life with Becki and his children seemed equally as dreamlike, as though it, too, had never existed, or, if it had, was lived by someone else. From time to time, he would come across a photo of Becki, or his children, who dutifully called every Sunday to confirm that he was still alive, phone calls marked by long silences and awkward interchanges, and Pincus would wonder who these strangers were and how they had ever been a part of his life.

It had all ended peacefully, without rancor, and now those twenty-six years seemed like a cloud that had settled early one morning on a pond and, as the dawn turned to day, disappeared.

At first, Pincus spent his time acquiring the basics for his one-bedroom Upper West Side Manhattan apartment, shelving his books, purchasing pots and pans and dishes for meals he would never make, having found it easier to call out and have his dinners delivered.

The shelving of books was, for Pincus, a priority. Pincus had many books — thin picture-books that went back to his childhood and he was now saving to read to his grandchildren; college textbooks that were twenty or more years out-of-date; thick elaborately-illustrated medical works that seemed medieval compared to the current state of medical practice, including one volume that devoted some substantial space to the use of leeches.

At first, Pincus arranged all books alphabetically by author, but, when this process came to an end several months later (Pincus leafed through each book as it was shelved), he took the volumes off the shelves and rearranged them by subject.

What complicated matters to no small extent was that Pincus had not actually read many of these books through which he leafed. For it seems that as Pincus perused his biweekly copies of *The New York Review of Books*, his attention would be caught by one advertisement or another, mostly by the university presses, and picking up the phone to dial the phone-order line of the publisher was the smallest of next steps.

At one point, Pincus even considered reserving a single section of his shelves solely for those books he had not yet read, and even considered a section-within-a-section that might be labeled "Books Not Read But Still of Some Interest To Be Read Some Day."

This exercise in Information Management occupied no small portion of Pincus's time in his new apartment and left little spare time for furnishing. But, finally, tired of sleeping on a futon he had bought from the former tenant of the apartment as the young man was moving out, Pincus decided it was time to decorate.

He found, to his delight, a surprising number of imitation oriental carpets at the larger home supply stores, and soon had placed five small fake oriental rugs on the floor, like stepping stones in a Japanese garden. To these he added to the corner of the living room a mahogany desk he found in a secondhand furniture shop, on which he planned to fill journals with poetry, but the journals sat empty months later, although he wondered, from time to time whether it might be possible to compile a book of verse based entirely on the phrases brought to his door in the bags holding the Moo Goo Gai Pan, the latest being, "*To avoid stress, get a cat.*"

The year 1980 passed quickly for Pincus, his time filled with details, the details of the divorce, the details of finding and furnishing the apartment, the details of selling his practice. But now, as Christmas arrived, so did the ache within him. The bright twinkling lights, the decorated store windows, the carols, things that once had filled him with hope and a childish sense of wonder, now served only as dull reminders of a life yet to be lived and love still to be found.

Ronald Reagan was soon to become, as he had predicted, his next president, and there was something Pincus found appropriate about having a movie star in the White House. It was all pretend, anyway, and now, at last, there was a trained actor to perform it. There were vague rumblings on the horizon of something called "Reaganomics," in which the richer the country made the rich, the more they would have to spend, and this would "trickle down" — a phrase that suggested to Pincus a recurrent problem he seemed to be having with his plumbing — to the impoverished and less rich, actually, Pincus learned in his research to follow, *much* less rich, as there were at that moment in the world, in the vicinity of two billion, four hundred and fifty-two million individuals living on less than a dollar a day. Pincus was encouraged to learn that all the destitute had to do now was hold out their hands to catch the trickle from above.

All in all, the year that was coming to an end had not been especially auspicious. Mt. St. Helens had erupted. The hostages were still being held in Iran. Apartheid was still alive and well in South Africa. The Soviets were still decimating the population of Afghanistan in spite of our having barred our athletes from attending the Moscow Olympics, something which surely should have brought the entire Soviet army to its knees. And, as though hostages, racial bigotry, and war were not irksome enough, John Lennon had shuffled off this mortal coil, with a little help from someone who was clearly not one of his friends.

This last event was for Pincus so catastrophic, that the Beatles would now never reunite, that, to determine where exactly this fit into the misfortunes to befall mankind, Pincus embarked on an intense period of research into the worst things ever to happen to human beings.

The flood of the Yellow River in China in the summer of 1931 had taken the lives of 3,700,000 people, exceeding the previous Yellow River flood of 1931 that swept away nearly 2,000,000 men, women, and children. Add to this the Shaanxi earthquake in China of 1556 that killed upwards of 830,000 people, and China, it seemed to Pincus, had had especially bad luck. In fact, Pincus was soon to learn that four of the five deadliest earthquakes in history had happened in China, but all of this was small potatoes, so to speak, compared to the Great Chinese Famine of 1958–1961 that killed 43,000,000, along with the Chinese famine of 1907 that took another 24,000,000 lives.

Pincus decided to stay away from China, a country that had always been on his short list of those destinations he would have liked to visit before his death, but not necessarily to induce it.

The misfortune of China occupied a lot of Pincus's thought over this year. What had China done to displease God so completely? What *could* they possibly have done that the Almighty would single them out for such devastation, over and again? The numbers were mind-boggling to Pincus, and he imagined people being swept away by walls of water, struggling, arms flailing, holding their children in their arms — hundreds of thousands of people sinking forever beneath the muddy water. It was beyond his imagination. Pincus wanted to understand this. Pincus wanted to know where divine providence was in all this. It became his passion.

He would go every morning to the New York City library at 42nd Street and Fifth Avenue and pore through historical tomes, looking for clues that might lead to an answer.

And then he came upon a number that took his breath away and put an end to his search. Smallpox had so far taken over 300,000,000 lives in the twentieth century alone; the Bubonic plague had claimed another 300,000,000 over its three appearances since the year 540; and malaria another 250,000,000 in the century in which he was now living. Pincus knew for certain that no explanation for any of this could be found in the spiritual world. Death was simply a fact, and death in great numbers, in huge unimaginable numbers, was an even more certain fact.

Pincus felt like running away, far far away, before he was inevitably swept up with the next disaster, but he didn't know where to run. He tried to bring his scientific training to the problem, but it led him nowhere. This was all beyond science. And this is where Pincus made his first great turn.

Pincus decided that the external world, the world of sense perceptions, must be a work of art, certainly not a scientific fact. He decided that the reason he could make no sense of the bodies floating down the rivers and the smoldering ashes that were once human beings was because he was locked up in his receiving instruments, such mundane apparati as his ears, eyes, and nose. In this world, this world that could be permanently cut from us by drops of rain, or microbes too small to see, each man must adventure for himself. Not only is the world imperfect, as he had learned far too well over his year in the bowels of the New York Public Library, but it was most likely an illusion. To make sense of the world, he had to see in Nature something beyond the phenomena, something that, for him, would transcend the death that was sure to come.

For the very first time Pincus saw the light, his own particular light. Pincus concluded that there must be something to know and to love more durable and greater than that provided by the illusions of sense, those senses that led him to experience the world as a place of imminent and unavoidable disaster. That love could be possible in such a place was its great secret, a secret that eluded Pincus as the secret of life eludes the biologist, but he was going to find this love and unearth its unknown. No matter what.

And, as if to prove his point, that there was something operating in the universe beyond what our senses will ever know, it was now that Rosalie, two decades older than when they had first met that snowy night, showed up at his door, forcing Pincus to put aside an interesting news item he had come across in that day's paper, first reports about an especially virulent form of pneumonia, coupled with the sudden appearance of Karposi's sarcoma, which seemed to be targeting homosexual men. As he walked to the door to his apartment to answer the persistent knocking, he was comforted to know that the Centers for Disease Control was on top of the situation and all would soon be resolved. There was nothing to worry about.

CHAPTER 2

The chubby thirty-five-year-old woman with curly hair, wearing jeans that might have fit better a few pounds ago, and now standing at his open door, was a stranger to Pincus.

"Hi," she said.

"Hi," Pincus answered.

"I'm Rosalie," she said, and then continued when it became evident that Pincus didn't recognize her. "You saw me when I was pregnant, twenty years ago.... It was winter. There was a blizzard. You came to my house."

"Ah, yes, Rosalie," Pincus finally registered. "How are you?"

"Not as well as I'd like, actually. May I come in?"

"Well, I'm not really practicing medicine any longer, Rosalie. But I can give you the name of the physician who took over my practice."

"It's not a medical problem. May I?"

Pincus turned around to assess the state of his apartment. It was in moderate disarray, but not so disastrous that he couldn't invite Rosalie in, so he stepped aside and gestured for her to enter.

"Thank you," Rosalie said, came into the room, and removed a rather large backpack and then her coat. She looked around for a place to put them, and Pincus nodded toward a chair against the wall. There was something about the backpack that made Pincus nervous.

"Can I get you something to drink?" he asked.

"You wouldn't by any chance have something to eat, would you?"

"I have some leftover pizza. I can heat it up."

"That'd be very kind of you. I haven't had anything to eat for a few days now."

Pincus felt the concern grow, the one that began when he saw the backpack, as he went to the kitchen in the back of the large open-plan room — a living room, dining room, kitchen all combined, the latest trend in what the ad for his apartment had called "loft-like living." He took the pizza from the refrigerator, put two slices on a plate, then stuck the plate in the microwave.

"If you place a paper towel over the pizza, it'll keep the crust from getting soggy," Rosalie advised, then studied Pincus. "You've put on some weight since I last saw you, haven't you?"

"Yes, I have," Pincus responded.

"It makes you look a little like a turkey — you know, the chins," Rosalie commented.

"So, Rosalie, how can I help you?" Pincus asked, as he tore off a paper towel, placed it over the pizza, placed the pizza back in the microwave, and pushed the start button.

"I'm not sure you can," Rosalie answered.

"Then why are you here?"

"My father told me to come here. Do you remember my father?"

Pincus pulled his mind back to that night, to Pantera, his long hair and chest-length beard, the dark eyes, the lab in which he had captured his animalcula.

"A little, yes. It was a long time ago."

"Well, he told me to come here."

"Did he say why?"

"Not really, but I learned long ago that it's not a good idea to question him. When he says 'go,' it's a good idea to go."

"He didn't want to come with you?"

"Not really. He and my mother have moved to Arizona, to one of those senior communities. They've taken up golf."

"He's playing golf?" Pincus was surprised.

"He's retired. Why not play golf?"

"Well," Pincus ran the image around in his head, "there was something about him that reminded me of ..."

"John the Baptist."

"I hadn't thought of that, actually."

"I had. I think that's who he wants people to think he is, or, at least that he's like him."

"I don't know — John the Baptist retiring to a golf community — I suppose if it weren't for Salome, and there'd *been* golf, he *could* have spent his last years playing golf...." Pincus's voice trailed off, trying to imagine the man who purified Jesus and called on all to repent their sins at the eleventh hour now teeing up on the tenth.

Rosalie looked around the apartment.

"It looks like you got rid of a lot of stuff. I mean, other than the books and some furniture, there's not much else here," Rosalie remarked. "No paintings, photos, plants — nothing."

"I don't like clutter. But you're right, I got rid of a lot of things that had accumulated over the years," Pincus said. "It's a blessing in disguise."

"As what?" Rosalie asked.

"As what?" Pincus asked.

"Yes, what is the blessing disguised *as*?" Rosalie asked and wandered over to the kitchen where the pizza was warming in the microwave.

"Poverty, I suppose," Pincus answered. "Maybe desperation. It depends on my mood."

"Well, I disagree. I think it's terrific to live simply. You shouldn't worry. Things couldn't be better, right?" Rosalie tried to be upbeat.

"No, they could be better. I could have a twenty-two-room house overlooking the sea, staffed with people waiting on me hand and foot, be obscenely wealthy and living with a breathtakingly beautiful nymphomaniac who thinks I'm a god. That could be better."

"You wouldn't *really* be happy."

"Maybe not *really*," Pincus conceded, "but it might *seem* so much like it that it wouldn't matter."

Rosalie didn't smile. Instead she looked up at Pincus with deep sad eyes.

"I can't find Her," Rosalie said.

"Who?"

"Her. She."

A light dawned for Pincus.

"Your daughter?" he asked.

"Yes."

"You call her 'She'?"

"My father called her 'She,' so it stuck. I never much liked it, but She was okay with it. Of course, it didn't sit too well with Her teachers. Actually, it made them rather crazy. But by then, that's who She was, and it was too late. After six years, you don't change a child's name."

Pincus nodded, as the bell sounded on the microwave. "And now you can't find Her?"

"We talked every week, no matter what, and then, suddenly, it stopped. When I called the convent, She'd left. I haven't heard from Her since. It's been years now. Not a word."

"Convent? She became a nun?"

"Her? No way. She was a student there. I knew it wasn't going all that well. I mean, it was going well, but there were certain — problems."

"What kind of problems?"

"It's kind of complicated. But, anyway, I don't think that's why She left and just — disappeared."

"Maybe She found a boyfriend and She's all involved in a relationship," Pincus suggested as he removed the pizza from the microwave and handed it to Rosalie.

"Thanks," Rosalie took the pizza and then bit off a chunk of it. She continued to talk as she chewed. "I doubt it's a boyfriend. It's something else."

"Like what?"

"Well, the truth is that my father thinks She's waiting for you. May I have something to drink with this?"

CHAPTER 3

"The way my father carried on about who was in my womb, you would have thought that I'd have had some sort of special birth," Rosalie said as she sucked on the end of the bottle of beer Pincus had given to her.

"Angels floating overhead, singing some sort of beautiful song, surrounded by inspirational light — *something*. Instead, She was ass-backwards, and the pain was beyond anything I can possibly describe. It was as though She was holding on to every organ in my body and wouldn't let go. I thought She was going to take my entire insides with Her. For someone who was supposedly a great divinity, one thing was clear — She did not want to be here, and since She couldn't take it out on my father, it was going to be me.

"Even the doctor said he'd never seen anything like it. He'd turn Her, and She'd turn right back. He'd pull and the second he let go, She'd go back in. It was a tug-of-war, and it went on for so long that I thought I was going to pass out.

"Finally, the doctor said, 'Okay, we're doing a Caesarean,' and the second She heard that, it was like She was shot from a cannon. She popped out like a cork.

"The doctor looked at this newborn thing wriggling in his hand, and She looked up at him, and they stared at each other, and then — now get this — the doctor swears that She *winked* at him, like She was saying, 'Well, you got me out, so now what?' until finally I said, 'I'd like to see my baby.'

The doctor handed Her to me, and, I have to tell you, this was the ugliest thing I had ever seen. She was wrinkled up like a dried fig, and purple, and I thought, if this is Her, if this is the divine spirit who is the Mother of all Gods, then we are in deep shit."

Rosalie took a long sip of her beer, emptying the bottle, while Pincus waited for the story to continue.

"You would've thought after all that, things would settle down. They didn't. Actually, giving birth to Her may have been the *easiest* part. She set a new record for colicky babies. And nothing we could do could quiet Her for more than ten minutes at a time. One thing was obvious — this child did not want to be here in this world.

"Then came the allergies. My breast milk didn't agree with Her, so I had to stop breast-feeding Her, which hurt – not the feeding part, the having to stop part. It made me feel terrible, completely inadequate as a mother.

"We tried soy milk, and then all the different powdered formulas that were supposed to be hypoallergenic, but they didn't work, either. We tried goat's milk, and that didn't work.

"Did you know that kangaroos have milk for their baby joeys? I didn't. So, we tried that. It didn't work.

"Whales give milk. You can get it in Japan. It's not cheap, but they've got it, and I really don't want to know how they get it. It's not as though they've got whale corrals where the whale farmers go early every morning to squeeze – what? And where do the whales have their boobs? Have *you* ever seen them? *I* haven't. And they're whales, so their boobs must be *enormous*, right? But where *are* they? And how in God's name do you *milk* a whale? Have you ever seen a group of guys out in the Pacific in black scuba suits kicking their flippers back and forth from a whale, holding little metal pails of *milk* over their goggles?

"But, She *loved* whale milk. We had UPS at our door every Thursday with cartons containing dozens of little metal cans, and She drank them up like they were *piña coladas*.

"Whale milk smells awful. It smells like rotten fish, which is, of course, what you'd expect from an animal that eats plankton all day.

So, the letters started coming again from the people who lived in the building. They thought we were canning sardines in our apartment. I don't really blame them. It was rank.

"We tried everything — air filters, incense, perfumed candles. Nothing worked. No matter what you did, everything smelled like tuna fish gone bad. But it made Her healthy, so what choice did we have?

"By the time She hit the terrible twos, I was exhausted. I wanted to jump off a building. Then she started crawling. I want you to know that there is no form of babyproofing that works with God. Just think for a moment of what Mary would have had to do to babyproof her place for Jesus. Most people don't think about that. Why even bother, right?"

Pincus tried to imagine the Virgin Mother securing cabinet doors and putting her cleaning supplies on the top shelves.

"And then one day, I remember this as though it was yesterday: she was three, and we went out to a diner to eat, because people interested Her and She would keep still and quiet for a while, and I was walking down the aisle between the booths, and a woman looked up at me and said, 'She's the most beautiful child I have ever seen.'

"I was dumbstruck. I looked at Her, and it was as if I was looking at Her for the very first time, and the woman was right. She was absolutely beautiful, just radiant, with a lovely light in her eyes, and I didn't know when that happened, and how I missed it, and most of all, She was mine.

"Then the most terrible sadness came over me, because I realized that She wasn't really mine. She came from me, but She would never be *only* mine.

"It was as though She understood what I was thinking, and She took my hand, and that was the first time She'd done that. She reached out for my hand, and She held it tightly, and She looked up at me with this beautiful smile, and there was this silent communication between us, and I understood what She was saying to me.

"'Yes, I am everyone's, but that means I'm yours, too.' And we walked to our booth, Her hand in mine, and I had tears pouring down my face, like *I* was the child."

CHAPTER 4

Pincus took Rosalie's words in with what could be described as a state of *fascinated detachment* (accompanied by disbelief) from where he sat on the overstuffed sofa he had purchased on sale at the Pottery Barn the year before — a deep burgundy with a design on the upholstery that could have been flowers, or perhaps birds in flight, but was in reality nothing, just blotches of brown and blue.

Across from him on the brown faux-leather chair he had gotten from Ikea, sat Rosalie, and, as her tale unwound, he inexplicably found himself thinking back to the first time he had seen a praying mantis on his grandfather's New Hampshire farm at age six.

What could the function be of this spindly creature? What possible purpose could there be in this design? It was, to Pincus at that age, already a challenge of understanding, unlike anything he had so far encountered in his life, as though this creature had been placed on earth to demonstrate to all who encountered it that this was a strange universe, indeed, as he would later read, not only stranger than we suppose, but stranger than we *can* suppose.

And so he listened to Rosalie with the same attention he had placed on the praying mantis. He observed the way she would move forward in her chair to make a point, and then retreat, as though seeking refuge. He watched how her hands never stopped moving, tapping her knee, her fingers playing in the air, fiddling with a button, pushing back her hair.

He had followed the praying mantis all day, watching it rise up on its legs, its long neck held absolutely still, its triangular head with the bulging eyes fixed intently on young Pincus, and then it would move on, Pincus a step behind, until finally it reached the neighbor's pond.

As the afternoon wore on and became evening, Pincus could hear his grandfather calling for him, but he dared not answer in fear of startling the mantis. Finally, as he could hear his grandfather's voice growing closer, Pincus reached out his hand, and, after a brief hesitation, the mantis climbed into his open palm and stood on his hind legs, spreading his tuxedo tail in an act that seemed to Pincus, kingly.

"Max!" His grandfather's voice boomed out, and the mantis jumped instantly from Pincus's hand on to a leaf floating by in the pond and drifted off into the darkness of an overhanging tree, lost forever.

When his grandfather arrived, Pincus had tears welling in his eyes.

"Well, if you wander off like this, you *will* get lost eventually," his grandfather told Pincus.

But, in fact, Pincus did not feel lost. He felt found, as he felt now, studying Rosalie, who he knew was to become a part of his life. He wondered for how long and whether one day she, too, would startle and jump from his hand to the nearest leaf that floated by.

CHAPTER 5

"She taught Herself to read when She was three," Rosalie continued to tell her tale, scarcely taking a breath. "How do you do that? How can a child teach Herself to read? I could never figure it out. But She loved words. She'd study them and listen to people say them, and, somehow She made the connections, and then one day we were at the grocery store, in front of all the Campbell soups, and there She was saying to me, 'Chicken with rice? No. Tomato? I don't think so. Bean with bacon, yuk! Broccoli and cheese. No thank you. Italian wedding soup. That sounds interesting. Let's have that.'

"Did I say She was three? Well, She was. Three years old and two months. Where did this come from? By the time She was four, She had run out of interesting English words and She started looking for words in other languages. Ramen noodles, Roquefort cheese, Bratwurst, Dorito tortilla chips and salsa, Barilla pasta, pita, yogurt — she found the foreign words on the packages and then she started saying words in Japanese, French, German, Spanish, Italian, Arabic, and Turkish. Other kids are outside playing in their sandboxes — she's sitting by the radio, switching stations from one language to the next. We must have thirty foreign language stations in New York. By the time She was four, I didn't have a clue what She was saying to me or even what language She was saying it in.

"So I took her to a child psychiatrist, and he listened to her garble on for ten minutes, and he said She was an 'idiot savant polyglot' and would probably never have an I.Q. over seventy, although, if we were lucky, She could probably play on the piano from memory everything

Mozart wrote in his lifetime just from hearing it once. Would you like to know how she responded?

Pincus, transfixed by this tale, nodded his head.

"She said to him, 'You're the idiot and the sad thing is, there's nothing savant about you that'll make up for it. You're just a plain idiot. Let's go home, Mommy.' And that was that. She got up, started to leave, then turned back to the shrink before She went out the door."

"You speak Hungarian, Dr. Szarka?" She asked.

"Yes, I speak Hungarian," Szarka said.

"Good," She says, and then She said a few sentences in Hungarian that, by the time She was done, had turned Dr. Szarka's professional demeanor into something very much like goulash.

"It wasn't that She didn't have friends as a child," Roslaie was on a roll. "She did. But the children who met her, either they adored her and would do anything she said, or they couldn't stand her and found her too bossy, so they wouldn't have anything to do with her.

And then She started school and that's where the real trouble began, because She was a very strong-willed child and had a lot of very specific ideas. The teachers tried to be supportive, but eventually it got to them. In fourth grade poor Mrs. Mirshon had a nervous breakdown trying to use reason to deal with Her, because She always had an answer. It just wore out Mrs. Mirshon's brain until there wasn't much left that was any good.

"That was when we first began to think that it might be wise to send Her away to a boarding school where things might be more structured.

"The final straw came a few months later when I was in the kitchen, cooking dinner for us, and I heard this strange sound coming from Her room. Actually, it wasn't the first time I'd heard strange sounds coming from Her room, but, as She was now a teenager, we had reached an agreement that Her room was Her own private area, and I would not enter it. But this time there was a racket that couldn't be ignored, and I began to get worried.

"I went upstairs and knocked on Her door. Then I knocked again, louder this time to be heard over the racket, and finally I just started pounding. She opened the door a crack.

'What?' She asked.

'What's going on in there?' I asked.

'Nothing.'

'What do you mean 'nothing'? It sounds like — well, I don't know what it sounds like. I've never heard anything like it before. I'm coming in.'

'Okay, it's just some friends of mine,' and She turned around and shouted, 'Shut up, will ya?' But all that did was increase the racket, and then, out of nowhere, a pigeon flew on to her shoulder.

'What's that?'

'It's a bird.'

'I can see it's a bird.'

'A pigeon. Gabrielle. That's her name. Gabrielle.'

'How sweet. And appropriate. Now let me in there,' I stood my ground.

'No way,' and then She started to stroke the pigeon's neck with the back of her finger. 'We're going to stand right here, aren't we, Gabrielle,' She cooed to the bird as She continued to stroke its neck. 'And nooo-body can come in, because this is our place, isn't it?'

'Guess what, dear? I'm coming in' I said.

"So I pushed on the door before she could react. There was a menagerie in her room. Two squirrels chased each other from window to window, leaping up on the glass and then sliding back down. There was something that looked a lot like a ferret or weasel that was burrowing under the pillow on her bed. Birds flew everywhere, flapping and whistling away. A large snake hung off the clothes rod in her closet, beneath which a number of lizards sat, staring out of the darkness.

'You see,' She said. 'I told you that you shouldn't have come in.'

"And that was when we sent Her away to the Convent of the Sisters of Perpetual Sorrow."

Pincus looked at Rosalie, who was quiet for the first time since she had entered his apartment.

"You can sleep on the sofa," he said, and Pincus went to fetch blankets, towels, and a pillow for Rosalie.

"Thank you," Rosalie smiled, the red lipstick on her mouth framing her words like a tulip.

CHAPTER 6

In the morning, after a sleepless night, Pincus found himself sitting in the easy chair once more, across from Rosalie, who was now sleeping peacefully on the sofa.

Her blond hair, he noticed, was fine strands of silk, and, being tied up on top of her head as it was, left little stray wisps extending from her neck, like lace filigree. Strangely, her ears, he decided, were much too large for her slender neck, and her neck too slender for her double chin. All in all, the more he studied her, the more he became aware that her anatomical parts didn't work as a cohesive whole at all. And, yet, in their not fitting together in any aesthetic way, they made a sort of organization that seemed, when considered in their entirety, rather pleasing, Pincus thought.

As Pincus watched Rosalie sleeping across from him, he now felt a certain comfort being in Rosalie's presence. In fact, this is what most impressed him as he sat there, his hands folded neatly in his lap like a school child listening attentively to a teacher — the presence of someone else, another human before him. Is this why he had married Becki and spent twenty-six years living with her, to have someone else there? Just there.

And, of course, the ultimate result of this new and important insight was that the ache returned, the ache that had caused him to walk away from Becki and his children, as though they had never existed.

What this proved to Pincus at that moment was that, in spite of his caring for his family, the presence he desired could not be any presence. It had to be a presence linked to his soul. It had to be Her.

And now poor Pincus's fantasy life rose up like a leviathan emerging from the brackish waters of his life. And once the monster was there, it slowly transformed into Her, into a thing of beauty — an angel-like being walking gracefully from the water toward him, glorious and radiant, with an extraordinary inner beauty and, Pincus was absolutely certain, a desire for him, only him.

Rosalie stirred, mumbled something in her sleep, and turned so she no longer faced Pincus. And now Pincus's thoughts turned to Her creation.

He did not for a minute believe Pantera, the Thaumaturge's, tale of animalcula. No, God must have done this. But how and why now? For that matter, why had God bothered to create anything at all? Assuming that God must have, by His very nature, been doing just fine, whatever on earth made Him decide he needed a universe?

And now, as Pincus settled back in his armchair, his eyes begin to droop, and drowsiness started to overcome Pincus while he sorted out the great questions of the cosmos.

Was God just something of a watchmaker, creating a universe, winding it up, and then standing back, uninvolved, while the hands of time moved on?

You don't get a watch without a watchmaker, and so, Pincus concluded, God must be necessary. And if God is necessary, then the universe He created, and all that is contained within it, including man, is necessary, not the least of which is the reasoning function He has given man, reasoning that had allowed Pincus to consider all this and arrive at such irrefutable conclusions. Surely, the mind of man was a gift of God, if for no other reason than because it served no evolutionary purpose. What is the selective advantage of music? Even more importantly, what is the survival value of knowing God?

It is here that Pincus came upon an insight that was to direct his behavior from this point on. It went like this:

God had no choice other than to create man as he is, conscious and contemplative, because to do otherwise would have meant that

His creation, His universe, would have gone unnoticed. And what fun is there in that? If you're going to create a universe, you might as well get some credit for doing it.

The great insight of Pincus was this: God needs applause. That is the explanation for the Universe.

Nevertheless, Pincus was willing to concede that there were, in many respects — putting aside the incessant catastrophes with which Pincus was now intimately familiar, and the issue of human self-interest and war-mongering — an undeniable beauty to this creation. And God had the good sense to make a mankind who could appreciate this beauty, the beauty of a landscape, of art and music and literature, of an elegant equation, and of curves, especially those curves of the female form. And this led Pincus to what he considered to be an obvious (and others considered unique) conclusion.

Ultimately, it all came down to sex. God had made a universe with the kind of curved beauty that would get women wet and give men erections.

And it was at this moment that Rosalie turned toward Pincus, opened her eyes, smiled at him, then closed her eyes and went back to sleep, as did Pincus.

CHAPTER 7

Deep among the dwellings,
Long since shuttered,
Doors now firmly locked,
Against the winds of fortune,
A light within appears
At midnight,
Spreading frosty pane,
To frosty pane,
And then another —

Pincus awakened from this dream in which he was, at long last, writing his poetry. He was awakened by the clanging of pots and pans, a clanging that had, in fact, been going on for some time. He was still in the armchair in which he had fallen asleep and was, at first, annoyed to be awakened prior to his finishing a poem he considered extremely promising.

"You should go wash up," Rosalie, seeing that Pincus had awakened, said from the kitchen from which the clanging came.

"Wash up?" Pincus asked, trying to orient himself to the presence of Rosalie, the smells of cooking, and no longer being asleep.

"Exactly. Go wash up. Your hands and your face. Your teeth as well. You can change your clothes later, because your breakfast is almost ready," Rosalie explained.

Pincus studied the situation in the same way he might study a fallen object, trying to determine whence it had come and what had caused it to fall, and then he forced himself to rise from the chair and walk toward his bedroom. On the stove he could see bacon and eggs cooking. The small kitchen table was set, glasses of orange juice beside each plate. The last gasps of steam were coming from the electric coffeemaker, which hissed as it finished its work.

"How did you know what I have for breakfast?" Pincus asked Rosalie.

"I opened the refrigerator and saw a carton of orange juice, a carton of eggs, a package of bacon, a loaf of bread, butter, jam, and a container of coffee, and I just took a gamble that this was your breakfast. Don't forget to wash between your fingers. Most people miss that," and Rosalie went back to her cooking.

"I like my eggs scrambled."

"You seemed like scrambled, so that's what I did."

"I seem like scrambled?"

"Sunny-side up requires a certain skill and concentration if you don't want the yolk to break, and even then there can be problems. I decided that you probably cracked them into a bowl and beat the hell out of them."

"I'll go wash up," and Pincus disappeared into the bedroom.

"Use a washcloth," Rosalie called after him, and then lowered the burner under the bacon.

When Pincus returned, Rosalie was in front of him like a bouncer at a disco.

"Show me," she demanded.

"Show you what?" Pincus asked.

"Your hands."

"You're kidding."

"I'm not kidding. I want to see your hands."

"What am I, three years old?"

"Hands, please. If you want breakfast, I need to see your hands."

Pincus looked over at the plate of steaming bacon and eggs sitting on the table. Then he held out his hands.

"Over, please."

Pincus flipped his hands over.

"When was the last time you cut your nails?"

"I don't remember."

"I didn't think so. Okay, we'll do your nails after breakfast. Otherwise it'll get cold," and Rosalie stepped aside to let Pincus pass.

Pincus studied Rosalie's eyes before moving on to the breakfast table. They were deep pools of concern — as though she knew the turmoil within him. There was something about these dark rosettes that seemed comforting. He smiled at her. She smiled back, and they took their places at the table.

"I was writing poetry," Pincus said as he started his orange juice. "In a dream. It seemed like a good start. I've been wanting to write a book of poetry since I moved back to New York, but there always seem to be things getting in the way."

"You moved away from the city?"

"When the kids got ready for school, we left New York. Becki – my ex-wife – and I never believed much in private schools, and the cost is outrageous, so we moved to Greenwich."

Rosalie nodded as she bit into a slice of bacon.

"And now you've stopped practicing medicine and moved back to Manhattan," Rosalie stated what she already knew as a way of confirming that she had been paying attention since the night before.

"I had plans for a new life here. I thought this would be a good place to be. Lots of people. Stimulating. The energy of the city. It was perfect."

In reality, the move to Manhattan had not been what Pincus expected or desired. He imagined himself steeped in the culture of New York. He imagined himself giving readings of his poetry – from what would have been his sixth book of verse, now in its third printing — in Greenwich Village book shops, perhaps even the 92nd Street Y. He saw himself at concerts, museums, and opera performances, drinking up culture like a camel having come upon an oasis.

Within days of his moving back to Manhattan, he had bought sea-son tickets to the New York Philharmonic Orchestra, the Metropolitan Opera, and yearly memberships to the Metropolitan Museum, the Museum of Modern Art, the Whitney, and the Guggenheim. After two years, he had been to each of the museums twice, and found himself in front of paintings he had either seen countless times in books or paintings he neither liked nor understood.

While he faithfully attended every subscribed performance of the New York Philharmonic and the Metropolitan Opera the first year, he found the second year that most of the operas were being repeated, and the Philharmonic Orchestra had decided to devote itself to Russian composers, something he soon decided one could take in very limited doses, like a medication with extremely serious side effects, and determined rather quickly that the angst of the great Russian composers was one of those cases where the cure was far worse than the disease.

He had chosen an apartment right on Central Park, expecting to go for lengthy contemplative walks, à la Emerson, or Whitman, or Thoreau. In fact, he began to read about muggings and murders in the park at night, then evenings, and then in the early mornings, leaving poor Pincus with a ten-minute window in which he would have felt safe venturing into the greens and arbors of Central Park, and then only heavily armed.

No, moving to New York City had not been a huge success for Pincus, and, as though in response, Rosalie looked up from her now-empty breakfast plate and nodded to Pincus.

"Do you want some more coffee? Because you really should start packing."

And before Pincus knew what was happening, he found himself in his bedroom with Rosalie, who was going through his drawers and closets and laying things out on the bed.

"Do you have a large backpack?" Rosalie asked Pincus, who shook his head.

"Well, then, we'll have to go buy one, because you can't go dragging a suitcase around."

"What's wrong with a suitcase?"

"On a pilgrimage? You're going to take a suitcase on a pilgrimage?"

"What pilgrimage?" Pincus asked.

"To find Her. You are going to help me, aren't you? She's waiting for you, not for me."

"Suppose She's staying at a hotel. I've been to hotels. People have suitcases there. I've seen them."

"She's not at a hotel, believe me. What would She be doing at a hotel?"

"I don't know. People don't usually do anything at hotels. Unless it's a convention. Or Las Vegas. They stay in hotels because they're doing something else nearby."

"She's not at a hotel. Do you have any pants that aren't all ragged at the cuffs? There's not a single one that isn't all frayed at the bottom. Why don't you buy shorter pants?"

"These are the size I've always worn. The pants tend to descend as I walk."

"What about blue jeans? Do you have blue jeans?"

"I have blue jeans," and Pincus removed a pair of jeans from his closet. Rosalie took them, examined the cuffs, placed them on the bed, and then went to the bureau and opened another drawer.

"You wear jockey underwear?"

"Can I please do this? I really would prefer if you didn't go through my drawers."

"Do men your age still wear jockey shorts?" Rosalie ignored Pincus's request.

"Apparently some do."

"Do you have a good pair of walking shoes?"

"I have sneakers."

"Sneakers aren't walking shoes."

"Really? What do people do in them?" Pincus was getting into what his ex-wife often described as a state.

"People run in them. You need walking shoes," Rosalie moved on. "We'll get you a good pair when we buy the backpack."

"You know, Rosalie, I don't remember saying that I'd be going with you to find Her."

"You didn't. But you will, won't you." This was not a question.

Pincus said nothing, but his eyes were the answer.

"I'm dreading going into your sock drawer, but —"

Pincus slammed his hands against the drawer before she could open it.

"I thought so," Rosalie nodded.

PART IV

The Nun's Tale

CHAPTER 1

They had spent several hours at a sporting goods store with an extensive section on camping, and it was here that Pincus had spent more time than he wished trying on heavy leather ankle-high hiking boots with rawhide laces and metal hooks until he finally found a pair that didn't seem to him as though he would be walking in leg irons.

Then it was on to socks that had to be, according to Rosalie, thick enough to absorb the sweat from the walking. Socks were followed by shorts and pants, constructed, it seemed to Pincus, almost entirely of pockets.

His outfit was completed with a poncho, a "slicker," as Rosalie called it, and a cap with a visor, on the front of which was embroidered an image of a carp jumping from the water, a hook in its mouth. It was Pincus who selected this, as he felt a certain rapport with the ensnared fish.

"Okay," Rosalie nodded to Pincus when the clothing aspect of the shopping seemed to be completed to her satisfaction, "now let's find the tent."

"What tent?" Pincus asked in alarm.

"We're not sleeping at hotels," Rosalie replied. "I have some savings, but I need them for our meals. I can't afford to waste money on hotels."

"I'll pay for the hotels, and exactly how long a pilgrimage were you expecting this to be?"

"I have absolutely no idea, but obviously not into the winter, or we'll need to entirely re-provision ourselves."

"Suppose She went south — where it's warm?"

"Why would She go south?"

"Why wouldn't She?"

"Because there's nothing there."

"In the entire southern half of the United States? Surely there must be something there. There're a heck of a lot of people living there."

"And even more who don't. She'd never go south."

"Because?..."

"Because I'm her mother, and I know which direction She'd go."

"What kind of tent?" Pincus asked.

"Light. Not too big."

"But not too small, either," Pincus said, studying Rosalie. "And don't we need sleeping bags and air mattresses?"

Rosalie nodded and a smile came to her lips.

"I knew you'd get into this," she said, and less than an hour later Pincus found himself at Grand Central Terminal, where they would be taking the train on the first leg of their journey.

Grand Central was mobbed that afternoon. There had been torrential thunderstorms off and on during the day, and the long wooden benches in the waiting room had become a temporary residence to scores of the homeless, their heads propped up on the green trash bags in which they kept their belongings. Pincus felt a comradeship with them.

As he walked into the main part of the terminal, past the long lines at the central information booth with the gold and ornate antique clock on top, he encountered hundreds of children being assembled for journeys to summer camp. Counselors ran about herding the campers into manageable groups, an exercise that seemed fruitless as ten-year-olds chased other ten-year-olds around the huge open space.

Before Pincus had the time to give much thought to this, he noticed a young boy of, perhaps, seven or eight, short-clipped blond hair, tan shorts, his hands folded on his lap, sitting quietly on his trunk, the blue of his eyes stilled with sadness. Rosalie had seen him as well, and Pincus watched her walk over and sit beside the boy. They talked for a moment, and then the boy began to smile. Rosalie gave the child a tight hug and a long kiss on his cheek, and then the boy leapt from the trunk and ran over to the rest of the group, which were now being shepherded to the train platform.

"Did you know him?" Pincus asked when Rosalie returned.

"No. His father is away on business, and his mother had to work, so he came with the family of one of his friends. He had nobody from his family to say good-bye to him, so I told him I was a very close friend of his mother, and she had sent me especially to give him a big hug and kiss and say good-bye for her."

Pincus looked at Rosalie, a pang in his heart.

"He told you this?" Pincus asked.

"No, I just knew," Rosalie said.

"How did you just know?" Pincus asked.

"Mothers just know these things, Max. May I call you, Max?"

But Rosalie never waited for an answer. She just took his hand, as though he were another camper, and led him off to the gate for their train for New Haven, Pincus struggling under the weight of the giant aluminum-framed backpack held firmly in place on his back by shoulder straps and several large buckled belts across his chest. As he walked, he imagined himself in a long line of peasants, plodding blindly up a mountain, a heavy burlap bag of coffee beans strapped to his back, dodging the dung that issued from the backsides of the mules directly in front of him.

And so it was with great relief that, once on the train, he began the process of disengaging himself from his load. This turned out to be no less arduous a task than it had been to get into the rig, and was accompanied by Rosalie's frequent warnings of "Watch out, Max!" as he knocked into one passenger after another who were trying to pass by.

"It's a good thing you never had to parachute into hostile territory," Rosalie commented, as she disengaged the last buckle and the backpack fell with a crash to the floor. "By the time you got out of the parachute, you'd have been shot so many times you'd look like Swiss cheese."

"Help me get this damn thing up into the overhead rack," Pincus said, and then he took his seat by the window, through which he saw only the dark of the tunnel and the reflection of his own face. He did not like what he saw and turned to Rosalie, who was now peeling an orange.

"How far from New Haven is the convent?" he asked.

"We're not going to New Haven," Rosalie answered as she dug her fingernails into the rind of the orange. "We're changing in Norwalk for the train to Danbury."

"The convent is in Danbury?"

"No, it's in Canaan."

"There's really a Canaan in New York?"

"Connecticut."

"Like the Canaan from which the Canaanites of Israel are descended, the Canaan with the Curse of Ham?"

"I don't know. At the convent I think they eat bacon, like with eggs, and maybe ham."

"Ham was not pork — he was Canaan's elder brother. The curse was put on him by Noah for not sharing in his brother's allotment of land. He insisted in staying on the Eastern shores of the Mediterranean."

"Oh, I thought it was the prohibition about eating pigs. Why wouldn't Ham leave the Eastern shore?"

"I don't know. Maybe he liked the view better. Jews are very particular about getting a good view of the sea wherever they stay. Or it could have been the way brothers can get sometimes."

"You have brothers?"

Pincus shook his head.

"Sisters?"

Pincus shook his head again.

"Only child?"

"It would seem that way."

"Your parents still alive?"

"No, my father died a few years ago. He had a bad heart ... and lungs ... and a lot of other things. And my mother died of pneumonia when I was thirteen. You're not supposed to die of pneumonia, but she did."

"Did you give them a hard time and wear out their organs?"

"No, I was a model child. They doted on me. Their organs weren't so good to begin with. Both their parents died young. How far is Canaan from Danbury?"

"Fifty miles."

"Is there another train to Canaan?"

"No."

"A bus?"

"No."

"Then what?"

"Feet," and Rosalie held out a section of orange for Pincus.

"I'm not hungry," Pincus pouted. He began to calculate. "A person walks four miles an hour, without a backpack. With a backpack, if we do three miles an hour, we'll be lucky. That's seventeen hours of walking."

"I'm not especially good at math, but I'll take your word for it," Rosalie answered.

"We can rent a car. I'll pay for it," Pincus pleaded.

 "A pilgrimage in a car? Get serious, Max. Here," and Rosalie held out the orange once more.

"No thanks," Pincus grumbled.

"You should take it, Max. You'll need it to keep up your blood sugar."

CHAPTER 2

For the next hour Pincus stared out the window in silence. He was disturbed by what he saw. The ground beside the rails was an almost endless pile of trash — rusted cans, empty oil containers, plastic debris of every kind — papers and scraps of metal and wood. He wondered how the trash had gotten there. The windows of the train didn't open, and he'd never seen people standing in the junction between the rail cars throwing debris.

But it was not this subject, in spite of the considerable thought Pincus gave to it, that most interested him. It was the graffiti. It was everywhere. On walls and buildings, on the carcasses of the rusted and abandoned cars, on the sides of trains parked on sidings, on bridges and inside the tunnels, giant swirling colorful graffiti filled every once-empty space. Pincus found it discomforting. If this was the writing on the wall, it was nonsense, indecipherable, not even intended to have meaning. It meant nothing. Absolutely nothing. It was gibberish, highly stylized, brilliantly colorful gibberish.

Pincus thought of bringing the matter to Rosalie's attention, soliciting her opinion, but before he could say anything, Rosalie stood up and announced that the next stop was theirs.

This was not welcome news to Pincus, not only for the trek that lay ahead of him, but for what would now be required to reinsert himself into the harness of his backpack, an exercise that he knew would result in a certain level of catastrophe for nearby passengers. He could not have been more prescient, and, even with Rosalie assisting him, the entire enterprise ended with two rather large men with shaved heads pushing poor Pincus out onto the platform just before the train's doors slid closed behind him.

Pincus managed to grab onto a railing as he hurtled ahead and, by holding to it tightly, was able to keep himself upright. Rosalie said nothing as she shifted her own backpack, but looked at Pincus in the way a mother might regard a child who, after many years and exhortations, had still not managed to learn the technique for keeping his shirt tucked into his pants.

She let out a long sigh and pointed toward a train waiting on the opposite track.

"That's our train to Danbury," she said, as she started off. "I'd say 'Follow me,' but under the circumstances, you should probably use the handicap ramp, Max."

CHAPTER 3

The journey that followed was a definite improvement over the first leg, Pincus decided, as he watched the countryside roll by. He passed ponds and lakes, shores full with trees, leaves overhanging the water, rustling in the breezes that moved across the blue mirror surfaces, shaking the trees as if, Pincus thought, to prevent them from developing a deep-rooted complacency.

There were wide open fields with knee-high grasses, and vast expanses of wild flowers; abandoned factories, windows long ago broken out, their concrete interiors empty except for the rusting hulk of a machine, too gigantic to move.

Every now and then they would pass a war memorial, its bronze plates green with age, listing the dead of one war or another. And then another lake, or stream, or farm, or a reservoir, followed by a single house, set down in the midst of nothing. Could a family possibly be living in such isolation, Pincus wondered, or were these, too, like old factories, abandoned remnants of another time?

As they approached Danbury, there was an abrupt change. The countryside ended abruptly, and suddenly there was a city, houses closely packed together, neighborhoods, and, as the train began to slow and the conductor announced they were arriving in Danbury, stores appeared: supermarkets, strip malls, fast food franchises.

Pincus's heart sank. The pastoral settings outside his window had put him in a receptive mood and reminded him of his journey, at the end of which he hoped to find the woman who would calm his tumultuous heart. Perhaps, were fortune to smile upon him, he would find peace at long last, the same peace he had felt in looking out the window at the fields of wild flowers and the still waters of the small ponds. And now this — this Danbury. It was unsettling. As the train pulled into its final destination, Pincus thought of the trek that awaited him. A cold feeling filled his heart. He looked up in dismay at the backpack in the rack over his head and let out a sigh.

"We'll let everyone else get off before us," Rosalie said, smiling maternally, "and then we can do the backpack thing."

Pincus nodded with some relief, and then looked out the window at the city of Danbury, which immediately displeased him.

"I don't see the problem," Rosalie replied, as they walked down Danbury's Main Street, divided by a grass median that had once been the town green and was now a park in desperate need of repair.

"The problem is that the street looks like someone bought a book on architecture of the last two hundred years and then leafed through it, picking a different style for each structure every ten pages," grumbled Pincus.

"So?" Rosalie asked.

"So?" Pincus answered in astonishment.

"I'm hungry," was Rosalie's answer, and she took Pincus by the arm and led him across the street off toward a luncheonette, where they buried themselves behind their menus in a windowside booth.

"I don't see the problem, Max," Rosalie's voice came from behind the folded cardboard in front of her face, as she scanned the offerings. "Okay, so they varied the styles of the buildings on Main Street. What of it?"

But before Pincus could respond, a waitress appeared at the table to take their order.

"I'll have the chili burger with fries, a side of cole slaw, and a Coke," Pincus told the round waitress with bleached-blond hair, a giant ornate crucifix on her well-developed chest, and a name tag to the right of it that identified her as May.

"He'll have a salad with a scoop of tuna, no fries or slaw, and a grapefruit juice," Rosalie told May.

"No, I won't," Pincus protested. "I'll have a chili burger, fries, cole slaw, and a Coke."

"You won't get ten minutes down the road with a lunch like that," Rosalie informed Max. "It'll weigh on your stomach like a sack of cement, and I think you've got enough to handle right now with the backpack," and Rosalie looked back up at May. "Tuna salad, grapefruit juice," she advised the waitress, who looked over at Pincus, who just waved his arms helplessly.

"You can make that two," Rosalie added.

May nodded, jotted down the order, smiled, and departed.

"So, what's the problem, Max?" Rosalie resumed their conversation.

"With my food or the town?"

"The town. We've already discussed the food, and I don't want to re-discuss it. It's been resolved."

"It doesn't feel like it's been resolved," Pincus answered. "I still keep seeing, sitting on a large plate in front of me, a great big burger, with chili spilling out of its sides, a giant mound of fries smothered in ketchup, a bowl of cole slaw swimming in mayo, and a glass of Coke fizzing away. I can hear the fizz right now."

"If you have something more to say about the town's architectural failings, I would be more than delighted to listen."

"It's a hodge-podge," Pincus moved on.

"And New York City is not?"

"New York is New York," Pincus answered. "New York City has ten million people from a hundred and fifty different countries. Variety can't be helped."

"There it's variety. Here's it's a hodge-podge."

"Here it's ugly. It's what happens when you don't have town planning. If God had created the universe like this, it would be one big chaotic mess, and we'd probably have two heads and no brain."

"The universe turned out okay because God was a Town Planner?"

"There's a disconnect," Pincus informed Rosalie.

"What kind of disconnect?"

"Between God and Danbury."

"Well," Rosalie offered, "maybe God sees Danbury differently. Maybe He thinks it's just the coolest hodgepodgist place."

"Not possible."

"Why is that, Max?"

"Aquinas."

"St. Thomas Aquinas?"

"Exactly."

"He's been to Danbury?"

"No, but he pointed out that God is a necessary, timeless, immutable, perfect, unchanging being on which the universe depends utterly for its existence, but, on the other hand, who is completely unaffected by the universe. God couldn't care one way or the other about Danbury. He probably isn't even aware it exists. The question is — how could He have created such perfection, which has led to such ridiculous imperfection?"

"Danbury?"

"Danbury," and Pincus looked down unhappily at the tuna salad and grapefruit juice being placed in front of him.

CHAPTER 4

Having passed through Danbury, Pincus and Rosalie found themselves on a winding country road beneath a canopy of full trees that provided welcome shade from the sun. The road was bordered by knee-high stone walls, centuries old, serving, as far as Pincus could tell, no practical purpose other than a place to sit and rest his weary legs while he sipped at his water bottle.

Rosalie was not pleased by this rest stop, but decided not to fuss, and joined Max on the wall.

"We probably haven't gone two miles, yet, Max," Rosalie commented.

"I'm thirsty and I'm tired," was Max's reply, as he took a long drink from his water bottle.

"How do you expect to get to Canaan, if we stop every two miles?" Rosalie fussed.

"I expect, assuming it's fifty miles away, that we'll get there after twenty-five stops."

"This is a pilgrimage, Max. Pilgrims can find no rest until they've reached their destination," Rosalie reminded Max.

"So I've heard. But this pilgrim needs frequent hydration," and Pincus took a long drink from his water bottle, screwed the cap back on, struggled to his feet, and, to Rosalie's relief, they resumed walking, finally arriving, several hours later, at the steep road that led into the town of New Milford.

A green ran the length of the main street, at the beginning of which was a large white church with the usual incongruous mixture of architectures to which Pincus was becoming more accustomed as his journey continued. The church had a Greek front, a Roman middle, and a Victorian top with a steeple, on each face of which was an exceptionally large clock. This intrigued Pincus, who was finding giant clocks in every town he passed through, as though the population was being reminded, in accordance with good Puritan ethic, that time was a wastin'. Surely, the clock on the steeple served as such a reminder to one and all that the hour of judgment, if not near for one and all, was also not getting any farther away.

A small brass band started to play in the hexagonal bandstand that stood at the beginning of the green, a green that was more brown than green. There was the obligatory war memorial, and a short distance from it, in the middle of the green, stood a World War II tank, its turret facing the bandstand and inducing, Pincus imagined, a certain dedication to task by the musicians who played while facing, exactly at eye level, a 120-millimeter cannon. Just across from the tank, under the shade of a large oak tree, a half-dozen elderly women sat in folding lawn chairs which, curiously, faced the tank, rather than the bandstand where the horns now played out a rousing Sousa march.

"Isn't New Milford charming," Rosalie extolled.

"No, it is not," Pincus responded as, to the strains of "The Stars and Stripes Forever," Rosalie and Pincus walked down the sidewalk that ran alongside the "green," past the old clapboard building that housed Village Hardware.

"I need to stop," Pincus announced.

"Do you realize how many stops we've made so far, Max? Do you really have to?" Rosalie whined.

"Yes. I have to pee."

Rosalie looked around. There was no sign of a restroom that might be considered public. And, she could find no luncheonettes or other eating establishments that might provide the necessary facility.

As she turned about, she saw behind her a shop with a tasteful wooden sign that read: WAINWRIGHT AND SONS, ANTIQUES.

Hooked on the bottom of the sign was a small board with the word "OPEN," and sitting in a rocking chair on the porch beside a spinning wheel was a man in his late sixties or early seventies, unkempt white hair, wire-rimmed glasses, a plaid flannel shirt, suspenders, and khaki trousers. He smoked a pipe as he rocked back and forth. Rosalie poked Pincus in his side and nodded toward the man on the porch, a gesture to encourage Pincus to ask whether he might use his restroom.

Uncertain how to proceed, Pincus smiled at the man.

The man smiled back, then took a puff on his pipe.

"Something I can help you with?" he asked.

"Well, actually, I was wondering whether you might have a restroom I could use?"

The man nodded.

"Back of the shop, on the right. The light switch is on the wall outside."

"Thanks," Pincus said, slid out of his backpack, laid it on the steps, then ascended and disappeared into the shop.

Rosalie stood facing the man, shifting from foot to foot.

"You want to rest your feet, you can sit on the bench up here," the man said.

"That's okay. You mind if I sit here?" and Rosalie slid out of her backpack and sat down on the wooden steps that led up to the porch.

"Afraid I'm going to try to sell you something?" the man asked.

"Nah, I just like the way I can prop my feet up on steps. You mind?"

"Not at all."

Rosalie sat in silence, elbows on knees, chin propped in her hands, staring out at the green, as the man rocked and puffed.

"Can I offer you something to drink? I suppose I should have an Orange Crush or Royal Crown or something from the past, but all I've got are Cokes and ginger ales.

"That's kind of you to offer," Rosalie said, "but I'm okay."

They sat in silence for a moment, as Rosalie studied the sign hanging on the post in front of her.

"You Mr. Wainwright?"

"Yep. Theodore C. Wainwright, Jr. though everybody calls me Theo. My father was Theodore. He founded the business."

"And you took over, and now your sons are going to take over for you?" Rosalie continued to examine the "Wainwright and Sons, Antiques" sign.

"They already have. Robert's off getting some supplies. We're touching up a wardrobe. And Phillip's got his kids this afternoon. He divorced last year. He should've done it a long time ago – well, he never should have gotten married in the first place. It was all about sex – just a couple horny kids who couldn't keep their clothes on, but that's another story."

Behind them there came the sound of a toilet flushing, and then water running in a sink.

"I don't think there're any paper towels left, but we'll know soon enough," Theo mused.

The running water stopped, and in a few seconds Pincus appeared, shaking the water off his wet hands.

"Thanks for letting me use your john," Pincus told Theo.

"You want a beverage?" Theo asked. "Like I told your, uh —"

Theo studied Rosalie, as all three searched for the right word.

"Associate," Pincus finally offered.

"Associate? Really?" Theo was amused. "Well, that's one I never would have guessed. You in some sort of enterprise together?"

"You could say that," Pincus answered.

There was an awkward silence while Theo waited for more.

"I take it you're not inclined to tell me what that is," Theo finally said.

"It's a long story."

"I got nothing but time," Theo responded.

"And complicated," Pincus answered.

"You don't think I'd be able to follow along, huh?" Theo responded.

Pincus didn't know how to answer. Rosalie came to his rescue.

"Maybe I will have that ginger ale, Mr. Wainwright. How about you, Max?"

Pincus looked at Rosalie, then Theo, and finally nodded, as Theo got up and walked to the end of the porch where there stood an old Coca-Cola cooler chest. He flipped open the lid on one side, reached in, and his hand emerged with two bottles of ginger ale, much to Pincus's surprise.

"The soda chest still works?" Pincus said.

"We don't accept things to sell if they don't work, or, at least, if we can't get them to work. Why would anybody want to buy an old Coke cooler chest that doesn't work?" and Theo handed Rosalie and then Pincus bottles of ginger ale and resumed his place on the rocking chair. "Take a load off your feet," he said to Pincus, who then sat down on a bench against the wall of the shop.

For a moment, Rosalie and Pincus sipped in silence, while Theo puffed on his pipe, which had long ago gone out.

"It's amazing that you've been able to stay in business through three generations," Rosalie finally said.

"Why is that?" Theo asked.

"Well, things change, you know. Times change. Interests change. What could be popular ten years ago, could be unpopular now."

"We sell antiques. They're over a hundred years old, some over two hundred years old."

"The Coke chest can't be that old," Rosalie pointed out.

"No, but there're probably not three functioning Coke chests left in the country. Still I take your point. Truth is, every so often we take in something that's not real old, and there it sits. We've had that damn Coke machine over forty years now. Rare as a feather on a frog. Can't give it away. If it isn't old, they don't want it. First thing they ask when they see something — how old is it? I could try to sell them one of my sons and they'd want to know what year he was made in."

Rosalie laughed.

"And that's not the half of it. More than that, they want to know who made it. Come inside, I want to show you something," and, before Rosalie and Pincus could respond, Theo popped up out of his chair and walked inside the shop, then poked his head back outside momentarily.

"I'd bring your backpacks inside if I were you or they won't be here when you come back out."

"They won't?" Rosalie asked in surprise, and she turned and looked at the quaint and quiet small town.

"Yes. I know what you're thinking. We don't lock our doors. The kids are always safe. You can leave your bike leaning against a lamppost all day and it'll still be there when you come back. Don't you believe it. Time has not missed New Milford, no matter how many brass bands they get to play the worst music that's been written since the invention of the tuba. We've got deadbolts on our doors, and whatever isn't locked up is going to walk. A few years back they stole the tank off the green."

"The tank?" Rosalie asked. "Where'd they find it?"

"They never did. That's the third tank we've had in the last eight years," and Theo disappeared back into the shop.

CHAPTER 5

The inside of the shop was crowded with furniture. Every room in what was once the first floor of the house — living room, sitting room, dining room, kitchen — had desks, sideboards, bookcases, chests, dressers, tables large and small, and on every surface were porcelain dishes, silverware, vases, and a nearly unending amount of bric-a-brac. Theo guided Rosalie and Pincus through the labyrinth until they came to a large, wide dining room table of dark polished wood.

"Cuban mahogany," Theo said.

Theo walked around the table, running his stubby worn fingers, the fingers of a workman, gently across the mahogany.

"This table is from 1750, maybe 1760, not much later. You like it?"

"It's gorgeous," Rosalie said, genuinely impressed.

"It's yours for twenty grand. And that's a bargain."

There was a brief silence, punctuated only by the sound of Rosalie and Pincus sucking in their breaths. Then Theo broke up in laughter.

"Well, probably wouldn't fit in your backpacks, anyway," Theo said when he'd stopped laughing. "But when you look at this, look beyond the beauty of the piece. Think of the people who must have sat at this table for the last two hundred years."

"Now come look at this," Theo said and walked into another room, followed by Rosalie and Pincus, who was strangely silent through all of this. They stopped in front of a sideboard.

"Hepplewhite," Theo said. "About the same time as the French table, maybe twenty years later. Hepplewhite took a lot from

Chippendale, who preceded him, but refined it. The finish is original. The brasses are original. Hepplewhite loved tapered legs with that little foot at the bottom, though sometimes he used the French cabriole leg. And he adored inlay. He'd rather die than have a section without inlay — wheatears, husks, urns, draped cloth, Prince of Wales feathers. Almost all sideboards ever since have copied Hepplewhite one way or another. So, do you like it?"

"It's a beautiful piece," Pincus said cautiously.

"One hundred forty-eight grand and it's yours."

Pincus gasped.

"Why?" Pincus asked in astonishment.

"Why?" Theo pulled out a drawer. On the bottom was signed, G. Hepplewhite. "Everybody wants to know the maker."

Theo carefully put the drawer back.

"Now I'll tell you what's interesting about this. So far as we know, not a single piece of furniture made by Hepplewhite exists — except this, and I doubt that this is genuine. I tell people that I can't warranty that the signature is genuine. One of the problems is that there's no document that can be found that has Hepplewhite's signature on it in order to match the signatures, not anything at all in his handwriting. It's not even clear he ever made a stick of furniture. He became famous for the furniture design books he published. Of course, if anyone bothers to look, they'll find that the design books that George Hepplewhite wrote were done long after he was dead and gone, so they must've been done by his widow, Alice, and there's not a little conjecture that Mrs. Hepplewhite was the one who actually made the furniture and just used his name, as furniture making was not a suitable profession for a lady."

Rosalie and Pincus, enraptured by Theo's tale, shifted their gaze between Theo and the sideboard.

Theo smiled, satisfied that he had properly educated Rosalie and Pincus.

"One last thing," Theo added. "Hepplewhite's construction was faulty, which is a nice way of saying that his furniture had a tendency to fall apart. And that, probably more than anything, including the questionable signature, is why this particular piece is worth so much. It's stayed in one piece — for two hundred years if you're counting, something of a small miracle, considering it's a genuine Hepplewhite," and Theo winked and laughed. "You folks got any plans for dinner tonight? We're having lamb."

"Actually, we have to get going," Rosalie said.

"Well, it's been nice meeting you. Hope you didn't mind my rambling, but I try my best when I sense I might have the opportunity to provide a little education."

Pincus and Rosalie nodded, as they followed Theo back out to the porch, but, just before they walked through the doorway, Theo turned to them.

"Sometimes," Theo ruminated, "I imagine Our Maker is a lot like George Hepplewhite — that He created the universe in a large workshop, lots of apprentice gods running around, doing this and that — one does the laws of physics, another puts together the biology of life, and so on. At the end of it all, God just kind of nods and says, 'Yep, that looks good.' Genesis. And God saw that it was good. You sure you don't want that lamb dinner? It's no trouble at all, and I'd enjoy the company."

"That's really very nice of you, Mr. Wainwright, but we really have to —" but, before Rosalie could finish, Theo interrupted.

"Wait here a moment," and Theo pushed past Rosalie and Pincus back into the house and headed up a set of stairs. "I'll be right back."

Rosalie and Pincus looked up the stairs that Theo was ascending, then at each other.

"It wouldn't hurt to join him for some dinner. What could it take, an hour?" Pincus asked quietly. "It's not as though we have a deadline."

"Well, we don't know, do we, Max?" Rosalie answered. "An hour here, an hour there, and we can end up just missing Her."

"We're going to hurt his feelings if we don't stay. I think he's taken a liking to us. I'm sure he doesn't invite every customer who shows up to stay for dinner. I don't see the harm in —" and Pincus broke off at the sound of Theo's footsteps on the stairs.

Pincus and Rosalie watched Theo descend, a bowl and spoon in each hand. When Theo reached the bottom of the stairs, he held a bowl out to each of them.

"You take a taste. Then tell me you won't have dinner," Theo grinned.

"Thank you," Pincus said as he took the bowl.

"This is very kind of you, Mr. Wainwright," Rosalie said with noticeable reservations, "but —"

"No buts until you've tasted," Theo stopped her.

Rosalie nodded, and she and Pincus took a spoonful of the lamb stew.

"It's really delicious," Rosalie said, beginning to accept the inevitable. "I mean, really it is."

"It is," Pincus joined it. "Absolutely."

"Did you make this?" Rosalie asked.

"I did," Theo said proudly. "Bernice, my late wife, always wanted one of those automatic stockpots. You know, you throw everything in the pot in the morning, put on the lid, turn it on, and when you come back at dinnertime, you've got a stew. Bernice called it her "pot au feu," which made it sound a lot more glamorous than it was, but she thought calling it that would open my mind to it, as I never much saw the sense in eating something that's been cooking all day long. So, finally, one Christmas I bought her the pot, and you would've thought I just gave her the Badminton Cabinet."

"You have a cabinet for badminton?" Rosalie asked.

"Wish I did. The Badminton Cabinet's the most expensive piece of furniture ever made. It took thirty men six years to make it for the third Duke of Beaufort in 1726. It has more precious stones in it than you'll find at Tiffany's. It's worth $30,000,000 now, if not more. The stockpot cost me $12.99. I got off good," Theo smiled.

"Is this her recipe?" Pincus asked.

Theo nodded quietly.

"She knew she only had a few more weeks before the cancer would get her, so she wrote down where I could find everything — phone numbers, addresses, dates, and all my favorite recipes. She died two days after she finished."

Rosalie stifled her breath and nodded.

"Well, it's a wonderful stew, and we'd be happy to stay for dinner, wouldn't we, Max?" Rosalie smiled through tears that were brimming in her eyes.

"It would be our pleasure," Pincus agreed.

CHAPTER 6

"What can we do to help?" Rosalie asked, as she and Pincus sat in the kitchen at the white metal table where Theo was now setting plates and silverware.

"You can just make yourselves comfortable," Theo responded, as he retrieved some wine glasses from a cabinet and set them on the table. "You folks like Bordeaux? It's a good one."

"Love it," Pincus said.

"Good," Theo said. "You can open the bottle," and Theo gave Pincus the bottle and a corkscrew. "I always end up breaking the damn cork."

As Pincus opened the wine, Theo started filling up bowls with the lamb stew, and Rosalie looked around. It was obvious that the kitchen hadn't been changed since Theo's wife had died. Pots and pans hung from a rack over the stove, behind which spices were perfectly aligned. A teapot had a padded cover over it, as did the toaster. Lined up against the wall, were old ceramic canisters labeled "Sugar," "Flour," "Coffee," and "Tea." Everywhere she looked, the sense of Theo's wife remained.

"I like this kitchen," said Rosalie, as Theo set the bowls of stew in front of her and Pincus, then took his own and sat down.

"Yes," Theo said. "It was difficult coming into the kitchen after she passed away. It was her place. She spent most of her time here, even if there was no cooking to be done. She'd write letters at the table or pay the bills here. Once she was gone, I'd do whatever I could to avoid coming in here. Then one day I found myself overwhelmed by such loneliness, and I found that the kitchen was the only place that helped. I could pretend as I ate that she was behind me at the sink, or gathering up the laundry and would be coming in here in just a few minutes. I could hear her calling, asking me whether I wanted my pajamas washed now or I wanted to wait until the next wash."

There is a silence as the three ate their stew, finally broken by Rosalie.

"How long ago did she die?"

"Twelve years and two months," Theo said, and then he looked over his shoulder at nothing in particular, at everything, at the potholders hanging by the stove. "I wonder sometimes," he continued, "whether it's love or loneliness, or if they can be separated. Is the loneliness because of how much I loved her and now she's gone, or simply because of the company I had for so many years and now I'm alone. You read that loneliness can kill you, and I believe that. It can weigh on you like a giant stone until it crushes all the life out of you. What kind of God would make a creature like that, a man who would suffer so from being alone? Six billion people in the world. You would think it could be avoided."

Theo said all this with his eyes looking down into his bowl, as though he were staring into the darkness of a bottomless hole. He looked up and smiled.

"I apologize. I didn't invite you for dinner to complain," he said.

"No," Rosalie said quickly. "We understand completely."

"Completely," Pincus seconded Rosalie.

Suddenly, Theo changed the subject. "So," he said, "where you all going?"

Rosalie and Pincus looked at each other.

"I'm trying to find my daughter," Rosalie spoke before Pincus could say anything.

"Actually —" Pincus started.

"Actually," Rosalie broke in, "She's been gone for some time, and I have no idea where she is."

"Actually —" Pincus tried again.

"Actually, it's been really tough, you know, being Her mother. You're right, Mr. Wainwright, you need someone. You need to know you're not alone."

"It's Her," Pincus said.

"Her?" Theo looked over at Pincus in interest.

"Capital 'H.' Her," Pincus answered.

"She's come?" Theo asked with mounting excitement. "How do you know?"

"I know," Rosalie said with a long sigh. "I know."

"You're absolutely sure?" Theo asked.

Pincus nodded.

"Well, that's good enough for me. Can I come?" Theo asked.

"Come where?" Rosalie asked with alarm, knowing exactly where.

"To see Her," Theo said.

"We don't really know it's Her," Pincus tried to help out Rosalie.

"That's right, we don't really know," explained Rosalie.

"But you just said you knew," Theo said to Rosalie.

"I may have misspoken, overspoken...." Rosalie tried to dodge the inevitable.

"I'll take my chances," Theo said.

"She's not God, you know, or even the Daughter of God. She's the Mother of all Gods," Pincus explained.

"Even better," Theo said. "I've had nothing to say to God since He did this to me. Nothing. But I do have a few things I'd like to say to His Mother."

CHAPTER 7

Pincus wasn't sure how he felt about Theo joining them. Although he and Rosalie had been together less than forty-eight hours, he had begun to feel a certain bonding — the two of them with the same goal, on the same journey — and the thought of Theo disturbing this connection, however tentative it might be, made Pincus uncomfortable.

On the other hand, there were some undeniable advantages to having Theo along. All Rosalie's attention would not be focused on him. There would be three now, which might allow for more democracy should a vote be required, and Pincus sensed that he might have more in common with Theo than with Rosalie on this account. Theo also seemed, in spite of his pain and loneliness, to be a rather spirited person, spirited in a far different way from Rosalie. He also had a sense of humor, something that Pincus had not noticed in Rosalie to date.

"So, does that mean you're in favor of him coming or not, Max?" Rosalie asked, as they stood side by side, washing and drying dishes after dinner, while Theo saw to customers in the shop below.

"Ultimately, I think it might be a good idea," Pincus answered as he placed a dish in the dish drainer.

"Ultimately? What does that mean?"

"It means that I don't see any real problem with it."

"He's seventy years old if he's a day, Max. You don't think that might slow us down?"

"Based on my own pace, it might actually speed us up. Maybe he'll try to prove that he's no drag on us," and Max took a handful of silverware from Rosalie and began drying.

"Where's he going to sleep, Max?" Rosalie asked. "Have you thought of that?"

"There's a sports shop across the green." Theo appeared at the kitchen door. "I can get a small tent tomorrow. You can spend the night here. And, actually, I'm sixty-nine. Won't be seventy for another six weeks."

Theo looked around at the clean kitchen.

"You did a good job here. Get your things, and I'll show you your rooms."

Rosalie and Pincus stood frozen, not knowing what to say, where to go.

"I'm not sure we can really stay here tonight, Mr. Wainwright," Rosalie gave it one more try.

"Sure you can," Theo answered. "Follow me," and off he went, Rosalie and Pincus being drawn behind him like leaves in a current.

When they reached the adjoining bedrooms, a large smile appeared on Rosalie's face. A giant four-poster bed, with a down comforter enclosed in a toile de jouy duvet, was against the wall. There was an antique dresser and chintz curtains. It seemed to Rosalie to be more than just a visit to another century, a time when everything, especially the pace, was different. It was out of a distant dream.

"This is very nice," Rosalie said.

"Glad you like it," Theo was pleased. "There's a bath through that door over there. It's got a claw-foot tub from the nineteenth century, but we had it fitted with a shower gizmo, for those who prefer. What time you want breakfast?"

Rosalie said "Seven," and Pincus said "Ten" simultaneously.

"How about we compromise and say 8:30," Theo smiled. "The shop across the street opens at 9:30, and that way I can get my gear, and we can be on the road by 10:30."

Rosalie and Pincus nodded, and Theo turned and started to leave. He stopped when he came to the stairs leading down to the shop.

"I appreciate your letting me come along," Theo said.

"No problem," Rosalie answered. "It'll be a pleasure to have you join us." And for that moment Rosalie meant it.

Theo nodded back and disappeared down the stairs.

"What changed your mind?" Pincus asked when Theo was gone.

"Yeah, well, it's obvious that he's coming, whether I want him to or not, so no use making him feel bad about it. He's already suffering from enough loneliness as it is without us abandoning him. We might as well make him feel wanted, right?"

"Right," Pincus nodded and disappeared into his room.

The situation would have remained settled had there not been a knocking on the doors to the rooms of Pincus and Rosalie sometime after midnight, waking them both. When they opened the doors, they found two men in their late thirties standing there. One, by the name of Robert Wainwright, was a carbon copy of his father, including the wire-rimmed glasses. The other, Phillip Wainwright, appeared to come from another family entirely. He was round, with puffy cheeks, a barrel chest, and a beard.

"We need to talk to you," Robert said. "Outside."

"It's important," Phillip added. "I'm Phillip and he's Robert. We're Theo's sons, and we think there's something you should know about Dad before you go trotting off with him."

"He told you?" Rosalie asked groggily.

"Oh, yeah," Robert said. "He told us. You should get a jacket. It's chilly out there tonight."

"We'll meet you outside," Phillip said, and when they finally assembled, by the monument on the green so they could not be overheard by Theo, it was Phillip who began the conversation.

"Dad's not all there," Phillip stated flatly.

"Really," Pincus commented. "Where is he?"

Rosalie placed her hand on Pincus's arm with a gentleness Pincus had not hitherto noticed. "No, no, please, let's let him finish," Rosalie said, her hope restored that Theo might not be joining them after all.

"He can be lucid at times," Robert said.

"Very lucid," Phillip seconded. "Like he is now."

"But then the next day, or the next week, or the next hour — he's gone," Robert reported.

"Where does he go?" Pincus asked once more.

"Max, please," Rosalie said.

"He's got dementia," Phillip said. "Well, he's getting dementia, that is, sometimes he's demented, and sometimes he's not. He says he's been 'visited.'"

"Really," Pincus remarked with some interest. "Did he mention who had come to see him?"

"Not really," Phillip replied. "He just says that he's been visited. He's been 'spoken to.'"

"What did they have to say?' Pincus asked. "Did he say that?"

Robert and Phillip looked at each other. Robert picked up the ball and ran with it.

"He said that he was told that they'd be coming for him," Robert explained.

"I think that'd be us," Pincus notified the brothers.

"You?" Phillip asked.

"Yep. And guess what. Behold, I bring you glad tidings of great joy. We're here."By now it had become evident to Robert and Phillip that they were not making the kind of headway for which they'd hoped, at least with Pincus. They decided to become more assertive.

"We really can't let you take him," Phillip informed them.

"Because he says he's been visited and been spoken to?" Pincus asked.

"No, because he's nuts," Phillip answered.

"It's getting worse," Robert upped the ante. "Since Mom died, he's become less and less himself."

"And more and more whom?" Pincus asked, suddenly feeling a genuine bond with Theo and a need to protect the elder statesman.

"Okay, I can see we're not making much progress here," Robert said.

"Not necessarily," Rosalie said.

The two brothers' heads turned to Rosalie, in the way a child who has prayed for snow on Christmas might watch the first flakes falling.

"I'm not sure it's appropriate for us to take on this kind of responsibility. I mean, what do we do if he completely flips out and we're, like, in the middle of nowhere?" asked Rosalie.

"We're going into the middle of nowhere?" Pincus was not a happy man. "You think She's in the middle of nowhere?"

"I didn't say that, Max."

"Yes, you did. I definitely heard the words 'middle' and 'nowhere.'"

"It's an expression, Max. I meant — nowhere near a hospital."

"That sounds a lot like nowhere to me, or, if not nowhere, at least right down the road from it," Pincus commented.

"Could you please let Rosalie finish," Robert said.

"Okay, finish," Pincus demurred.

"It's a big responsibility," Rosalie continued. "He could need medication, a protected environment so he doesn't harm himself, a constant supply of Depends. I mean, if he's demented, or even becoming demented, then we really don't have a right to jeopardize his health."

"Exactly," Robert agreed. "That's why we really can't let you take him wherever you're going. Where are you going, by the way?" Robert asked.

"We're going to see Her — the Mother of all Gods," Pincus informed them. "Or, at least, we're trying to find Her."

Robert and Phillip looked at Pincus, then at Rosalie, then at each other. They knew now that they were no longer dealing with one crazy person, but three.

"The Mother of all Gods?" Robert finally inquired.

"You bet," Pincus answered.

Robert looked over at Rosalie and couldn't help noticing that she was not correcting Pincus.

"And," Pincus continued, "it would seem to me that unless you have some sort of papers giving you custodial authority over your father — Do you have custodial papers?"

The two brothers shook their heads.

"— then," Pincus went on, "it's up to your father whether he comes with us or not."

"You don't have any say in it?" Robert asked with some irritation.

"Oh, we do," Pincus said. "But Rosalie and I agreed earlier this evening that he could come with us, and that's what we told him, didn't we, dear?"

Rosalie looked at Pincus and nodded her head reluctantly.

"And we're people of our word, so, while we're very grateful for your sharing all this with us, and you can rest assured that we will keep an eye out for your father's mental and physical well-being at all times, he's coming with us. Did I mention that I'm a physician?"

And this is how Rosalie, Pincus, and Theo found themselves the next morning somewhere after 10:30, laden with backpacks, moving down a lovely shaded lane on their way toward Kent, and thence to Canaan and the Convent of the Sisters of Perpetual Sorrow.

CHAPTER 8

As it turned out, Pincus and Rosalie had some difficulty keeping up with Theo, who skipped on ahead, tapping an antique gnarled-wood cane with a silver cap on the road as he moved on through the countryside, passing farmland intermixed with surprisingly large homes set on vast acreages.

"Second homes — summer homes," Theo nodded at an especially giant specimen. "The owners come up from the city in June and leave on Labor Day. The more poetic ones stay through the change in the foliage, or, at least, come back on the weekends to catch the colors, but, by the beginning of November, the pipes are drained so they don't freeze up, and the houses are empty for the next seven months. Never did understand the thinking behind all that. But they never move up here, even when they retire, and they never see what it's like around here when we're under a foot of fresh powder snow and the kids get out their sleds. Jonathan McKenzie's got a real sleigh from the turn of the century and a team of Clydesdale horses, and he takes whoever's interested on rides and then serves them hot cider around his wood stove. Never charges a cent. t just gives him pleasure. You sit there under wool blankets and listen to the bells on the horses, and everything else is silence. You ever hear the sound of the runners of a sleigh on the snow?"

Rosalie and Pincus, now entranced, shake their heads.

"It's like the wings of angels," Theo mused. "It's a whisper, the faintest sound, like two hands rubbing together. That's all you hear."

And so it was as they walked on toward Kent, passing signs that pointed in the direction of Dogtail Corners, Bulls Bridge, Dover Furnace, Wingdale, Cricket Hill, and Pleasant Ridge Roads — Theo describing the genealogy of one farm or another through the centuries or the history of a now-defunct foundry.

"They made the links for the chain here that Washington put across the Hudson to keep the British from advancing beyond West Point," and Pincus and Rosalie looked to their right at the remains of a stone chimney.

"Did it work?" Rosalie asked, as they passed a covered bridge beside them, over a section of the Housatonic River.

"It changed the war," Theo responded, his cane tapping the ground rhythmically as he walked on.

Rosalie stopped for a moment and looked back at the foundry, now in the distance behind them.

"The chain became a testament to good old-fashioned American ingenuity," Theo continued. "John Abbey, a young New York odds-and-ends man with a keen sense of history, concocted a story about how he had found the links from the chain after it had been forgotten in an old storage facility at West Point for over a hundred years. He then proceeded to sell his fake 'fully authenticated links' of the West Point Chain for rather large sums and made a small fortune doing it. It's generally regarded as the first great con in American history, the equivalent of selling the Brooklyn Bridge. As it turned out, Mr. Westminster Abbey had obtained an old mooring ground anchor chain, and cut up its links. The last report was that there are no fewer than a hundred and thirty museums and historical sites still displaying Abbey's 'fully-authenticated links' of the West Point chain that won the war for America."

And now, ahead of them, they saw the main intersection that indicated the town of Kent.

The first thing that caught the eye of Pincus and Theo simultaneously was the gasoline station on the corner, and they increased their pace substantially.

"Where're you racing to?" Rosalie asked, but her question was answered in short order as both men headed for the men's room at breakneck speed, reaching the door simultaneously.

"I can wait," Pincus said in great discomfort.

"Thank you," Theo said. "I can't."

"You know," Rosalie called to the two men, "you guys are able to just go in a field or behind a tree."

Pincus was biting his bottom lip and didn't respond, as a sound not unlike a fire hose running into Lake Erie came from the men's room.

"God, I hope the entire trip isn't going to be like this, racing from toilet to toilet," Rosalie commented.

"Can we discuss this another time?" Pincus called back, as there was, behind them, the sound of a toilet flushing, followed by a loud sigh from Pincus.

"Oh, for godsakes, Max, you're like a three-year-old. Surely, you've got more self-control than that."

Before Pincus could respond, the men's room door opened, and Pincus jumped inside, as a smiling Theo Wainwright emerged.

"You don't want to go?" he asked her, as the restroom door slammed shut behind him.

"No, I don't want to go."

"Why not?"

"Because I don't have to go, Mr. Wainwright."

"Why not?"

"Why don't I have to go?"

"Yes."

"Frankly, I don't know how to answer that. I just don't have to go, that's all. There's nothing inside me that says that it's time for me to go now."

"You don't want to try?"

"No, I don't want to try," and Rosalie was beginning to wonder whether she was beginning to encounter some of Theo's deteriorating mental state.

"It might be a long time before we reach another facility," Theo informed her. "Maybe you should try. I'm only saying this for your own good."

From behind them came the sound of a toilet flushing. Rosalie tried to ignore it but couldn't. The conversation had made it impossible to think about anything else, and now she looked up at Theo, sighed, and then headed off toward the restroom, from which Pincus was just exiting. She slammed the door behind her.

"What's that all about?" Pincus asked Theo.

"Guess she had the urge to go," smiled Theo.

Pincus nodded, then looked behind him at the foothills of the Berkshire Mountains rimming the north and western edges of the town. They seemed substantial, and he hoped their route would not require him to ascend them.

As Rosalie finished her business and reemerged, Pincus noticed, for the first time, a front of darkening clouds in the distance, indisputably heading in their direction.

"Let's go before the rain comes," Rosalie's voice came from behind Pincus and Theo, and they started down the street, past the large grey stone church on the corner, where, behind it, was an enormous cemetery surrounded by a wrought-iron fence.

Victorian homes lined the street, all with porches bordered in elaborate dentil molding, homes once filled with family life but now serving as shops, the large bay windows on the first floor displaying dresses or china.

There was something about this that disturbed Pincus. This was once a street of family homes, and now it was, in fact, a strip mall. These grand homes would never hear the sound of children's feet nor would the rooms fill with the smell of cooking. It saddened Pincus.

"I think we should stop in here and buy some things for lunch," Rosalie nodded toward a small one-story wooden building with a sign overhead that read "Ken's Market," and off she went, Pincus and Theo a step behind.

By the time the trio exited, there was a steady rain falling. Pincus and Rosalie hastily draped their ponchos over themselves. Theo, on the other hand, had brought a small collapsible umbrella, not much larger than what one might see a circus clown carrying, and now he marched on ahead, holding his umbrella high with one hand, his cane still tapping the ground with the other hand, as though he was a drum major leading a tiny band of two in lock-step behind him.

After passing a church and a number of clapboard homes, they came to a flat area in which the town had placed a baseball field with, to the trio's good fortune, a dugout. Theo decided this would be a good shelter in which to have their lunch, and so he led his marchers around the chain-link fence into the dugout.

For some time they sat there in silence, eating and watching the rain.

"There's something comforting about rain, don't you think?" Theo broke the silence.

"How is that?" Pincus asked.

"Just is. Moisture rises up, clouds form, rain falls. Makes you think of the Almighty, if you're so inclined, which I am not. Although I've often wondered whether He created rain, or the weather cycles that allowed for rain, or simply the physics which would allow water to form."

"I'd have to say the latter," Pincus answered. "I've never thought of Him as a micromanager. He doesn't tinker. I'd have to say that He just started the ball rolling."

"*Forty days and forty nights*, He told Noah," Theo pointed out. "Then came the rains."

"I think that was a special circumstance," Pincus remarked, and he took a long drink of his blueberry Gatorade. "It was a reflex reaction to a lot of bad behavior. He grabbed the first thing around."

"He parted the Red Sea for Moes. Jonah was swallowed by a whale of the ocean. Christ walked upon the waters. You think about it, God seems to be especially attuned to the aquatic," Theo pointed out, extending his hand into the rain, then showing it to both Pincus and Rosalie, as if this confirmed his point.

"You think God made your hand wet?" Rosalie was finding the conversation uninspiring. "Rain is rain. If God created the universe, then *everything* is God, Mr. Wainwright — rain, sun, fire, wind, snow – the whole meteorological smorgasbord."

"What about asphalt?" Theo asked.

"Asphalt?" Rosalie asked in some dismay.

"What they pave roads with?" Pincus thought he'd help out.

"I know what asphalt is, Max," Rosalie turned to Pincus.

"Well," Theo explained, "if God created everything, then He must have created asphalt. But it's always seemed to me that asphalt, among a lot of other things like Styrofoam and vinyl, is a uniquely human endeavor, don't you think?"

Rosalie turned to Theo.

"You want to know whether God created asphalt?"

Theo nodded as he swallowed the last of his ham and cheese and wiped his lips with the back of his hand.

"I think this is a very good question for Her, Mr. Wainwright. Why don't you ask Her when we see Her? And now it's time to go," was Rosalie's response.

Theo saw the seriousness in Rosalie's eyes, nodded, slid into his backpack, as Rosalie and Pincus did the same, and then Theo took his cane in one hand, popped open his umbrella with the other, and once again, umbrella held high, Theo led his band of two into the rain.

"What I was going to ask before you insisted we move on," Theo said as they climbed a rather steep hill, Rosalie now on his right, Pincus on his left, "was whether She is considered to be the Second Coming?"

"I don't know. She never mentioned having been here before," Rosalie thought about this. "How would we know?"

"We could ask Her," Pincus suggested. "But I seriously doubt She is. The Second Coming is of Christ. You know — *Christ has died, Christ has risen, Christ will come again*. And She's not Christ. She's the Mother of all Gods."

"We don't know what form Christ will take when He — or She — reappears," Theo pointed out.

"Isn't the Second Coming supposed to be like, the Kingdom of God on Earth, the last judgment, some sort of Heaven on Earth, where all evil is gone and there's only good, and all the dead are resurrected? Because, if it is, then I, myself, just don't see it," Rosalie commented. "And, besides, I'm not sure I know what to do with this thing about *all* the dead being resurrected. Are they being resurrected in heaven or here on earth? Because, we don't have a lot of room here, and the thought of *everybody* who ever was – the Neanderthals and the Visigoths and a lot of Popes who never should have been Popes to begin with, not to mention Vlad the Impaler and Adolph Hitler – all walking around again, well it's kind of creepy, don't you think?"

"Well, to tell you the truth," Theo said, as they passed a sign reading "Canaan – 1 Mile," making Pincus's heart skip a beat, "the whole notion of a Second Coming has never made much sense to me. It seems something of a waste of effort. Not to be overly morose about the whole thing, but, as I understand it, the entire universe is condemned to final futility. So why bother with all the Coming and Going and Recoming? Life will have been nothing more than a tiny moment in the history of a universe that no longer exists. It all becomes a bit meaningless, don't you think?"

"I'm not sure that the eventual death of the universe on a time scale of tens of billions of years is any more perplexing a problem than the knowledge of our own deaths on a time scale of tens of years," Pincus mused.

The rain had stopped, and they continued to walk, now in silence, digesting the conundrums their conversation had brought up.

And then there they were. They turned a bend in the road and found themselves facing, on their left, two huge iron gates with crucifixes worked into the metalwork. In a sweeping arch over the gates were the words THE CONVENT OF THE SISTERS OF PERPETUAL SORROW.

"Not a very comforting name," Pincus noted.

"He's got a point," Theo chimed in. "It doesn't exactly make you want to race inside for spiritual renewal."

Rosalie didn't respond, but pulled a chain, and a bell over the gates rang loudly. Almost before she had finished, the large oak door to the convent opened and a nun in a black habit appeared. She was short and round and appeared to be in her sixties. She wore wire-rimmed glasses and had a dark shadow on her upper lip, the sign of an incipient moustache never bleached.

"The *perpetual* definitely doesn't help," Theo continued to comment, still looking up at the sign.

"If you guys could say something *positive* just for once, I'd be most grateful," Rosalie said.

"Mrs. Heiligenschein?" the nun asked, as she continued to approach.

"Yes, it's me," Rosalie answered.

Pincus turned in astonishment to Rosalie.

"Mrs. Who?" he asked.

"It's nice to see you again, Mrs. Heiligenschein," the nun was almost at the gates.

"Heiligenschein?" Pincus asked again.

"Not now, Max," Rosalie said under her breath to Pincus.

"Mrs. Heiligenschein?" Pincus persisted.

"And it's nice to see you again, too, Sister," Rosalie responded, as the nun arrived at the gate. "And these are two of my dear friends — Max Pincus and Theodore Wainwright."

The nun unlocked the gate and swung it open.

"Mrs. Heiligenschein?" Pincus said again quietly under his breath to Rosalie.

"Later, Max," Rosalie answered sotto voce, her lips motionless.

"I'm Sister Gloria Gloria," the nun said and shook each one's hand, then ushered them past the gate, which she closed and locked behind her.

"We do have a lot to talk about, don't we?" Sister Gloria Gloria looked at Rosalie and smiled much too pleasantly as she marched onward, her new wards in tow.

"Mrs. Heiligenschein?" Pincus said to Rosalie.

CHAPTER 9

As a child, one of Pincus's favorite books had been *The Secret Garden*. He was too young to see any Christian analogy, nor did Pincus find himself moved by the miracle that Mary worked, if, indeed it was a miracle. It was the ivy-covered door that excited him, how it was found, and how it opened to reveal a garden paradise Pincus had drawn so completely in his mind that he knew every flower, every path, every statue, and fountain.

And so it was now as Sister Gloria Gloria pushed open the heavy oak door and revealed the interior of the convent. Pincus found his secret garden.

A long hall extended to his left and right, a hall with a marble floor, pink stucco walls, and gothic windows — some with stained glass depicting saints or scenes from the life of the Messiah, and others with clear glass, through which Pincus could see a glorious sun-drenched garden. And directly across this lush paradise, and rising high above everything else, was a church, nearly a cathedral, its size and majesty were so imposing.

Suddenly, there was the sound of a bell ringing, and, as though by magic, coming down the hall and heading toward them from both directions there appeared girls in short blue and green plaid pleated skirts and white blouses, clustered in small groups, gabbing away as only young girls do. Pincus watched as they stopped halfway down the long hall, turned, and exited out doors to the garden, crossing toward the church, as the bell continued to ring.

"Vespers," Sister Gloria Gloria announced. "Would you like to join us?"

Pincus, Theo, and Rosalie were frozen in place, speechless. How exactly does one say to a woman of the cloth, "Not especially, but thanks for the invitation." One does not. One turns and follows Sister Gloria Gloria like chicks behind a mother hen.

Inside the church, all was a hushed quiet, save for the slight rustling of skirts and the wooden creaking of people taking their places in the pews. Several dozen nuns were in the front rows to the left of the center aisle, and, on the right, Franciscan monks in their brown tunics were entering a small door in the front right of the church and taking their places. Behind the nuns and monks, on both sides, some three hundred young women were sliding into the aisles and settling, as the last sounds of the bell were heard.

Sister Gloria Gloria nodded toward a pew in the back where Pincus, Rosalie, and Theo took their places, and Sister Gloria Gloria walked slowly to the front of the church, turned to face the congregation, and instantly there was the sound of the monks chanting, their song resonating through the large vaulted church.

"Deus, in adiutorium meum intende. Domine, ad adiuvandum me festina. Gloria Patri, et Filio, et Spiritui Sancto."

O God, come to my assistance. O Lord, make haste to help me. Glory be to the Father, and to the Son, and to the Holy Spirit — Pincus looked down at the pamphlet for vespers he now held in his hand and read the English translation. He felt himself overcome with a deep sadness, as though he had suddenly suffered a profound and unexpected loss. He followed along in his hymnal.

"As it was in the beginning, is now, and ever shall be, world without end. Amen. Alleluia."

Religion had never been a significant part of Pincus's life. In fact, it had been, for all intents and purposes, and with only a few exceptions, no part at all. As a child, he had never thought about what religion he was, and his parents offered no help in that regard. Had he not come upon a baptismal certificate while disposing of his father's papers following his death, Pincus would never have known that he was Catholic. And the same could be said regarding his mother, who, he discovered, when going through her jewelry drawer after her death and finding a star of David on a silver chain, was Jewish.

Growing up, he would go to weddings and funerals of his aunts and uncles and never know whether he would find a priest or a rabbi or a reverend officiating. It was not at all confusing to Pincus. It was just the way it was. If you were being joined in holy matrimony or going to your final resting place, you collared whomever was available to preside, he imagined.

The congregation started singing the Magnificat.

"Magníficat ánima mea Dóminum..."

Pincus looked over at Rosalie, who stood beside him. Her eyes were flooded with tears. Then he looked over at Theo, who stood on the other side of Rosalie. Theo was frozen in place, as though he had been sculpted from a block of ice.

The high-pitched voices of the young girls in the cavernous church seemed to him as though they were made of crystal, sending chills up Pincus's spine.

And now one of the monks approached the altar and began the benediction of the Blessed Sacrament.

"Blessed be God.

Blessed be His Holy Name.

Blessed be Jesus Christ, true God and true Man...."

As the monk recited the prayer, Pincus's eyes were fixed on the monstrance, the lights from the chandeliers reflecting off its gleaming gold. The monstrance consisted of a four-legged pedestal on which several cherubs were placed, one holding a crucifix. At the top was an elaborate gold sunburst, surrounded by angels, in the midst of which was the round opening into which the host was being placed. Pincus was impressed with its opulence. He imagined the artist who had spent months, perhaps even years, crafting this piece. He saw him leaning over it, peering through his glasses, a small tool in his hand, working slowly, patiently, a smile of contentment on his face as he finished the face of one angel or another.

While such devotion moved Pincus, the relationship of religious worship and God had always been a confusing one for Pincus. He could see the potential benefit in men and women assembling as a community in a place of worship, and the goals of the community seemed to Pincus exemplary. However, that being said, he had the impression that the repetitive uttering of certain words and phrases were of no meaning to those saying them, any more than the responsive readings, or the rising and kneeling. Did anyone actually think about the words they were saying, know their meaning, take them to heart? Finally, how does one pray to atoms and molecules, to the law of physics and the workings of biology? How many in the congregation had actually seen their pleadings to the Lord God Almighty bear fruit? And yet for centuries now, for millennia, people had done this. It made no sense to Pincus. Organized religion and God the maker of the universe had, to the mind of Pincus, absolutely no relationship whatsoever.

As for Theo, he remained in his frozen state. He and Bernice had been regular church-goers, devoted worshippers, active in their congregation, generous givers to their faith, and what did it get him? At the end of a life well-lived, Theo expected his last days to be joyful, celebratory, and now this. It had all been for naught. Where was God now? Certainly not here.

The church in which Theo and Pincus and Rosalie now found themselves suddenly resounded with several hundred voices, Pincus's and Theo's not among them, saying "Amen," followed by Sister Gloria Gloria walking down the aisle. When she reached the pew where Pincus, Rosalie, and Theo sat, she stopped, beckoned them with a nod to follow her, and instantaneously the church began to empty — first the nuns, then the monks, and finally the girls, who had been taught to maintain their silence until they had at least one foot out the door.

Pincus was already in the office of Sister Gloria Gloria when he could see out the gothic windows the last of the young girls exiting from the church, accompanied by what sounded like a loud frantic buzzing of bees but was, in fact, the multitude of girls gabbing with each other after having restrained themselves from talking for what seemed to them the kind of eternity found only in the hereafter depicted only a few moments before.

"As we have discussed a number of times, Mrs. Heiligenschein," Sister Gloria Gloria informed Rosalie from the leather armchair in which she sat, "I have absolutely no idea where your daughter has gone."

"She," Rosalie said. "Her name is She."

"And we have discussed this on even more occasions, as I'm sure you're well aware," Sister Gloria Gloria responded. Her tone was not one of being perturbed, but more of quiet resignation, a sort of weariness from having gone over the same issues many times with no sign of progress.

"I do remember," Rosalie answered. "But, nevertheless, it is Her name."

"We refer to the young women here by their family name — also discussed numerous times," Sister Gloria Gloria continued. "But, however that may be, the end result is that your daughter departed, leaving no indication of her destination or how she might be contacted."

"I can't believe you did that — something *I've* discussed on numerous occasions," Rosalie told Sister Gloria Gloria. "You don't think that I should have been notified before She left?"

"She had already left by the time we called you, Mrs. Heiligenschein, and, just for the record, she was going to be nineteen the next day, so we had no authority to stop her."

Rosalie took a deep breath, aware that she was getting nowhere. There was a moment of silence, as Rosalie decided on her next approach, and Sister Gloria Gloria waited, feeling much as she suspected Pharaoh must have felt as he tried to anticipate whether frogs would come before or after the locusts.

It was at this point that Theo reached a decision.

"As I can't see what use I can be here, I am now going outside for a nice relaxing stroll through your delightful garden," Theo nodded toward the verdant quadrangle outside Sister Gloria Gloria's office. "But before I go, and since, having devoted my life to antiques, I tend to see things from an historical perspective, might I suggest that you review the pertinent details of Her time here in the likely event that it will give some indication of what She might have selected as Her next destination," and Theo headed for a door in Sister Gloria Gloria's office that led directly to the outdoors. "Off to Gethsemane," he smiled, opened the door, and left, closing it very quietly behind him.

"Your friend has an interesting sense of humor," Sister Gloria Gloria remarked after Theo had left.

"How's that?" Rosalie asked.

"Well, as I'm sure you are well aware, Gethsemane is where the disciples and Jesus prayed the night before he was crucified. Luke says that the Messiah's anguish was so great that it was as though his sweat was great drops of blood falling to the ground. Gethsemane is also where they buried the Blessed Virgin Mother, so, all in all, it's not exactly a place one would choose for a 'nice relaxing stroll' to unwind and get away from it all."

"Yes, but it is at the foot of the Mount of Olives, and the olive branch is traditionally a sign of peace, so one might see it in that way, especially since overlooking Gethsemane is the Church of All Nations," Pincus pointed out helpfully.

"Which is also known as theBasilica of Agony. I stand by my original position," Sister Gloria Gloria said, but she was impressed with Pincus's knowledge of Christianity, and his stock went up considerably.

"That being said," Pincus continued, "Mr. Wainwright's idea of reviewing Her time here may not be a bad one."

"She was here for a number of years, Mr. Pincus. I'm not sure —"

"Just the highlights, perhaps," Pincus interrupted Sister Gloria Gloria. "I suspect She left because of some unresolved issues. Maybe we could just discuss those."

Sister Gloria Gloria leaned back in her armchair and thought about whether this was a good idea, and, if so, where she might begin. More to the point, she thought very hard about whether she had the emotional resources to go over the various encounters that led to Rosalie's daughter leaving the sanctuary that she, Sister Gloria Gloria, so painstakingly and lovingly provided. Yet, as though it was beyond her control, she found herself responding.

"Well, of course, when Miss Heiligenschein first arrived, She was an absolute delight. More than that. Everyone took an immediate liking to her, myself included. She had a way about her that was warm and engaging. She was exceptionally attentive to others, we warmed up to her immediately, and were especially fond of her sense of humor. It was hard not to like Miss Heiligenschein at that time."

"But then…?" Pincus asked.

"Then she turned thirteen, and She — developed. While we are aware that this all took place over some time, it seemed to us that one night we put Pippi Longstocking to bed and the next morning we woke up Jayne Mansfield," Sister Gloria Gloria explained.

"And you all went nuts," Rosalie repeated.

"I'm not sure that's an accurate characterization of our reaction, but it was somewhat disturbing, not only to us sisters, but to the other girls, who were in something of a panic regarding whether the same thing could happen to them, and, what appeared to be of even greater concern, what if it did not, or did but to a much lesser extent. Within a few months, nearly half our girls were in counseling."

Rosalie turned to Pincus.

"She got tits," Rosalie explained to Pincus, as though he couldn't imagine what had transpired. "But not just tits. The most absolutely gorgeous gedoinkers you could imagine. If Michelangelo had seen Her chest, he would have thrown his tools into the Arno and taken up flower arranging. God had created something that no man would ever match."

Pincus tried not to laugh, but was unsuccessful.

"There was nothing amusing about it, I assure you, Mr. Pincus," Sister Gloria Gloria scolded. "As though this wasn't enough, along with this, what seemed to us, explosive burst of maturity, came a mind like a scalpel and a will that was not to be denied."

Rosalie turned to Pincus. "We had a lot of parent conferences about this," Rosalie added to the story.

"Yes, we did," Sister Gloria Gloria remarked tersely, and then turned back to Pincus.

"We encourage the children to ask questions about God and religious life, but Miss Heiligenschein's questions were not the usual ones. Most children will ask things like, 'If God is all-powerful, does He control everything we say and do?' and we're able then to have an enlightening discussion about God and free will with the entire class. Here is the first question, following Miss Heiligenschein's blossoming, that she submitted for class discussion."

Sister Gloria Gloria reached for a thick folder on a table beside her chair, opened it, extracted a lined sheet of paper with a young woman's handwriting on it, and she handed it to Pincus, who read aloud.

"If the Church forbids birth control because it is unnatural, then how come it requires priests and nuns to practice life-long celibacy which is even more unnatural?"

Pincus thought he was going to choke on his own breath from trying to suppress a laugh. He inhaled deeply to maintain his composure.

"I see," Pincus said. "How did the discussion go?"

"There was, of course," Sister Gloria Gloria explained tersely, "nothing to discuss."

"Ah, yes," Pincus nodded, trying to appear supportive.

"Next came this," Sister Gloria Gloria said, while fishing another handwritten paper from the folder and handed it to Pincus, who, once again, read aloud.

"I don't get it. How come with all of St. Jerome's deep feelings about the fall of the ancient world and all the horrible mutilations by the enemies, he thinks the preservation of virginity is so much more important than victory over the Huns, Vandal,s and Goths?"

"Because a theme was beginning to emerge," Sister Gloria Gloria explained, "I naturally called her down to my office to review with her the doctrine of original sin."

"Good thinking," Pincus continued in his supportive mode. "How'd it go?"

"This is what she wrote to me after our little tête-à-tête."

Sister Gloria Gloria extracted another, much longer, handwritten paper from her folder and handed it to Pincus, who read aloud once more.

"Dearest Sister Gloria Gloria, Thank you very much for our most instructive talk yesterday afternoon. It was kind of you to take the time. I will try much harder to think of the kind of questions you call appropriate for future religious classes. However, I did want you to know in regard to our conversation yesterday that there is, in fact, no such thing as original sin. Since, as you said, sin comes only from the soul, and as you have often taught us, the soul is not inherited but created anew with each person, so in order for us to have the sin of Adam and Eve, God would have to be putting it there with each new baby, which is hardly original, but just mean and stupid. And, since we all know that God is not mean or stupid, therefore, like I said, there is no original sin. But don't worry, I won't bring it up in class."

Pincus looked up from the paper at Sister Gloria Gloria.

"You see the problem," Sister Gloria Gloria explained.

"Ummm," Pincus nodded.

"And," Sister Gloria Gloria added, "this was only the beginning."

"I'm sorry to hear that," Pincus said soothingly. "What else?"

"Well," Sister Gloria Gloria was especially pleased that Pincus seemed to appreciate her plight, "I thought that, perhaps, if I established a closer relationship with Miss Heiligenschein, and if we became more like good friends than Sister and student, we might be able to understand each other on a less formal basis."

"It didn't work," Pincus conjectured.

Without responding, Sister Gloria Gloria reached into the folder, pulled out another letter, and handed it to Pincus. Pincus began reading:

"*Dear Glor, I've been reading St. Augustine the whole week like you suggested, and I'm sorry to say it's not at all what I had hoped. I know that he felt really lousy about pilfering the pears, but seven whole chapters of 'Foul soul, shame, shameful soul, foul me, foul and shameful me' is a bit much, don't you think? Besides, as we all know, the guy got away with murder, so to speak. What kind of prayer is 'Lord, give me chastity and continence, only not yet?' And how come in all the stuff we read about him nobody ever talks about his mistress? I mean, he had one, you know, and they had a kid. Then he ditched her and made her leave the kid with him. She was so bummed out that she took off for Africa and never saw the kid, or even another guy, for the whole rest of her sad life. The truth is that Augustine was kind of a creep, don't you think? What do you say you and I write to the Pope and start some kind of movement to get him unsainted before someone finds some parchment or something that exposes him, and we all look pretty stupid. Your pal, She.*"

"What she wrote about Augustine, is this true?" Rosalie asked with some interest.

"Your daughter claims to know a great many intimate details of the lives of the saints that are not of public record, and, as you can tell, these frequently depict the less saintly aspects of their lives."

"She was an early reader," Rosalie explained.

"She calls Aquinas 'Tommy,'" Sister Gloria Gloria said tersely. Then she reached for another paper which she handed to Rosalie this time, who read as follows:

"*Jesus says, 'When thou makest a feast, call the poor, the maimed, and lame and the blind.' Well, you're going to have a heck of a lot of food left over if the people you invite can't walk, have no money for transportation, and can't see where they're going."*

Rosalie stared for a moment in silence at the paper in her hand.

"I hadn't seen this before," Rosalie commented to Sister Gloria Gloria.

"This was just the beginning," Sister Gloria Gloria said, and she got up and walked over to her desk, on which sat a portable tape player.

"We had our usual differences, but the way things were going I felt it best to record our conversations. Miss Heiligenschein had no objection, and, in fact, on more than one occasion asked me if she could listen to one or another of our recorded interchanges and seemed quite pleased by what she heard. This is our last conversation," and Sister Gloria Gloria pushed the play button on the tape machine.

"I need to talk to you, Miss Heiligenschein," the voice was clearly that of Sister Gloria Gloria, "about something that has been brought to my attention recently."

"What's that?" She asked.

Pincus was surprised by Her voice. He expected something more mature, something more womanly, but instead found himself listening to the voice of an adolescent. And, yet, there was something about the voice, something beneath the voice, that was different, confident, ethereal, forceful without being offensive. It was the voice of an eighteen-year-old who seemed to have lived a long time and experienced a great deal. As Pincus listened, his heart raced and he tried desperately to imagine the face that went with the voice, but he had no luck. Faces flitted through his mind, but nothing stuck.

Rosalie, however, hearing, for the first time in years, the voice of her daughter, was in a state of great distress. Tears flooded her eyes and every muscle in her body tensed as she fought to keep from falling apart.

"Tell me about the Mother of God," Sister Gloria Gloria asked on the tape.

"Mary?"

"Well, apparently, according to Sister Grace, you feel there's another Mother of Jesus, as I understand it," Sister Gloria Gloria commented.

"No, there's only one Mother of Jesus, and that's Mary, the Virgin Mother."

"Well, I'm glad we've cleared that up."

"There is, however, the Mother of all Gods," She explained.

"Of which Gods? I thought there was one God."

"Only if you're a Christian or a Jew. But there're also Muslims, and Hindus, and Buddhists, and hundreds of tribes in Africa and South America, and these gods had to come from somewhere, too, and that's where the Mother of all Gods comes in. Jesus had a mother, and so did they. Of course, Jesus isn't exactly God, but that's something else."

"I beg your pardon."

"Jesus never claimed to be God."

"No, we claim he is God."

"How do you know?"

"From what He said, from what He did, from His miracles, from His arising from the dead, to name just a few things. You don't believe that Jesus is God?"

"I believe that Jesus had the highest awareness of God that man has ever had on earth. But he told people repeatedly that he was not God, and I take him at his word."

Pincus and Rosalie looked over at Sister Gloria Gloria, who was having a difficult time hearing this once more.

"You don't believe that Jesus was conceived of the Holy Ghost by the Virgin Mother from God?" Sister Gloria Gloria's voice was beginning to crack on the tape.

"No, and I don't think Matthew did, either. Otherwise he wouldn't have spent twenty verses tracing Jesus's ancestors back to King David."

There was a silence on the tape. Then the voice of Sister Gloria Gloria was heard, speaking in firm measured tones, the kind used to give a countdown to a firing squad.

"Let. Me. State. For. The. Record. Our. Position. At This. Convent. Miss Heiligenschein. We. Believe. That. The. Christian. Religion. Is. Founded. On. The. Premise. That. Christ. Is. God."

"Well. It. Doesn't. Have. To. Be."

"No, it *has* to be," Sister Gloria Gloria said through clenched teeth.

"Jesus said that God is in us, and he's right. To experience God, all we have to do is feel the world all around us, become a part of it. As St. Mechtilde of Hackeborn said —"

"Saint who?" Sister Gloria Gloria was clearly losing her patience.

"Saint Mechtilde."

"Of where?"

"Hackeborn."

"Hackeborn?"

"Right. Hackeborne. What she said was that we are in life like a fish in the sea, a bird in the air. That's what Saint Mechtilde said."

"Miss Heiligenschein, this would be a perfect time for you to leave my office before I do something very un-Christian-like.... I won't have you talking like this in the home of God."

"Home for you, Sister. For me, my heart is the home of God."

"You have an answer for everything, don't you?"

"Not really. I just try to <u>think</u> things out and see whether they make sense, that's all."

"Have you forgotten, my child, what Aquinas says, that God reveals Himself to us, not by logic, but by revelation and faith. He is too great for our puny intellects."

"What is that supposed to mean? That God is only for stupid people?"

"It means that God is too powerful for us to understand, so you should turn to your faith."

"Well, the truth is — and I know you're not going to especially like this — but God is not all that powerful."

There was something akin to a sputtering sound on the tape, a sound like the engine of an old car dying a slow death. The sound was from Sister Gloria Gloria.

"God is all powerful! God can do anything!" Sister Gloria Gloria shouted.

"Not really."

"What?! What?! What can't God do? Name me one thing!"

"I'll name you ten. He can't change Himself, fail, forget, repent, make us have no souls, make a circle have less than three hundred and sixty degrees, undo the past, commit sins, make another God, or make Himself not exist!"

"Out! Out! Get your grotesquely overdeveloped heretical body out of my office!"

Sister Gloria Gloria pushed the button to stop the tape player, then looked up at Rosalie and Pincus.

"And the next morning She was gone," Sister Gloria Gloria said.

There was a long of silence. Finally Rosalie spoke.

"You have to help us find Her," Rosalie said, torn with conflicting emotions. "You must come with us."

"I know," answered Sister Gloria Gloria quietly.

"Do you know how we can find Her?" Rosalie asked.

Sister Gloria Gloria nodded her head.

"Yes, I do. God will lead us to her," Sister Gloria Gloria said, and, unexpectedly, her eyes began to flood with tears.

PART V

The Singing Machine

CHAPTER 1

Love calling to love is the compelling gravity of human momentum. "My weight is my love," says Augustine, but for Pincus love was more than just mass, more than just a magnetic force.

Pincus was convinced that finding love in its purest form, that is, by finding Her, he would at long last overcome the vast inhibitory forces binding him to this mundane earth. Or so Pincus thought as he lay awake that night in the Convent of the Sisters of Perpetual Sorrow, visions of a female form of aesthetic qualities previously unknown to mankind dancing in front of him until he was nearly blinded by the perfection of Her proportions.

To give Sister Gloria Gloria time to prepare for her journey, they had agreed to stay for dinner and overnight, planning to leave just after breakfast the next morning. Pincus had been looking forward to a restful night of sleep, but it was not to be.

He spent the night, not tossing and turning, but staring motionlessly at the ceiling of a room that, Pincus reflected, gave new meaning to the term "monastic." The furnishings consisted entirely of one single metal bed, barely the width of his body, on which was a thin blanket and a pillow that resembled in size and texture the Sunday edition of *The New York Times*.

In addition to Pincus's usual musings on God, life, and neurophysiology, all of which had a way, if not preventing sleep entirely, certainly removing from it anything that might be considered restful, this night Pincus also found himself unable to sleep because of a voice that continually resonated through his brain — Her voice. Pincus was having a substantial problem assimilating the tale he had heard in Sister Gloria Gloria's office with the voice that now played in his mind.

Pincus had always imagined that, upon finding Her, he would encounter an adoring and submissive companion, one who accommodated his every desire. If there was one word that encapsulated the great and perfect love that he hoped to find at the end of his quest, that word was "easy." Their relationship, their profound love, would be one without dispute and complication. The story that Sister Gloria Gloria had to tell that afternoon now suggested that this might not be the case.

The barely post-adolescent She was obviously someone with strong opinions on a variety of subjects. His image of a living, adoring, and obliging God of All Gods was quickly dissipating. Pincus was beginning to consider that She might be a "handful," not unlike the only God he knew, and this was not at all what Pincus had in mind.

Still, Pincus decided, as the first light of dawn appeared and he still lay awake, caught up in his perpetual motion of love, that he would continue his journey. Perhaps, what he heard was just the usual adolescent obstinacy, and now, Her having passed through this phase, he would find the compliant love he was seeking. Pincus hadn't actually convinced himself of this, but it was enough to keep him going.

In the next room, Theo also couldn't sleep, simply because he didn't want to be there. God, or His Son, or His Son's Mother, or those who believed and worshiped all of the above, were everywhere he looked in this place. His devotion to God had long ago disappeared, though not his belief in God's existence. For to dismiss God altogether would deprive him of someone to blame for all that had befallen him, of his pain, and of the suddenness with which his beloved wife, Bernice, had had her glorious life rent to shreds.

And then there was Rosalie, who did sleep, but fitfully. Every hour or so she would awaken, and she would hear the voice of her daughter, a voice she had not heard for so long that its sound was almost a stranger to her, and Rosalie would weep inconsolably for a while, until she had cried herself back to sleep.

So it was a rather bedraggled and sleep-deprived group that started out after breakfast the next morning with Sister Gloria Gloria, who dragged an enormous black suitcase on wheels. Sister Gloria Gloria had taken over the lead for Theo, who seemed to have lost a step, now tapping his silver-handled cane erratically, not at all in synchronization with his feet.

Sister Gloria Gloria, prior to their start and after her daily Angelus and then breakfast, had assembled the group in the convent kitchen, where they made lunches of peanut butter and jelly sandwiches and placed them into small brown paper lunch bags along with an apple or pear, according to the preference of each. Then they filled their water bottles, from which Rosalie now drank, as Sister Gloria Gloria halted the group at a crossroads a mile past the convent.

"Oh, Lord come to my aide; O Lord make haste to help me," Sister Gloria Gloria said, head bowed, eyes closed.

"Excuse me?" Rosalie asked, not pleased to be stopping at such an early point in their travels. "What's going on here?"

"Memorare," Sister Gloria Gloria answered, equally displeased to be interrupted in the midst of prayer.

"Which is?" Rosalie asked.

"I am petitioning Our Blessed Virgin Mother," Sister Gloria Gloria responded.

"Mary?"

"Do you know of any other virgin mother?" Sister Gloria Gloria asked.

Rosalie turned to Pincus, who stood beside her.

"You think?" Rosalie asked Pincus.

"I think," Pincus answered in slow and measured words, "that this information is something that, in the case of Sister, should be presented gradually over time, and at just the right moment."

Rosalie thought about this, then nodded.

"Okay," Rosalie said, "but sooner or later . . ."

"Now if I may proceed?" Sister Gloria Gloria asked, not actually a question, and she resumed her prayer, concluding with,

"O Mother of the Word Incarnate, despise not my petitions, but in thy mercy hear and answer me. Amen."

Sister Gloria Gloria looked at Rosalie, Theo, and Pincus, her eyebrows raised in expectation.

"Amen," the three obliged.

"To the right," Sister Gloria Gloria informed everyone with firm conviction, and off she headed. The group stood dumbstruck for a moment, then followed behind Sister Gloria Gloria.

In a moment Rosalie caught up with her.

"I don't mean to pry into your private spiritual life, but the Virgin Mother actually told you to take the road to the right?"

"As I understood her," Sister Gloria Gloria answered.

"How much room would you say, offhand, there is for misunderstanding?" Rosalie continued her interrogatories. "You can express it in percentages, if you want."

"Very little," Sister Gloria Gloria answered.

"I see. Well, I mean, did Mary actually say, 'I'd take the road to the right, if it were me,' or was this, like, more of an interpretation on your part?"

"This was," and now Sister Gloria Gloria was losing her patience, "what I felt was given to me in answer to my prayer of petition."

"So, there weren't actually any words?" Rosalie asked. "I'm not trying to argue with you, just to understand for, like, future intersections we come to."

"When someone looks at you with love, do you need words to understand?" Sister Gloria Gloria asked. "Does the person actually have to say, 'I love you'? Or do you just know it in your heart?"

"Well, of course, I know it in my heart, but then there's this other person there right in front of me — eyes, mouth, nose, ears — all that — who I can actually see," Rosalie pointed out. "That *really* helps."

"But man does not see by eyes alone, does he?" Sister Gloria

Gloria said.

"Jesus actually said that?" Rosalie asked.

"No, I did. I see the Virgin Mother as clearly as if she were standing before me, speaking to me, and she fills my heart with her essence and benevolence."

"And her essence and benevolence says 'Make a right here'?" Rosalie asked.

Sister Gloria Gloria was surprised at how her heart, this same heart that had so completely filled just a moment before with the peace and wonder of the Blessed Virgin, was now filling with thoughts of grabbing Rosalie by the neck and shaking her until her teeth rattled in her head.

Pincus, just a step behind, reached out and grabbed Rosalie by the arm, causing her to fall back into step with him.

"Are you familiar, Rosalie, with the concept of leaving well-enough alone?" Pincus inquired.

"I'm aware of it," Rosalie snapped. "I'm also aware that I may never see my daughter again if our route is entirely determined by Sister Gloria Gloria's petitions to the Virgin Mother. Let's take, for example, the possibility that Mary might have meant, not this right, but the next right. It all could just be this gigantic misunderstanding between two impenetrable women, you know virgin to virgin. I mean, nobody's perfect, right?"

"I think the idea of the Virgin Mother," Pincus told Rosalie, "the immaculate conception, all that, suggests that Mary is considered to be, in fact, pretty much perfect."

"I meant *Sister*, not the Holy Mother," Rosalie said crisply and left Pincus.

Behind them, tapping erratically with his cane, was Theo, his head tilted upwards, inspecting various cloud formations as he walked.

"Perfect," Theo echoed. "Just perfect."

And so onward they moved, past pastures and fields, down winding roads, fortunate, Rosalie thought, not to have encountered any further intersections. From time to time a car or truck would pass by, and the driver or passenger would wave at Sister Gloria Gloria, as though by doing so a special blessing was bestowed upon him, and Sister Gloria Gloria would nod back in a way that very well could have been a blessing; it was hard to know.

Then they stopped — that is Sister Gloria Gloria stopped, placed her suitcase along the side of the road on a dirt pullout, opened a section of the top to reveal a small shrine, and knelt, while the others looked on with various emotions.

"Are we stopping for lunch?" Rosalie asked, trying not to sound sarcastic.

"Noooo," Sister Gloria Gloria said, deciding that Rosalie must, in fact, be sarcastic, as Rosalie couldn't possibly be looking at the small lace-covered shelf in front of her on which stood a gold crucifix, between statues of the Blessed Mother and St. Francis, and think she was about to have lunch. "Lunch is at 1 p.m. Now it is noon, and I am stopping to say the Angelus, as I do each day at noon."

Then Sister Gloria Gloria took a small vial from her pocket, pulled out the stopper, and flicked holy water on the three individuals who now stood beside her, hitting Rosalie, not entirely by accident, directly in the eyes.

"Did you say 'each day at noon'?" Rosalie inquired, as she wiped her eyes.

Sister Gloria Gloria's answer was to pull a small bell from another pocket and ring it three times.

"Someone should get that," Theo said.

"The Angel of the Lord declared unto Mary. And she conceived of the Holy Spirit," Sister Gloria Gloria said.

"Hail Mary, full of grace, the Lord is with Thee, Blessed art Thou among women, and Blessed is the fruit of Thy womb, Jesus. Holy Mary, Mother of God, pray for us sinners, now and at the hour of our death. Amen."

"Amen," they all said.

"I'm just wondering — " Rosalie started to say, but she never finished, as Sister Gloria Gloria rang her little bell three more times.

"Isn't anybody going to answer that?" Theo asked.

"Behold the handmaid of the Lord," Sister Gloria Gloria continued. "Be it done unto me according to thy word. Hail Mary, full of grace, the Lord is with Thee, Blessed art Thou among women, and Blessed is the fruit of Thy womb, Jesus. Holy Mary, Mother of God, pray for us sinners, now and at the hour of our death. Amen."

There was a rousing chorus of "Amen" from the congregation.

Sister Gloria Gloria rang her bell three more times.

"Oh, Jesus," Rosalie said, but it was not said in prayer.

Sister Gloria Gloria looked up sternly at Rosalie.

"Sorry, sorry. I'm just wondering how many times you're going to ring that damn —" Rosalie started.

"And the Word was made Flesh," Sister Gloria Gloria said. "And dwelt among us. Hail Mary, full of grace, the Lord is with thee, Blessed art Thou among women, and Blessed is the fruit of Thy womb, Jesus. Holy Mary, Mother of God, pray for us sinners, now and at the hour of our death. Amen."

"Amen," the others chorused, but with somewhat less enthusiasm.

They waited for the bell, but there was none, just a moment of silence as Sister Gloria Gloria closed her eyes and bowed her head.

"They'll call back," Theo reassured everyone.

"Pray for us, O holy Mother of God. That we may be made worthy of the promises of Christ. Let us pray," Sister Gloria Gloria said. She looked beside her at Rosalie, Theo, and Pincus. Rosalie and Theo knelt.

"I'm Jewish," Pincus explained, "more or less. My mother."

Sister Gloria Gloria looked Pincus in the eyes with a cold stare that penetrated down to his circumcised penis.

Pincus knelt and clasped his hands together in prayer.

"Pour forth, we beseech Thee, O Lord, Thy grace into our hearts, that we to whom the Incarnation of Christ Thy Son was made known by the message of an angel, may by His Passion and Cross be brought to the glory of His Resurrection. Through the same Christ Our Lord. Amen."

"Amen," once again said the three supplicants beside Sister Gloria Gloria, who smiled and started to close her suitcase, a signal for the others to rise.

"Every day at noon?" Rosalie asked. "You say the Angelus every day at noon?"

"And at 6:00 a.m. and 6:00 p.m.," Sister Gloria Gloria said, as she snapped the last clasp of her suitcase shut.

"Any other prayers I should know about?" Rosalie asked, not especially wanting to hear the answer.

"The Gloria at 9:00 a.m., the Our Father at 10:00 a.m., and the Prayer to St. Francis at 3:00 p.m. And, of course, we say the Act of Contrition at 8:00 p.m. to end the day," Sister Gloria Gloria said and started off down the road.

"*We* say?" Rosalie asked, but Sister Gloria Gloria didn't answer, so Rosalie turned to Pincus. "That's every two hours," Rosalie told Pincus. "And that doesn't include asking the Virgin Mother for directions. At this rate, my daughter will be a hundred and four before I ever see her again. You have to talk to her, Max. Jews are great at persuading people to do things they don't really want to do."

"And then they get crucified," Pincus pointed out, "and now we have to stop every two hours and pray because of it."

"Well, if you won't talk to her, then who will?" Rosalie asked and nodded toward Theo, shuffling along behind them. "Not him. Theo's still waiting for them to call back."

"I think we just have to play this out," Pincus said. "Patience is a virtue. What could be better to have on a religious pilgrimage than regular prayer?"

"Roller blades?" Rosalie asked, and so it went that first day.

They crossed from Litchfield into Berkshire County and were now in Massachusetts, at which point, it now being exactly 1:00 p.m.

and having sighted a picnic table in a cut-out along the side of the road next to a stream, Sister Gloria Gloria indicated that this would be a very good time to break out the packed peanut butter sandwiches and fruit.

By now Theo seemed to be regaining contact with reality and commented from time to time on the species of various trees, how they had come to be there, which were native and which were not. The group was impressed, asked questions at intervals, and so the time passed until they found themselves sitting at the picnic table, sinking their front teeth into apples, beneath a quite spectacular tulip poplar tree that was nearly a hundred feet tall.

"This is about as far north as you'll see a tulip poplar," Theo said while biting into a Macintosh. "If you've ever seen one in bloom in the spring, the flowers are quite spectacular, with a ring of scarlet around the base inside the flower. People see them in bloom, and they run right out and plant a bunch around their house. What they don't know is that a tulip poplar excretes a sticky sap that is going to turn their lawn black and attract every flying bug known to man. But for a couple weeks there, the tree is one of the most beautiful in nature."

"How do you know so much about trees?" Rosalie asked Theo.

"Guess from living in the world," Theo answered. "I have a natural curiosity. And I like a good story."

"You know what that is over there?" Theo asked.

"Another interesting tree?" Rosalie asked tersely.

"More than interesting. It's an eastern hophornbeam," Theo informed them.

"You're kidding," Rosalie said facetiously. "I can't believe it. And I'm here to see it."

"Eastern hophornbeam," Theo said again. "Its wood is hard enough for making tool handles and mallets, which is exactly what the first settlers here did with it. Rabbits and deer feed off its bark and twigs. And the nutlets and buds feed the birds — grouse, pheasant, and quail, along with the rabbits. There're not a lot of hophornbeams left, but the trees provided a living and provisions for most everybody who came here to make a home."

Pincus wondered at the economy of it all. It was hard for him to imagine the ecology of this as just being accidental, yet Pincus had doubts that the Almighty had said to Himself one moment during the Creation, "Hey, here's an idea. I think I'll make a tree that will provide tools for mankind and sustenance for my creatures who will be tasty to the human beings I create — deer, rabbits, pheasant, who, of course, must be fruitful and multiply at a rate greater than they can be eaten."

Something didn't compute for Pincus. He doubted God got that involved in the details. Pincus felt that with the heavens, sun and moon, oceans, giraffes, and hippos to come up with, not to mention mankind and womankind, this seemed not to be worth God's time, given all that had to be done in only six days, if the Creator was ever going to get that seventh day off. But then, if not Him, who — and how?

Unable to resolve his conundrum at this moment, Pincus hoisted his backpack on his shoulders, followed by Rosalie and Theo. Sister Gloria Gloria replaced her leftover half sandwich in the rolling suitcase, closed the zipper on the outside pocket, and all was ready to roll.

An hour and a half later they found themselves in South Egremont, where Rosalie and Sister Gloria Gloria once again locked horns.

CHAPTER 2

South Egremont was something of a haven. There were a half-dozen shops on the tree-lined main street, all facing a large white clapboard church, which Rosalie passed, hoping that Sister Gloria Gloria had no desire to check it out.

So it was with great relief that the group passed by the church, patronized a small market where they purchased provisions for dinner, and finally entered a pharmacy with an old-fashioned soda fountain, behind which was a large barrel with the words "Hires Root Beer" on it in large letters.

"It's the real stuff," the young man behind the counter told them, and, in fact, it was — a keg of fresh root beer such as Theo and Pincus had not tasted since their youth and Rosalie had never tasted. Sister Gloria Gloria, in spite of assurances that this beer had no relation to that sold by Budweiser, abstained, had a glass of ice water, and notified the rest that she would be outside.

After a second round of root beers, Rosalie, Theo, and Pincus walked out into the bright sunlit day and found Sister Gloria Gloria standing in front of an old stone water trough that had been placed there for horses several centuries ago. Behind the fountain was a road at right angles to Main Street, and Rosalie guessed instantly what was transpiring as she approached Sister Gloria Gloria and heard her chanting.

"O Mother of the Word Incarnate, despise not my petitions, but in thy mercy hear and answer me," Sister Gloria Gloria was finishing her prayer, concluding with, "Amen."

The group, well-trained by now, chorused their Amens, and then Sister Gloria Gloria turned and faced them.

"We go this way," she informed them, pointing to the road on the other side of the horse trough.

Rosalie looked at the signpost at the start of the road. It read "Mt. Washington," followed by an arrow pointing up the road.

"We're going to go up a mountain?" Rosalie asked.

"It's not a mountain," Sister Gloria Gloria responded. "It's a large hill."

"The letters 'M,' 'T,' and then the period," Rosalie pointed her arm at the sign. "What do you think they mean, Sister?"

"I think they refer to the name of the hill," Sister Gloria Gloria answered.

"Why do you think," Rosalie tried to maintain calm, "they didn't write 'Hill Washington'"?

"Because that's not what it's called," Sister Gloria Gloria responded tersely.

"You don't think it's because somebody, maybe even a lot of people, considered it to be a mountain?" Rosalie responded.

"Perhaps, but it's not. I've taken my students there. It's a hill," Sister Gloria Gloria answered.

"A big steep hill?" Rosalie queried.

"Well, a hill is a hill," Sister Gloria Gloria answered. "It's obviously bigger and steeper than a usual road."

"Okay," Rosalie tried another approach. "Let's assume that the Virgin Mother told you to go up this steep hill which is called Mount Washington."

"Yes, let's," but, once again, Sister Gloria Gloria was beginning to lose her patience.

"But I'm wondering," Rosalie asked, "whether there might be some way you could conference me in to the Virgin Mother so we might talk directly to one another."

"If this is a joke, I don't find it amusing," Sister Gloria Gloria responded.

"I assume the answer is no, then, and this means we're going up the mountain?" Rosalie said glumly.

"Guess it does," Pincus smiled pleasantly. "What a great adventure it will be for us all, won't it Sister?"

Rosalie spun back to Sister Gloria Gloria before she could answer.

"Where does it go? Do you know that? When you go down the other side, where are you?" Rosalie asked.

"There is no road down the other side. There're just trails. We go up from here, and we come right back down to here," Sister Gloria Gloria informed Rosalie.

"We're climbing a dead-end mountain?" Rosalie could barely get out the words.

"Mountains have great religious significance," Theo pointed out. "The Ten Commandments. The Sermon on the Mount...."

Rosalie spun back to Theo.

"You think we're getting commandments from God or a sermon from Jesus when we get up to the top?" Rosalie asked incredulously. "And just for the record —"

"Maybe this isn't the best time to set the record straight," Pincus opined.

"Just for the record," Rosalie continued, "it makes no sense to climb a mountain to talk to God. You think that God can't penetrate the clouds? What is He made of, helium? And, when you think about it, how much closer can you actually be to God at the top of a mountain, even Mt. Everest? You think God hovers in the upper troposphere, dodging commercial aircraft?"

"Perhaps," Theo joined in the discussion, "men go up mountains to communicate with God where there is a certain kind of peace and silence. It tends to get very noisy down here."

Rosalie looked at Theo. This was something she hadn't considered.

"Maybe," she finally responded, "but you'd think with God being all-powerful, we could get just as good radio reception down here on earth."

"I think we should start, since we're losing time," Pincus said.

"Losing time for what?" Rosalie asked. "Not to find my daughter. We're just going up the mountain and back down the mountain, and, I don't care what anybody says, this is a mountain."

Then Rosalie turned to Sister Gloria Gloria.

"Did Mary actually say my daughter was up there?" Rosalie asked.

"No, but she didn't say she wasn't."

"Would you excuse me for a moment," and off Rosalie went, across the street, and back into the pharmacy. In a moment she emerged and entered the shop beside it, then exited, and repeated this until she had entered and exited all six shops. Then she returned to the group, which was now sitting on the edge of the horse trough, awaiting her.

"I have shown Her photo to everybody in every shop, and no one has ever seen Her. Since She needs to eat, unless She's been living on the nutlets and buds of the hophornbeam tree, She would have had to come down here to get food. She's not up there. She's just not. So why are we going?"

"Because that is what we have been told to do," Sister Gloria Gloria responded tersely. "As the Bible tells us, 'Ours not to reason why....'"

"That's not the Bible," Rosalie erupted. "That's Alfred Lloyd Tennyson. We read it in tenth grade. And it's not '*Ours* not to reason why,' it's '*Theirs not to reason why, Theirs but to do and die: Into the valley of Death, Rode the six hundred.*' *This* is supposed to make me want to climb the mountain? They all died, Sister! Every one of them! That's why he called it the '*Valley of Death*'! I want to talk to Mary. How do I do it? *Conference me in!*"

"Are we all ready?" Sister Gloria Gloria ignored Rosalie's tirade. "You can stay here if you want," she told Rosalie, "but if the Virgin Mother has told us to climb this so-called mountain, then that's exactly what we're doing." And off Sister Gloria Gloria went, followed by Pincus and Theo.

Rosalie stood stewing, watching them leave, then, walked across the street and sat on a bench in front of a hardware store, her arms folded defiantly across her chest, all the while mumbling unintelligible sounds of frustration, as she watched the group finally disappear up the mountain road.

"What if my daughter is somewhere up there?" she thought. "Maybe She just went up this morning to find peace and tranquility. Just suppose there's some sort of clue up there, some indication that She'd been there and where She was heading — sort of like a spiritual treasure hunt. By now, Rosalie's rear end was up from the bench and she was crossing the street toward the mountain road.

Rosalie found that the mountain road was not as steep as she had feared, but clearly not a hill, either. Soon, in the distance, she heard Theo singing. She could see him bringing up the rear of the trio, his cane waving in the air.

"We are climbing Jacob's ladder, We are climbing Jacob's ladder, We are climbing Jacob's ladder, Soldiers of the cross," Theo's voice boomed out.

Rosalie broke into a near-run and reached Theo as he launched into the next verse, with great determination on his face.

"Every round goes higher, higher, Every round goes higher, higher, Every round goes higher, higher, Soldiers of the cross."

Rosalie skipped ahead to Pincus, trying to catch her breath.

"Is this really necessary?" she asked Pincus.

"Probably not," Pincus responded, who, not knowing all the words, had been humming along with Theo, "but I don't see the harm, and Sister Gloria Gloria seems to be especially pleased by it. This is, after all, something of a crusade we're on, right?"

A hand tapped Rosalie on the shoulder. It was Theo. He gestured with his cane for Rosalie to join in.

"Sinner, do you love my Jesus? Sinner, do you love my Jesus? Sinner, do you love my Jesus? Soldiers of the cross," Theo continued to beckon for Rosalie to join in.

Then he sang directly to Rosalie, who found it unsettling, even more so when Sister Gloria Gloria joined in the last verse.

And so it was that the soldiers of the Lord marched onward like this for some time, Sister Gloria Gloria at the front, followed by Pincus, then Rosalie, and, finally, Theo, who walked with his head bowed, as though in prayer.

It had been many years since Pincus had been out in the woods. He had taken his children camping each year when they were smaller, just him and the two children, having developed the notion that the distance he already sensed developing with them could be breached if he could spend some quality time. But the camping trips never closed this mysterious gap between a father and his own children.

He always undertook this outing with his children the week of his birthday. For a reason he never completely understood, he wanted to be alone on this natal day on which the rest of the world gathered friends and family and celebrated together with gifts and candlelit cakes. His gifts were the moments alone with his children, and his candles were the billions of stars he could see through the pines.

Beside the campfire, after the children had gone to sleep in the tent, Pincus would set goals for the next year. Once set, he assumed that all would follow of its own accord. And when he returned the next year to his campfire, he would recall each goal and tick off whether or not he had accomplished it. The answer was no different from one year to the next. He had written one poem in the new leather-bound journal he had purchased the week after he had returned from camping. Actually, the poem wasn't quite finished, but he had made what he considered to be an excellent start.

And so it went, as he would go down the list, until, finally, Pincus reached the conclusion that his life was an unaccomplished one and, therefore, entirely meaningless.

But now there was She. She would bring him what he had always needed and longed for — meaning. Pincus was as certain of this as he was that his feet had swollen at least two sizes since he started his journey. Perhaps, meaning was simply a love unlike any other, a perfect love.

Such were the thoughts of Pincus as he trudged up the steep hill, inhaling the intoxicating smell of the evergreens that brought back all these memories, perspiration dripping from his forehead and soaking his shirt.

CHAPTER 3

When Pincus and Theo caught up with Rosalie, she stood perplexed at an intersection. The road they were on had turned to blacktop, and now Falls Road, also blacktop, was on their right, with a large sign reading BASH BISH FALLS, an arrow beneath the words pointing down the side road. Wright Brook ran alongside Falls Road, its clear waters moving over the pebbles that lined its bed.

The three looked at each other.

"This is just terrific," Rosalie said irritably. "You would have thought she'd have waited here for us, or at least left some sort of —"

But Rosalie never finished, as Theo had approached the Bash Bish Falls sign and was now pointing to a crucifix that had been scratched into it with a stone. At the end of the horizontal arm of the cross was an arrow.

"Seems to be recent," Pincus said and started down Falls Road, Theo joining him.

Rosalie watched them go, looked at the sign, looked behind her just to be sure there wasn't another crucifix pointing in another direction, and then, with a shrug, followed the two men.

After a mile, the road turned sharply to the right, and Wright Brook was joined by Bash Bish Brook, causing the stream to swell and flow rapidly, white bubbles of foam appearing as the water hit the larger stones and now splashed over them.

Pincus found something exhilarating about this, the way he felt as a child when he knew in a short time his father would be coming up the front walk, briefcase in hand, or when, he himself, would pull into the driveway early in his marriage to Becki, an anticipation both known and unknown.

He could begin to hear the sound of the falls ahead, and, as they approached the falls, there was the unmistakable sound of Sister Gloria Gloria's voice.

"Lord, make me an instrument of Thy peace …"

"Oh, my God," Rosalie whined, as she, Pincus, and Theo emerged from the path through the woods and found themselves in a grotto composed of huge boulders, in front of which was a pool, across from which an eighty-foot-high plunge of water rushed down the rock face. It was a falls unlike any Pincus had seen.

A giant boulder that reminded Pincus of a skull stood at the very top of the falls and divided it into two parts. The numerous rocks over which the falls fell on the right side shattered the water so that it reached the pool like a rainfall shower; while the falls on the right fell unabated to the pool below with a loud rush, its force sending up a spray that drifted over to where Sister Gloria Gloria stood saying her prayer to St. Francis.

She did not turn to them for their responses as she finished her prayer, but, instinctively, and quietly under their breath, the three pilgrims behind her said, "Amen," at which point Sister Gloria Gloria knelt on the boulder, facing the falls.

Pincus removed his backpack and sat a few feet away from Sister Gloria Gloria, taking in the cascading water before him, saying nothing.

"I think of Golgatha," Sister Gloria Gloria said after a few moments. "Forthwith there came out blood and water," she nodded toward the twin falls.

Pincus wondered whether he should mention that there had been an egregiously bad Bible translation, that in the Hebrew it is not the Son of God who is pierced, but God, himself – and that the world will not mourn the "Son of God," but the world will mourn "as though one had lost one's favorite son, one's firstborn."

"They shall look toward Me," God says, "because of those who have been thrust through with swords," was mistranslated to "They shall look toward Him, who has been pierced with a sword," and so a story was concocted about a soldier piercing the side of Christ to fulfill the Old Testament Zechariah. But, Pincus looked over at Sister Gloria Gloria, and, considering the beatific look on her face, he decided to let well-enough alone.

Behind Pincus, Rosalie sat not far away on another boulder, equally mesmerized by the falls. This seemed to her to be a gift — for her to come upon a falls halfway up a mountain. It said something to her about the unexpected, that it might not always be something to avoid.

Rosalie removed her shoes and socks, and, after reaching behind her and pulling a granola bar from her backpack, she slid forward and dropped her feet into the water, which was, at first, startlingly cold, but soon became refreshing. And there she sat, munching and soaking.

Seeing this, Pincus decided to do the same, removed his shoes and socks with a great sigh of relief, and slowly inserted his feet into the pool.

"Jesus, Mary, and Joseph!" Pincus exclaimed, as the cold water hit his toes and seemed to freeze them solid. "Sorry," Pincus mumbled when Sister Gloria Gloria turned sharply to him in reproach. "Just an expression," he explained to her. "No offense meant. Just names."

"Just names?" Sister Gloria Gloria asked in disbelief.

"Okay, not just names — big important sacred names — but I could just as easily have said 'Jimmy, Myrtle, and Jasper.'"

"Why don't you do that next time," Sister Gloria Gloria requested and started to remove her own shoes and knee-length stockings.

All the while, Theo sat motionless and in silence on a boulder some distance behind them, nearly hidden by the shade from an overhanging tree.

"Holy Mary, Mother of God!" shouted Sister Gloria Gloria as her feet hit the ice cold water.

Pincus and Rosalie looked over at Sister Gloria Gloria, who shrugged and began mumbling what was to become a very long series of prayers of contrition.

And so the three sat, feet dipped in the cool water, side by side, not unlike the proverbial monkeys who could speak, hear, and see no evil. They said nothing, but watched the water fall, transfixed by forces they contemplated but were unsuccessful in understanding — Pincus, Rosalie, and Sister Gloria Gloria in a strange unity.

Still behind them on the shaded boulder, sat Theo, his eyes brimming with tears because Bernice was not there to see this; and, no matter how he wished, she never would be there to share this or anything else in his life. So, he stared silently at the falling water, until suddenly his attention was caught by a pigeon flapping noisily over his head, landing finally in Rosalie's lap.

Rosalie startled, sat up, and looked in disbelief at the pigeon.

"It's Gabrielle," Rosalie announced.

"Who's Gabrielle?" Pincus asked.

Rosalie pointed to the pigeon pecking at the crumbs of the granola bar in her lap. "She sent Gabrielle to lead us to Her."

"The pigeon is Gabrielle?" Pincus asked.

"Exactly," Rosalie said with great joy, and now Sister Gloria Gloria was beginning to pay attention.

"The Angel Gabriel?" Sister Gloria Gloria asked.

"No, the pigeon Gabrielle," Rosalie explained.

"I heard you the first time," Sister Gloria Gloria replied. "I'm asking whether you're saying that this pigeon is the Archangel Gabriel, the same one who announced the birth of our Savior?"

"I don't think so," Rosalie said upon further consideration.

"But you're not certain?" Sister Gloria Gloria pursued the subject.

"She named it Gabrielle. I never thought it could actually be the Angel Gabrielle, but I suppose it could be her," Rosalie ran this over in her head.

"Do you think it could also just be a pigeon that landed in your lap to eat the crumbs of your granola bar?" asked Sister Gloria Gloria.

"The fact is, Gabrielle has been sent by my daughter to lead us to Her," Rosalie informed both Sister Gloria Gloria and Pincus. "I know that for sure."

"Well, dear," Sister Gloria Gloria suggested with more than a little irony, "why don't we wait until Gabrielle the pigeon has finished all the granola crumbs and then see what transpires."

"It's why the Blessed Virgin sent us up here," Rosalie said.

"Well, " Sister Gloria Gloria responded, "I am not following a pigeon all over creation trying to find your daughter."

"No, you're going to stop at every intersection all over creation and file a petition with the Virgin Mother," Rosalie snapped.

"Are you comparing Blessed Mary, Mother of God, to a pigeon?!" Sister Gloria Gloria's dander was up.

"No, but I don't think she's a Hopi scout, either," Rosalie answered.

"Now, now," Pincus tried to counsel, "let's not get all worked up over this."

"Not get 'all worked up'?" Sister Gloria Gloria retorted. "She just compared the Virgin Mother to a common bird!"

"That's not what I said," Rosalie answered. And now it was time to take out the heavy artillery. "And just for the record, Mary is not the only Virgin Mother around here."

The only sounds were the falls and Sister Gloria Gloria gagging on her own breath. Pincus and Theo raced to the rescue, pounding Sister on the back, but she brushed them aside.

"Might I ask," Sister Gloria Gloria said after she had regained her ability to breathe and speak at the same time, "who exactly around here is also a Virgin Mother?"

"That would be me," Rosalie smiled.

"Really," Sister said.

"Really," Rosalie nodded.

"You are the Virgin Mother and the pigeon eating crumbs out of your lap is the Archangel Gabrielle?"

"Don't get all worked up. I am not *the* Virgin Mother," Rosalie responded, "just *a* virgin mother. And the pigeon is not the Archangel Gabrielle, at least I don't think so, just a pigeon who was a pet of my daughter and she named Gabrielle."

"I see," Sister Gloria Gloria said, though it was not apparent she did. "And may I assume that the result of the virgin birth was your daughter?"

"You may assume that because it's true," Rosalie answered.

"And your daughter was conceived without any man being involved?" Sister asked.

"You mean except my father?" Rosalie asked back.

"I beg your pardon. You were impregnated by your father?"

"Well, yes, but not in the way you're thinking. He just had me breathe the air," Rosalie explained.

"Breathing the air made you pregnant?" Sister Gloria Gloria tried to follow the logic.

"The air he had, yes. There were these little beings in the air, kind of like souls, and I breathed it, and, well — that was it. I was pregnant. So, it's not like there was some annunciation, and God came down, or his angel, including Gabrielle, and there was no room in the inn and She was born in a manger or anything," Rosalie tried to comfort Sister Gloria Gloria.

"May I say something here?" Theo asked.

All heads turned to take in his contribution.

"I don't want to rain on your parade, but the fact is," Theo explained, "the prophesy in Isaiah that the Messiah would be conceived by a 'virgin' was a mistranslation. Isaiah prophesied that the Messiah would be born of an 'almah,' which means a 'young woman,' not a 'virgin.' It just says that a 'young woman shall conceive' — not a virgin."

The three looked at Theo as though he had been speaking Greek.

"I majored in philosophy and religion at Dartmouth," Theo smiled.

"Well, that was really helpful," Pincus finally commented, as he reached out to steady Sister Gloria Gloria, who was not doing well, having dealt in rapid succession with a pigeon who was the Archangel Gabrielle, with Rosalie being a second Virgin Mother, and now with the loss of the virgin birth of the Messiah, substantially more than a woman of the cloth is intended to endure in one sitting.

"I think," Pincus said, clutching the arm of Sister Gloria Gloria to keep her upright, "that we should put a pin in all this for now and come back to it another time."

"Hey, look! She's still here," Rosalie said. "Gabrielle has finished all the crumbs, and she's still sitting in my lap. I'll bet when we wake up tomorrow morning, she'll still be here, too."

And she was.

CHAPTER 4

Pincus was the first to awaken. Theo was still asleep, wrapped in his sleeping bag, his head not visible. Pincus had given his tent to Sister Gloria Gloria, and the sound of her heavy breathing issued from it. A short distance away, Rosalie was asleep in her tent, the pigeon Gabrielle perched on its top, serving as a weather vane pointing to the ultimate destination, Pincus thought. Rosalie would neglect to tell her companions that she had awakened every half hour to feed the pigeon small chunks of her granola bars, and this may have had something to do with the bird's continued presence.

In following Rosalie's pigeon the evening before, they had retraced their steps from Bash Bish Falls, continued on Mt. Washington Road, then taken a sharp U-turn up Pond Road, and found themselves at Lake Riga, a large lake at the top of the mountain, where the pigeon drank copious amounts of water to wash down the granola.

A haze had settled over the lake as though it were a large cloud, and, as the sun rose, the haze glowed orange and rose. It seemed to Pincus as though the glowing mist was not a reflection of the sun as it rose behind it, but the light emanated directly from within, or was all light source — a divine presence itself — and this created in Pincus a serenity he had rarely experienced.

Rosalie crawled from her tent, took one look at what lay before her sleepy eyes, and turned to Gabrielle. "Good work, Gabe," she said softly to her, and then walked over to join Pincus. Theo and Sister Gloria Gloria were now sitting beside him.

"Tell me that we are not being led by a divine presence," Rosalie said, directing her comment at Sister Gloria Gloria. "Would we ever have found this without Gabrielle?"

"Perhaps not," Sister Gloria Gloria responded, "but I suspect that if your bird were under a park bench in the Boston Common at this very moment, pecking at the remains of peanut shells, what we are seeing would be the same."

"You know what I don't understand," Rosalie responded. "How can somebody who has devoted her life to spiritual pursuits have the same sense of wonder as a slug. I have to take a pee," and off Rosalie went into the woods.

"I'll make breakfast," Sister Gloria Gloria said, "if one of you will set a fire."

"I can do that," Theo offered, and off he went into the woods to gather sticks, followed very shortly by a loud shriek from Rosalie.

"Sorry, sorry," Theo's voice could be heard coming from the woods, "I forgot you'd come in here."

An hour later, they found themselves once again on Mt. Washington Road, retracing their steps.

"Look," said Rosalie with great pleasure, "Gabrielle the dove is still leading us."

"First of all," Sister Gloria Gloria commented, "it is following us, not leading us."

"How do you know?" Rosalie asked.

"Because," Sister Gloria Gloria said, her teeth clenched tightly, "it is behind us, not ahead of us. And second, it is a pigeon not a dove."

"I think they're the same," Rosalie responded. "Pigeons and doves."

"Doves are white. Pigeons are not," Sister Gloria Gloria settled the matter.

"That's not true at all," Rosalie responded.

"Have you ever seen a dove of peace that is anything other than white?" Sister Gloria Gloria pressed her case. "Once it becomes gray, it becomes a pigeon of peace. Doves are white; pigeons are —

whatever — but not white," Sister Gloria Gloria completed what she considered to be an irrefutable proof.

"I think Rosalie's right," Theo decided to add to the dialogue, having now carefully considered both positions. "Pigeons and doves are pretty much synonymous."

"Not if you're a Christian," Sister Gloria Gloria said tersely.

"You mean the Holy Spirit?" Rosalie asked.

"Clever girl," Sister Gloria Gloria responded.

"Well, seeing as how smart you think I am," Rosalie answered with scarcely a beat between Sister Gloria Gloria's last word and her first, "you might want to check your Bible, Sister, because the Bible doesn't say that the Holy Spirit is a dove."

"I beg your pardon?" Sister Gloria Gloria could barely get the words out, ire so filled her throat.

"What the Bible says is that, when Jesus was baptized, the Spirit descended upon him like a dove, not as a dove. It could just have easily have said that the Spirit descended upon him like sleet."

"Six hundred wings," Sister Gloria Gloria said after she had regained her composure.

"Six hundred wings what?" asked Rosalie.

"That's how the Angel Gabriel is described," Sister Gloria Gloria explained. "He's described as having six hundred wings. Now take a look at your pigeon and count. I get two. What do you get?"

"Sister, with all due respect," replied Rosalie, who was becoming bored by the conversation, "I don't know where you got this from, but the only place you can find six hundred wings in one place is at Kentucky Fried Chicken. Now, seeing as how we have now reached the bottom of the mountain, I think we should give this conversation a decent burial and move on to which direction we should walk."

Sister Gloria Gloria, perhaps for the first time, and probably the last, couldn't have been more in agreement with Rosalie, opened her suitcase and began setting up her shrine to make her usual plea to Mary for guidance.

Rosalie watched this, as she ran through in her mind how she might approach an obviously delicate matter.

"Sister," Rosalie finally said, "I really don't want to get into a competition here —"

"Good. Then don't," Sister Gloria Gloria said before Rosalie could finish her sentence, "Oh, Lord come to my aide; O Lord make haste to help me," Sister Gloria Gloria began, her head bowed, her eyes closed.

"However," Rosalie continued, "I'm following the bird that my daughter sent to guide us. Anybody who wants to come with me is welcome."

"The Holy Mother says that we should continue straight ahead," Sister Gloria Gloria announced.

"Then that's where the Holy Mother should go. Gabrielle is taking a right turn here, and that's where I'm going," Rosalie announced.

"You're defying the Holy Mother?" Sister Gloria Gloria asked.

"No, I'm obeying the directive of the Holy Spirit. One would think there'd be some agreement here between your divine spokesperson and mine, but since, obviously, there is not, and, just spit-balling here that we're not likely to reach an agreement, it looks like it's one way or the other. So — seeya," and Rosalie walked a few steps and made a right turn.

Sister Gloria Gloria watched aghast.

"I'm kind of here at Rosalie's invitation …" Pincus said apologetically to Sister Gloria Gloria and followed after Rosalie.

"I guess I'd have to say the same," Theo mumbled, dug his cane into the ground, and off he went with Pincus, leaving Sister Gloria Gloria with an open shrine and very few options.

"God help that bird if I ever get my hands on it," Sister Gloria Gloria said, as she packed up her portable place of worship.

And that is how all four of them ended up at Pym's Lodge.

CHAPTER 5

Beauty is truth, truth beauty — that is all ye need to know on earth, and all ye need to know.

These words reverberated around the cranium of Pincus as he walked on, breathing in the sweet intoxicating smell of the corn growing in the fields that lined the road.

"Keats," he thought. "The words must be from Keats," but he wasn't certain. *Ode on a Grecian Urn,* Pincus decided as he proceeded down the dirt road, the pigeon still fluttering overhead, Rosalie in the lead, Theo, walking stick in hand, a few steps behind, then Pincus, and finally Sister Gloria Gloria bringing up the rear, dragging her rolling shrine over the pebbles in the road, perspiration pouring from under the yellowing headband of her habit, quietly praying, Pincus supposed, although she could just as well have been cursing.

Mathematicians had long known that beauty was a reliable guide to truth, as they searched for proofs that showed elegance, so it all made perfect sense to Pincus. Perhaps, all that existed, including us, was just elegant numbers. And God was a formula, a proof, a digit — the most beautiful of all from which everything else was derived.

Such were the thoughts of Pincus as they walked by the pastures of Blue Hill Road, past the clear flowing waters along Stony Brook Road, through the tiny town of Stockbridge where guests rocked back and forth on the porch of the Red Lion Inn, stopping finally for lunch at a picnic table under the pines bordering Laurel Lake, after which they made a detour to avoid the trendy boutiques sprouting like crabgrass in Lenox, through the gray city of Pittsfield that seemed to Pincus to be a purposeless place, made all the more so by the tiny college town of Williamstown. Upon arriving there, Sister Gloria Gloria made the local bookstore into a personal retreat, settling into an armchair in the air-conditioned shop and quickly dozing off, well aware that no employee would dare disturb a woman of the cloth.

Upon awakening several hours later, the group returned to their pilgrimage, Gabrielle guiding them ever onward, at Rosalie's urging.

"Shoo, shoo!" Rosalie said to the pigeon in her hand, who immediately flapped into the air, down Route 100, and very soon into the state of Vermont, the group following as they passed by the tiny hamlets of Heartwellville, Searsburg, Medburyville, Wilmington, West Dover, and then, finally stopping at the east edge of the National Park where they came to a large farmhouse with a sign that read "Welcome to Pym's Lodge."

"Does anyone have a clue where we are?" Sister Gloria Gloria asked.

"I do," Theo said proudly, and pointed to a sign facing the opposite direction with the words "You are now leaving Podunk, Vermont. Thank you for visiting and come back soon."

"There can't possibly be a real Podunk," Sister Gloria Gloria said with dismay.

"Seems there is," Pincus remarked.

"Your Angel Gabrielle has led us to Podunk?" Sister Gloria Gloria was having difficulty assimilating this. "Is this a joke?"

"No, it's a quaint country inn," Rosalie said and headed up the path that led to the front of the house.

As Rosalie approached, an attractive woman in her late thirties, wearing an apron on which she wiped the flour from her hands, emerged from the screen door and stood on the porch.

"Welcome to Podunk," Florence Pym said to Rosalie. "Oh, I do enjoy saying that," Florence laughed. "Better still, welcome to Pym's Lodge. I know you'll enjoy your stay here." Then she called toward the large red barn a short distance from the house. "Elliot! Sparky!

We have guests!"

Two men emerged from the barn, one of them, even from a distance, immediately presented as strange. He was in his early fifties, bald, with tufts of gray hair sticking out at the temples, a round face and a bent Roman nose. He was wearing an old plaid flannel shirt, even in the summer heat, and had khakis with the cuffs rolled up to mid-calf, white socks, and old black shoes that once could have been part of a tuxedo outfit.

"This is Elliot," Florence said. "He'll show you to your rooms."

"Pleased to meet you. Welcome," he said in a deep rasping voice.

Coming up behind Elliot was a man in his late thirties, very thin, a shock of thick hair that had turned prematurely gray, an oval face and wire-rimmed glasses. He seemed to be a quiet, ascetic type, and stood with his hands thrust deeply in his jeans pockets.

"And this is Sparky." Florence introduced the shy man who was shuffling from foot to foot. "Him and Elliot are brothers. His real name is John, but he's always been called 'Sparky.' He'll help you all with your bags."

By now Theo, Sister Gloria Gloria, and Pincus had reached the front steps of the porch. Sparky took Pincus's backpack and slung one strap over one shoulder, then did the same with Theo's over his other shoulder, grabbed Sister Gloria Gloria's suitcase as well, and headed up the steps with a load that easily outweighed him.

"I can take my own," Rosalie said and followed the group into a house that appeared not to have been touched for the last hundred years. The walls were covered with faded flowered wallpaper, hooked rugs were scattered here and there, and the sofa and armchairs were covered with a bristly brown fabric, doilies strategically placed to cover the worn spots.

The bedrooms were no different, both bathed in faded flowered wallpaper, hooked rugs, a large four-poster bed, and wall-sconces with frosted glass, converted from gas lights.

Rosalie found all this comforting, and after placing her backpack on an armchair, she tried out the bed, finding that the softness suited her. She could imagine staying in this house for some time.

Rosalie lay there on the bed, taking in the flowers on the wallpaper and the chintz curtains blowing slightly in and out from the open windows, and she realized that, if she didn't get up and shower right then and there, she would be asleep in a few seconds. So, with some effort, she undressed, showered, got into clean clothing, and collapsed on to the bed, where she instantly dozed off.

An hour later, she was awakened by a sound that came from the red barn from which she had seen Elliot and Sparky emerge. The sound was at first a creaking noise, like joints moving, and then it was followed by a musical sound resembling an orchestra tuning up, but more in unison, fragments of tunes emerging here and there. There was a strange quality to it all — engaging but mysterious; playful, but with a serious overtone — and, ultimately, unlike anything Rosalie had ever heard.

Pincus also now lay awake in his bed, listening to the music, as did Theo and Sister Gloria Gloria. In short order they all found themselves in the hallway outside their bedrooms on the second floor in the small country house, drawn to the music, sensing that their fates were inextricably bound in whatever was responsible for this music.

The moon was full and illuminated the cornstalks in the field behind the house as the foursome approached the barn and slid open the large doors.

Before them was one of the strangest objects they had ever seen. It was a huge construction of red pipes, joined here and there with couplings, holes of various sizes drilled into them, cables running across them, as though the device was a giant harp that could also be played like a flute. The exterior was the shape of a dodecahedron supported all around by a spherical structure. Its innards were composed of other polyhedrons — a pyramid, a cube, an octagon, and an icosahedron, their vertices on a vast and complex arrangement of tracks such that the inner shapes were able to rotate within each other, and, in fact, it became apparent that the pipes were both expandable and collapsible, allowing them to exchange positions. Before their eyes, the pyramid went from being inside the octahedron to completely incorporating it, in the process losing segments to the larger structure and assimilating others. The result was that a time came when everything merged into an undefined assembly of pipes and wires, it being impossible to determine what parts belonged to what figures, until shapes and forms emerged once again, whole and integral.

It was like watching the inner workings of an immense clock, a clock of which the universe was made, and out of it the formation of the heavens and the creation of life, all that had been and will be. But what captured their hearts was the music that emanated from the machine, music unlike anything they had ever heard — slow, methodical, seductive harmonies that should not have been harmonic — diatonic, chromatic, whole tone, Phrygian, echoic — it was impossible to tell, but the music filled their being, as though their insides were instruments, their bones resonating like reeds on a pipe organ. What was most surprising was how the music seamlessly integrated with the turning strings and the pipes rumbling on their tracks. The music made it seem as though the machine were alive, a vast celestial being, living and yet mechanical, as though the equations of physics had been brought to life.

"Like Xerxes encountering the Athenian phalanx, we have found the transcendental rift, loosed the fury of fortune's forelock, and made it ours," Elliot announced, as he appeared from the darkness, startling the assemblage.

"I'm sorry," Pincus said. "We didn't mean to pry. We were drawn by the music."

"No need to apologize," said Sparky, appearing from behind a long row of electronic equipment from which a thick cable ran to the machine. "It happens all the time."

"What is it?" Rosalie asked.

"Well, now that's a very good question. For me, it's a very cool merging of art and science," Sparky answered. "We wanted to build something aesthetically pleasing and technically perfect that had absolutely no purpose whatsoever. This is pretty damn close."

"The pipes are hollow, and like Pan's Pipes, sing of love, and whatever else is on its mind, in the way that woodwinds do," Elliot explained.

"We began making something that could convert words to music. I'll show you," Sparky said, walked over to a keyboard and typed, speaking out loud as he did, "The wind blows leaves in the rain."

Slowly the structure began to shift its form and a sound began to appear, not a replica of leaves rustling in a windy storm, but a musical suggestion that matched the concept perfectly, and that they all found exceptionally pleasant.

"We started with simple concepts that we felt would be easy for it to interpret," and now Sparky was bouncing excitedly on the balls of his feet as he talked, "and then one night I was getting bored. I'd had too much to drink, and I started typing whatever I could think of — stuff out of textbooks, data from math and weather tables, weird thoughts that were racing through my mind, and the machine made the coolest music. We've been doing that ever since."

"Like the sceptre of Apollo, encompassed by the suppliant's wreath, we implored the machine to accept our offerings and have since entered the entire encyclopedia, all the *World Almanacs* since their inception, the Holy Bible — King James version, of course, as the machine had no interest in any other and rejected all other versions we tried —, the writings of all the great philosophers, the great equations and some not so great, newspapers and magazines as far back as we could reach, and everything else we could get our hands on," Elliot explained.

"We want to see what kind of music it's going to make when it knows everything we do, collectively, as humans," Sparky continued. "We feel we're pretty damn close."

"Can we hear something else?" Rosalie asked.

"Sure. But I need input from you," Sparky answered. "Type in 'I miss Her terribly.'"

Sparky sat down at the console and typed in the words. The machine shuddered for an instant, then came to life. Slowly its parts began to move and then music came out. The music that emerged was a largo, sad but with a sense of rejoicing to it, as well. As Rosalie listened, tears filled her eyes and quickly streaked her cheeks.

"Tell it to stop," Rosalie said quietly. "Please."

Sparky nodded, typed on the keyboard, and the machine was silent. But there was something different Rosalie thought. It wasn't quite in its original state. She said this to Elliot.

"It's never exactly the same after each entry," Sparky said. "We still haven't figured this out. We measure everything before, and we measure everything afterwards, and everything stays the same. But we know it's not. I can't explain how."

"Why is that?" Rosalie asked.

"Because it's something that can't be measured, at least not by anything we have yet for measuring. Does anyone want to try giving something else to the machine?" Sparky asked.

The group immediately shook their heads. Although Pincus was tempted, he was concerned that it might reveal things he'd rather not have revealed. Theo was simply overwhelmed. It was too much to deal with. Sister Gloria Gloria was afraid of it. The machine frightened her, as though it possessed a terrible destructive potential. She didn't like it at all.

"Well, then," said Elliot, "I suppose we should go back to the house for dinner."

CHAPTER 6

"What do you do around here?" Rosalie asked Florence when they were all seated around the large dinner table. "You know, for fun — for anything?"

"Not much," Florence answered. "Elliot and Sparky are always working on their contraption in the barn, and that seems to keep them occupied most of the time and out of my hair. That puts me in charge of running the Inn by default. Sparky and I were married for fifteen years, and that provided a lot of excitement, but we ended that a couple years ago."

This immediately caught the attention of Sister Gloria Gloria, who had a long-standing issue with divorce.

"You took a vow before God," Sister Gloria Gloria reminded Florence.

"Yep, we did do that," Florence agreed. "Otherwise, we probably wouldn't have lasted two weeks, Sister. But I'm one of those who thinks that marriage should be something more than just a contract. There's got to be feeling."

Pincus was now hanging on every word Florence said, as though the words were his own.

"But you're still living here with him," Rosalie said to Florence.

"I am. And Sparky and I still get along, just like we always did, except that now we're not married any longer, and somehow that seems right. I keep thinking that I'll leave, but I don't. I haven't figured out where I'd go and what I'd do differently than what I'm doing now, so here I stay until I figure it out, but the truth is, I don't see myself going anywhere at all. I told my mother before she passed away last year what I'd come to realize. I'm a woman without dreams. She said that was impossible. Everybody has dreams. What I lacked was hope, and once I got out of this house set down in the middle of nowhere, hope would surface and I'd have dreams, big dreams. But I don't think so. It's just the way I am, and sometimes I wonder whether it should bother me, because it doesn't."

There was a long silence at the table — only the sound of silverware against china plates. From time to time, people would look over at Sparky to see how he was taking all that Florence had to say.

"I don't really mind," Sparky finally said. "She's still around, and that's what really matters. I get to talk to her, and we even kiss goodnight, not like we used to, but it's still good."

Rosalie thought she would cry. Sparky was still in love with Florence, and it was clear to her that Florence didn't know it. Maybe she had never known it. Or maybe, being a woman without dreams also meant being a woman who can't know love. And, yet, Florence didn't seem to be a cold woman. To Rosalie, she was warm and lovely, so there was something missing from her story.

"Well," Rosalie finally said, "you make a wonderful meal. This chicken is great."

"Thanks," Florence answered. "But that's not the chicken you're eating. The chicken's in the dish over there. You're eating the squab, because I didn't think we'd have enough chicken to go around. Well, it's probably not squab, either. It was too big to be squab. But, it was just sitting there forever on the front porch railing while you were all upstairs showering and napping and over at the barn with the machine, and it just let me walk right up to it and take it in my hands, and I thought, maybe with currant jelly and mint, some sliced peaches, and a nice red wine sauce, the thing to have with the chicken tonight is pigeon. I'm glad you like it."

CHAPTER 7

Rosalie had never fainted before, but when she looked at the flesh on her fork, her eyes rolled up into her head, and she toppled off her chair and hit the floor like the proverbial bag of cement.

Sister Gloria Gloria dipped her napkin in her glass of water and walked slowly over to the other side of the table, where she knelt and placed the wet cloth on Rosalie's forehead, a most Christian gesture, indeed, considering that Sister's mind was reaching out to the Blessed Virgin and thanking her profusely for answering her prayers.

Pincus had never been convinced that there was anything divine about the pigeon, but, for the sake of expedience, had been willing to go along with the notion that Gabrielle had been sent by Her to guide them to where She now resided. He now knelt beside Rosalie, who was slowly reviving.

Theo, for his part, wasn't quite sure what was happening. While it was not in his nature to eat what he considered to be a pet of Rosalie, he was impressed by how tasty the bird had been, and especially found the combination of the currant jelly, the red wine, and peaches much to his liking.

"Is she all right?" Florence asked, looking down at the fluttering eyes of Rosalie coming back to a state of consciousness. "What happened?"

"Well, depending on how you look at it," Pincus explained, "you either cooked the Holy Spirit, or a messenger sent by Her to guide us to where She now is, or a pigeon with a particular liking for granola bars."

"What Holy Spirit?" Florence tried to sort this out.

"The Holy Spirit," Pincus responded.

"It was a pigeon," Florence answered. "It couldn't possibly be the Holy Spirit."

"I agree," Pincus answered. "It was only an hypothesis that was floated for consideration."

"I mean," Florence her concern growing, "I don't think you can chop off the head of the Holy Spirit, bleed it out, pull off its feathers and cook it in a cheap Bordeaux," Florence explained, and Rosalie was out cold again.

Florence stood up and looked down at Rosalie lying on the floor.

"Why does she keep passing out?" Florence asked.

"I think the bird had special meaning for her," Sparky concluded, evaluating the information coming in.

"The bird was leading us to — well, Her," Pincus explained. "She's the Mother of Her."

"Her, like the Her, the Her who will one day come again, that Her?" Florence asked, considering the implications.

Pincus nodded.

"Oh, my God," Florence gasped. "I cooked Christ."

"With currant jelly, peaches, and a Bordeaux reduction," Theo added. "And you did one heck of a job with it, if I may say so."

"You didn't cook Christ," Pincus tried to comfort the woman. "At the worst, you cooked the messenger of Christ."

"This is really quite disturbing," Florence said, as she wrung her hands. "What do I do with the bones?"

"You throw them in the trash," Sister said. "It's a pigeon. It's not the Holy Spirit, and it's not a Divine Messenger. It's a bird, and I agree with Mr. Wainwright: you did an excellent job of preparing it," and Sister Gloria Gloria, and Pincus hoisted Rosalie, raising her from the near-dead, upright, back into her chair.

"Feeling better, dear?" Sister Gloria Gloria employed her most sympathetic tone.

"Don't talk to me," Rosalie responded. "I know you were responsible for this."

"She seems to be coming back to life," Sister Gloria Gloria remarked tartly.

"Why don't we help you clean up," Pincus suggested, hoping to move on.

"Not necessary," Florence said. "I'll do that. It comes with the Inn."

"Then we're going to go back to work," Sparky announced, and got up, Elliot joining him.

"And I think I need to go to bed," said Rosalie, an idea the others instantly agreed was a good one, and off they went to bed, where they would have stayed through the night, had the machine not started singing on its own.

CHAPTER 8

Pincus had barely fallen asleep when he awakened. He had been having an especially pleasant dream. It was, of course, of a woman, in this case a young woman, a young woman in her twenties. He stood talking to her, and he told her how beautiful he thought she was. It seemed to him that they had had a relationship before, although he couldn't remember it. They stood closer, and Pincus rested his hand on her hips, which were naked. He could feel the way they curved and how soft the skin felt beneath his hands. He liked the way she felt, how wide her hips were, how womanly, and this excited him. And it was at this point that Pincus realized that he was awake, that he may have been awake for some time, and this was not a dream but the fantasy of a waking mind. It was the music.

Pincus looked around him, trying to get his bearings. At first he thought he was back home with Becki, and finally he understood that he was at Pym's Lodge and that there was music outside.

Putting aside the woman with the wide naked hips, who was still there in Pincus's mind as he held on to his vision just as long as he possibly could, Pincus forced himself to get out of bed and walk to the window.

Outside in the moonlight was the machine of Elliot and Sparky. It rested on its giant balloon tires, like those of a dune buggy, and stood in the pasture beside the house. Its framework against the sky was a sight unlike any Pincus had ever seen. From within the machine came the music, the music that had awakened Pincus from his reverie, and Pincus wondered whether the music, itself, could have induced his libidinal vision. Had his naked female been the music from the machine?

Pincus dressed, walked softly down the dark stairs, and went outside. The others were already there, drawn to the machine the way that crowds are drawn to an event in the sky, like an eclipse or a comet.

The machine was silent now, as they all stood there, waiting for something to happen, more music, something beyond the music. The machine with its pipes and wires loomed against the sky like a giant skeleton, something prehistoric and simultaneously futuristic. It made Pincus feel insignificant.

"It started last year," Sparky, who now stood next to Pincus, told him.

"What started?" Pincus asked.

"We had just finished loading in the bulk of the information," Sparky explained, "and Elliot and I pulled it out here and went inside."

There was a long silence. Finally Elliot spoke. "*The soul is a heavenly melody, intolerably sweet ...*" Elliot said. "St. Francis of Assisi. The machine started singing on its own."

And then, on cue, a single note emerged from within the device. It was a deep tone that made Pincus's bones vibrate. Then, before Pincus could remark on it, another tone came, and then several more tones, and then it was music.

It seemed to Pincus that there had never been, in the history of mankind, music like this. The richness of its melody swelled within Pincus until he felt he would burst with the fullness of it. There were, as before, harmonies he had never heard, notes he had not known existed, cadences and rhythms that swept him along with them, as though he had fallen into a swiftly moving river and was being carried with its current toward some unknown paradise that would eventually appear.

And, as the machine sang, it changed shape in concert with the music — turning about itself, shapes transforming into new shapes, leaving behind no sign of the form that had existed before. It was to Pincus and to the others, entrancing, like finding a secret world of the kind children dream about.

"There are three kinds of music," Elliot commented as the machine sang. "The music of the worlds, the music of humanity, and the music of instruments. Of the music of the worlds, one is of the elements, another of the planets, another of time. Of that which is of the elements, one is of number, another of weights, another of measure. Of that which is of the planets, one is of place, another of motion, another of nature. Of that which is of time, one is of the days and the vicissitudes of light and darkness; another of the months and the waxing and waning of the moon; another of the years and the changes of spring, summer, autumn, and winter. Of the music of humanity, one is of the body, another of the soul, another is the connection that is between them. The life of the visible and invisible universe consists of a supernal fugue."

All heads turned to Elliot.

"Hugh of Saint-Victor," Elliot said.

"Who of Saint What?" Sister Gloria Gloria asked in dismay. "Where do you people come *up* with these saints?"

But nobody actually heard Sister's words over the music.

For the next hour the Machine sang, its frame reaching out toward the sky in the way some tethered-winged mythical beast might be imagined to grasp for the heavens, hoping once more to fly.

It was Pincus who first described the machine as "singing" because, to Pincus, there was a voice to the music. These were not simply the tones of instruments. The Machine was a being, alive with yearning. After a while, the music became a heart-wrenching lament such that Pincus found himself shaking. Sister Gloria Gloria fell to her knees, and Rosalie buried her head into Theo's chest and held on tightly, as Theo wrapped his arms around her, seeking comfort even as he gave it.

And then, suddenly, a bird flew into the Machine and disappeared. There was no puff of smoke or flash of light. The bird was there and then it was not.

The group looked on in astonishment, as the Machine came to the end of its song.

"Anything that enters the Machine while it is singing on its own is gone," Elliot explained quietly. "It just disappears. There's enough energy in there to turn anything instantly into nothing."

"Where did it go?" Pincus asked.

"Nowhere," Elliot answered.

"Where does a snowball go when you put it in a microwave?" Rosalie asked.

"There's a puddle," Theo pointed out.

"Not always," Rosalie was quick to respond.

"Or steam, vapor," Theo clarified.

"Are you saying that what my brother and I have constructed is a giant microwave?" Sparky said with indignation.

"It could be a portal to another realm," Florence tried to be helpful. "Like some sort of black hole. I saw a television show about them once."

"Yes, maybe the bird is now in an alternative universe. That's what's on the other side of a black hole, isn't it?" Rosalie offered.

"How do you know? Have you ever been to the other side of a black hole?" Elliot was becoming irritated by the unfounded conjectures. "The bird did not get transported to some 'alternative universe,' whatever the hell that is. It's just gone."

"I think the issue here is not where it's gone," Pincus said, "but whether it's coming back."

"You want to know whether this little bird is going to be resurrected?" Sister Gloria Gloria asked, incensed.

"Do things come back from the microwave?" Theo asked.

"It's not a microwave!" Sparky shouted. "The Machine is not for warming up leftovers!"

There was a moment of silence. Rosalie spoke what was on everyone's mind.

"Just how dangerous is the Machine?" Rosalie asked.

"As long as you don't go into it when it sings on its own at night, you have nothing to worry about," Elliot comforted the group, but they were not entirely comforted.

"And it sings on its own only at midnight," Sparky said.

"What happens if you keep it in the barn?" Rosalie asked.

"Then it makes such a deafening racket that we have no choice but to take it out."

"What is it saying?" Florence asked and turned to Sparky for an answer.

"You need an algorithm to sort it out, and I haven't given it any algorithms. It makes its own algorithms — so I don't have a clue what it means."

"Perhaps," mused Pincus, "it's God singing in the shower."

"You think God takes showers?" Sister asked.

"It's no more godlike than I am," said Sparky. "Undo a couple bolts and it'll be nothing but a pile of scrap."

"Did you give it a name?" Rosalie asked.

"Nope," Sparky said, and he grabbed a handle, and slowly he and Elliot began to move the huge structure into the barn, as Sparky answered Rosalie's question without turning around.

"We just call it 'The Singing Machine.'"

CHAPTER 9

Throughout the night, Pincus lay in bed, staring at the ceiling, thinking about The Singing Machine. He was convinced that there was something about it that Sparky and Elliot knew but had kept from them. And, if it had been kept from them, then it couldn't be anything good. He thought of bringing it up at breakfast that morning, but he never had the opportunity, as the conversation centered only on what the song could mean.

It was agreed that machines don't just start singing on their own without a good reason, but, beyond that, there was something about the song, itself, something both sacred and profane, that made it more than simply music.

"There are times that I think we're hearing the sound of the earth moving through the ether of the cosmos," Sparky commented as he dug into an enormous stack of blueberry pancakes that Florence had prepared for them.

"It's a vacuum," Sister Gloria Gloria was quick to put the kibosh on that notion. "Out there in the cosmos is nothing, nothing at all."

"Not even God?" Elliot asked as he spread more butter on his pancakes and then doused them with a generous amount of fresh, genuine A-grade Vermont maple syrup.

"God does not exist in a *place*," Sister Gloria Gloria was quick to retort. "God is everywhere."

"Then He must be out there, as well, unless you don't consider the cosmos as part of everywhere," Elliot pointed out.

"You're twisting my words," Sister Gloria Gloria snapped back, although it seemed that Sister Gloria Gloria was doing considerably more twisting at that point than her words. "What I'm saying is that there is no single *place* where one finds God. He's not sitting somewhere out there on a gold throne."

Theo's ears picked up. "*And immediately I was in the spirit: and, behold, a throne was set in heaven, and One sat on the throne,*" Theo said without looking up from his pancakes. "*And out of the throne proceeded lightnings and thunderings and voices. And in the midst of the throne, and round about the throne, were four beasts full of eyes before and behind. And when those beasts give glory and honour and thanks to Him that sat on the throne, who liveth for ever and ever, four and twenty elders fall down before Him that sat on the throne, saying, Thou art worthy, O Lord, to receive glory and honour and power: for thou hast created all things, and for thy pleasure they are and were created.*"

There was a moment of silence.

"Revelation chapter 4, verses 2 through 11," Theo looked up for the first time at those sitting around the large wood-plank kitchen table and grinned. "It's worth memorizing, don't you think? But I'd say it leaves little doubt about a throne and Who's on it."

There was the briefest moment of silence, followed by the voice of Sister Gloria Gloria.

"Hyperbole," Sister Gloria Gloria said. "Plain and simple hyperbole."

"That's a heck of a lot of detail for hyperbole," Pincus said.

"There's a lot of poetry in the Bible that we're not meant to take literally," Sister Gloria Gloria attempted to fight her way out of a hole that seemed to be growing deeper with each comment she made.

"Like God had a son, who came to earth, was crucified, and then arose from the dead — that kind of not taking literally?" asked Florence, immediately creating a permanent rift between her and Sister Gloria Gloria. "I mean, I agree that there's a lot in the Bible that we shouldn't take absolutely as its written. The problem for me is what things those are and what things those are not."

Sister was ready to launch into vitriol, but before she could answer, Florence asked the question on everyone's mind.

"What I really want to know is what the song of The Singing Machine *means*?"

"She'll know," Rosalie said.

And that's how it all began, and how it was finally decided, after some debate, that Florence, Sparky, and Elliot, all of whom, like the others, felt they could find no peace until they knew the meaning of the song of The Singing Machine, would join the pilgrimage.

They would bring The Singing Machine to Her, and She would tell them the meaning of the song.

Of course, there remained one small problem. Now that the messenger pigeon sent to guide them to Her had been digested, nobody actually knew how to find Her, as Rosalie deftly informed the group.

"The Singing Machine will guide us," Elliot announced. "Tell us all you know about Her, each one of you, we will enter it into The Singing Machine, and ask it to direct us to Her."

"You think that'll work?" Rosalie's mood brightened.

"It's certainly worth a shot," Elliot responded.

"Not to me, it isn't," Sister Gloria Gloria announced. "Mary has led me along the right path all these years, and I have faith that she will continue to do so," although, even as Sister Gloria Gloria said these words, she knew that she would be going along with the others and following the guidance of The Singing Machine. Sister Gloria Gloria was not of a disposition to go it alone.

"Fine. Then you go with her, and we'll follow The Singing Machine, and God bless," Rosalie said tartly.

"You know, I'm getting a little tired of you constantly taking the name of our Lord in vain," Sister Gloria Gloria snapped back, as the heads of those at the table flicked back and forth from Sister Gloria Gloria to Rosalie.

"*God bless* is taking the name of the Lord in vain?" Rosalie asked in amazement.

"It was the way you said it." Sister Gloria Gloria held her ground. "Your tone made it the religious equivalent of giving someone the finger."

"*God bless* is flipping someone the bird?" Rosalie asked. "What is *The Lord be with you* F— off?"

"More pancakes, anyone?" Florence tried to calm things down.

Florence's words, in fact, had the desired effect, and the conversation turned to issues that Pincus raised about whether The Singing Machine would fit under various overpasses, and whether, in some towns, they might need a parade permit, as there were now seven of them, plus The Singing Machine, and they might now be construed by some authorities, if the machine became musical, to be a marching band.

But it was decided that these were issues that could be dealt with as they came up, so following breakfast, Theo, Pincus, Sister Gloria Gloria, and Rosalie headed off to the barn with Elliot and Sparky Pym to tell what they knew about Her and have it all fed appropriately into The Singing Machine.

That night The Singing Machine sang again. There seemed to Pincus to be a sense of rejoicing in the song, the kind one might hear in the words of two lovers, long separated, at last coming together.

PART VI

The Ecclesia

CHAPTER 1

Three days later, they all gathered on the road in front of Pym's Lodge, The Singing Machine standing in their midst, and they waited for a sign that would start them on their journey. Pincus was hoping that one of the rods of The Singing Machine would extend, like an arm with a pointed finger, to show them the way, much like Moses signifying where the Promised Land could be found, but there was no such gesture. Finally, Sparky and Elliot let go of the machine and sat on the grassy side of the road. Almost immediately, The Singing Machine began to move ahead on its large balloon tires.

"Well," said Sparky, "we're on our way. The Singing Machine has found the path to Her."

"It's just rolling down the hill," Sister Gloria Gloria said as she walked up to Pincus. "What else did they think it would do?" she asked Pincus. But Pincus didn't answer. He just marched onward, feeling a sudden exhilaration for no reason he could explain, pleased to be part of this group, now of seven.

Florence soon assumed the lead position, Theo hobbling beside her with his cane. Directly behind them, Sparky pulled The Singing Machine and Elliot pushed from behind. Pincus walked alongside Elliot, Rosalie beside him, and, finally, came Sister Gloria Gloria, pulling her suitcase-shrine.

And so it was that the seven, plus The Singing Machine, continued along the narrow road, not without considerable complications. Drivers honked their horns and made various obscene comments and gestures, as often it was impossible for their vehicles to pass, either because of the width of The Singing Machine, or because individuals in the group were not especially adept at keeping a straight line.

Although they made a number of turns as they headed north through Vermont, it was never clear to Pincus whether The Singing Machine was guiding them or they were guiding The Singing Machine, and because neither Sparky nor Elliot would allow anyone else to handle the machine, there was no way for anyone to know for certain.

CHAPTER 2

The sun had just begun to set as they neared a house that seemed to be known to Elliot. Set close to the road, with a porch from which hung baskets of flowers, it was the residence of Meyer Steinmeyer, a man Elliot had met when Meyer had lodged at Pym's Lodge on the way to the meeting of an international cell of Neo-Marxists, of which Meyer was a charter member.

Meyer was of uncertain origin. Depending on the day, he claimed his parentage to be of French and German mixture, his mother being a Parisian cabaret singer, while his father was a professor of philosophy at the University of Marburg, where he was a colleague of Martin Heidegger, specializing in phenomenology. On other days, his father was French, a frequent patron of Café Les Deux Magots and a member of the faculty of the Sorbonne, where he made several important contributions to existentialism, and his mother worked in a well-known beer garden in Munich, where she had affairs with Gustav Klimt, Oskar Kokoschka, Gustav Mahler, Walter Gropius, and Franz Werfel, a succession of lovers remarkably similar to those of Alma Schindler Mahler-Gropius-Werfel, leading one to wonder whether her affairs paved the way for or picked up the crumbs left by Fraulein Schindler.

But on this particular evening, Meyer's heritage was Russian, and his father, Yuri, had been a Soviet shot put champion, as well as a close confident to both Lenin and Trotsky, and his mother, Olga, was Stalin's bastard daughter, as everyone knew. Meyer's father had been expelled from his motherland, then the Soviet Union, when he made the mistake of offering his own personal interpretation of the thinking of Karl. Unfortunately, his special reading of Marx was at considerable variance with what was then Soviet doctrine, and having to choose between a revision of Marx or the revision of Yuri, the authorities elected not to modify Marx. This was how Meyer came to America.

"Marx," Meyer explained over a dinner of cabbage and pirozhki, "is nothing more than the reworking of the New Testament. The Communist Party is the Church, the Proletariat is the Elect, the Revolution is the Second Coming, the Communist Commonwealth is the Millennium, the punishment of Capitalism is Hell, and," Meyer smiled broadly, "Karl Marx is, of course, the Messiah."

"I beg your pardon," said Sister Gloria Gloria, but this was not a request for forgiveness.

Meyer leaned toward Sister Gloria Gloria, "I'm working on a new formulation," Meyer said, "in which I reveal the hidden erotic content of *Das Kapital*."

"Marx was an atheist and impotent," Elliot mumbled, but loud enough to catch Meyer's attention.

"Exactly," Meyer did not disagree, "and that it is why it is so hidden. Very clever, this Marx."

"Marks?" Theo asked. "Are we being graded on this?"

"There's a test?" Florence looked up from her plate with some alarm.

"I never did especially well on tests," Sparky commented. "I never knew how to study for them. I always got back exams with 'Careless mistake' written all over them because I misread something or left out a word in my answer. Elliot, though, was a whiz. He still has this box of exams with 'A+'s' and 'Superbs' written all over them, and he hardly studied at all. I once took a class in how to take an exam, and I failed that. I asked to take the course again, and they wouldn't let me. They said they couldn't, in good conscious, take my money any longer."

And so the evening continued.

Pincus, alone, gave some actual consideration to Meyer's interpretation of Marx, noting that there was, in fact, some sort of strange symmetry between the teachings of Karl Marx and the Christian religion, at least to the extent that, for both, material possessions seemed to be in disfavor, and each held in high esteem those who were willing to share.

When dinner finally came to an end and the contents of the two bottles of vodka on the table were depleted, this might very well have concluded their excursion into dialectical materialism, had the machine not sung its song that night.

CHAPTER 3

Pincus had been unable to sleep as he lay on his bed, listening to the sounds of the katydids that came through the screens of his open windows on this unusually humid and warm summer night for Vermont. He was becoming concerned that they might not ever find Her, unable to accept that The Singing Machine was a reliable compass. He imagined them dragging themselves all over northern New England on a fruitless search for someone who, actually, now that he considered it, might not really exist at all, or if She did, might be nothing more than another human, like himself, with the same neuroses to which Pincus had long ago resigned himself. And then The Singing Machine began its song.

At first, just a few notes drifted in the open window. Pincus, his head embedded in the down pillow, listened motionless, allowing the music to sweep over him.

As though in a trance, Pincus lifted himself from the bed, descended the stairs, and went out the back kitchen door, where The Singing Machine stood in the yard, slowly moving against a moonless sky across which was a dazzling array of stars.

One by one the others arrived, the last being Meyer, who stood, arms folded across his chest, studying the giant structure as it folded and unfolded into one shape and then another, its music becoming more melodic but never more than a few notes in concert, more like a small ensemble, a string or woodwind quartet, not at all like the full symphony Pincus had heard before.

"I hear Marx singing in this song," Meyer told the group.

"Oh, shut up," Sister Gloria Gloria explained.

"Isn't Marx dead?" Rosalie asked.

"He is resurrected in this song," Meyer responded, his dark eyes gleaming.

Sister Gloria Gloria's head perked up at the word "resurrected," a concept to which she felt she had a certain ownership. "Okay, now you look here — " Sister Gloria Gloria began but never had a chance to finish, as Meyer continued his exegesis.

"We are hearing the voice of workers crying out for freedom from slavery of property, so weighted down they are by capitalist oppression that they cannot experience full sexual release."

"Actually," Theo commented, "I found that whenever I had an unusually good day of antiques sales, my sexual release couldn't have been better. I had a Lord Archer Georgian mahogany pedestal desk that I sold for $31,000, and that night I had an orgasm that came real close to blowing off Bernice's back."

"Wow," said Florence, feeling a tingling in her loins.

"In this song," Meyer continued as though Theo had not spoken a word, "the workers shout, 'Why must we sublimate our erotic drives to profit incentives!' and they writhe in agony."

"That's a lot for one song to say," Florence remarked.

"Only when the inevitable domination of socialism occurs will we achieve full and satisfying climax," Meyer announced emphatically.

There was a moment of silence as all were under the spell of the music.

"So what is it?" Meyer asked a question that Pincus thought would have been his first remark on encountering this vast skeleton singing in his backyard.

"What is what?" Sparky asked.

"That. This," Meyer pointed to The Singing Machine, which was now ending its song.

"We don't really know," Spark responded. "That's why we're on our way to Her. We're convinced that She will know."

"To *Her*? *The* She?" Meyer's mind was whirling.

"Yes," Sparky answered. "Rosalie is her mother."

Meyer looked over Rosalie.

"Isn't She to be born of a virgin?" Meyer remarked.

"And that would be me," Rosalie smiled sweetly.

"Yes, Rosalie is a virgin," Sparky answered decisively, leaving out that the conversation at the dinner table had had a profound effect on his libido, and he had appeared at Rosalie's bedroom door and made the unfortunate mistake in judgment of attempting to test Rosalie's claim of maidenhood, and he was now healing, a plastic bag of ice tucked surreptitiously in his jockey shorts. Sparky was somewhat less sparky tonight.

"She's come. Again. I knew She would," Meyer rolled this over in his mind with a growing sense of excitement.

No one had expected Meyer to accompany them, largely because no one had invited him, but this turned out not to matter.

"I must go with you. Only She," Meyer explained, "will know the true meaning of politics —and love — and belief — and orgasm."

"That's a lot for one Savior to deal with," Theo mused out loud. "Would She have to do them all at the same time?"

But nobody was listening to Theo, as Meyer's passion was so great that the group caved in and agreed that he could join them.

CHAPTER 4

The next morning, after a group breakfast of kasha, Meyer, joined the group, now eight in number.

Sister Gloria Gloria was in the lead, accompanied by Florence and followed by Rosalie, who now kept Meyer beside her as protection against Sparky's libido, which she was not entirely certain had fully retreated to a quieter place. Sparky was next, pulling The Singing Machine, and, behind it was Elliot, pushing and panting, as they were encountering hills that seemed to have an almost unending ascent. Bringing up the rear were Theo and Pincus, who were in a reverie over the spectacular Vermont day, exchanging poetic comments on the landscape, the sky, and the air.

It was, in fact, one of those memorable Vermont summer days. The humidity was gone and the air was crisp. The road was bordered by a brook, its clear waters still racing from the last runoff of the Green Mountain snow-pack that had disappeared, except for small dots of white here and there at the very apex of the mountains.

When they reached the ski resort town of Ludlow and marched down Main Street, pushing and pulling The Singing Machine, they encountered their first major problem. Before they had gotten from one end of the town to the other, they were surrounded by six police cars and detained for several hours until it was determined that they weren't transporting a gigantic bomb. They were allowed to continue, no thanks to Meyer, who decided that, facing a police state, he had the perfect audience with whom to share his thoughts of a Marxist revolution.

They had barely recovered from this ordeal, when, on the way into Rutland, Sister Gloria Gloria slipped off a curb and broke her ankle, and after spending most of the afternoon in the emergency room, Sister Gloria Gloria, her leg in a cast, was now in a wheelchair, Pincus pushing.

Pincus was not sure how this chore had been assigned to him, but, passing a medical supply store on the way out of the next town, and deciding that he had no intention of spending the days ahead pushing Sister Gloria Gloria up and down hills, Pincus pulled out his credit card and $1599.95 later, Sister Gloria Gloria found herself in a motorized wheelchair.

This may have proven to be a mistake, as Sister Gloria Gloria now considered herself as the leader of the entourage, riding in front, chastising everyone to keep up and creating not a small amount of dissension in the ranks as she called back to them, "Remember, we walk by faith, not by sight! Let us set our affections on things above, not on things on earth! Onward and upward!"

Such entreaties were met with loud, and not infrequently blasphemous, responses from those in the group who were not motorized and, consequently, hot and tired.

"I will suffer ye fools gladly, for I have the ornament of a meek and quiet spirit," Sister Gloria Gloria would counter. "The Lord be with you. And also with me."

"And you will be with Him sooner than you'd planned, Sister, if you keep this up," Meyer informed her.

"All in all," Pincus remarked to Theo as they reached the road that led into the woods where one found the Abbott Tavern and Inn of North Sherburne, "this has not been an easy trip today," and Pincus headed off to arrange accommodations, the last light of dusk rapidly fading.

CHAPTER 5

The next morning it was still raining, making the interaction among the pilgrims even more contentious. Sister Gloria Gloria opened her suitcase and set up her portable shrine, where she kneeled and asked the Virgin Mother for guidance. Simultaneously, Elliot and Sparky consulted The Singing Machine for an indication of the next step in their journey, while the others huddled on the front porch of the Tavern and watched the rain come down in buckets.

When Sister, Elliot, and Sparky reassembled, the signs given by their prognosticators had turned out to be equivocal. It seemed that their "compasses" were temporarily out of commission.

"I think we should just continue down the highway," Elliot said. "That seemed to be the general direction indicated by both The Singing Machine and the Blessed Mother."

This seemed to be a workable compromise, and so, draped with ponchos or holding umbrellas, the group made its way back down the muddy road and out on to the highway.

Pincus had not slept much of that night, and for good reason. Shortly after he had turned out the light, there was a knocking on the door. It was Meyer.

"Can we talk? There's something I must share with you," Meyer said, his Russian accent now replaced with something vaguely French.

Pincus thought it over briefly, then nodded and let Meyer enter.

For a moment, Meyer stood uncomfortably in front of Pincus, then nodded toward a chair in the corner, asking permission to sit.

"What I am going to tell you must be kept in strict confidence,"

Meyer said.

Pincus nodded in agreement.

"She lived with me for almost a year. I didn't know it was Her, but now that you've come and I've had a chance to think it over, I believe it was Her."

"You had a relationship with Her?" Pincus asked in dismay.

"No, no, nothing of the kind. I taught Her philosophy, and she did the cooking and cleaning and kept up the house. It was an exchange. At first, I had wanted Her to assist me with my research. When I saw Her in town, I knew She would be exactly what I needed."

"What research?" Pincus tried to assimilate it all.

"Funklein," Meyer announced.

"I thought you said you didn't have sex with Her."

"I didn't. Funk, not Fuck. Funklein is the spark of our soul, the point where our souls come into contact with the heavens. For women, their bodies, their entire being, becomes at one with the universe, their periods and moods are determined by the cycles of the moon, and, perhaps, the stars, as well. There comes a moment, a single moment, when the human female joins the heavens — menarche, the first menstruation. Up until then she is an innocent, but then starts a celestial change in her being toward cosmic perfection. My professional life has been devoted to determining the exact moment of femaleness, that instant when a girl becomes a woman — their funklein."

"What'd you find?" asked Pincus.

"My results, unfortunately," Meyer said sadly, "were inconclusive. Then She left. But now there is new hope. She is certainly female taken to its most perfect condition. Once we find Her, I have only to determine what those characteristics of womanly perfection are that She possesses, and my pre- and post-menarchal measurements of other females will reveal to me the genesis of woman, God willing."

"God is involved in this?" Pincus asked. "You're a Marxist who believes in God?"

"I have to be going," and Meyer got up from the chair. "Not a word of this to anyone," Meyer continued as he went to the door. Before leaving, he turned to Pincus.

"This is no idle pursuit," Meyer Steinmeyer explained with great gravity. "In other words," he continued, "as all of us issue from the female, the key to understanding our place in the universe rests entirely on determining that instant when the female becomes another heavenly body."

The next morning, as Pincus walked down the road, lost in thought over the possibility that Meyer might actually have seen Her, he waited until Meyer had separated from the group, then drifted back until he was walking beside Meyer and couldn't be overheard by the others.

"She was petite and reminded me of a porcelain doll, except that her skin was tanned," Meyer responded to Pincus's request for a description of Her. "At first I thought she might be from a Mediterranean country, or India, but her skin wasn't olive-toned, or as deep as those others — just tan, but not the kind one gets from spending a week at the beach."

Pincus ran the image through his mind, trying to picture a china doll with a tan.

"Her features were fine — thin lips, an oval face, gentle eyes, that were a translucent blue and seemed even more so because her hair was blond, blond as wheat, so her eyes seemed to blaze out from her face.

"She had an hourglass figure, and while She had developed into a woman of perfect dimensions, the kind of female form a man might conjure to inhabit his dreams, there was still something girlish about Her. She had a way of carrying Herself that was not at all seductive, as though womanhood was something She had recently accomplished and wasn't quite certain what to do with it. It gave Her an undeniable appeal without any suggestion of sexuality. To think of Her erotically would have been as absurd as imagining sex with an angel.

"Her voice was quiet, but She had no problem raising it if she became passionate about something. In fact, She could become alarmingly intense one minute, and then go for long periods being a very gentle creature. It made the outbursts even more startling.

"She had a way of talking to you, to *you*, not to whom you pretended to be, or to what defenses you put up, but the you inside, who you really were, and you felt all the layers you had built up over the years fall away. It was comforting. It was disarming. It was — there's no other word for it — spiritual. You found yourself connecting on an entirely different plane. And, yet, you had no sense that She was anything other than just another young woman, one who knew how to listen, one who had strong opinions, one with no sense that there was anything about Her that was special. Yes, She was divine, but there was certainly nothing that would make one think that She was a god, unless one considers all beautiful and charming women to be gods, which is not out of the question. Ask any Frenchman.

"When She left I was filled with a sadness that lasted for months. It was not that I missed her company. It was that I had an intense desire to have some sort of union with her, that without it, it would be nearly impossible for me to survive, but, again, the union was not a sexual one, but the kind of bond that can happen only through the joining of souls."

Pincus thought he would cry. "Yes, yes," he said. "This is what has led me here, what has eaten up my insides, what can be made whole again only by Her."

Theo had been walking some distance behind Pincus and Meyer during their discourse, unable to hear exactly what they were saying, but assuming that they were talking about Her. Now he joined them having something to offer of his own.

"I think She's going to have some major new religious theories and everything will be turned topsy-turvy," Theo mused. "I'm not sure I like that. It's difficult enough dealing with what we have now without introducing something new."

"I'd be surprised if She changes anything much," Meyer responded.

"You don't think She's come to change everything for the better?" Theo asked. "Or, at the very least, to straighten out a number of very confusing matters."

"No, I don't," answered Meyer. "Religion has always been the result of individual inspiration, not doctrine. Catholicism is because of Jesus, and someone else preaching the same thing would not have had the same effect, if, in fact, Jesus actually preached anything at all, and it wasn't invented by his apostles after his death. The Reformation was because of Luther and Calvin, not because of a new theory of justification and redemption."

"Did somebody say 'Luther and Calvin'?" came an irritated voice from the front of the entourage.

"Relax, Sister," Elliot called up to Sister Gloria Gloria, "they're just batting a few things about religion back and forth. It's okay."

"Calvin and Luther have nothing to do with religion," Sister shifted into a lower gear so she was within earshot of the conversation.

"You don't think they were dealing with God?" Sparky decided to share his perspective with Sister Gloria Gloria. "You don't think that God is about religion?"

"Luther and Calvin knew nothing about God," Sister Gloria Gloria barked back at Sparky.

"Don't be ridiculous," Meyer joined in. "They were trying to understand the meaning of God, just like the rest of us."

"You're not making any sense," Florence said. "God is just God, that's all. I don't understand why you keep talking about meaning. What does *this* mean? What does *that* mean? Nobody knows what God *means*. That's just how it is."

Sister Gloria Gloria lit up like a Christmas tree.

"Well, she said, "if anyone is interested, 'Deus' *means* shining and transcendent light. And 'Theos' *means* supreme desire or inward love. That's what God *means.* So there you have it," and Sister Gloria Gloria shifted her wheelchair into high gear and zipped back to the front to resume her leadership.

CHAPTER 6

Sister Gloria Gloria announced that she was not about to implore the Mother Mary for directions that afternoon, explaining that she had the sense that she might be wearing out her welcome by continually using the Blessed Virgin as a navigational instrument.

Elliot and Sparky, likewise, felt that The Singing Machine might be reaching a point of exhaustion. They certainly were. And it might be judicious to utilize its power on a more selective, as-needed basis.

No sooner had Elliot and Sparky decided this than The Singing Machine, as though sensing the fatigue of the group, resumed directing them on their way, seeming in some undefinable way, to have homed in on Her location. After some discussion, the group decided that because they really had no other option, they would go wherever it was The Singing Machine was leading them.

It was at this time that Pincus had a premonition. He had no idea from whence it had come, but suddenly he felt that they were getting close. His pulse quickened and an excitement started to grow within him. The image that Meyer had painted of Her began to fill his brain, and he imagined Her voice, and, most importantly, what he would say to Her when they finally, inevitably, met.

Pincus decided, as he reviewed his physical attributes, that he had never looked better. The daily exercise of walking for endless hours had trimmed the flab off, and the sun had tanned him to a radiant healthiness, a tan he hoped would match Hers.

Pincus was not the only one who sensed they were getting close, and a conversation ensued regarding whether She had returned for a specific reason.

"There is only one reason for the Savior," Meyer Steinmeyer answered.

"I hope it's not to die for our sins again," Rosalie said with some concern.

"It is to restate metaphysics in terms of personality," Meyer informed the group. "It is to act as a living mediator between unknowable God and finite man."

"Well, all I can say," said Theo, who also sensed that their destination was growing near, "is I hope She has some answers."

"Not everything has an answer, Theo," Sparky offered his insight. "Especially regarding religious matters."

"For example?" Theo was not pleased that his journey might be for naught.

"I don't know," Sparky responded. "Maybe, like why the universe was created in six days? Why not four or ten or seven hundred and four?"

"The universe was created in six days," Meyer answered, "because six is a perfect number, equal to its factors — 1 x 2 x 3."

"I think there has to be a reason for the Savior to return," Pincus said. "She doesn't just show up because She's bored. There's got to be a message."

"There's no message," Meyer said mischievously. "And that is the message."

"What kind of message?" Florence was intrigued.

"I don't know. Maybe it's to reform Christianity like the last time," Pincus tried out.

"First of all," Elliot said, as he turned over pushing the machine to Pincus, "there *was* no Christianity to reform the last time."

"Well, I doubt if She's going to reform Judaism," Pincus snapped back as he pushed The Singing Machine up the hill.

"And second," Elliot disregarded Pincus's response, "the last Savior didn't reform anything at all. He came to found a universal religion of humanity."

"All I know is that there's got to be a message," Pincus was insistent.

"What message?!" half a dozen voices rang out simultaneously.

"I don't know exactly," Pincus held his ground, "but everybody's got a message. That's mostly what we spend our time doing — trying to get other people to accept our message, to sell people on who and what we are."

"And that's what you want?" Sister Gloria Gloria asked. "You want to find out Her message?"

"Exactly," Pincus felt he had at last been understood, neglecting to mention that he was much less interested in selling Her message than in buying into it, and that the real reason he wanted to know Her message was to respond with his own message in a way that would mesh their messages into the kind of romantic bliss not seen since Aphrodite and Adonis were messaging back and forth.

"Well, I do hope that this Savior doesn't get crucified, like the last one," Florence commented.

"Christ wasn't crucified," Meyer announced.

"I beg your pardon," Sister gasped.

"How do you know that?" Theo became interested.

"Well," Meyer said with some relish about being called upon to educate his colleagues, "let's take the Gospels as a starter. Mark says that the Last Supper is the Passover Day on which the lamb is eaten. That would have to be Nissan 14. Mark also tells us that the priests have specifically said that they will not arrest Jesus on that day, which is exactly what he then says they do, even though, as they knew, that would be breaking Jewish law. Mark also identifies Nissan 14 as the day that Simon the Cyrenian is compelled to help Jesus carry the cross, and also the day that the shroud was bought. In addition, no executions were permitted to take place during Passover. They were quite strict about that. This means that, in order for the Gospels to be correct, Jesus would have had to have been crucified and then eaten the Passover dinner that night, which, to say the least, is more than a little strange, even for the Son of God, and certainly raises some real questions about whether Christ was actually crucified. You want to hear about the resurrection?"

Sister Gloria Gloria had a few things to say in response, and was determining how to do so without using expletives that would surely have condemned her to hell for all eternity, when The Singing Machine let out a triumphant volley of music.

"She's around here somewhere," Sparky announced.

The stunned pilgrims stopped and looked around. In front of them was an exceptionally large country inn, white clapboard, a white picket fence with gardens in front, a welcoming porch on which was comfortably arranged white wicker furniture with colorful cushions. It was perfect after so many days on the road.

"We'll stay here," Pincus said and went inside to check the availability for such a large group. This required answering a significant number of probing questions which, seeing the rag-tag group and the large machine in their midst, were more than simple inquiries.

The inquisitor was a hefty woman in her fifties, Gladys Fogg, who had the physique and demeanor to have fit inconspicuously in with Meyer's father's shot-put squad. Finally, while not entirely satisfied, Gladys reached the conclusion that this was, pure and simple, too large a financial windfall to turn away, and so the group was permitted to register, and, in short order, all were showering and doing their best to look presentable for a dinner at the Inn that was surprisingly tasty. For the first time, they were too exhausted for arguments, and so the meal was surprisingly cordial, and they went off to bed with good-natured good-nights, vowing to get rested for the glorious encounter they were confident would occur, even though those in the Inn who they had asked had no idea where She might be.

Meyer was the first to retrieve the local newspaper the next morning. He opened the paper to glance at the headlines. There was an article in the upper left of the front page describing the care given by a young woman who worked in a nearby hospice. The headline read, "The Angel of Jericho, Vermont." The photograph was of Her.

There was pandemonium — people knocking on doors, shouting down the hall, calling out windows, running from one to the other. The Savior was in the next town over, in Jericho.

There was a knock on the door to Pincus's room, and the door opened, already being slightly ajar. As Rosalie walked into the room, she found Pincus sitting on the edge of the unmade bed, staring at the newspaper in his hand, a copy of which Rosalie also held in hers.

Rosalie had tears streaming down her cheeks.

"Is She …?" Pincus asked.

"Yes," Rosalie said.

Then Rosalie buried her head in Pincus's chest and, as Pincus wrapped his arms around Rosalie, she wept along with Pincus.

PART VII

The Savior

CHAPTER 1

The town of Jericho, Vermont, population 5,704, is not a town, nor is it even a village, in spite of its legal incorporation as such. There is a town green, but the only store on it is the small Jericho Center Country Store, the oldest continually-operating general store in America, looking every inch the general store it did when horses and wagons were hitched out front.

On the town green, among the historic homes, is the town library and the town hall, and several churches, along with the old red mill, now a museum, which sits alongside the Browns River and houses the famous photographic collection of Wilson "Snowflake" Bentley, so nicknamed for having photographed over five thousand snowflakes, and, indeed, each one is different.

The strangely-assembled group walked past the town green, having decided a short time before, at the urging of Elliot Pym, to refer to themselves henceforth and collectively as "The Ecclesia," much to the outrage of Sister Gloria Gloria, who considered this to be a presumption nearing, if not actually achieving, blasphemy.

Pincus had taken the precaution of booking rooms at the Sinclair Bed and Breakfast, a charming Victorian bed and breakfast, centrally located in Jericho, owned and operated by Doris Pratt, a no-nonsense woman in her sixties. He made the reservation for a party of seven, plus one virgin mother. Doris Pratt laughed for several minutes before accepting the reservation. She was not one to turn down the business because of some mental abberations of the customer.

Now, as the others trudged on toward the inn, Pincus felt a terrible dread. He told the others to go on without him for now, and he would join them later. Then Pincus slid out of his backpack and sat on a bench bordering the town green, trying to come to terms with the realization that his journey had reached its objective, or soon would — the resolution of that yearning that — it seemed decades ago — had caused him to awaken one morning in a panic, hand the keys to his Mercedes to the nearest passer-by, leave his wife and children, and quit his profession. Somewhere, not far away, She could be found, the Angel of Jericho, his angel, the One who could make his life whole again and bring meaning to his existence.

Of course, at the inception, Pincus never imagined that the object of his desire would be a divinity, and this complicated matters somewhat. Pincus was confident that the skill required to establish a close and lasting relationship with a female, while, perhaps a bit rusty, would reassert itself, as one spoke of riding a bicycle after a long absence. But now he found himself concerned about how his attentions might be received by, well, a Higher Power.

He tried to conceive of what reaction Jesus might have had to, as the vernacular has it, being hit upon by an interested female. He realized that the New Testament was conspicuously lacking in any mention of the Messiah's interest in the many wonderful things offered by the other gender, and Pincus did not have in mind a female's skills at housekeeping and laundry.

Pincus found all this to be a bit curious, as Christ was quick to inform one and all at every turn that he was a man, like all others, and wasn't this the point, that God had sent the Savior to experience life as a mortal, to live and to die as a mortal, and what is mortal man without at least some moderate interest in mortal female? The writers of the Gospels made no stab at depicting their Savior as lacking in any way the very human emotions of anger, frustration, grief, and despair, so how is one to consider a man a man if he has no desire to have a physical relationship with a female? Putting aside the place sexuality plays in the perpetuation of the species, to suggest by omission that there was something profane about physical love certainly made it difficult, at least for Pincus, to see the Lord Jesus Christ as just another one of the guys, the son of anybody, least of all Man.

What these mental gymnastics on the part of Pincus came down to was that he had not come all this way to get an autographed photo of Her for his mantelpiece, but Pincus was very much interested in establishing a relationship of a particular kind, and this was not of the kind that would result in years of stimulating correspondence one day to be published by a University Press, but the correspondence he had in mind had to do with certain anatomy of his corresponding with certain anatomy of Hers.

"That large contraption sitting on my front lawn," began the owner of the Sinclair Inn, the previously mentioned Doris Pratt, "might I ask what it is and whether you intend to keep it there?" she asked when the group had checked in.

"It's a Singing Machine," Sparky informed her. "We've come here to find out the meaning of its song."

"I see," said Doris Pratt, deciding instantly that further inquiries would be a waste of her time. "Would you please be so kind as to remove it from my front lawn," she said.

"Is there another place we might put it?" Florence asked. "It's really quite important that we keep it with us," Florence adopted the warmest and most engaging tone she could muster.

Doris Pratt thought about this.

"Well, you certainly can't park it on the street, that's for sure," Doris ran the alternatives around in her mind. "I suppose," Doris finally said, "you can keep it behind my house, on the other side of the fence. George Thatcher has a grazing area for his cows there, but he's moved them over to the east meadow because it's pretty much eaten up in the back, so I could talk to him about whether you could keep it there."

"That would be very kind of you," Florence smiled her most ingratiating smile.

And so it was, a phone call later, that The Singing Machine, was, as they say, put out to pasture.

As the men went about this, Doris spoke to Rosalie, one eye on Rosalie, the other on those moving The Singing Machine across her well-maintained lawn.

"May I ask you something?" Doris began.

"Certainly," Rosalie answered.

"Your friend said that you all had come here to find out the meaning of the song of The Singing Machine?"

"Among other things," Rosalie answered, "but basically yes."

"I was wondering how you intend to go about this?" Doris asked.

"We all feel that my daughter will know the meaning," Rosalie responded.

"Your daughter?" Doris asked.

"Yes. She's the one who was in the newspaper. You know — the Angel of Jericho, Vermont," Rosalie answered.

"The woman with no name — well, at least no name that she'll tell us. We just have to use pronouns — 'she' and 'her' and so on."

"That is her name," Rosalie told Doris.

"What is her name?"

"'She.' Her name is 'She.'"

Slowly a light began to dawn for Doris. She looked out at the men returning from setting The Singing Machine in the pasture, and then she looked back at Rosalie.

"*The* She?" Doris asked. "The one who was prophesied to one day come a second time?"

Rosalie nodded. "I'm Her mother."

"You're the one Mr. Pincus said was the Virgin Mother?" Doris was about to erupt in another episode of laughter, but, seeing the sincerity in Rosalie's eyes, stifled it.

"That's me," Rosalie smiled.

"And that monstrosity that's now in my backyard — is that supposed to catapult her back from where She's come?" Doris asked.

"No, I don't think so," Rosalie answered.

"But you're not sure?"

"Only because none of us knows what it is exactly — except, we think She knows. Which reminds me. Where is She? Do you know where we can find Her?" Rosalie asked.

"Well, usually she's up at the hospice. She lives there."

"She works in a hospice?" Rosalie asked in surprise, realizing for the first time that she had been so overwhelmed in seeing her daughter's picture in the paper that she never bothered to read the article. "What does she do there? Is she a nurse?"

"Oh, no, exactly the opposite, I'd say," Doris informed Rosalie. "Nurses help people to live. She helps people to die."

CHAPTER 2

Because the Sinclair was a bed and breakfast, this left the issue of lunches and dinners still to be resolved, as it was obvious from the moment that the Ecclesia entered Jericho that this was a town where citizens ate their meals at home. There was only Joe's Snack Bar in town and that was a considerable distance away and open only for breakfast and lunch.

The solution suggested by Doris was to utilize the town's community center, which had a rather large commercial kitchen for various events, such as the Snowflake Festival and the Green-up Day Breakfast. Doris also suggested that Helga Von Hippel — who was known for her Valentine's Day cherry pies, Thanksgiving Day pumpkin pies, and Christmas Eve fruitcakes that she gave out liberally on these occasions — would, for a modest fee, most likely be more than happy to provide what meals the group needed. And so Rosalie had arranged for them to reconvene for dinner at the community center at 6:00 p.m. But now, before heading for their rooms, Rosalie thought they should discuss how to proceed, it being obvious that all eight of them presenting themselves simultaneously to Her might be somewhat overwhelming, and Rosalie had determined that it was essential for the protection of her daughter that her role be that of Mother Hen. Her child being assaulted by a hoard of people all asking simultaneously for explanations of one sort or another was simply not going to happen.

"The last Savior didn't seem to have any problem dealing with all the apostles at the same time," Florence suggested.

"Apostles?" Sister Gloria Gloria gasped. "Now we're apostles? Where did this come from?"

"Other than the Last Supper, I don't recall any instances in the New Testament where they were all together at the same time," Theo remarked. "I'm not even sure they were all there for the crucifixion."

"Well, if there ever was a crucifiction, there weren't exactly bleacher seats set up," Meyer was losing his patience, "but I do think that this was probably an important enough event for them to rearrange their schedules and move conflicting obligations to another day."

"I'd always thought of them all traveling together, to tell you the truth," Florence offered.

"You really think they all followed after Jesus every place he went, like a Cub Scout troop?" Meyer asked, not exactly sure where all this was heading.

"I think we're getting off the topic here," Rosalie tried to shepherd the group back to the issue.

"What is the topic here?" Sister Gloria Gloria asked, "because I haven't the slightest idea."

Pincus decided to get to the heart of the matter.

"I think," he said, "we've been waiting so long to see Her that none of us wants to wait any longer. But I do think that it could be somewhat daunting for Her to be confronted with all of us at one time."

"I think what it all boils down to," Theo offered, "is that everybody wants to be first, and nobody wants to be last."

"I thought the last shall be first, and the first last," Sparky commented.

"Now that is just plain unhelpful," Florence remarked.

"Well, I think this is all rather silly," Rosalie entered the fray. "I'm Her mother, and I haven't seen Her for several years now, and I'm not standing in line to do so. And I'm bringing Max with me, since I asked him to come, and my father says She's waiting for him."

Pincus felt a chill go up his spine at these words.

"The rest of you," Rosalie continued, "can work out whatever you want, but, as soon as we're done here, Max and I are going up to the hospice to see Her."

There was a silence, nobody wanting to confront Rosalie, and, the truth was, nobody actually objected to what she had said, even though it would mean postponing their own encounters.

"And I think I should be next," Sister Gloria Gloria announced.

"And why is that?" Meyer challenged.

"This is why," and Sister Gloria Gloria pointed to her habit and the large silver cross resting on her chest. "You don't think this gives me a certain priority?"

"Because you're dressed like a nun?" Meyer asked.

"No, not *dressed* like a nun, I *am* a nun, and I have *been* a nun for longer than you have been alive," Sister Gloria Gloria snapped back.

"I think we're getting off the subject here," Elliot suggested. "What we really should be discussing is how exactly it is we'll know that it's really Her."

"I beg your pardon," Rosalie's head spun toward Elliot.

"Well, anybody can say they're the Savior, but how do we know for certain?" Elliot continued to pursue the subject.

"Well," Rosalie took a deep breath to control her emotions, "I had the impression that the last time the Savior appeared, people could kind of tell."

"Not until He died and was resurrected, it seems," Meyer pointed out.

"You want Her to die and come back to life so you can know whether She's telling the truth?" Rosalie asked in disbelief.

"Well," Sparky said, "that's kind of what He did the last time."

"It's not kind of what He did, it's exactly what He did the last time," Sister Gloria Gloria said.

"Yeah, well this isn't the last time," Rosalie snapped. "This is this time."

"Still," Elliot remarked, "you all have to admit that without the resurrection, Christ'd just be another guy on a cross who didn't make it."

Meyer instantly grabbed the back of Sister Gloria Gloria's wheelchair, as she surely would have run over Elliot had he not.

"He also, if I recall, was responsible for a number of miracles," Sister Gloria Gloria pointed out.

"That's not a bad idea," Meyer Steinmeyer said. "I don't think it's absolutely necessary for Her to die and come back to life."

"How kind of you," Rosalie commented.

"I'd be satisfied if She performs a miracle every now and then," Meyer suggested.

"I have an announcement to make," Rosalie said, having had enough of this. "Max and I are going now to see my daughter. I think that anybody here who finds themselves in the presence of the Savior and can't figure out who She is, will need a whole lot more than a miracle to convince them. That's what I think. Let's go, Max," and off Rosalie went, yanking Max by the hand behind her.

As soon as they left the building, Pincus turned to Rosalie.

"Well, I think that went well, don't you?" Pincus noted with sarcasm.

"There's always going to be some dissension," Rosalie responded, as they walked past the green and turned on to the street that would lead them to the hospice.

"For the most part, I think everyone wants to hear some justification for their suffering," Pincus replied, "and I don't want to think about what's going to happen if they don't get it. In fact, the more I think about it, the more likely I think it is that they won't get what they're looking for than it is that they will, at least if this Savior is anything like the last one."

"You're in a real mood," Rosalie remarked.

"I have a bad feeling about all this," Pincus confessed. "Everybody's expectations are far too high."

Rosalie suddenly stopped walking, jerking Pincus to a halt with her. She turned him to face her and placed her hands maternally on his shoulders.

"You're going to be okay, Max. You really will. She's going to like you — She will. You two are going to get along like bread and butter."

"I can't have butter," Pincus answered.

Rosalie dropped her hands off Pincus's shoulders.

"I think that's it there, down that lane," she nodded to large metal gates at the end of the street, down which a pebbled road led to a large, and somewhat strange-looking, building. The sign across the top read, "HOSPICE OF OUR LADY OF LAMENT."

"Not exactly the cheeriest name for a place in which people want to find themselves when they're terminally ill," Pincus commented as he read the words several times to make certain he hadn't missed anything.

"You worry too much, Max," Rosalie told him, and opened the large doors that led inside.

Immediately upon entering, they found themselves in what very well could have been someone's home. The floors were carpeted, the walls wallpapered with toile fabric on which various domesticated animals grazed; china table lamps provided a warm yellowish light and rested on mahogany tables beside velvet-covered armchairs and sofas. Oil paintings of landscapes and bowls of fruit hung on the walls, illuminated by picture lamps.

To their right as they entered, sitting at a large Regency desk, was a young woman in her early twenties with curly red hair, Barbara Bissel.

"Good evening," she smiled warmly to Rosalie and Pincus, as they looked about the large room where men and women sat quietly talking, or playing cards, or watching television — and, Pincus couldn't help thinking — dying.

"Good evening," Rosalie answered. "We're here to —

"Oh, yes, we knew you'd be coming," Barbara smiled again.

"You did?" Rosalie asked. "How did you know that?"

"Well, you're Her mother, aren't you?" Barbara asked.

Rosalie nodded.

"Let me see whether She's available. She's been expecting you, but She's been busy helping someone depart," Barbara says.

"Depart?" Rosalie asked.

"You know, pass away. It's always so hard. Nobody wants to go, and it takes so much support to help them let go. I don't know what we'd do without Her. I'll be right back," Barbara said sweetly and danced off.

After she had gone, Pincus looked around him at the patients in the room. There was something that wasn't quite right to Pincus's mind. These did not seem like dying people, not people who would one day die, but, as this was a hospice, people who were going to die soon, like tomorrow or next week. He had seen these people in his practice, patients to whom he'd given a terminal diagnosis, and they didn't sit around playing cards and watching Johnny Carson. They went home and told their wives and their children and their parents and their friends, and then they all wept, and then they did research into treatments, and then they read articles about people who were told they would be dead in twenty-four hours and were still alive twenty-four years later, and that could be them, they told him on the phone within minutes after finishing the articles on miraculous recoveries.

Then they went to their lawyers, and returned home after putting everything in order, and they went sky-diving and visited the pyramids or the Taj Mahal or started to learn the cello. Some of them talked to their priests and rabbis, and prayed for themselves, making elaborate bargains with God if He would save them, and then they prayed for those they loved. But what they did not do is what these people sitting quietly and comfortably around the living room did. No, no — someone had filled this room with normal healthy people to give false hope to those entering this building that they would never leave alive.

"She can see you now," Barbara's voice interrupted Pincus's reverie, "but just for a few minutes. As I said, She's in the middle of Her work."

"How kind that she could squeeze us into her life," the mother of the Savior said tartly, and Pincus got his first hint of what was to come.

It is difficult to describe Pincus's first reaction to seeing Her. First, She was in her early twenties, not much older than his own children. Pincus had expected Her to be young, but the sheer sight of someone so vibrantly young made Pincus feel three times his age. Then, She was wearing cut-off jeans, a sky blue t-shirt, and sneakers with short white socks that had a little pink pom-pom sticking out the back to keep the socks from sliding down into the sneaker. The only jewelry She had were earrings, silver with small turquoise stones.

She was just as Meyer had described Her. Her face was oval, and Her hair was a bright blond, pulled back to display a widow's peak, the triangle perfectly splitting the middle of her brow, and making Her face seem, Pincus didn't know how to describe it, a face you couldn't take your eyes from, as though it were a portrait, something Vermeer might have painted — wheat eye-brows arching over blazing blue eyes, and a gentle sloping nose that was unremarkable except in the way it led one's eyes to the thin lips that formed Her mouth, a mouth that, to Pincus's mind, Vermeer might have spent months trying to capture, as he would have the entire face, without success. The way the deep blue translucent eyes were surrounded by the blond hair and eyebrows, the wisps of hair falling by Her ears, the ruby lips, resulted in something that would be nearly impossible to capture faithfully with camera or brush.

Pincus had to catch his breath.

There was no question that, if this was really Her, come back a second time as prophesied, no one would doubt that She had come back as one of us — only more so.

She stood now at the bedside of a dark-haired woman, who couldn't have been more than a few years older than She was. The young woman had her eyes closed — in a coma, or near-coma. The Savior — Pincus thought of Her as that already, but couldn't explain why — had one hand on the woman's head, stroking her hair gently, while Her other hand held the young woman's hand in Hers.

She talked to the young woman, but so quietly that neither Pincus nor Rosalie could discern what She was saying.

In a moment, She looked up and saw Pincus and Rosalie standing in the hall. She said something more to the woman, and then slowly walked from the room and over to Rosalie.

"Hello, Mother," She said, and kissed Her mother on the cheek. "How are you?"

"That's it?" Rosalie asked. "Hello and how are you? You disappear for years, and it's hello and how are you? How about, I'm sorry I disappeared from your life. I'm sorry I never told you where I was, or called, or even sent you a postcard. They still do have postcards, don't they? And, I think you still probably remember our address. Hello and how are you, Mother?"

"Can we not do this, Mother?" She said. "You're always doing this. Is it any wonder you never heard from me? Who wouldn't want to get away from this?"

"You did get away from this, if I remember correctly," Rosalie answered. "I seem to recall you were in a convent several hundred miles away from this, a convent where I also never heard from you. And now it's my fault?"

"I didn't say that, Mother," She said.

"Really? Then what is 'Is it any wonder you never heard from me?' supposed to mean?"

"Mother! There's somebody dying in here!"

"Am I stopping her from dying? Is that my fault, too?" Rosalie snapped back.

"You know, Rosalie, maybe you should let Her go back to what She was doing," suggested Pincus.

She turned to Pincus as though unaware of his presence up to now.

"Who's he?" She asked Her mother. "You aren't —?"

"This is Max Pincus. The man your grandfather told you about."

"This is Max?" She asked in disbelief.

"I think maybe I should be going. Obviously I'm interrupting a family reunion, and I should be —" Max said hastily.

"You're a lot older than I thought you'd be," She said.

"Yes, I am," Pincus answered. "Actually, I think I'm a lot older than I thought I'd be — so I'll be going now."

"Grandpop said you were in your late twenties or thirties," She said.

"Well, I was — once. Actually, the last time I saw him, that's what I was. But now I'm older. A lot older, actually. And I feel like I'm getting even older every second I stand here. Sooo — like I said — I think I'll go."

"I don't think you should go," She said, staring into Pincus's eyes until, it seemed to Pincus, they penetrated his brain and came out the back of his head.

"No, I really think I should go," Pincus persisted.

"Why?" She asked.

"Because I'm older now. Actually, too old, much too old."

"Too old for what?" She asked.

"For whatever you thought I was older for. For that," Pincus replied.

"Why, what was I thinking?" She asked.

"I don't really know what you were thinking," Pincus conceded.

"You're right. You don't. So stay. I want you to stay."

"Why?" Pincus tried to sort this out.

"Because I think you should. This is interesting to me. You are."

"And I'm not interesting?" Rosalie said.

She spun to Her mother.

"Oh, for godsakes, Mother. Puh-lease...."

Pincus was surprised, and his face showed it.

"What?" She asked.

"Well, I hadn't really expected you to take the name of the Lord in vain," Pincus explained.

"Because I said 'for godsakes'? That's not on the list of profanities."

"It's not?" Pincus asked. "There's a list? Who keeps the list? Can I see it?"

She sighed, and at this exact moment, for just a fleeting second, Pincus thought he saw the head of Sparky appear at the window, lock eyes with Her, and then, with a wane little smile, slide back down out of view. It wasn't clear to Pincus that She had actually seen Sparky, and there was no indication from Her either that She had, because She returned immediately to business.

"I have to get back to work or she's never going to die," She said.

Pincus reacted with surprise, half at seeing Sparky, an appearance that filled his being with an inexplicable dread, and half at Her words.

"Now what?" She asked Pincus, seeing his surprise.

"Nothing," Pincus said quickly, deciding it was better not to address the issue of the face at the window because he could not be absolutely certain She had seen it. "I was just — Well, is it such a bad thing if she doesn't die?"

"It is if you're in constant pain, or at least you would be if you didn't have enough opiates in you to put every cartel in Columbia out of business. Now, if you will excuse me," and She turned and started back toward the room. But before She could go half a step, Rosalie's voice rang out.

"I think I'm entitled to an apology," Rosalie informed her daughter.

"Okay, I'm sorry. I should've called, Ma. Now can I please go?"

"A sincere apology," Rosalie said.

She turned to Max.

"I will do anything for you, Max, anything, well almost anything, if you can get this woman to think about somebody other than herself for just one minute — sixty seconds, that's all. Now I will see you both as soon as I get this poor soul out of here."

"I just want to say," Pincus thought it might be time to show a positive side to himself, "that I think that what you're doing is extraordinary, guiding this woman's way to heaven."

"Sorry, Max. There is no heaven. But there's also no hell, so it all kind of balances out," She informed him.

"There isn't? Not either?"

"No, there isn't. Not either," She said.

"Then what is there?" Max asked in some distress.

"There's only this, Max — otherwise I wouldn't have to work my ass off like this to get people out of here," and She turned and went back into the room, where She took the hand of the young woman, stroked her hair, and whispered gently into her ear.

The only words that Pincus could make out were, "Let go, Phyllis. You can let go. It's okay to let go...."

CHAPTER 3

Pincus did not stay. But he did not go, either. It felt intrusive for him to remain in the room while She coaxed the dying woman off to a better place, a concept that Pincus refused to relinquish even in the face of Her startling pronouncement that there was, in fact, no better (or worse) place. Pincus would not accept that this place, these cold stone steps on which Pincus now sat waiting for Her reappearance, looking out at the flowering beds of marigolds that lined the driveway and the evergreen trees in the distance, that this was it. After this, there was nothing.

Now the reader should be advised that, because of the large number of individuals involved, coupled with the haphazard journal entries kept by Pincus as his attention turned elsewhere, elsewhere being almost exclusively toward Her, it is impossible to determine with any accuracy the time frame during which the events that follow unfolded.

However, based on references found in various documents of the time, it is reasonable to assume that they occurred over a period of years, as opposed to weeks or months. And these years were, the historical record confirms, not without a certain initiative shown by those elsewhere on the globe, especially those who held passionate beliefs contrary to those who passionately believed otherwise — the Soviets and the Afghans, the Iraqis and the Iranians, the Muslims and anti-Muslims, the Islamists and the Christians, and the Serbs and Croatians. Those who felt that the wars raging between these factions were insufficient expressions of their discontent showed even more initiative. The Rome and Vienna airports were attacked, the barracks in Beirut were bombed, the Soviets shot down Korean Airlines Flight 007, Pan Am Flight 103 was blown up, and Anwar Sadat, Indira Gandhi, and Swedish Prime Minister Olof Palme were assassinated. It was during this same time that, to make absolutely certain that CNN did not run dry of material to air during its 24-hour news cycle, the NASA Space Shuttle Challenger disintegrated 73 seconds after launch, and when this event had exhausted its newsworthiness six months later, there was a nuclear meltdown in Chernobyl. The decade ended with the crushing of the protests of Tiananmen Square, and while the future looked bleak if the past was any indicator, there were compensations that arrived on the scene during this same decade that provided a means to cope — Pac-Man and the Boombox.

To be sure, this was not the primary subject on the mind of Pincus. Having met Her, there was now a great deal to process. She was not at all what he had expected. She was no doubt beautiful, but her beauty was not the kind that could easily be categorized. She did not have the looks or stature of a fashion model, nor the appearance of the sort of classic beauty one might find in a Botticelli painting, nor did She have the visual attraction and sexuality of a film star, although in some way She reminded Pincus of the kind of beauty found in Audrey Hepburn, as much eyes and radiance, a way of holding herself, leaning forward when she talked as though you were the only person in the room, the oval contours of her face capturing the light the way the marble of a Bernini sculpture might — perfect, unblemished, flawless. While Her face dominated her appearance, Pincus had taken the time to inspect the full package as he had stood there — the delicate arms with the blond down on them, the deep curve at Her waist that swept in a perfect arc to Her hips, and then back again to Her thighs and down Her legs. She had a beauty that was to Pincus, simply, in a word, transcendent.

Still, She was less than half his age. What possible interest could She have in him? Perhaps, Pincus thought, She was not intended to be the love of his life, the great salvation for which he had hoped, but could, at the very least, show him the way.

"So now what?"

Pincus's reverie was broken by Rosalie's voice. He looked up and watched her sit on the opposite side of the steps, not looking directly at Pincus, her fingers playing with loose strands of her hair.

"Well, you've found Her. That's what you wanted, yes?"

"I wanted more than that," Rosalie answered.

"You wanted Her to run into your arms and embrace you, something like that?" Pincus hypothesized.

"Don't be stupid. She's about as likely to run into my arms and embrace me as you are to lay an egg. That's not Her."

"She seemed to be showing a lot of affection and compassion for her patient."

"The woman was dying, Max. How much effort does it take to be kind to a dying woman? Everybody's kind to someone who's dying. You say sweet things to them, you hold their hands, you give them a big hug, and then they're dead, and you can go back to thinking about yourself," Rosalie said this more as a fact of human nature than with vitriol.

"Children always disappoint their parents in one way or another," Pincus tried to reframe things with a more global perspective.

"Connection," Rosalie said.

Then there was silence. Pincus and Rosalie looked out at a few puffy clouds floating by.

"I would have liked to have felt a connection," Rosalie finally said.

"Yes, connection with your child is a good thing," Pincus said with a weariness borne of his relationship with his own distant children.

The silence returned, and would have remained if it hadn't suddenly been broken by a heartrending wail that came from inside the building. The sound was chilling in its grief and anguish and shook Pincus's bones.

Rosalie reacted with an instinctive sigh.

"Well, I guess she's dead now," Rosalie said.

"Yes, she's dead," She appeared at the top of the steps. "It's her husband. It always happens. There's nothing I can do about it. Husband. Mother. Son. Daughter. They see that their loved one is gone, and they let it all out — the loss, the life they had together gone forever, the empty life ahead without them, the end. And it doesn't matter whether they believe that their loved one has gone to Paradise, or that it's a blessing they're out of their misery. It just happens. The last breath leaves the lungs of the dead and fills the chests of those they left behind, and the living exhale it so that they might keep living, and when the air of death leaves them, it makes this sound. I don't know whether this is good or bad. It just is. It's the sound of something beautiful becoming nothing. It's what nothing sounds like."

"That's terribly sad, dear," Rosalie tried to comfort her daughter.

"I don't think so. It's not sad. It's something else. I used to be worried that it would frighten everyone here, because none of them is far away from the same end. But it doesn't seem to bother them. I think it's reassuring for them to know that they may have meant so much to someone else."

She turned her attention from her mother to Max.

"So ..." She said, looking at Pincus.

Pincus had no response. He attempted a smile to cover his inability to generate an engaging and witty reply.

"So ..." Pincus finally decided to go with the flow.

"So, here you are," She said.

"I am here, yes. Here I am," Pincus confirmed. "And I've brought a few friends along with me."

She nodded.

"Well, I can certainly see why my grandfather wanted us to meet," She said.

"You can?" Pincus didn't know what to make of this, whether this was good or not, but for a reason unknown to Pincus, he found tears beginning to well in his eyes.

But tears were not something that escaped Her notice, even the faint beginnings, the moisture that turns the landscape of the eyes into a lightly shimmering pool.

"Ah, Max," She said, walked slowly over, sat beside Pincus and took his hand, stroking it gently in the same manner as she moved her alabaster fingers over the hands of the dying and the dead.

"What friends?" She asked.

CHAPTER 4

As it turns out, at this very moment, the "friends" of Max were involved in an intense conclave at the Sinclair Inn. How this came to be is a story, in itself.

Sister Gloria Gloria, feeling weary from the events of the day, decided that a cup of tea might restore her. En route to the kitchen at the Sinclair Inn, she encountered Florence, who agreed that a spot of tea would be just the ticket to energize themselves for what might lie ahead of them. By the time they reached the kitchen, Sparky and Elliot had joined them.

They encountered Doris, who was standing at the sink, peeling potatoes.

"We're wondering," Sister led the expedition, "whether we might trouble you for some tea," Sister asked in her most amiable voice, something of an effort, as Sister was not accustomed to asking for things from others, as opposed to demanding them.

"I'm sorry, but the kitchen is closed," Doris answered without turning from the sink.

"Exactly in what way is the kitchen closed?" Sister asked, "as it appears to me that you are currently in the kitchen at the sink."

"Yes, I am that," Doris responded with only the slightest edge of annoyance in her voice, but fully recognizing the dangerous road on which she had embarked. "The kitchen is closed to guests. This is a Bed and Breakfast," Doris explained. "It is not a Bed and Breakfast and Afternoon Tea."

"But it could be, could it not?" Sister almost bit her tongue under the strain of remaining even-tempered.

"Actually, it could not," Doris continued to explain, and now she turned from the sink and wiped her hands on her apron. "It's a matter of insurance. We're covered during the breakfast hours for anything that might happen in the kitchen to one of our guests. After that, we have no insurance coverage, and so the kitchen is closed to guests."

Sister decided to pull out her trump card.

"Mrs. Platt, you see before you a holy woman of the cloth, a handicapped holy woman of the cloth, weary from travel, who has come to your door in search of spiritual renewal — "

"And a cup of tea," Doris offered. "And the name is Pratt, not Platt."

"I apologize, but you do understand," Sister continued.

"I understand that you are trying to use your religious standing in a desperate attempt to get me to do something which, in all good conscience, any truly religious person would never do. Now, if you will excuse me, I have work to do."

"Madame — " Meyer began, reverting to his French heritage.

"Ah, yes, the French have entered the fray," Doris said as she peeled away. "This should be interesting."

"We are on our way to see the Savior, as you most likely know," Meyer continued.

This caused Doris to stop her peeling, as she recognized this to be an unexpected Gallic approach.

"Well, no, I didn't actually know that," Doris answered. "Which Savior is this, and where might He be?"

"It is the Savoir, and it is She. She lives in your town."

"She is the Savior? Like Christ?" And this was enough to make Doris turn off the tap and turn from her endeavors.

"Yes," Meyer affirmed. "It is She. Didn't you know?"

"No, actually, I didn't. The subject never came up, at least when I was around Her," Doris told them. "Are you going to tell on me? Will I be damned for all eternity for not serving afternoon tea?"

"You never asked Her if She was the Savior?" Meyer continued.

"No, I did not ask Her if She was the Messiah, and She is not the only one in my life I haven't asked. There's a long line of them," Doris offered.

"And you couldn't tell?" Meyer asked.

"How could I tell? We broke bread, but there was just enough to go around and no more. We ate fish, but once the fish was eaten, that was it."

"I think we should be going," Meyer responded. "If nobody can tell that She's the Savior, and She's not outright demonstrating it, I think we all need to talk."

Sister, while not wanting to yield on the tea, feeling she had several promising avenues yet to explore, nevertheless understood that a Savior who is not obviously a Savior and might actually deny being a Savior presented a problem that needed to be addressed immediately.

And this is how the conclave at the Sinclair Inn occurred.

"But didn't Christ insist that he was not the Messiah, that he was absolutely not the Son of God, that he was simply the Son of Man?" Florence asked, confused about what all the fuss was about.

"He was speaking in metaphors. He was too humble to admit his true nature," Sister answered.

"That may be," Meyer said, "but if She denies that She's the Messiah, then how will we know, and let's not get into the miracle business again."

"I think," said Elliot, attempting to create an order to the chaos that was slowly developing in the room, but feeling, as with all things, the proof must eventually come down to constructing certain experiments and validating the results, "we should each determine for ourselves what we would need to confirm that She is who we believe She is. And for this, we need to create an orderly progression of inquiry, who shall go in what order."

"I don't see what difference the order makes," Florence responded, who felt that it was all a matter of love, of divine love, that would no doubt display itself in Her presence no matter what system was employed.

"No, he's right. We need proof," Meyer offered, as he wondered how Schopenhauer, Sartre, and Mikhaylovsky might have handled the situation. They certainly would have required reason to be the ultimate determinate. "We need to build to the truth in an orderly way, so that one proposition follows another, as in a syllogism."

"You want to develop a syllogism to determine if someone is God? How would it go? All who deny that they are God are God. She denies that she is God. Therefore, She is God?" Elliot asked, believing that the Cartesian approach, the ontological proof, had already resolved all questions regarding the undeniable existence of a Supreme Being.

"I will not have Her divinity determined by a syllogism, whatever that may be," Sister said. "There is only one among us who has the religious and spiritual wherewithal to know whether She is truly what She is said to be or not."

"The religious and spiritual wherewithal to throw Her out of a convent for not fitting perfectly into your preconceived notions of spirituality?" Meyer asked.

"There is nothing preconceived about them," Sister snapped. "They are a doctrine that has been passed down for two thousand years."

"Wasn't that the doctrine that was used for the Inquisitions?" Theo asked, whose mind during this discussion had been primarily occupied with thoughts of what would be served for breakfast in the morning, hoping it would be pancakes with the Agrade Vermont maple syrup he so loved.

Sister whirled around in her wheelchair to face Theo, but as her mouth opened, Sparky spoke to prevent what was surely to come.

"I think we agreed that we shouldn't all go at once, that it would be overwhelming and unproductive," Sparky remarked, his heart still racing from the beauty he beheld from his brief appearance at Her window and planning his next steps to bring this radiance even closer to his heart. "I see nothing wrong in there being an order, and if Sister would like to be first among us —"

"I *am* first among us," Sister clarified.

"... then," Sparky continued without taking a breath, "I can agree to that, and, I'll even volunteer to take my turn last," Sparky ended, feeling that his chances to win Her would be better if all others had gone before him.

There was a general mumbling of reluctant agreement among the Ecclesia, primarily to defuse the volatility of the situation.

"I think that I should follow Sister," Florence said. "It might be good to have a woman-to-woman chat, let her feel comfortable speaking her mind, as a woman."

"I don't think it's a good idea for two women to go back-to-back," Meyer remarked.

"And why is that?" Florence alerted to what she suspected to be gender-bias.

"Because," Meyer responded, "females have a way of ganging up on men, to be perfectly frank about it, and after two women have made up their minds, the chance of a man having a different opinion is, for all intents and purposes, impossible. Women instantly turn it into, not just a difference of opinion, but a personal insult, a statement of their intelligence and worth as human beings, respect for their humanity, lack of consideration for the travails they have had to endure with menstruation and childbirth and the constant pressure to focus on their appearance. The possibility of prevailing in the face of all this stands about the same chance as having your wife cater a birthday party celebration for your mistress."

Florence looked around at the grins on the faces of the men in the group and decided she would be willing to go third, but no lower.

It would not aid the reader to relate further the discussions that continued until darkness fell and dinner hour arrived, but the final order was determined to be the following: Sister Gloria Gloria followed by Meyer Steinmeyer in order to establish a sound rational approach grounded in precise philosophical reasoning followed by Florence, who would soften any bad feelings that may have resulted from Her sensing that Meyer was conducting an interrogation, Florence joining with Her in the understanding that this is what men, basically, do, and it should not be taken personally, followed by Elliot, who intended to present several well-constructed experiments that could, at an acceptable level of significance (Elliot suggested no less than .001) establish the truth of Her divinity beyond reasonable doub, followed by Theo, who simply wanted to know what had happened to his dear wife once she left the world, where exactly she was now, and whether she was happy, followed at the end by Sparky, who informed the group that he wanted nothing more than to know Her better, neglecting to mention how much better.

"Of course," said Rosalie, who had been standing in the doorway for some time, unnoticed by all, "if She can tell us the meaning of the song of The Singing Machine, all the rest might not matter."

CHAPTER 5

Behind the Hospice of the Lady of Lament was a garden of such exceptional beauty that it nearly took Pincus's breath away. Flagstone paths led through brilliantly blossoming flowers everywhere, and surrounding the garden was an eight-foot-tall, worn-brick wall on which varieties of climbing roses grew.

"I tried to select roses for their meaning," She explained, as they walked side by side down the flagstone path. "For example, the red ones over here are Super Excelsa, and those small orange ones over there are Breath of Life."

"The gardens are all perennials," She continued as they walked. "I thought originally that I would only do annuals, since it seemed like a good idea for the patients to watch something they planted bloom into flower, but too many of the patients never lived long enough for that to happen, so I changed to perennials, which isn't really a bad idea, when you think about it. Every year they blossom, and then they die, and then they come back to life, even more beautiful than the year before."

"Dormant," Pincus finally broke from his reverie.

"What?"

"They're dormant. They don't actually die. They just go into a sleep state. They don't really come back from the dead," Pincus explained quietly, trying not to negate the sentiment behind Her words.

"Yes, but you shouldn't be so literal, Max, should you, because it seems as though they have died and come back. So it doesn't really matter if they're really dead or not, does it?" She gave Pincus a gentle smile.

They walked that afternoon, Max and Her, down the meandering paths, through deep purple lavender, golden Peruvian lilies, blush pink sedum, mango-orange coreopsis. They came upon small waterfalls, the sunlight reflecting from them as though they were lit from within.

"I didn't think it out completely," Pincus said, explaining why he had come. "I just knew that there was something more, that something was missing, and I imagined something better. No, better than better — perfect."

"None of us is perfect, Max," She said.

"I know," Pincus agreed. "But I didn't mean that you were perfect — although, of course, you certainly could be," Pincus hastily added.

"Well, I'm definitely not," She said.

"I meant the relationship, that there would be a love that would be effortless. Perfect."

"Love?" She asked. "You've come to me for love?"

"Well, liking, anyway — immense liking."

They had come to a small koi pond, water cascading down steps of stone into the small pond in which a dozen large goldfish swam around each other. Beside the pond was a bench, and they sat there.

"How does that work?" She asked.

"How does what work?" Pincus asked.

"A love like that? Effortless. Perfect."

She leaned back against the bench and looked up at Pincus, who thought that she must be joking, but then decided not when he looked into the blue of Her eyes.

"You've never had a love like that?" Pincus asked.

"I was raised by my mother, so it was out of the question, and then I went to a convent of all girls where there really wasn't much opportunity for that kind of thing."

"I thought you lived with Meyer for a while."

"I did. He was my teacher. That was all. Nothing romantic. I took care of his home and showed him how he could memorize the Bible, and, in exchange, he taught me philosophy. Is he one of the friends who have come with you, because I would very much like to see him again?" She asked.

Pincus nodded, but was concerned about the competition.

For several minutes they sat in silence. Pincus watched the fish swim about, and then he looked around at the red, yellow, and orange blanket of flowers that surrounded the pond. Every so often Pincus could feel Her eyes looking over at him, inspecting him, as though She had a question and his eyes held the answer.

"Would you show me?" She finally asked.

Pincus suspected what She was asking, but didn't want to assume it.

"Show you what?"

"How to love like that?" She said.

"You need two people for that to happen," Pincus said.

"You can't fall deeply and effortlessly in love with yourself? It seems to me it would be so much less complicated," and Her eyes flashed with delight.

"It seems to work better when two different people are involved. You're playing with me, right?"

"Why do you say that?" She asked.

"Well, you can't not know this," Pincus explained.

"Why is that? If I've never experienced it, how would I know it?"

"Well, maybe you haven't experienced the feelings, but you certainly know the mechanics and how it all happens. Who doesn't know about love?" and now Pincus wanted to touch Her, and he had to stick his hands in his pockets.

"I've known a different kind of love, Max. Something higher, but if you don't want to show me how this all works …" She started to turn away from Pincus.

"I didn't say that," Pincus said quickly.

"It seems like that's what you're saying," She said.

"No, no. What I'm saying is —" Pincus stopped. He didn't know what he was saying.

"Look at me," he finally said. He held out his arm. "Look at my skin. It's beginning to shrivel. I look like an elephant. My skin is falling off my bones. That's how old I am."

"I love elephants," She teased him.

"How old are you?"

"Why, does this all depend on how old the two people are? Is there, like, an expiration date on loving someone?" and now She was no longer joking. "How old are you, Max? I mean, really. Inside. In your heart and your soul. How old are you?"

Pincus thought about this. How old was he?

"Ten," he said. "I'm actually ten years old."

"Well, then, you're much too young for me," She laughed, and She stood and started to walk away. Pincus watched her leave, and then got up to follow her. When he caught up with Her, her took her arm.

"You open yourself up and expose your vulnerabilities, because you know that you are totally safe with this person, and then your hearts begin to connect," Pincus said, but he couldn't help wondering whether this was all a ruse to get him to learn something more about love, to cure him of his heartache, in the way Socrates might question, knowing the answers all along.

"These flowers are my favorites," She said, and She leaned against Pincus, pleased at Her small victory, looking down at a bed of hooded yellow blossoms.

"What are they?" Pincus asked.

"Jerusalem sage," She answered, and She broke into a laughter of such delight that it coursed down to Pincus's toes, and Pincus knew, at that moment, that whatever happened, he would be helpless.

CHAPTER 6

When Pincus arrived at the town center, the Ecclesia were well into their meals. Helga Von Hippel had decided to start them off with her most popular meal — Shepherd's Pie with fresh green beans, and Apple Brown Betty for dessert. As Pincus took his seat, the group, which had been noisy with chatter, suddenly silenced, all eyes turning in the direction of Pincus, who was involved in inspecting the plate piled with a mixture of whipped potatoes and ground burger that Helga was setting in front of him.

"Well?" Meyer broke the silence, looking up from a stack of index cards on which he had been making notes for a coherent and consistently logical approach to his meeting with Her.

"Well what?" Pincus asked through a mouthful of Shepard's Pie.

"Is She or isn't She?" Meyer continued.

"Is She or isn't She what?" Pincus said as he swallowed.

"Don't play with us," Meyer said.

"I'm not playing," Pincus said. "But I don't know what you're asking."

In fact, though it should have been obvious to Pincus, in his current state his own name called out would not have been obvious to him. His head had no room for anything other than the encounter he had just experienced. He realized that he had only half-listened to what She had said, and hardly remembered a word he had spoken in reply. He could only think of Her lips as She formed the words, of Her hands as they rested in her lap, of Her feet as she walked beside him, of the feel of Her against him. And now She wanted him to show

Her what it was for a man and woman to love. And, on that front, there was good news. He was halfway there. He was already in love with Her.

"Oh, for Lord's sake," Sister Gloria Gloria finally barked out. "Is She or is She not the Messiah come back for the second time?"

"I don't know," Pincus answered. "I didn't see anything that would disqualify Her."

"There're qualifications?" Meyer asked, unhappy with the inconclusiveness of Pincus's answer. "There's some sort of certification process? You can get a degree in Messiahship?"

"I just meant that She could be," Pincus said calmly.

"What is that supposed to mean?" Elliot asked, no more pleased than Meyer with what he considered to be Pincus's evasiveness. There was a good possibility, he thought, that Pincus knew something that he was keeping to himself and didn't want to share, giving him a certain leg up on the rest of them.

"It means," Pincus said, "that the subject never came up."

"Didn't you ask Her?" Sparky joined the conversation.

"No," Pincus answered. "I didn't. As I said, the subject never came up."

"I would have thought that you would have brought it up," Elliot told Pincus. "How long were you together?"

"Two hours, maybe three," Pincus.

"Three fucking hours and the issue of Her divinity never came up?!" Meyer shouted in anguish, expressing what all the other members of the assembly were thinking.

"Umm hmmm," Pincus said as he ate.

"How come you didn't ask?" Florence had been following the proceedings, and thought that, perhaps, there might be an explanation.

"I don't think it's all that unusual," Pincus said as he chewed on a bean. "I don't recall Christ ever being asked if he was God."

"Three hours...?" Sparky said with a plaintive whine, seeing his chances with Her slipping away. "What did you do for three hours?"

Sparky asked, already dreading a number of possible answers to his question.

"We just walked and talked," Pincus said.

"For three hours, and the subject of her divinity never came up," Meyer was apoplectic. "What did you walk and talk about?"

Pincus tried to replay the time with Her in his mind, but was having no more success than earlier, just a general notion that he had been in a state of bliss.

"I'm not sure," Pincus said.

"Weren't you there? Were you conscious? It was only a few minutes ago, and you can't remember?" Meyer asked.

"Max, dear," Florence said with a sweetness that rivaled the Apple Brown Betty before her, "please tell us what impression She had on you and whether you had the sense that She might be God."

Pincus thought it best to throw his fellow pilgrims a crumb.

"She is absolutely radiant, in the way a divine creature might be," Pincus said. "That's my impression from the first meeting."

There was silence at the table, as the group considered Pincus's words.

"That's not proof of anything," Elliot finally said.

"Yes," said Pincus. "It's certainly not proof, just an impression, as I said."

More silence. They turned to their desserts.

"Why isn't Her mother here?" Sister asked, and licked the brown sugar of the dessert off her top lip.

And, while there was no response, the answer was obvious. Rosalie was at this moment with her daughter, sitting in a gazebo in the garden, imploring her child to leave this town as quickly as Her divine little feet could carry Her.

"I have a very bad feeling about all this," She told Her. "You should get out of here as soon as you possibly can."

"I can handle it, Mom," She said.

"No, you can't," Rosalie told Her. "That's the point. You can't."

"Why? Because a bunch of people have come here, thinking I'm God?"

"Well that, but because they also want answers, and you don't have any answers, at least not so far as I know, and they won't be happy when they don't get their answers, and then God only knows what will happen when you multiply disappointment times seven," Rosalie tried to illustrate the situation as best she could.

"Don't be so dramatic. It won't be the first time they've faced disappointment. And, if they really think I'm a God, then they'll know there isn't anything they can do about it," She answered, and She looked out at the sun starting to set over the wall covered with yellow Summertime roses.

"That's just it, honey. There're going to be big problems because they believe that you're a divine being who can explain their misfortunes and change their lives. They're sure you have some sort of direct connection to God and can intervene on their behalf."

"Well, then they're going to be in for one heck of a surprise, because God has thrown up His hands. Really, Mom. He has. He doesn't care anymore. Mankind has made such a mess of things that He's just given up. Free will has turned out to be a complete disaster. He's kicking himself for ever thinking of it in the first place. And taking free will away and doing everything Himself is out of the question. Even an eternal being has only so much time to waste, and, besides, what fun is it to move everybody around like you're playing some sort of game against yourself. God is not a puppeteer. And, let me tell you, He's just heartbroken over the whole business. He had this idea that He would set everything in motion and then lean back and say, 'Wow! What a *terrific* idea this was — mankind. Just look at what they can do! Holy gomoly, this is better than the dinosaurs, which I have to admit were a total mistake to eradicate. Just total.' No, Mommy, you can pray to God until your knees need replacements and it won't do any good. The Almighty has had it with us. We're on our own. God just isn't interested in us any longer."

Rosalie listened in shock.

"Sweetheart, please do not tell this to anyone. I am begging you. You absolutely must keep all of this to yourself. It's our little secret. Right?"

"Tell me about Max," was Her response.

"Did you hear what I just said?" Rosalie asked Her.

"I heard, I heard. Now tell me about Max."

"Don't go there, either, dear," Rosalie told Her.

"Why?"

"Because Max is a confused and tormented soul," Rosalie informed Her.

"That's not true," She said quietly. "That's not true at all. He's an innocent. He's like a child reaching for the moon."

"And he thinks that you're the moon — and the sun and the stars — so let it be. It's only going to end badly. For you both. You have to trust me on this."

"Do you think he's a good lover?" She asked.

"A good what? Is he what?!" Rosalie asked in dismay.

"I don't necessarily mean physically — unless, of course, you know that from experience, Mom."

"Well, I don't know it, and you should put any notions of finding out for yourself right out of your mind, dear. Don't even think about it!"

"Okay," She answered, but it was not an expression of agreement. "Okay," She repeated to calm Her mother, and then She looked out at the gardens surrounding them.

"Don't you absolutely love the way the red of the sunset plays off the flowers?" She said. "It's inspiring,"

And She got up, and, leaving her mother behind to soak in the colors, She walked back to the house of the Hospice of Our Lady of Lament, in front of which sat Sister Gloria Gloria in her wheelchair, an envelope on her lap in which could be found a Certificate of Good Citizenship signed by the sisters of the convent, and embossed with a gold seal out of which two thin red ribbons descended.

"Mother Gloria?" She asked in surprise when She saw her. "Why are you here? And what happened to you?"

"Nothing serious. I'll be fine in a couple months. Here," and Sister extended the envelope toward Her.

"What's this?" She asked. "You brought my report card?"

Sister smiled.

"Open it, dear," Sister said.

"And why are you calling me 'dear'? You never called me 'dear' before. There's something that's not right here," She said.

Sister had promised herself that, no matter what happened between them this time, she would maintain her composure.

"Please open it. Please," Sister said.

She opened the envelope, and pulled out the certificate.

"A Certificate of Good Citizenship? What for?" She asked, Her brow furrowing as She read the text, and inspected the gold seal with the red ribbons.

"We all feel badly about the way things ended, because we all feel that, all things considered, you did your very best," Sister said, hoping to make some inroads toward absolution.

"Everyone felt that? Even Sister Margaret and Sister Ignatius, because they were organizing an exorcism to deal with me when I left," She pointed out.

"I don't think it's productive for us to discuss Sister Margaret and Sister Ignatius," Sister tried to calm the waters, feeling a certain pride about how well she was maintaining her self-control.

She reread the certificate, while Sister watched in silence.

"There's a rumor going around," Sister decided to address the issue head-on, "that you might be the Messiah come back a second time."

"I'm the Messiah?" She asked, trying to suppress a smile.

"Well, not *the* Messiah. That would be Jesus Christ, our Lord," Sister clarified.

"Jesus is not the Messiah," She told Sister.

"He's not?" Sister said, beginning to realize that maintaining her composure might be somewhat more difficult than she had imagined.

"No way. You don't really believe that, do you?" She asked.

"Well, yes, I do. I absolutely do. You see before you, my dear, a believer, a true believer, a woman who has devoted her life, her entire being, to the proposition that our Lord Jesus Christ is the Messiah."

"Okay," She said, as Sister sucked in a huge breath, Sister knowing instantly that this "okay" was the gateway to certain disaster.

"Putting aside," She continued, "that it is absolutely ludicrous to believe that someone who has so completely transformed history was totally unnoticed during his lifetime — not a single mention of him in any text among thousands that have survived — his entire life is simply a pasting together after his death of verses from the Old Testament. In Micah it says that the Messiah would be born in Bethlehem and in Isaiah that he would be born from a virgin, although, as I'm sure you must know by now, this was a mistranslation and the correct word is 'young woman' not virgin, so the apostles screwed that up and gave themselves away by trying to apply a virgin birth to him. In Isaiah it says that he will be called 'Immanuel,' that he would be rejected by his own people, that he would speak in parables, that he would be silent before his accusers, that he would be spat upon and struck, that he would be crucified with criminals, and he would be a sacrifice for sin. In Psalms it says that he would be declared the Son of God, that he would be called 'King,' that he would be betrayed and falsely accused, that he would be hated without cause, that he would be given vinegar to drink, that soldiers would gamble for his garments, that he would resurrect from the dead, and he would ascend to heaven, where he would be seated at God's right hand. Now, Sister, the chances that all of this would have happened to Christ, word for word, exactly as it was described in the Old Testament thousands of years before he was born, is, of course, not only improbable, it is inconceivable. The apostles were absolutely not interested in reporting what they knew, but in proving what they believed. The idea of a Messiah had already been established, and Jesus had to fit it. But apostles giving arguments for a conclusion they knew in advance has nothing to do with what's true. It's just a kind of begging for belief. And Jesus's genuine teaching didn't even survive him. Since Christianity grew from eleven people trying to figure out his person and his mission, Christ wasn't even its founder. It never entered his mind. He didn't foresee it, and, what's even crazier when you think about it, he didn't *want* it. It was against everything he taught. He said, 'When thou prayest, enter into thy closet, and when thou hast shut the door, pray to thy Father which is in secret, but when ye pray, use not vain repetitions' — and there goes Sunday morning mass and St. Peter's Cathedral. If Christ had anything to tell us, it was that virtue doesn't consist of a fanatical attachment to fixed religious institutions. Christianity was just an expression of the enthusiasm of the apostles, along with a whole bunch of things they borrowed from other places like the philosophy of Plato and the Stoics, the morals and history of the Jews, and salvation from Orphism, and then they threw them all into one pot to make Christianity. The truth is that Christianity was founded by Paul, not by Jesus, and by a bunch of people, some who knew him, some who had never even met him, who were more interested in proving what they believed and what they wanted us to believe than in what they actually knew, and so they cooked up some stupid story of his life to fit what they'd read in the Old Testament so everyone would believe that Jesus was really the Messiah, which, of course, he was not. Okay?"

"An exorcism," said Sister Gloria Gloria, "would have been the kindest thing they could do to you." Then Sister turned her wheelchair and started to roll away.

She watched, then decided to make an attempt to redeem Herself, and scooted up to Sister as she rolled along.

"I love Jesus, Sister. I do. He was in constant communication with God, because God was in him. He didn't need to see God to understand Him. He could be at one with God without needing a burning bush like Moses, or the agony of Job. The hallucinations of St. Theresa would have been useless to him. God was already in his heart. Christ's theology is that Christ consisted of only one thing — God is our Father."

"Get the hell away from me," Sister said as she rolled along, damning the wheelchair for not having a faster speed.

"I believe that Jesus was a great teacher and a very good Jew, in spite of all the tsuris they caused him, and he would be really really happy with all the things that Christianity stole from the Jews, you know, like a sacred history, a chosen people, righteousness, the law, belief being as important as virtuous action, the Kingdom of heaven, revenge psychology so that the bad get theirs, even the idea of a Messiah, like I said, so I don't think, if Jesus was still around, he'd really have any problem at all with what happened to Christianity, because it all turned out just to be Judaism with a little fairy tale thrown in."

Sister stopped her chair and turned to Her, the words spitting out of her mouth.

"Jesus is still around. He is sitting at the right hand of God! Now please show some mercy from whatever denomination you want — Jewish, Christian, or Jewish-Christian-Fairytale — and leave me in peace, I beg of you," and Sister turned back, shifted into gear, and rolled away.

She watched her go, wishing sincerely that things had gone better, and then She walked back toward the entrance to the Hospice of Our Lady of Lament.

She stopped in her tracks when She opened the door and saw Meyer Steinmeyer, second in line, sitting in the living room, leafing through his notecards.

"Hello, Meyer," She said as graciously as She could muster. "It's good to see you again, and I'm sorry I'm not able to spend any time with you right now, but this has been a very long day, and I'm really pooped."

"This won't take long. I just have a few thoughts to share with you, and I'd like your opinion on them," Meyer said.

"I'm not really in a state where my opinion would be worth much," She tried to smile, hoping that might be enough for Meyer to yield, but, at the same time, knowing better.

"Five minutes," Meyer pleaded. "I've come a very long way."

She let out a sigh and sat in a large armchair across from him.

"Okay, five minutes," She answered in defeat, "but if you want to know whether I'm the Messiah or not, you're wasting your time, and mine."

"What do you know about our funklein?" Meyer dived right in.

"Our what?"

"The spark of our soul, the point where our souls come into contact with the heavens," Meyer went on. "Surely, as a woman, you would know that, since, in becoming a woman, your body, your entire being, became at one with the heavens, your periods and moods now determined by the cycles of the moon, and, perhaps, the stars, as well. And as the ideal woman, as the perfect woman, then you would know this better than anyone, yes?"

"I am in no way a perfect anything," She responded. "Now can I go to my room, please? I'm really exhausted."

"How do you know that?" Meyer pressed on. "For that matter, how do we know anything? Isn't that the real question? There are those who say that you're the Messiah come back for the second time, but how would we ever know that? Because we never have direct experience of things, of the noumenal world, and what we do experience, the phenomenal world is conveyed by our senses, and we know how little we can trust these. So, the question is —"

And now Meyer looked down at his cards and quickly flipped through them until he came to the card he needed, having coursed through those before it more rapidly than he had anticipated.

"—no matter what you might tell us, or what you might do, is there any way of knowing, with any certainty, whether it's true? And to what extent?" and Meyer looked up at Her the way a dog might look up at its master when it's time to be taken out for a walk. She even thought for an instant that She heard a canine whimper escape Meyer's lips.

"Meyer," She explained patiently and with some effort, drawing on the philosophical education that Meyer, himself, had provided Her, "I could not agree more, that experience is subjective, and, if you don't filter it through reason, you only end up with illusions. But, even so, what you are looking for is, by definition, not able to be determined by either experience or reason, as you've just said, because our reason is limited and there will never be any irrefutable evidence, and that leaves us only faith. And faith is the opposite of reason. So, Meyer, who or what I am, who or what *God* is, whether there is an afterlife, all that — it can only be known through faith. So you're barking up the wrong tree. Sorry. Goodnight."

"Yes, yes, I know," Meyer said with an urgency that he hoped would keep Her there. "But if we cannot prove that something is, we might be able to prove that it is not."

"And if you can prove neither," She re-engaged, hoping to do so only briefly, "then you have to ask yourself whether it might be in your interest to accept one of the alternatives hypothetically. Maybe it's okay just to presuppose that God, the soul, and freedom exist, and, perhaps, even that I am what you want me to be. I mean, what's wrong with that?"

"What's wrong is that we still cannot transcend the bounds of our own mind. We can never access the *Ding an sich*, the thing-in-itself, or the *Ding an sich selbst*, the thing in itself-self," Meyer countered.

"Did you just say the thing-in-itself-self?" She asked, thinking that She had perhaps misheard Meyer because of her fatigue.

"Yes, I know that Kant is a little hazy on this, the transcendental object, but, the point is, that this leads us inevitably to the notion that we must rely solely on synthetic *a priori* knowledge, like mathematics, and logic, things that are not derived from experience, in order to obtain any certainty. Take logic. Logic tells us, for example, that God must exist, because, if God is defined as being greater than anything that can exist, and if He did not have existence as one of His qualities, then logic tells us that I could imagine something even greater that also had existence as a quality. So, therefore, God must have existence as an attribute, and so He exists, *quod erat demonstrandum*. See how I arrive at this by pure logic."

"Not so pure, Meyer," She answered. "I can imagine an island greater than any other island, one that has existence as a quality, so does this island exist or not?"

This silenced Meyer, if only momentarily, as he ran various alternative refutations through his mind, but, before he could continue, She stood up and spoke, saying verily:

"Meyer, I'm going to go to bed now. I leave you with only this. What you are looking for does not exist, I can assure you of that. You will never find objective reality of any kind for a theoretical idea, and, if ever there was a theoretical idea, God would take the cake. And the reason for this is so simple that I'm surprised some brilliant German or Frenchman or Russian, whoever you are today, hasn't thought of it. The reality of the idea of God, of who or what I am, can only be proved by the means of this same idea, by our looking at the way the world works, the universe works, and the way we work, in other words, in all the works of the same God we are trying to prove exists, using what might be called 'our God-given faculties.' You can't use God to prove God. So, when it comes right down to it, the existence of God is only for a practical purpose, so that, under the best of circumstances, we can act with a pure moral disposition of the heart, and, in that way, we can be pleasing to God, who we assume exists. So, as I said at the beginning when I was awake enough to still see straight, why not act as though there is a God, and as though I am whatever you want me to be, without bothering to prove anything? Give your brain a rest. And now, speaking of rest, and for the last time, goodnight. Good luck with your funklein," and She headed down the hall.

Meyer watched Her disappear down the hall, then looked down with profound disappointment at the remaining stack of cards in his lap, cards in which could be found a clear elucidation of the differences between *das Verstehen* and *der Verstand*, a distinction that Meyer was convinced would have given him the upper hand at the end of it all.

CHAPTER 7

Rosalie had remained in the gazebo, hoping to regain her composure after a trying encounter with her daughter. She was absolutely certain that no good would come of any of this.

Rosalie ran through in her mind various alternatives to rescuing her sole offspring, or at least protecting Her, but nothing seemed a solution. Certainly, speaking to the Ecclesia and telling them to go elsewhere with their complaints and unanswerable questions would not be successful, and, if she did speak to them, the more adamant she became, the more convinced they would all be that she was preventing them from something that was of greater and greater value to them.

Speaking to Pincus, she knew would be fruitless.

So went Rosalie's thoughts as she looked out at the many hues of the garden and darkness fell.

From time to time, Rosalie thought she could see a crouching figure moving stealthily through the garden, perhaps a gardener sneaking up on various pests that came out only at night, but, had she confronted the nefarious being, she would have discovered this particular pest to be Sparky, and the occasional snip-snip she heard to be his scissors.

After darting furtively from the garden, Sparky took up residence just outside the window of the living room where She was engaged in Her dialogue with Meyer, focusing on Her every move with all the wide-eyed wonder of a child seeing its first soap bubble.

Afterwards, when he had watched this effervescence float off toward Her room, Sparky stood back from the building, waiting to see where a light might come on, signaling Her room. He hadn't long to wait. To his good fortune, a ground-floor light came on, causing Sparky to scamper toward the end of the building and wait behind the boxwood.

Sparky waited until Her light went off, not wanting Her to think that he was some sort of Peeping Tom, and, once he felt certain that She must have by now climbed into her bed, Sparky ducked behind the hedge, and placed his face against the screen.

"Hello?" Sparky whispered into the room.

There was a short shrill shriek.

"I won't harm you," he whispered. "I just want to introduce myself. I'm Sparky."

"Sparky?" She said.

"Yes," Sparky answered, excited that he had elicited a response from the object of his deepest desires.

"Would you please be so kind as to get the hell away from my window!?" the voice inside said to him.

"It's okay. I just want to introduce myself," he replied, undaunted.

"Yes, you told me," She said. "But it's not okay, Sparky. It's rude and it's creepy. Now please go away."

"I can't."

"Why can't you, Sparky?"

"I can't because I have something for you. I'll leave, once I give it to you."

She thought about this. She had the impression that, if She did not do as Sparky asked, this could go on for a very long time, and, because it seemed to Her that Sparky was sincere, and he would, in fact, leave as promised after giving Her whatever he had brought with him, She decided that obliging Sparky would probably be the best way to get some sleep.

"Turn around," She said to Sparky.

"Why?" Sparky asked.

"Sparky! If you want me to come to the window, you have to turn around until I tell you to turn back."

A light dawned. "Oh. Okay, I'm around," Sparky said, his back now to the window, images of a naked female Messiah flooding into his poor brain until it was so saturated that he thought he very well might drown of overactive imagination.

She slowly got out of bed, wearing only bikini panties, and took up the robe that always lay at the foot of her bed for use in the event that she should be called in the middle of the night to ease some poor suffering soul from this world.

"Okay, you can turn back around, Sparky," she said as she tied the terrycloth belt around her waist and walked toward the window.

Sparky turned back to the window and let out a tiny gasp at the sight of Her face so close to his. He took a deep breath, and then Sparky spoke.

"Open the screen please," Sparky asked.

"No way, Sparky."

"If you don't open the screen, I can't give you what I want to give you."

She thought about this. Sparky, of course, had a point, but he would also have easy access to Her room. On the other hand, She realized, the screen was not much of a barrier, and, if this was Sparky's intention, he easily could have broken through it already. She raised the screen.

Sparky stared at her, his eyes the size of a communion plate.

"Oh, my God," he said, enraptured by Her beauty.

"I'm not your God. God is your God. Now what do you want?"

"You are ... you are ... beyond words."

"Thank you. What do you want to give me, Sparky?"

"Here," Sparky said, and held out a bouquet of flowers.

She gasped.

"Are those my Gaillardia?" She asked, looking in shock at the large yellow, orange, and red daisy-like flowers Sparky held out. "You stole them from my garden? They were at the height of their bloom, Sparky. And my asters? You clipped my asters?"

"These are yours? I didn't know they were yours," Sparky sensed that things were not proceeding as he had envisioned. "If I had known these were yours, I never would have —"

"Whoever they are, they're not yours, Sparky," She explained. "You don't go into other people's gardens and take their flowers."

"Yes, I know. I'm really sorry. Do you still want them?" Sparky said in a voice that was barely audible and so soaked with remorse that She had no choice but to take pity on him.

"I'll take them. But you must never do something like this again, Sparky. You have to promise me that."

"Oh, yes, I do. I promise. With all my heart, I promise. Never again," Sparky, said, somewhat cheered that She was taking his gift.

She reached out and took the flowers from Sparky.

"Now, go as you promised, Sparky."

"Aren't you going to say 'thank you'? I went to a lot of trouble to get these."

"No, Sparky, I'm not going to say 'thank you,'" and She closed the screen.

"Why not?" Sparky asked. "What about Jesus when he met the woman at the well?"

"What about her?" She asked.

"Well, he thanked her for giving him a drink, even though she was a Samaritan and had so many husbands she couldn't keep track of them."

"She never gave him a drink, Sparky. And he didn't thank her."

"She never gave him a drink?"

"No, she didn't. Jesus offered the woman his living water which would lead her toward eternal life, and it's not clear she even drank that."

"This is all very confusing," Sparky said.

"Goodnight, Sparky."

"Yes, goodnight," and Sparky left the window and walked slowly around the boxwood hedges until he could see the crescent moon rising for the night.

"I was sure she gave him a drink of water and he said 'thank you,'" Sparky said as he slowly walked away.

And, while Sparky was walking back to the inn, Sister Gloria was rolling into the living room of the Sinclair Inn, where Theo was playing checkers with Florence, while Elliot was reading a *Reader's Digest* from 1974 that he had found on the shelves behind him.

"This Savior is going to be a problem," Sister announced to the threesome.

Theo and Florence did not look up from their game, but Elliot decided this might be interesting to pursue.

"It didn't go well?" Elliot asked, although it was not exactly a question.

"If She is truly the Messiah, then I'm Bugs Bunny," Sister declared. "We're never going to get what we want out of Her. We might as well go home."

"You haven't seen Sparky, by any chance, have you?" Elliot paid no attention to Sister's admonition.

"No, but it wouldn't be hard to guess where he is, would it?" Sister stated.

"He wanted to go last," Theo finally spoke up, as Florence did a triple jump, slamming the checker down on the board as emphatically as she could. She was already far behind in the game and hoped that this might put a little fear into Theo of what she could do, given the chance.

"Did he?" Sister said sarcastically. "Then I guess I didn't see him dodging through the bushes toward the hospice this evening."

"It wasn't really a formal meeting," Sparky said from the doorway, as he entered the room and dropped down on the large antique sofa with the carriages and wagon wheels on the slipcover. "I just gave her some flowers as a welcome from all of us."

"You should have told us you were going to do that, Sparky," Florence said as kindly as she could. "We agreed to an order we would all go in."

"I just gave her flowers," Sparky said.

"What did She say?" Theo asked.

Sparky had to think about how to answer this.

"I think She was pleased," Sparky said.

"She wasn't pleased," Sister snapped. "You could bathe Her in warm milk and shower Her with rose petals, and she wouldn't be pleased. It's not in Her nature. Take my word for it."

"But what did She actually say?" Theo pursued. "Exactly."

"Exactly?"

"Word for word," and Elliot put down his *Reader's Digest*.

"Well," Sparky said slowly, "exactly, She said, 'Get the hell away from my window.'"

There was a sudden silence, suddenly broken by the first notes coming from The Singing Machine.

CHAPTER 8

When The Singing Machine sang that night, it was unlike any song it had sung, a thousand thousand voices singing in concert, a song of such beauty that it stirred the soul in places the spirit had never known. And to those who heard this song, it froze them in place, as though the slightest movement would break the spell of the song, and it brought them back to times and places lost long ago.

Elliot and Theo and Florence and Sister Gloria Gloria had turned to statues, a film come to a halt on one particular frame.

Elliot held the *Reader's Digest* before him, but he was not there. He was in a classroom in first grade, watching Mrs. Donnelly write numbers on the blackboard — 1 through 10 — and, as he watched each number form, his eyes widened at the wonder of it all. It was to the six-year-old Elliot like magic. He knew that a door had been opened, and that these shapes would reveal a world that he could not even begin to imagine. It seemed that they were speaking to him, that each had a different personality: 1 was full of himself, being the first and standing alone; 2 was a friendly number, not apt to cause trouble, and getting along with so many other numbers; 3 could be difficult and it was hard to pin him down, helpful at some times, a trouble-maker at other times; 4 was a nice enough fellow, playful and fun; 5 was the smartest of the numbers, doing many things that the other numbers couldn't do and proud of it; 6 was not especially smart and could be silly; 7 was arrogant, and could often cause trouble; 8 was a funny number, and liked to play when he should have been doing work; and 9 was a very stern number, not at all easy to deal with, and could often throw a monkey wrench into things and gum up the works, at times seeming just downright mean. And now, as the song of The Singing Machine continued, the excitement that filled every cell in his body when he first encountered numbers came back, and he wondered how he ever could have lost it. He hoped that the song would never end.

Florence, leaning back from the checkerboard, was in her mother's kitchen, mixing flour and eggs. She was five years old, and it was the first time her mother had let her cook. She was making a cake, and when she poured the batter into the round pans and placed them into the oven, she could feel, right there at the checker table, the blast of warmth from the oven. Every few minutes Florence would stand on her toes and peer through the glass on the door of the oven, her mother frequently warning her not to open the oven door, but when they did, there was a cake! She spread the white icing on the cake, a cake she didn't want to eat, but just look at, enraptured at what could be done with things that were not "cake" at all — eggs and flour and oil and butter and sugar. She was certain that God had a hand in this.

Across the checkerboard, Theo found himself in his father's workshop. He was eight years old, and he heard the sound of the table saw and the planer, as he watched his father at work building a table. He stood beside his father at the lathe, as the table legs turned, rings forming as the chisel etched into the wood. His father had given him sandpaper, and now Theo, the music of The Singing Machine filling his frame, felt in his fingertips how the paper moved back and forth on the wood, and how his fingers ran over the wood, brushing away the sawdust to determine how smooth the surface had become. And then, his favorite part, his father had let him rub the varnish into the wood, coat after coat, until he could see his young face in the shine. When, at last the table had found its way to the dining room, Theo sat toward the end, and, as he ate with one hand, his other hand would feel the edge of the table, moving around the curve that joined the long side with the short side, stroking it slowly in the same manner he would pet the Labrador Retriever, Baxter, who lay at his feet, because, after all, wasn't the table alive, in the same way that the song of The Singing Machine was a living breathing thing?

Standing in the doorway as when he had first arrived, Sparky was lost in the fabrication of a crystal radio from a kit he had found in the attic of his grandfather's home. He was seven, and, at first, had absolutely no idea what would come of this, but it interested him, and he could still feel the smooth copper wires that he had wound around a tube to make a coil. He remembered the parts' numbers as he assembled them — the 365pf variable tuning capacitor, the IN34A germanium diode. He had thrown a ball of wire out the window of the attic, and now he could feel the rough bark of the maple tree by the street that he climbed with the wire in hand until, at last, he reached a height even with the attic window and had wrapped the wire around a thick branch. And then, when he returned to the attic and placed the phones on his ears, there was the sound of music and voices of announcers, and he was filled with an indescribable joy. He had built a radio! He could not imagine that anything he built could ever be better. But now there was The Singing Machine, and maybe this was better, but only slightly — only slightly.

In front of Sparky, Sister Gloria Gloria sat in her wheelchair, her eyes closed, back at the age of five, walking with her grandmother to church in Cleveland. Grandmama decided they would go to St. Stephens this Easter. At first young Gloria had been terribly disappointed since she so much enjoyed looking around at the beautiful stained glass windows at St. John, depicting the Annunication, the Nativity, the Presentation, Jesus in the Temple, the Resurrection, the Ascension and the Assumption — the whole story there in brilliant color, dazzling as the sunlight came through the windows, a spectacle far better than any film she had ever seen — and in the front, the rose window with the hand of God, and behind her the window with the Holy Spirit. She was encased in magic.

And now the five-year-old Gloria entered St. Stephens and she knew at once why they were there. Intricate wood hand carvings had been imported from Munich by the hundreds of German families who made up the congregation. In the front was a wooden sculpture of Christ on the cross, beneath which were wooden sculptures of Joseph and Mary looking up at their son. Beneath them, in small naves, were six angels, and in front of them lit candles. And as the large chorus began to sing, Gloria was called. There were no voices or visions, just the knowledge that filled every space in her body that she was home, that this is where she belonged, that this was to be her life. And, now, as she sat in her wheelchair, Sister Gloria Gloria felt so totally alone, vigilantly defending her love of Christ, her belief in him, her devotion to him. But she would never give up, not ever. She would stay forever her five-year-old self, looking in wonder at the church, filled with hope and peace and immense joy, and a tear dislodged from one eye and then the other and ran down her cheeks as The Singing Machine sang on.

The song of The Singing Machine drifted over the countryside that night and came to the bench behind the Sinclair Inn where Meyer Steinmeyer sat, his head leaning back, his hands rubbing back and forth on his knees. He had been transported to the age of 14 and found himself in the library of his tutor for the first time. He had been asked to wait there, as his tutor was behind schedule. From floor to ceiling were books, all bound in leather. He walked around the room until he came upon a small wooden stand in which were dictionaries — Latin, German, French — and Greek. He picked up the Greek dictionary and looked up the words — Ἐν ἀρχῇ ἦν ὁ λόγος, καὶ ὁ λόγος ἦν πρὸς τὸν θεόν, καὶ θεός ἦν ὁ λόγος.

Word after word, young Meyer shuffled through the pages, faster and faster, hoping to finish before his tutor returned. In. The. Beginning. Was. The. Word. And. The. Word. Was. With. God. And. The — But the tutor walked in and looked sternly at Meyer, who dropped the book in surprise. Slowly the tutor walked over. Meyer was certain he would get slapped, but, instead, the tutor picked up the book. "Did you finish?" he asked. "Not ... yet ..." Meyer had said, shivering in his shoes. "Then we should finish," said his tutor. And they sat down at a large desk, and they learned Greek — And. The. Word. Was. God. — and then the next year Latin, and the year after that four more languages. Meyer no longer needed a dictionary, except in the most difficult circumstances. At 14, Meyer knew that he had passed through the portals of paradise, never to return.

As for the citizens of the town who heard the song of The Singing Machine drift over the Vermont countryside that night, those who were not already asleep, such as Rosalie, imagined the sweet melody to be that of a stereo from a neighbor's house, or to be coming from a car parked up on Lover's Lane, or simply floating in the air from some unknown source; and those who were sleeping heard the music, as well, but it came to them in their dreams, dreams of childhood toys and past loves. For her part, Rosalie dreamt of sitting by a stream, her feet dangling in the clear water, as the sunlight filtered through the filigree of trees above, the secret place she had gone as a child to find perfect peace.

Pincus was neither asleep nor frozen in place. He was lying in bed, eyes wide open, when the song of The Singing Machine began. For a while, he lay there and listened. The song seemed to Pincus to be coming from the place where all life ended, the brightly-lit destination that those with near-death experiences describe. At that moment Pincus no longer feared death, because he knew that The Singing Machine sang of a place where he would spend eternity after life, a place so sublime that it could only be called Paradise.

Slowly, Pincus arose from his bed and walked to the window that looked out the back of the inn on to the field in which The Singing Machine had been placed. He was struck at first by a glow that emanated from The Singing Machine. Until now, there had only been music and matter. Now there was light.

And then Pincus saw Her. She stood before The Singing Machine in a thin white dress, her back to him, the glow of the machine shining through Her dress and illuminating her form. Pincus watched as She swayed gracefully to the music of The Singing Machine, in perfect synchrony, as though they were one.

As he looked upon Her joining with The Singing Machine, it was just as Pincus had imagined. At a certain point, Pincus believed, the harmony between two living things becomes so complete that the beautiful becomes sublime. Never was there, nor could there be imagined, it seemed to Pincus, such a love as he now felt. His poor heart was ready to burst with such terrible longing that he thought he was close to death.

He placed his hands on the sill to steady himself, and, at that moment She turned, looked up to where he watched through the window, and smiled at him, as the song of The Singing Machine began to fade until it was not much more than a whisper.

Slowly She turned back to The Singing Machine, her arms outstretched as if to embrace it, and She spoke softly to The Singing Machine.

"Daddy," She said.

PART VIII

Ecstasy

CHAPTER 1

Pincus didn't sleep that night. The vision of Her swaying before The Singing Machine danced before him throughout the dark night and into the light of dawn with a power of uncertain magnitude, calling to him and stirring feelings of both longing and foreboding. Although transfixed by a beauty, Pincus felt an undefinable dread. Her absorption in the song disturbed him in a way he couldn't put into words.

As soon as the sun's first rays spilled brightly into the bedroom, Pincus dressed and went immediately to the Hospice of Our Lady of Lament, where he found Sparky sitting on a bench on the porch, holding a chicken — actually a rooster, and not a happy one at that.

"I bought it off a guy down the road. Twelve bucks," Sparky said proudly, as he wrestled with the crowing bird. "I got it for Her."

"Why?" Pincus asked. "Did She say She wanted a rooster?"

"Not really."

"Was there something She did that suggested She was interested in having a rooster?" Pincus asked, raising his voice to be heard over the squawking bird.

"Before the cock crows thrice," Sparky said merrily. "It's a symbolic gesture to demonstrate my devotion to Her."

"It was not 'before the cock crows thrice,'" Pincus informed Sparky.

"Yes, it was" Sparky insisted.

"No, Sparky. Jesus said that he would be denied three times before the cock crows — meaning before the morning. 'Verily I say unto thee, That this night, before the cock crow, thou shalt deny me thrice.'"

"You're sure?" Sparky asked, his glee deflating.

"Absolutely positive. You can look it up if you like."

"I was certain that the cock crowed three times. Maybe the cock crowed one time for each denial. It could have been that," Sparky was not ready to concede. "'I deny him. Cock-a-doodle-do. I deny him. Cock-a-doodle-do. I deny him. Cock-a-doodle-do.' Like that."

"Peter denied him three times, and then came just one 'Cock-a-doodle-doo,'" Pincus said, as he sat on a wicker rocking chair across from Sparky. "'Even if I have to die with you, I will never deny you,' was what Peter told Christ at the Last Supper."

"And he denied Jesus, anyway?" Sparky asked in mounting dismay. "I don't remember Peter saying this."

"Well, he did," Pincus informed Sparky, "Three times Peter told the servant girl, 'Woman, I do not know this man.' Then the cock crowed. Then Peter wept profusely, and then, sixteen hundred years later, Caravaggio put it all down on canvas to remind us that Peter may have been the rock upon which the church was built, but not a small portion of his dedication may have been to compensate for his having been a two-faced sonofabitch, no matter how much tearful remorse he experienced after having thrown his best friend and arguably the Son of God to the wolves."

"This is very disturbing ..." Sparky had a lot to process.

"What's going on out here?" She appeared on the porch, the screen door slamming behind Her.

A smile came to Sparky's face, and he held out the rooster. "Here," he said.

For one of the rare times in Her life She had nothing to say. She just stared at the large terrified bird struggling to get free.

"It's for you," Sparky clarified the situation.

"You've woken up everyone in the hospice. These are dying people. They need their rest, Sparky," She said.

"If they're dying, they're going to have plenty of time to rest later," Sparky pointed out.

"Sparky, please take the bird back from wherever you stole it," She told Sparky, who wasn't really paying attention to the substance of Her words, only to the sweet sound of Her voice and the way her lips formed them.

"I didn't steal it. I bought it for twelve dollars," Sparky said, proud that he had learned his lesson from the flower incident the previous night.

"Why?" She asked.

"Why?" Sparky asked.

"Yes. Why are you giving me a chicken?" She asked.

"It's a rooster," Sparky mumbled, but wasn't quite sure now how to proceed, taking into account that he may have missed a few details in Matthew. Still, there was a rooster involved in the Last Supper and denial business, and putting aside a definitive computation of the number of times it crowed, it was symbolic of something, even if Sparky was no longer certain of exactly what, and so Sparky finally decided to go with his original formulation.

"I got it to show you that I will never deny you. Not ever. No matter what," Sparky said with great conviction. "It's a symbol that I am here for you through thick and thin. So, here," and Sparky held out the bird once more.

"Sparky...?" She said in soft measured tones.

"Uh huh," said Sparky.

"I am touched. Sincerely," She said.

"You are?" Sparky thought his heart would leap from his chest and fly around him in little circles, carried by angel wings.

"I am. Truly. But now I'm wondering whether you would do me a huge kindness," She said gently.

"Anything," Sparky panted.

"Do you think you might be able to take the rooster off the porch and carry it far away from here to wherever it came from, and never again bring me anything — not flowers, not poultry, nothing? What do you think? It would mean so much to me."

Sparky looked at Her, his eyes probing Hers, and then he nodded, got up from the bench, slowly descended the porch steps in silence, rooster in arms, and walked away, turning back every now and then to glance at Her.

As Sparky disappeared in the distance, the sound of the squawking rooster trailing behind him, She turned to Pincus, her head tilted askance.

"I had absolutely nothing to do with this," Pincus pleaded his case. "He was already here with the bird when I arrived."

She stared at Pincus as though She had not heard his words, then spoke what was on Her mind, what had been incessantly on Her mind since she awoke.

"Tell me about that contraption behind the inn," She said.

"The Singing Machine?"

"Where did it come from?"

"We brought it with us."

"Where did you find it?"

"At Sparky's. He built it. He and his brother, Elliot."

She looked in surprise toward the path on to which She had dispatched the Masterbuilder of The Singing Machine. It seemed to Her something far beyond anything of which Sparky could be capable.

"Why did you bring it?" She asked Pincus.

"It sings by itself. Every night. We were hoping you could tell us why."

"It wasn't built to sing?"

"Not by itself."

"What made you think I would know?" She asked.

"We didn't know for certain, but we thought you might. Do you?"

"Know why it sings by itself?"

"And what it means. The song."

"That's why you've all come? You want me to tell you why the machine sings and the meaning of its song?"

"Among other things. Each of us has other agenda, as well, but, if anything unites us, and it would definitely be the only thing, we share a desire to know the meaning of the song."

"It's a song, Max. What does a song mean? A song is a song."

"Yes, I know. And we shouldn't read anything into the Hallelujah chorus. Handel was just in a good mood."

She smiled, and at that moment, to the surprise and delight of Pincus, he felt a spark. Just the tiniest electrical particle. It leaped between them and made a connection. Pincus could feel it enter his eyes and descend down to his toes.

"It's not just a song," Pincus said, trying to keep the electricity flowing.

"No, Max, you're right," She said. "It's not just a song."

Then She turned and walked into the hospice, leaving Pincus staring after Her. In a few seconds the screen door reopened and She stuck out Her head.

"I've got a busy day, Max. A ton of patients, but, if you want, we can have some coffee in the garden before I start my day."

And so Pincus headed for the garden, while She went inside to fetch them coffee.

"It's confusing to me," She told Pincus among the newly opened day lilies, when they settled on the bench in the garden. "I love everyone, so I've never understood what this other love is, this love of passion and desire."

"Everyone?" Max asked, not convinced that this was possible. Love, by its very nature, was, he had always thought, exclusive. It needed an object that called out one's affection. It was not so much that love for others was withheld, it just wasn't drawn out indiscriminately in all directions.

"Everyone," She confirmed, and She took a long sip of Her coffee, small wisps of steam rising from the cup and drifting toward the cloudless blue sky.

"Criminals and perverts?" Pincus tried to narrow things down.

"Them more than anyone, because they need it most of all."

Pincus said nothing in return, but studied Her eyes, wondering whether this was a test. How could she not know the love of romance, of passion, of desire, of the longing to complete oneself with another?

"Well, this is different," was the best Pincus could do.

"It has always seemed to me," She responded, and She placed Her hand on the knee of Pincus, as though to comfort him for the pain that would follow her words, "that lovers always overestimate love, and this inevitably leads to disillusionment, until, finally, one or the other of them wants to escape. They begin to feel alienated and come to hate each other. So," and now She smiled with an engaging sweetness to indicate that She was simply stating the facts as She knew them, and no offense was intended, "that's why I don't understand."

As Pincus watched Her put love on the anvil of life and pound it mercilessly into oblivion, Pincus knew that his work was cut out for him. His own experiences with love were not exactly refutations of the portrait She had so precisely painted. Pincus tried to think of how to respond, of which part of Her argument could be summarily rejected, but nothing came immediately to mind.

"It's a feeling," Pincus said to bide some time. "Once you have the feeling, you'll understand."

"I hope so, Max," She said, "because I have the feeling that when two people love like that, they experience an aspect of the divine. That's what I want," and She stood up, poured the remaining drops of her coffee onto the small white pebbles on the path, took Pincus's hand in Hers, and they walked together from the garden.

CHAPTER 2

When the Ecclesia met that next morning, there was great consternation. Once again, when The Singing Machine sang that night, She had appeared, swaying in rapture to its melody.

"Not so much rapture, I would say," reported Pincus, who had watched from his bedroom window. "More like a moth drawn to a flame. I'm concerned She'll go into The Singing Machine, and we'll never see Her again."

"Moths aren't drawn to flames," Theo explained. "They're simply disoriented. I used to think they were attracted to the light, but they're not. Moths find their way by using light as a compass. When the light is the sun or moon . . ."

"Theo...?" Rosalie tried to intervene.

"— the source is distant, and the light rays that strike the insect are parallel to each other."

"Theo?" and now Rosalie's voice was louder.

"So moths — and many other flying insects — mosquitos, horseflies, beetles, mayflies — have evolved to receive light at a fixed part of the eye," Theo continued unabated. "As long as the moth flies in a straight line, the visual pattern is unchanged. But when the light source is a nearby candle, the moth tries to maintain a constant angle to the source — and so it spirals in toward the light. The moth seems to be attracted to the light, but it is not really attracted. It's just confused."

"Thank you, Theo. That was very educational," Rosalie spit out in single syllables.

Florence saw trouble brewing and stepped in.

"Perhaps, being divine, She won't disappear if She goes into the machine," Florence offered.

"Really," Sister Gloria Gloria's ears perked up. "Did She happen to say that She was divine?"

There was silence.

"I don't suppose anybody actually bothered to ask Her?" Sister continued.

More silence.

"I thought you were going to ask Her when you saw Her again, Max," Florence attempted to be helpful.

"It didn't really come up," Pincus answered quietly.

"What precisely did come up?" Sparky asked, worried that what came up might have been him.

"Well, precisely," Pincus answered even more quietly, "what came up was that She wants me to show Her how to fall in love with me."

The outburst from the members of the Ecclesia caused Doris Pratt, the innkeeper, to appear at the entrance to the room.

"Please," she said firmly. "You're disturbing the other guests."

"What other guests?" Sister responded just as firmly. "We've got every room. Are you hiding someone in the attic?"

"Okay, then you're disturbing me, so quiet down," and Doris nodded emphatically, threw a cold smile Sister's way, turned left, Doris's now-vacant spot by the door being instantly filled by Meyer.

"What's happening?" Meyer asked.

"She's asked Pincus for instructions on how to fall in love with him," Sparky moaned, although the expression of anguish was not entirely necessary, since, truth be told, Sparky, in spite of his intense wooing, did not actually want Her to fall in love with him. Sparky's intention was simply to demonstrate to Florence, for whom his love was more profound than ever, that he was still desirable. He had absolutely no idea what he would do if She, in fact, responded to his attentions. He was hoping that his childlike nature would allow for success in all eventualities — both Her becoming attracted to him and him extricating himself should he, miraculously, succeed.

"Why him?" Meyer asked, his look fixed on Pincus.

"Why *not* me?" Pincus was quick to respond.

"You want the list alphabetically or numerically?" Meyer was just as quick to respond.

"The truth is," Pincus conceded, "that I'm really not sure what to do."

"Well then," Meyer offered, "maybe you should just stop."

"I haven't started," Pincus responded.

"Then you have nothing to lose by not continuing," Ellot remarked. "It will only end badly, not only for you, but for us all."

"How is that?" Pincus asked, genuinely confused.

"Well," Elliot explained, "if She falls in love with you, where does that leave the rest of us?"

"You don't think She can love more than one person at a time?" Pincus asked. "Love does not have to be exclusive, especially if She's the Savoir."

"I do wish someone would finally ask Her," Sister chimed in. "It's a simple question, amenable to a 'yes' or a 'no' reply. 'Are you the Messiah? Yes or no?'"

"Doesn't God love us all equally?" Pincus continued, ignoring Sister.

"Yes, but so far as we know, God is not having a sexual relationship on the side," Meyer countered.

It was not that Meyer was concerned about Her affection being divided, as much as it was that he considered her being romantically involved to be an unnecessary complication. There was a certain purity in Her not being in a relationship, especially a sexual one, something that could easily contaminate what he hoped to discover — how perfection in a woman could provide a clue to perfection in mankind and the universe. It seemed to Meyer that she became something else after losing her virginity. Up to that time, sex had simply been an interesting notion. Once she found that another person could satisfy these desires, a man in most instances, the entire business became more complicated, and a female who had, until that time, been perfectly content with being exclusively what she was — she could have her nails painted hand and foot, cover her face with a multitude of cosmetic products, wear a wide assortment of glorious garments, do countless things with her hair, deck herself with an inexhaustible supply of baubles — now discovered the penis, an organ that, until someone introduced it into her body, she had never known she had a need for with so many other things she could do to her body all by herself. And this diluted the purity for which Meyer was searching. For penises came attached to men, and this required certain efforts on her part to obtain, and these efforts changed a self-reliant, perfectly content female into a dependent, discontented, incoherent pudding head, hungering for something for which she had absolutely no need until she encountered, up close and personal, the male organ.

"Do you intend to have sex with Her?" Florence spoke what was on Meyer's mind, and did so as calmly as she could, not an easy task for her, as it had been a very long time since she had experienced physical intimacy and the thought of it stirred long-dormant feelings that headed directly and rapidly to exactly where in her body she would have preferred them not to have directed themselves. Sex had always been somewhat confusing to Florence, and, if there was one thing she hoped to learn from Her, it was whether, with the daily deluge of sexual content everywhere she looked, it was possible for sex ever to be sacred again.

"I hadn't thought about having sex with Her," Pincus answered.

"You're not having sex with the Messiah," Sister confronted Pincus, "so don't even think about it."

CHAPTER 3

Lunch was just ending when Pincus arrived at the Hospice of Our Lady of Lament, and, as the room emptied, it was accompanied by the usual bustle of residents talking loudly to one another, wait staff cleaning tables, and the nursing staff herding those in need of medication off to the medication station.

Meals were a focal point of life at the hospice. There was much conversation about what had been served and its quality (lacking in all respects), followed in short order by what might (or should) be served at the next meal.

Seating arrangements were also of great interest. Often married couples wished to sit together, off by themselves, as they had been doing for decades prior to arriving at the hospice, and this was not of much concern to the inhabitants of the hospice — until one or the other of them decided not to sit as a couple, and this now became a subject worthy of a full hearing of the United Nations General Assembly.

One of the first items on the agenda of every individual on arriving at the meal was to assess the seating arrangement to detect any significant changes and attempt to determine the cause. This would provide food for the meal of far greater importance than that being served. The only changes in seating that were passed over, so to speak, were the ones occasioned by those passing on, hospices being what they are, not a rare occurrence.

And now, as the guests walked, rolled, or were pushed from the dining room, Pincus waited at the exit, hoping to catch Her before she went back to work. He had planned to decline Her request for instruction in romance, not because of anything that had occurred at the conclave that morning, but because he had reached the conclusion that it was not something that could be taught.

The meeting, itself, had broken up not long after Pincus had been instructed by Sister Gloria Gloria and Rosalie to abstain from fornication, and various members drifted off one by one to do other things, but not before one final plea from Sister to demand a straight answer from Her about Her Messiahship.

"For what purpose?" Elliot asked. "Will you believe Her? If She says She is or says She is not, will that resolve the issue? If you meet Her and you can't tell, then nothing She says is going to help."

"Then how will we know?" Sparky asked.

"You just know," Florence said. "Elliot is right. You meet Her and then you know. That's what happened with the last one. The apostles just knew, that's all."

"They knew," Sister said emphatically, "because the 'last one' fulfilled prophesies that provide material for half the Old Testament, performed more miracles than you can count, and was resurrected from the dead. John didn't just take one look at Jesus and say, 'He seems like the Christ to me. What do you think, Simon Peter?'"

And this seemed to end the meeting. Elliot left quickly for town, and others headed off to walk through the countryside, now brushed lightly with the first colors of autumn, fallen leaves crunching under their feet as they walked with no particular destination in mind.

Elliott knew his destination. It was to the Resurrection Funeral Parlor and Cremation Services, an odd name Elliot thought, in spite of its intended comfort to the bereaved.

George Crowley, the undertaker, was a rotund man in his sixties with thick silver hair that could have used a good combing and a wispy goatee that matched his hair in color and care.

"What for?" Crowley asked in astonishment.

"It's for an experiment, but I assure you that she'll be returned in the same state in which you give her to me, maybe even better," Elliott explained.

"She's dead," Crowley explained.

"Yes, that's the idea," Elliott answered. "I just want to borrow her. I only need her for a few hours. I'll bring her right back, I swear. No one will ever know."

"I can't loan out one of my corpses!" Crowley responded emphatically. "It's just not done. And I'm sure it's illegal, or immoral, or if neither, then in very bad taste."

"Look," Elliott explained, "I'm offering you a rare opportunity that could make your business explode overnight."

"The last thing I want is for my business to explode. I had that happen once. The refrigeration went out one summer, and the gasses built up in Mrs. Paasch, and it was like she had swallowed a grenade. For the next year I was finding Mrs. Paasch all over the basement, and I was in litigation for six years. No thank you," Crowley said, his left eye twitching as he relived it all.

"Perhaps, I chose the wrong word," Elliott tried to set a new tone. "Look, you know about Her, yes?"

"Her who?"

"Her. She. She who is up at the Hospice of Our Lady of Lament."

"Yes …" Crowley said cautiously. "We have all heard of Her."

"And you know who She is believed to be?"

"I know who She's rumored to be. And I know that nobody in his right mind would believe any of it," Crowley said, beginning to see where all this was heading.

"But suppose, just suppose, that She really is what She is rumored to be. And just suppose that She raises — what's her name?" Elliott asked, nodding toward the deceased, gray-haired woman lying on the metal table to his right.

"I'm not telling you."

"Very well, but just suppose that this woman is, in fact, raised from the dead by Her — just imagine what it will mean for business at the Resurrection Funeral Parlor," Elliott continued his sales pitch.

"What it means, Mr. Pym, is that I'd be bankrupt. How am I supposed to earn a living if she starts raising the dead? We're working at cross-purposes here. There's a real comfort in my profession in knowing that, when they bring in someone who's expired, they're going to stay that way. They start coming back from the dead, and my business goes into the toilet," Crowley explained.

"I only need her for two hours, three at the most," Elliot pleaded.

"Mr. Pym, let me explain the situation with Mrs. Bagwell here. She has no blood. Every vein and artery in her body is filled with formaldehyde. All her internal organs have been removed, drained, and are now sitting in a plastic bag in her chest. And her mouth and anus have been sewn shut."

"Then you will have to admit," Elliott said, "that Mrs. Bagwell's resurrection will truly be a miracle."

While all this was transpiring, Pincus had determined that She was not there in the dining hall, it now being empty, with the exception of a lone worker vacuuming a vast amount of food particles from the carpet.

"This is Her day off," he was informed by a young nurse's aide. "She's in town, but I'll tell Her that you've been looking for Her when She returns."

"Do you know where in town? We were supposed to meet," Pincus told her, not entirely a lie, although an exact time for their next rendezvous had not been set.

"No clue. Sorry," she smiled and left, swinging her hips, Pincus thought, more than actually necessary to propel her.

Pincus finally caught up with Her in town. She was sitting on the rocks across from the Old Red Mill that sat alongside Browns River.

The mill was exactly what one would imagine of a red wooden New England grist mill, the kind found on postcards. But times changed, and after a hundred and fifty years of grist production, it became a museum, grist mills sitting idle on the first floor. Now on the second floor of the Old Red Mill the vast snowflake photograph collection of William A. Bentley, Jericho's very own "Snowflake Man."

"He took over five thousand photographs of snowflakes," She told Pincus when he had joined Her. She was resting back on the stone, her eyes closed to protect them from the sun that illuminated her. "Since you seem to be so interested in meeting God, if you want to see God, you should go look at them, Max," She said. "Every unique crystal is a masterpiece of design. When a snowflake melts, the design is forever lost — the beauty gone, without leaving any record behind."

Then She opened her eyes and looked at Max.

"You and I can leave a record behind, Max. That's what we can do before we melt away," She said with a voice that had such a soothing quality to it that it made Max want to lay his head on Her chest and never move it again. "Snowflakes can't leave any part of their beauty behind. Actually, nothing can. Except us. We can leave the beauty of our lives behind for everyone else."

She reached up and ran Her fingers through Pincus's hair.

"Would you like to go for a walk with me? We could continue to talk and get to know each other better," She said.

Pincus nodded, wondering how someone could fall so in love so quickly.

CHAPTER 4

Jericho being what it was, there were not many places to walk and talk. In addition to the Red Mill, there was Joe's Snack Bar, the Post Office, the Town Hall, the Town Library, and the Jericho Center Town Green, and that was Jericho. None of them seemed ideal to Pincus, who, the night before, had explored in great depth all the pamphlets neatly arranged on a rack beside the Sinclair Inn public telephone. He now had a fuller understanding, not only of what Jericho had to offer, but what it had to offer in decades passed. Forty-nine men from Jericho who died in the Civil War, all of them, it seemed, eighteen years old at the time, give or take a year. The population of Jericho was officially 1,687 back then. What a sad place this must have been, Pincus thought, turning pages in the pamphlet. An entire generation gone, the youth of their town no longer. How many other towns there must have been like them, and how many of the young men who fought and died knew what it was they were fighting for? That a government of the people, by the people, and for the people shall not perish from this earth? It has not. A more perfect union? It is not.

But it was Pincus's own more perfect union that occupied his mind now. He was a lost man, convinced that he would be unable to lead her, step by step, into love, certainly not the love that he now felt for Her.

"Do you like chocolate chip cookies?" She asked, aware of Pincus's state of mind and feeling some gentle coaching might be in order. "We could walk to the Country Store, if you like chocolate chip cookies. Abby makes the best."

"You like chocolate chip cookies?" Pincus asked in surprise.

"Why not? You think the Messiah wouldn't like cookies?" She teased.

"Are you saying you're the Messiah?" Pincus thought he'd struck pay dirt.

"No, I'm saying that I like chocolate chip cookies, Max, especially ones that are fresh-baked and still warm from the oven. How about you?"

"I had never actually thought about what Christ had to eat," Pincus mused. "The Bible doesn't have much to say about it, now that you think about it. You don't read, 'And thus Matthew and Jesus sitteth down for a quite palatable lamb pot-au-feu, with a side of pommes frites, and a mixed salad of fresh greens.'"

"Fish and bread I believe are mentioned," She advised Pincus, "and, if I remember correctly, in great and unending quantities," and She took Pincus's arm and led him in the direction of the Jericho Center Country Store.

"It must be difficult for you," Pincus launched into a first attempt at getting to know Her better.

"How is that?" She asked.

"Being the Messiah, being God," Pincus getting right to the heart of it.

"The Messiah was not God. God is God. Jesus said it quite clearly, I think. 'The Father is greater than I. John 14:28.'"

"Yes, but if Jesus is the Son of God, doesn't that also make him a God?"

"There is no such thing as a God. There is only one God, and that is God. It's a pretty simple concept, Max. One equals one."

"I get the concept," Pincus persisted, "But just because I consider my father to be greater than I am, that doesn't make me less of a human being than he is. Didn't I read that everything that belongs to the Father, except being the Father, the Son has also eternally from the Father, from whom He is eternally born?"

"Yes, the catechism says that. But it was written more than fifteen hundred years after Christ died by hundreds of cardinals trying to come up with something to sidetrack Martin Luther, and not without a lot of screaming and yelling along the way. The real miracle is that they could agree on anything at all."

"Christ wasn't the divine hypostasis, the wisdom of the world?"

"Nothing divine about him. Sorry, Max. And he never claimed to be. He was an advocate, counselor, and interpreter of celestial truths, and that's all."

"I am the Peraklit," Pincus quoted Christ.

"His word, not mine, but yes, Max. That's what he was, and all he wanted to be. But, as for your original question, yes it's hard for me. Very hard, in fact," and there was a catch in her voice, more from a weariness than a sadness.

Pincus looked over at her, surprised at both the answer and the emotion.

"Would you like to say something more about that, in the interest of our getting to know each other better?"

"Well, Max, I'm not like anyone else. I've always known that. People relate to me. I think they like me. But we're never close. There's always this wall between us. I don't like it, but there's nothing I can do about it. It hurts."

"I'm sure that people like you," Pincus said. "No — more than that, I'm sure they love you. You must know that."

"I do. But it's a strange kind of love, Max, a distant, respectful love, not the joining of hearts. I want to experience the joining of two hearts," She said, and was about to say more when a voice rang out from the porch of a house they were passing.

"Afternoon," a woman in her forties with blond hair called out, waving.

"Afternoon," She called back, as they continued to walk on.

"That's Sally Burkett. She teaches second grade. She and Dennis have been trying to have a baby forever, and she thinks it'll never happen, but it will. And soon," and now a smile returned to her face.

"You know that?" Pincus asked in surprise.

"I do," She said.

"And the Messiah is not God," Pincus confirmed.

"That's right. Have you ever awakened one day and said to yourself, something good is going to happen today. I can feel it. And it does. Does that make you God?" She asked.

Pincus was going to answer, but he was distracted by a sudden wind that picked up, causing a flurry of leaves to fall. The wind had a scent of winter to come, just the slightest chill. Pincus found himself breathing deeply to experience it.

He turned to keep looking behind him at the falling leaves and found, to his surprise, that Sally Burkett was walking twenty yards or so behind them, along with her husband and a half dozen others.

"We're being followed," Pincus said to Her.

"Not really. They just want to see where I'm going," She explained.

"Why don't they join us?" Pincus asked.

"Because they see we're talking to each other and don't want to disturb us, but, if I were alone, they wouldn't join me, either."

"Because of what you were saying about your relationships?"

"No, because I'm walking alone, and so they leave me to walk alone."

"Does this happen often?"

"Always. Ever since I was a child. Whenever I walk anywhere, after a while, I turn around, and there's a crowd behind me."

"And you don't mind it?"

"It just is. Once I get where I'm going, they'll catch up, and we'll talk. That's all they really want, just to talk."

"What about?"

"Life. They'll tell me what's been happening with them. Sometimes they'll ask what I think about this or that. They'll ask me questions. I'll ask them questions. We laugh. Sometimes we cry. It's like that."

"And you don't think that's being close to people?" Pincus puzzled.

"No. It isn't. The kind of closeness I imagine is something that lasts. This never lasts. It's for the moment. Then they go off on their own way, and I go off on mine. Sometimes their lives change. Mine never does."

It was exactly as She described. When they arrived at the Jericho Center Country Store and had purchased their cookies, they settled on the porch bench next to an ice chest, a bench that would soon be buried in pumpkins for sale. Behind them on the left was a mailbox, and on the right a bulletin board with small papers tacked to it offering services for babysitting, leaf-raking, septic cleaning, and general repairs. On the other side of the porch was a red Coca-Cola cooler, the kind that Theo had on the porch of his antique business, and in front of it, two Citgo gas pumps. Other than a laundry, Pincus couldn't imagine what a citizen of Jericho could possibly need that couldn't be found in this small, white wooden building.

The crowd that had been following them had grown to thirty or more, and were now inside purchasing drinks and cookies from Abby, a woman, to Pincus's surprise, in her mid-twenties, a one-year-old in a high chair beside her.

"Abby took over when her father died last year," She informed Pincus. "She started baking the cookies for him. He had colon cancer. When it was discovered, they all knew it was a death sentence. The cookies cheered him up, for as long as he could eat." Pincus had been fixed on her eyes, and now looked up and found, standing around them and sitting on the porch, a small crowd of people who had been listening to their conversation and now nodded.

"Abby gives the money she gets from the cookies to the Cancer Society," said a woman in her thirties with a Red Sox baseball hat out the back of which flopped a brunette ponytail. "And we all send in a little each month."

For the next hour they all talked and Pincus just listened. They talked about their children and their jobs, about their homes and their gardens, about their parents and grandparents, about birthdays and deaths. She said very little, other than every now and then repeating what she had just been told.

"Yes, taking care of a parent is very difficult," She would say, or, "It will take weeks before the bubblegum is entirely out of her hair," and this would be followed by laughter. And there was laughter, and the silence of people choking back tears, and, here and there a sigh of sympathy or recognition.

It was not group therapy, or neighborly conversation, but something else, something that Pincus couldn't describe, a sense of the community being human, being alive in this world now, and out of it there seemed to Pincus to come a certain joy, as if those there were receiving a spiritual infusion.

How this happened with Her was impossible to know. She made no great pronouncements, provided no special insights. But it was clear to Pincus that it was all because of Her. Pincus had no doubt that She was who She was reputed to be. The love for Her that had been in his heart transformed into a kind of love he had never before experienced, unlike the love for which he had been searching. It was as though to love Her was to love something so mysterious and so profound that it existed beyond his senses and could never be described.

"Do you know the story of the woman who was offered the choice between unlimited money for as long as she lived, or to live forever but in poverty?" She asked, and eighteen heads shook that they did not. 'Well,' the woman said, 'this is a tough one. Suppose I choose the money but then die tomorrow? On the other hand, what good would it be to live forever if I am constantly struggling to make ends meet? Today I am neither poor nor rich, nor do I know when I will die, so this is what I will do. I will stay as I am now and think it over, and I will let you know my decision the moment I know the hour of my death.' 'But then it will be too late,' she was told. 'No,' she said, 'because then I will have lived knowing that I had a choice between great wealth and eternal life, and I chose to live as I am.'"

Some laughed, though Pincus did not know why, and some wiped tears from their eyes, and then, as if all their meetings ended with her telling one tale or another, they said their goodbyes and drifted away.

"And still you don't believe you're loved?" Pincus asked in disbelief as they walked back toward the hospice.

"What did you think of the cookie?" She asked.

"It was very good. Now answer my question," Pincus persisted.

"I did answer your question, several hours ago, and now it's your turn," She responded, and She wrapped Her arms across Her chest in response to the chill that arrived as the sun began to set over the trees.

"What answer? My answer to what?"

"I thought we were getting to know each other better. You haven't told me anything about you, although my mother has filled me in on some of the more interesting details, but, then, it's my mother, so who knows what's true or not. She still insists I was created by her breathing microscopic souls when she was suffering from a severe case of nasal congestion, which, of course, makes absolutely no sense at all, because if her nose was all stopped up, how did the little souls get inside her, wiggle their way through the mucus?"

"Where is your mother by the way? After all the fuss she made about finding you, I was sure you'd be spending a lot of time together," Max decided not to deal with the issues regarding Her creation and the Thaumaturge.

"Why?"

"Well, because she was the one who brought me along on this expedition. She turned heaven and earth to see you."

"And she saw me, and she knows I'm doing just fine. And she tucks me in at night, if you really want to know."

"She tucks you in?"

"Well, not literally. But she comes to talk to me each night before I go to bed, even if I'm really late because of my going to see The Singing Machine. She'll still wait up in my room, and then we talk. Actually, it's the first time we've really talked. I won't pretend that she's always coherent, and that she doesn't fret over me like I'm a child, but, all in all, it's been good. So, how much did you love your wife?"

"What's the scale?" Pincus asked, his head whirling. While he was aware that, from time to time, she employed an approach best described as nonconsecutive reasoning, this didn't make it any easier to follow.

"You know what I mean, Max," and now She took his arm as they walked through the dappled shade, and leaning against him to share his warmth. "Did you love — really love her?"

"I think I did. But, somehow, it doesn't work like that. There's the initial attraction, the physical attraction, and then you're with each other a lot, and then you decide that you want to be with each other longer, and have a family together, and so you get married. She worked two jobs to put me through medical school, and it was hard, and we didn't see much of each other, but I finished. We felt we made it, so we started having children, and there was caring, and you call it love. You've gone through a lot together, and you know that nobody would have done it unless you meant something very special to them, nor would you have allowed them to do it if you hadn't felt deeply for them. But somewhere along the way the question of love goes unanswered until, in my case, one day it appears again, not with someone else, but as an idea, as a belief, as a longing."

She erupted in deep, prolonged laughter. He stopped and watched Her.

"Do you want to tell me what's so funny?" Pincus asked.

"Sure, Max," She answered. "That was simply the most depressing depiction of a relationship I've ever heard. I mean ever. If that's what getting close to someone is all about, then forget I ever asked you to show me what it's like."

"It's not like that," Pincus tried to regain his equilibrium. "You don't live with someone all those years if there's not something good about it."

"I didn't hear much good. It sounded like a business. She provided the revenue for your education. You then provided the revenue for your family. You engineered children. You formed an industrial partnership for their upbringing. Then, you dissolved the partnership. Are they all like that, or just yours?"

"Well," Pincus was becoming defensive, "every couple is different, but a lot of it is the same for everyone, I think. It's just the way it is. You can't expect that initial flame to burn forever, at least not as brightly as it did at first."

"Unless you keep fueling it."

"What fuel?" Pincus was becoming angry. "You don't have time for fuel. There're too many other things going on, things that you need to do just to live."

"But didn't you choose each other because of the feelings you had for each other?"

"Yes, but it doesn't work like that. You chose someone with whom you want to spend your life —"

"Which you didn't."

"Why are you doing this? You're making me angry," Pincus stopped walking and put his hands on Her shoulders.

And then, as they looked into each other's eyes, something between them crossed an invisible boundary, like a wave breaching a wall. Their voices lowered and came close to whispers.

"I'm doing this, Max, because I hate it when someone lies to himself, which we all do, but it still bothers me. You never gave up on the kind of love you had when you first met. You just buried it. Only it wouldn't stay buried, and that's why you left. That's why you're here, and it makes me angry."

Small tears began to work their way into Her eyes.

"It also hurts," She said, "because the pain would be unbearable if what we might have turns into what you've just described. It would be unbearable."

Pincus knew what was going to happen next. He would have done it, himself, were he not trembling with uncertainty about how it would be received.

She leaned forward, and their lips barely touched in a kiss of the kind a young child might give. But this kiss didn't end as a child's might. Her lips stayed on his, and Pincus placed his arm around Her waist, pulling Her to him, and She did the same. Slowly the kiss ended, and She rested Her head on Pincus's chest.

As Pincus enveloped Her in his arms, a thousand thoughts went through his mind, but it was all a muddle. The only thing that he could understand was how good it felt to have Her resting against his chest.

In a moment they separated and resumed walking down the road, now in dusk, as the sun had set. They held hands and said nothing. At the end of it all, when Pincus recalled that late afternoon, he remembered thinking how happy he had felt and how he had known then that it could only end badly.

"Will you come back to my room with me?" She asked. "Just to spend a little more time together, nothing more," She made certain that Pincus didn't misunderstand Her intentions. "I have to go to dinner in a while, but until then?"

Pincus nodded, grasped Her hand more tightly, and they continued down the wooded lane.

Of course, what She did not know was that, while She was away, Elliott and Sparky had carried a very bulky carpet into the hospice, claiming to a staff member that She had ordered it and they were to deposit it in Her room. Inside the carpet was Mrs. Bagwell.

She found out soon enough.

She had asked Pincus to wait outside the door to Her room while She tidied up. She disappeared inside, and then Pincus heard a strange noise, halfway between a cry and a shout. He quickly threw open the door to see Her standing beside Her bed, hopping up and down, heel and toe.

"There's a dead person on my bed! And she's not from here. Why is there a dead woman on my bed?"

A voice came out of a dark corner of the room, where Elliott sat on an armchair.

"I did that. I'm Elliott Pym. The group has requested some irrefutable proof of your messianic nature. I thought this would be a good experiment."

"Get her out of here!" She said.

"Does this mean you're conceding that you can't raise her from the dead?"

"This means I want this dead woman off my bed right now," She replied.

"If you can revive this woman, it shouldn't take long. A few minutes of your time at most. Jesus just called Lazarus, and out Lazarus walked, alive again." Elliott tried to give the experiment the historical significance it required.

"Lazarus walked out because he was never dead in the first place, Elliott," She said. "Live people can do that. Try calling someone who's alive to come and see what happens."

"No, no — Jesus raised Lazarus from the dead. They tell Jesus that Lazarus is very sick, and Jesus says, 'This sickness will not end in death. No, it is for God's glory so that God's son may be gloried through it.' I know I read that. In the Bible," Elliott presented his case.

"Okay, then why did Jesus weep when they told him that Lazarus was dead? Why does it say that 'anger welled up within him'? If Jesus knew it was all going to be okay, and at the end he would only be glorified by it all, then what's he all upset about?" She asked.

"What? What is he all upset about?" Elliott started to search through his well-reasoned argument for a response.

"Exactly. What's all the agony for? Jesus said that he'd make sure Lazarus lived, so he could have just come back from whatever business he has in Capernaum or Sycar or wherever and say, 'Watch this, everybody. Now Lazarus is dead. Now Lazarus is alive. Another miracle. Write that down, Simon.' Only problem is that Lazarus didn't die."

"No, no," Elliot pushed on, "Lazarus was definitely dead in the tomb. His sister says to Jesus, 'By this time there is a bad odor, for he has been there four days.' That sounds dead to me."

"It's a prediction, Elliott. Martha hadn't been inside the tomb because there was a huge stone over it. She was simply predicting that, after four days, there would be a bad odor. She had not gone into the tomb and actually smelled it."

"You're saying that Lazarus was never dead," Elliott stalled for time.

"What I'm saying," She said emphatically, "is Jesus thought that Lazarus, his best friend, was going to be okay, and foolishly predicted it, relying on God to take care of things, so Jesus went off to do what Son of Men do, and then four days later Jesus finds out he blew it, that God kind of let him down, that his best friend died without Jesus being beside him. So Jesus is really upset with himself for not being there, as he should be, which is why he cries and berates himself. But he has one last shot at getting back in the game. Medicine being what it was in those days, it was not unusual for people thought to be dead not to be dead at all, but in a coma, or have shallow breathing, or something, so Jesus takes a shot, has them remove the stone from the tomb, crosses his fingers and calls out to Lazarus, who hears his name, stirs, and Jesus gets lucky and out the guy walks, probably happier at not being sealed in a tomb forever when he's not dead than angry at Jesus for leaving his bedside when he's about to croak. Now will you please get this dead lady out of my room!"

"What the hell is going on here?!"

They all turned to find a large man in his fifties with a salt-and-pepper beard, Seth Binder, standing in the open doorway.

"She's raising this poor woman from the dead," Elliott thought this might induce Her to perform. "You want to watch?"

"My ass, She's raising her from the dead. This is my mother-in-law, and I've been waiting half my life for her to die. You bring her back to life, and they'll be more than one dead person in this room. There's no way this woman is going anywhere except into her grave, six feet down, in a sealed box, with a ton of concrete on top of it, and it can't be soon enough."

"A lot of people think that She's the Messiah," Elliott offered.

"I've heard. And every December when I put on that red suit with the white fur trim there are a lot of people who think I'm Santy Claus," Seth responded, walked to the bed, picked up his mother-in-law, and hoisted her over his shoulder.

"Holy shit, she weighs a ton. For years I've been telling her to cut down on the donuts, but would she listen?" and out the door Seth went, Mrs. Bagwell's arms flapping up and down on his back like the ends of a large scarf.

Elliott watched the pair disappear, then shrugged.

"Well, I guess that's it. No resurrection from the dead this time, huh?" Elliott said and slid past her out the door, his eyes averting contact with Hers.

CHAPTER 5

It is not clear whether it was that night, or a night much later, that She was in the garden lighting candles after the death of Buster Pettigrew, a man in his eighties who, before dying, had wanted forgiveness for repeatedly cheating on his wife during late night calls to repair the furnaces of his heating business clients. He had wanted to confess to Sally, his wife, because the guilt was almost more than he could bear, but he realized that it would only hurt her and he suspected that she already knew. On her deathbed Sally had said to him, "I want you to know, Buster, that I understand. And that I still love you," and then she died. It had taken more than a month for Buster to stop weeping. He woke up weeping, and he went to sleep weeping. He ate weeping, and he peed weeping. Slowly it got better, but, even in his last days he would sometimes wake up in the middle of the night, and he'd find that his pillow was wet with tears, and he'd know why.

"Will I be forgiven?" he had asked Her with his last breath.

She had nodded, and leaned down and kissed Buster on his head. Buster smiled, flashing his porcelain teeth, and he died.

So now She lit candles for Buster in the garden. It was a tradition She had started that, when someone dies at the hospice, candles are lit along the paths and among the flowers. The candles sit in small paper bags, the type used for school lunches, and the glow brings a life to the garden that suggests dozen of souls still burning brightly, even after death. The residents look out their windows and see the flickering lights spread throughout the garden, and it gives them peace of mind. She was doing this when Florence appeared.

"They said I could find you here," Florence said. "Am I disturbing you?"

"Not at all. Would you mind helping?" She asked, reached in her pocket, and handed Florence a lighter.

"Of course," Florence said, as she kneeled and lit the candle in the bag by a bed of violets. "I'm so sorry about Elliott. I came to apologize for him, because I know he never would. None of the rest of us knew he'd be doing something crazy like putting a dead person in your bed."

"He's your husband?" She asked.

"No, my brother-in-law, well, former brother-in-law. His brother is Sparky, who I know you've met. We're no longer married, although we still live together in the same house, but we no longer share a bed, or a bedroom," and Florence looked up, wondering whether she was already becoming too personal, and she decided to redirect the conversation to the purpose of her visit, even though she knew that offering an apology for Elliott was just an excuse for coming and was in no way the purpose of her visit.

"Elliott didn't mean to be disrespectful," Florence explained, "only to obtain, the word he uses often, certitude. He wants proof for just about everything. It's not that he doesn't believe what you say, or even what he sees with his own eyes, but for certitude apparently everything has to be experimentally verified. It requires one to be very exact in what one tells him. If I told him I'd just flown, he would push me off the nearest building before I could explain that it was in an airplane."

They both laughed.

"Sparky is just the opposite," Florence continued. "He'll believe anything. He'll believe what he wants to believe. He invents the world as he goes along, and it's often not the same world that the rest of us inhabit. I used to love him for it. Then it became tiresome, but the truth is that sometimes I wonder whether it isn't better." Florence stopped and looked around her at all the glowing bags throughout the garden.

"Why are we doing this?" Florence asked. "What are we celebrating?"

"It's a memorial," She said.

Florence said nothing. She looked out at the small lights dotting the landscape and nodded, deciding not to question any further.

"If you sit on the bench over there by the fountain, there's an elevation, and you can get the best view," She told Florence, who followed Her over to the bench, where they sat side by side.

"It's quite lovely," Florence told Her. "I'm not really one for memorials, but, if I were, this would be special," and Florence let out the tiniest of sighs. "It's hard to find things in life that are special, whatever that means, 'special,' I've never been sure, because I think that all of us find life to be disappointing, don't you?" Florence went on, not waiting for Her to respond. "So little of what we dreamed our lives would be ever comes true. So why bother to have dreams at all? The joys are never as sweet, the loves are never as great, and the music is never as rich as we imagined — except, of course, for The Singing Machine."

She nodded.

"Sparky made The Singing Machine for me. He never said so, but I know he did it for me. He knows how disappointed I've been, and he wanted to build something that would show me something that was absolutely perfect," Florence said. "The song of The Singing Machine is perfect."

"Yes," She said. "It is perfect."

"The problem is that it's had exactly the opposite effect of what Sparky wanted," and Florence looked up at the sky, which she noticed was speckled with stars, as though someone had thrown a handful of silvery sand into a black pond. "Every time that damn machine sings its perfect song, it just reminds me of how imperfect everything else is."

Florence was going to continue, but her throat caught with emotion, so she just took a long, deep breath.

"I don't know. I think that every moment you experience shares in perfection to some extent," Her voice was still and thin, like a sustained note. "Nothing we know will ever achieve all of it, but, when it comes close to perfection, then it becomes 'special,'" and She placed Her hand lightly on Florence's arm. "I think that's what you mean when you say that something is special, that it shares in that perfection, that it reminds you that there's beauty, harmony, and grace that exist on a plane far beyond what we'll ever experience. I think these moments are like small windows that every so often open to give us a glimpse of the landscape of absolute perfection in which everything shares, more or less but never completely. Even us."

Florence nodded.

"I don't complain much, you know. I don't go around whining about how bad it all is, because it's not so bad, it's just less than what I wanted, but I'm used to it now, so, in a way, it's okay. It's the way it is."

Her head still tilted up toward the flickering sky, Florence found herself back at the age of six, her mother, who died years ago, tying the ribbon of a dress around her waist. It was a pale blue ribbon that went with a white organdy dress that billowed out like a bell from her waist, stiff and white as white, moving in tiny circles as she walked in her black patent leather shoes with the heels that went click-clack-click with each step. She had never felt so girly, and she liked this feeling. She felt beautiful. It was all new to her. It promised wonderful things to come, and she did a little girly beautiful dance that made her mother laugh. Florence couldn't remember where she had been going, whether to church, or a party, or for a visit. She only felt the hands of her mother on her back, tying the ribbon at her waist, and there in the garden, with the sky lit up with stars and the ground glowing with candles, she wanted to turn and face her mother and stand on her toes and kiss her on the cheek and reach up and put her arms around her neck once more.

And now, suddenly, Florence felt compelled to dance. She arose from the bench, placed her leg out like a ballerina, and then proceeded to dance in and out of the candlelit bags, arms waving, body swaying — feeling light as air, girly, beautiful, six years old.

She watched Florence's performance in silence, and might have joined in the dance, herself, had a voice not rang out from the far end of the garden.

"Hello?" Sparky called. "Are you there? They said you were here."

"Sparky?" Florence called back in shock, and she stopped her dance. "What are you doing here, Sparky?"

The answer came instantly. On the top of Sparky's head was a metal frame, and now it began to ignite, a line of fireworks spelling out letters — "G O D."

"Sparky, what are you doing?!" Florence shouted.

More letters ignited.

"I S"

"Florence? Is that you, Florence?"

"L O V E"

A small pinwheel on top of the letters began to spin, and fireworks started to shoot into the sky, sizzling and cracking, booming when they reached the apogee of their flight.

Florence dropped to her knees in dismay and buried her head in her hands, as She marched down the path, between the oleander and the hydrangea, in the direction of the man with the flaming "GOD IS LOVE" across his forehead, while roman candles and bottle rockets shot off from the top of his head. When She reached Sparky, She folded her arms tightly across her chest.

"You have to go home now, Sparky," She said between pursed lips.

"I think Florence has noticed me, what do you think?"

"What I think is that you can't keep waking people up like this, morning and night. Are you able to shut that thing off?"

"I thought you'd be impressed," Sparky said.

"I'm very impressed by what you've done here, Sparky, and even more so that you're not getting third-degree burns from it, but can — you — turn — it — off?"

"It's almost off already. Just wait." And at this, three croisettes shot off Sparky's head far into the sky, exploding in intersecting trails and forming an impressive star, while, simultaneously, the sign on his forehead slowly died out, leaving only a smoldering "D" from "GOD," "I" from "IS," and "E" from "LOVE."

"So, what do you think?" Sparky asked, a smile on his face, his eyes searching Hers for a sign, any sign, of approval, with "D I E" smoldering on his head.

It was not to come. At that moment a note sounded in the distance, and then another with the first, and then a third, and The Singing Machine began its song.

CHAPTER 6

Florence did not accompany Her to The Singing Machine, but stayed behind to soak Sparky's head in the fountain, hoping to cool it down enough to prevent blistering from the heat of his performance.

Meyer was already at The Singing Machine, whose song was in its full glory by the time She arrived. At first She gave no indication that She knew he was there. She swayed with the music, as though in a trance, and walked around The Singing Machine in the way a ballerina might cross a stage, toes pointed, one leg extended and then the other. It was not Machine and Woman, but Machinewoman, and it made Meyer wonder whether this wasn't what had been intended from the very start, that The Singing Machine had waited to be completed by Her appearance.

She looked over at Meyer and nodded, as though She had been reading his thoughts. Meyer took this as a sign that it was acceptable to engage Her.

"Will we ever understand its song?" Meyer asked Her, his accent now vaguely German. "We have been written into the laws of nature as conscious beings, but is it possible to step outside of ourselves to understand the very cosmic order that has produced us, that has produced a machine that sings when it wants and what it wants, but on a level of such magnificence that it goes beyond the realm of the physical and enters the mystical?"

Meyer had long ago learned that the best way to get a woman's attention was through philosophy. For women, philosophy was sensual. It signified that they were being addressed as more than sexual objects. For women, Meyer had quickly discovered that metaphysics was, in the vernacular, a turn-on. It was a source of immense disappointment that, in spite of numerous and exhaustive attempts during the year they lived together, She, alone in his experience, appeared to be immune to such an approach. Now, he claimed, to compensate, that his feelings for Her had been solely as mentor and student. At times he even believed it.

"Not that the mystical may not be as real as anything else," Meyer continued, hoping that at long last he might hit paydirt. "Abstract concepts such as logic, number, soul, and, yes, even God, recur throughout history as the firmest ground on which to build a picture of reality that has any hope of permanent dependability."

"God is not an abstract concept," She answered. "God's only abstract when we think of God as being some sort of being — omniscient, omnipotent, omnipresent. There's nothing abstract about God if God is everywhere and everything — the stars, oceans, daylight, and nighttime, what grows and what dies — us. All about us is an immense flowering into Deity, the beating of the heart of God," and She curtsied, as though her words were part of the dance, and then spun away in a series of pirouettes.

"Ah, yes, dear old Spinoza," he said in response to Her depiction of God as being all about us, but equally to indicate that he could hold his own in this dialogue. "But, for that, one has to assume that the world is both rational and intelligible. If, as with mysticism, there are facts that have to be accepted without reason, then rationality breaks down and the world is absurd."

She stopped dancing and spoke to Meyer from the other side of The Singing Machine as it sang on.

"The mystic world is no less real than your physical world simply because it's a world experienced only by the heart. Why do you even try to come up with great formulas to account for the 'facts,' because you'll never come up with a Theory of Everything. There is no formula that can deliver all truth, all harmony, all simplicity. No rational system can be proved to be both consistent and complete. There'll always be some openness and mystery, something unexplained. Your facts, your mathematics, get you only so far, and then you get stuck."

And now The Singing Machine sang out a glorious affirmation, surprising Meyer, and he would have stopped right there and let things stay as they were had he not found that Her last dialogue had given him a rather large erection. He wondered whether She was on to his game and was actually more adept at it than he was. Had She, so to speak, turned the tables on him, stimulating him as he had so often tried to do to Her?

"Are you suggesting that we abandon reason?" Meyer parried the best he could.

"Have you wondered," She continued as the music ended, "why the universe goes to all the bother of existing? What is it that breathes fire into your equations and makes a universe for them to describe? If you're looking for a rational explanation for nature, then you have to find that explanation outside the physical world — in something metaphysical, in God or something like God. The universe cannot contain within itself an explanation for itself, can it?"

Meyer turned his back to Her, and awkwardly moved to a large stone, where he sat down and crossed his legs.

"The universe exists because it's good that it does so, and that's it," She said as She appeared from the other side of The Singing Machine. "That goodness is compelled to create a universe because it's good that it does so."

"And that goodness is God?" Meyer guessed.

"Yes," She said, and The Singing Machine began a fugue.

"I will concede that, if the universe has an explanation, it can't explain itself, and it must be explained by something outside itself, for example God," Meyer tried to correct his problem with the equivalent of a philosophical cold shower. "But what, then, explains God?"

Meyer had hoped that this profound question would produce a salutary effect on his condition, which was becoming more extreme with every word, but it had the opposite effect, and Meyer now placed his hands discretely on his crotch, hoping She wouldn't notice, but having no choice in the matter, as he was beginning to hear the faint sound of his zipper pulling apart, link by link.

"The fact is that no one has really proved that God exists," Meyer said in desperation. "The universe has a very good design, but does a design imply a designer? A good universe might look designed to us, even if it had not been."

"Nor has anyone proved that God does not exist," She smiled and did a sweeping bow, as The Singing Machine broke into a waltz and She danced around to the back of it.

"Yes," Meyer riposted, "but, once again, what would it mean to say that something exists whose existence and nonexistence could never be proved?"

She looked at Meyer for a moment, then She sat on the ground, pulled up Her knees and wrapped her arms around them.

"Isn't that the point?" She asked. "There was once a man who was asked to play Twenty Questions. He asked questions, and the answers came back. 'Is it bigger than a breadbox?' 'Is it a living thing?' Eventually, he asked, 'Is it a cloud?' 'Yes!' he was told, and then everyone laughed because they revealed to him that they had not chosen an answer in advance. They had all agreed to answer his questions purely at random, as long as they were consistent with the other answers they had already given him. So this game wasn't arbitrary; the answers were determined by the questions he asked, but it was also by chance, since they might have given many different answers along the way as long as they were consistent, in spite of his questions being random. It's the same for us. Our questions determine the answers, and how fortunate we are that God has given us minds that can both ask and answer the questions. Our existence as rational conscious beings wasn't just an incidental blip in the great cosmic drama. Our involvement is too intimate. And that's that."

She stood up.

"It was nice talking to you," She said. "This discussion has been quite stimulating, don't you think?" She trilled merrily as She walked away. And The Singing Machine ended its song.

Throughout this pageant, Pincus sat on a wooden chair at the window of his bedroom, taking it all in. In the midst of the music, weaving in and out like counterpoint, he could make out a word, a phrase, a notion of what was being said, but no more. Rational, intelligible, mystical, goodness — the words were to Pincus like the buds of flowers opening to reveal their blossom, turning the spectacle of the music, the dialogue, and Her dance into a garden not unlike the one She had planted behind the Hospice of Our Lady of Lament.

Pincus might have worked harder to discern more meaning, but his mind was occupied now with one sensation: Her kiss. He could still feel the brush of Her lips against his that afternoon, but had no more sense of their meaning than he did of the events that he viewed distractedly from his window.

He remembered a Chekhov story he had read in his youth in which a military officer with no social skills, Ryabovich, finds himself at a General's party, and, being a poor conversationalist and graceless dancer, saves himself from embarrassment by ducking into a dark room, where a moment later a strange woman appears in the dark, wraps her arms about his neck, whispers "At last!" and kisses him passionately, only to pull back, shriek, and run from the room when she realizes her mistake. While he tries to tell himself that it was all an accident, he finds himself embracing it as a wondrously radiant event, and it transforms his life. Months later he realizes that his romantic dreams were wildly disproportionate to their cause, and the whole world becomes for him an aimless gest.

"Am I Ryabovich?" Pincus wondered.

Pincus had been pondering this since he had joined Her for dinner after the unfortunate incident with the experimental corpse Elliott had so decorously placed on Her bed. He hadn't been quite sure how to approach the subject of the kiss, and so he decided to deal with it obliquely.

"I'd like to ask you out for a date this weekend," Pincus had told Her over their salads.

"What's that?" She asked.

"What's a date? You don't know what a date is?" and Pincus looked around the room at the other diners, concerned that he might have asked too loudly, but no one seemed to notice. "Surely you've been out on a date before."

"Max, I already told you. I was with my mother until I was eleven, and then in a convent with all girls until I left for here, with very few stops along the way, and not the kind of stops where boys are asking you out on dates. So, just tell me what we're supposed to do, and, if this interests me, I promise to do my best, okay?" and She rested Her hand on Pincus's arm, aware of his confused state.

"When two people go out on a date, it's one of those ask-answer things. One or the other of them makes the request and then there is a response. So there's what might be called a declaration of intention. This is a date," Pincus felt that this was a very good introductory statement.

"I see," She tried to go with it, seeing how hard Pincus was working. "Then what?"

"Then what?" Pincus started to reflect.

"Well, yes. How is it different from when we're just together? Like before. Could we have been on a date, but I didn't know it?"

"Well, as I said, a date requires some sort of mutual declaration of intention," Pincus approached the subject axiomatically.

"What's the intention?" She asked, now seeming to become more interested in this phenomenon.

"To see how it feels to be together — whether we're comfortable with each other, whether we have things in common, whether we 'click,' whether we like each other — to become close, if that's the way things work out," Pincus thought he had given quite an informative description, although he was becoming concerned that he might be draining datehood of all things it was intended to be.

"Do we have sex at the end of it? Is that the goal — I mean, if we 'click'?" She asked with wide eyes.

Pincus felt he had to tread very carefully here. She waited, Her eyes fixed on those of Pincus.

"It's not the goal," Pincus said slowly. "It's something that might or might not develop, depending on how the evening goes."

"But it's something you would like, something you're hoping for, and that's why you're asking me out on a date?" She inquired.

Pincus thought hard and long.

"Okay, look, not so long ago you told me you wanted to know about love, the kind of love that happens between a man and a woman. A date is a small first step. I want to spend some time with you, that's all, just the two of us, for us to have a good time. I suppose that's the overall goal right now, if there is one — for it to be fun," Pincus said, deciding not to mention that he was now so in love with Her that he could barely breathe.

"What I'd like," Pincus formed his words with precision, "in terms of this 'date' business is simply to be with you, to show you that I care."

"But I already know that, Max."

Pincus said nothing. He just looked at Her, Her words washing over him like a mist on a May morning.

"Would you like to go out with me on a date this Saturday evening?" Pincus finally asked.

"Sure," She said.

CHAPTER 7

"You're taking her out on a date?" Sister Gloria Gloria cried out in disbelief the next morning. The Ecclesia had, one by one, drifted into the living room of the Sinclair Inn after breakfast to catch up on events and make plans.

"Yes," Pincus said, "and how do you know?"

"She told Her mother, who, by the way, is now out shopping for 'date attire,' and after Her mother told me, I felt I had an obligation to inform the others," Sister answered.

"You can't take Her out on a date, Max," Sparky pleaded.

"Why not?" Pincus asked.

"Because you don't date the Messiah," Elliott announced. "It's unseemly."

"Well, first of all, She's never said She was the Messiah," Pincus answered. "And if She were the Messiah and decided She wanted to date, that ought to settle things right there. The Messiah certainly knows what is and is not 'unseemly' for Her to do."

"I thought She was the Mother of all Gods," Meyer said sarcastically. "I'm not sure being the Mother of all Gods and the Messiah are compatible. I think She has to choose."

"You don't choose what kind of god you are, for chrissakes," Elliott told Meyer. "You are what you are. As far as I know, She hasn't said She is anything other than a woman who works at the local hospice, has a flair for arguing philosophy and religion, and has a strange attraction to our Singing Machine."

"I think The Singing Machine is becoming a problem," Meyer offered.

"How is that?" Florence asked, genuinely interested, as she, too, was beginning to feel that there was something about The Singing Machine that was getting in the way.

"The way She is drawn to it," Pincus said. "Meyer is right. It seems to have taken on an importance to Her that's distracting Her from why we're here."

"You can't date the Messiah, and that's final," Sister Gloria Gloria reiterated.

"I thought you didn't believe that She was the Messiah," Pincus retorted.

"I don't," Sister answered, "but there's nothing in this world that's one hundred percent certain."

"I think I know the real problem here," Theo offered, and a smile spread across his face. There was silence and all heads turned to face Theo.

"You all don't want Max to fuck Her," Theo said sweetly.

There was the expected uproar. Theo tried to calm the waters he had agitated.

"Maybe She's not interested," Theo offered. "Jesus was a virgin."

"And you know this because?..." Pincus asked.

"The Bible?" Theo responded, but it was not said with a great deal of certainty, and he was hoping to gather support elsewhere.

"Really?" a voice came from the doorway. It was Her. All heads spun toward Her.

"Jesus was a virgin? He was just a nice Jewish guy who remained a virgin for all thirty-three years of his life, typical of Jewish guys, as we all know," She said tartly. "More to the point, since all the Gospels make a very big deal about how Jesus is directly from the seed of David, we've got some genetics to deal with her. It's no secret that David had a sex life that makes one wonder how he had time for anything else. Chronicles is basically a Filofax of David's sex life. He had Amnon by Ahinoam, Daniel by Abigail, Absalom by Maacah,

Adonijah by Haggith, Shephatiah by Abital, and Ithream by Eglah. By Bathsheba his sons were Shammua, Shobab, Nathan, and Solomon. His sons born in Jerusalem by other wives and concubines included Ibhar, Elishua, Eliphelet, Nogah, Nepheg, Japhia, Elishama, and Eliada. He had at least one daughter, Tamar by Maacah. There were countless others, but I can only suppose that the scribes ran out of parchment. So, let's just say that, taking into account his religion and his genetics, the question of whether Jesus remained a virgin until the age of thirty-three remains kind of an open one. I need to talk to you, Max," She smiled sweetly.

"Me?" Pincus asked.

"Yes, that's why I'm here. So come on," She gestured to Pincus, and off they went.

There was a prolonged silence after She and Pincus had gone, and then it was Florence who spoke.

"I don't know the Bible well enough to contradict Her, but is that all true?" Florence asked the group. "And, if it is, how does She know all that?"

"She reads a lot," Theo answered.

"She's memorized the Bible," Meyer explained. "She had me do it, too. It's not that hard, actually — it just takes time. A lot of time."

"I must say I found what She said to be very unsatisfactory," Elliott said.

"Unsatisfactory?" Sister Gloria Gloria finally regained her ability to speak. "She made our Lord Jesus Christ out to be some sort of horny toad, hopping from bed to bed until they finally nailed him down."

"I believe you'll find it's a horned toad, not a horny toad," Theo said.

"What I meant by it being unsatisfactory," Elliott ignored Theo's comment, "is that this is the first time She has appeared before all of us, and what do we get, a detailed depiction of the escapades of a Biblical character of dubious distinction."

"Dubious distinction?" a head appeared on the other side of the large screened window. It was Her, with Pincus standing patiently and somewhat nervously behind Her.

"Of dubious distinction? You've got to be kidding. David, the King of the Jews — sound familiar — is mentioned in the Bible one thousand one hundred and thirty-five times. He was a superb statesman and warrior, not to mention a prophet, musician, and poet. Of the one hundred and fifty Psalms in the Bible, seventy-three are signed by David, and the rest most likely are his. God seemed to be impressed enough with him to make a covenant that David would produce a dynasty of kings that would never end, that would play a vital part in God's great plan of salvation, and, in fact, for the next five hundred years direct descendants of David ruled, until the Babylonians killed all the sons of King Zedekiah, making him watch as they did it, then gouged out his eyes, and led him in chains to Babylon, and that pretty much put an end to the reign of the Kings of David. But God still kept His word, which is why, and see whether this rings a bell for anybody, the Angel Gabriel says to Mary, 'Fear not, Mary, for thou hast found favor with God. And, behold, thou shalt conceive in thy womb, and bring forth a son, and shalt call his name Jesus. He shall be great, and shall be called the Son of the Highest, and the Lord God shall give unto him the throne of his father David.' Now, I truly apologize for not staying longer, but I have already had the very great pleasure of engaging in spirited conversation with many of you, and it seems to me that you've decided to run me through some sort of Ecclesiastical gauntlet that I pray to God I've nearly completed, and I can't for the life of me figure out what it is that you all really want from me that I can actually give you, but if anyone of you, or all of you, wish to continue this, I will make myself available on Sunday.

"However, I plan to be hiking, so those who wish to join me should wear good hiking shoes, not street shoes and not sneaks, and bring a backpack with water and some food and a bottle of wine if it interests you, although it's not recommended for a hike. In the meantime, I'm going," and She left with Pincus in tow, mumbling under her breath, "... dubious distinction ..."

"God, She's in a mood," Sparky noted.

"Okay, look," Meyer spoke with a most serious tone, "in a way She's right. It seems like we've been here forever, and what have we actually accomplished? Do we know whether She is the Messiah? No, we do not. Do we know why The Singing Machine sings? No, we do not. Do we know the meaning of its song? No, we do not."

"You have a plan?" Sparky asked hopefully.

"I do," Meyer announced. "We should accept Her invitation and we should go with Her on Her hike. By Sunday we will all have spoken individually with Her, and when we're all together with Her, we'll investigate further. We'll ask Her the questions we all want to know. Then on Monday morning, we should vote."

"On what? Is She running for some office?" Sister asked in disbelief. "We're going to elect Her God? Are you totally crazy?"

"We need to vote on whether She is our Savior come for the second time or not," Meyer said.

"We're going to vote on whether someone's God?" Elliot asked.

"We're going to put our minds together and give it serious thought and see whether, from our interactions with Her, we feel that it is likely that She is the Messiah. It will be a collective judgment," Meyer explained.

"And then?" Florence asked. "Do we give Her a throne and a scepter or something?"

"Then we ask Her to tell us the meaning of the song of The Singing Machine — if we feel that She is the Messiah," Meyer said.

There was a long silence as the Ecclesia considered Meyer's proposition.

"I don't like this at all," Sister finally said. "There's something undemocratic about voting for God."

"But I think Meyer is right," Elliott said. "It's time to get some resolution here."

"If She's not what we thought She was, then we're done here," Meyer said.

"And if She is?" Sparky asked hopefully.

Meyer reached over and placed his hand on Sparky's shoulder.

"Then we get religion," he said.

There was a moment of contemplative silence and then Theo spoke.

"Do you think She really counted all one thousand one hundred and thirty-five times the word 'David' appears in the Bible?" Theo asked.

It was this exact question that Pincus asked as he walked with Her through a canopy of the spindly branches of trees now mostly bare of their leaves. They seemed to have lost their foliage at an alarmingly rapid rate, the result of the cold Vermont nights and the breezes that swept down from Mount Mansfield, and Pincus was not at all pleased to see this.

"Don't be ridiculous," She answered Pincus's inquiry about the number of references to David. "I have other things to do with my time. I read it somewhere, and, while I don't normally accept any numbers that come from someone else unless I've counted myself, this seemed believable and I felt it could come in handy in the future, which it did."

"I must apologize for the others," he said to Her. "But, when it comes right down to it, they care about religion like I care about the mating ritual of the mollusk. You could be the Savior or you could not be the Savior. It's of absolutely no consequence to them, in spite of their bleating, just as long as their own pain is relieved. That's why they've come. That and the song of The Singing Machine. It drives them nuts, why it sings on its own, and what that means. They expect that when the mystery of it is unraveled, all will become clear and the world will have meaning for them."

These are the words that Pincus spoke, but within them could be discerned the smallest hope, that, in fact, something somewhere did make sense, and that, perhaps, The Singing Machine knew what it was.

"You don't have to apologize for them," She said. "I understand why they're here and what they want, and religion is not it. In fact, Meyer absolutely hates religion."

"The opiate of the people," Pincus remarked.

"As a Marxist, and not a very good one by the way, Meyer thinks that the world is unfair, even cruel. He thinks that all religion does is give those who are suffering hope, that things will get better in this life or in the next. But you know what Meyer has missed, Max?" She said, a light dancing in her eyes. "Besides that, Marx, who hated the bourgeoisie, spent most of his life begging his wealthy parents for money, and he's been totally misquoted. Totally. Yes, he said that religion is the opium of the people, but that's not the whole quote. The quote begins by his calling religion 'the sigh of the oppressed creature, the heart of a heartless world, the soul of soulless conditions.' Marx believed that religion helps us deal with an intolerable situation, and I don't see the problem with that."

"Well," Pincus offered, reverting to his medical training, "the thing about opium is that it relieves the pain but doesn't solve its cause. As long as people are dulled to the reality, nothing gets better. We grab on to religion to fill the void."

She said nothing in reply, just looked into his eyes, and continued walking. For the next few moments they walked in silence, as Pincus wondered why She had come and what She wanted with him. Overhead, a large flock of birds migrated south, what Pincus supposed were the last stragglers heading for warmer climes. He watched them disappear over the trees with envy.

"What Meyer's philosophy boils down to is this," Pincus finally said to break the silence. "How do we live together if self-interest will always win over everything else? Do you have an answer to that?" And, as he asked, it was clear that Meyer's question was also his.

"My answer is this. What would good be without evil? What

would pleasure be without pain, victory without defeat, light without the darkness? So why not have a radiance to light our way through the times of darkness? When we have to choose the path to take, what would guide us?"

"Our hearts," Pincus said. "And there would be a world without suffering."

"There will always be suffering. It's part of the human condition," She said.

"I thought the Second Coming was to bring heaven on earth, when evil would be no more."

"Yes, well," She countered, "there is no Second Coming and never was. Somebody made it up. Christ is quoted twice in Matthew, twice in Mark, and then again in Luke as telling the apostles, 'There are some standing here, which shall not taste death, till they see the Son of Man coming in His kingdom,' and they never got to see Him coming in His kingdom, which, by the way, is why the Church quickly changed its emphasis from the Second Coming to the Resurrection and the promise of eternal life, because a number of the faithful noted that the apostles weren't around any longer, nor had Jesus appeared, and this made for a problem. But if there were a Second Coming, it wouldn't be to war against evil. It would be to rejoice."

"Over what?" Pincus thought about the wars and catastrophes he had compiled in his year of research.

"To rejoice that good has always prevailed against evil. It has taken time, and sacrifice, and suffering, but eventually and always good has defeated evil."

"At what cost?"

"At great cost. And often it has taken centuries. But it is how it is, and it will never end. Would you like to know why?"

Pincus nodded, although he wasn't certain he did want to know.

"The eyes of the innocents," She said. "As long as there are the eyes of the innocents, good will prevail, even over self-interest. They light our way."

For a moment they stood there, looking into each other's eyes. Finally, Pincus asked the question that had been filling his brain.

"You came to see me. Is there something specific, besides Marxist doctrine, that you wanted to speak to me about?" he asked with some dread.

"Specific? Not really."

"Then something, perhaps, of a nonspecific nature?" and Pincus and She continued to stand, looking into each other's eyes.

"I wanted to take the pressure off our date, Max. I just wanted to be with you without any agenda."

"That's it?"

"That's it. I wanted to lower your expectations," She smiled.

"Thank you," he said, not as relieved as he thought he might have been.

"You're most welcome," She continued to smile, then leaned forward, and Pincus leaned and met Her halfway. They kissed, and, for that brief moment, Pincus believed that everything just might be fine.

CHAPTER 8

When She arrived back at Her room, She found Her bed covered with newly-bought clothes and Her mother sitting in the chair by the window, reading an old copy of *People* magazine.

"What are all these clothes doing on my bed, Mom?" She asked.

For your date," Rosalie smiled maternally. "You need to dress for your date, and I know you don't have anything decent."

"I thought you were against me going out with Max," She pointed out.

"I was when you told me. Now I'm not any longer," Rosalie responded. This was not entirely true. It had never occurred to her, considering the difference in their ages, that things would develop as they appeared to be between Pincus and her daughter. Now that they had, she had decided that the best way to put an end to everything would be for her daughter to learn as quickly as possible that She and Pincus had absolutely nothing in common, and then Rosalie would whisk Her away from this place at dawn's early light. To this end, Rosalie walked over to the bed and held up a white dress with red flowers.

"What do you think?" she asked. "I think you'd look stunning in it."

"It looks like wallpaper. I'm not wearing wallpaper, Mom. In fact, I'm not wearing any of these, so take them back."

"What do you think about this one?" she Rosalie asked, undeterred.

"Mother, please. I'm not a child. I really don't need you to dress me."

"Yes, you really do. I saw what was in your closet. Rags. All rags."

"You went into my closet?! Who said you could go into my closet?!"

"I'm your mother, dear. I'm entitled to go into your closet," Rosalie offered.

"No, you're not. You're not entitled to anything of the sort."

"I hate it when we get into these things. I just hate it," and Rosalie let out a long sigh of desperation to emphasize her point.

"Well, me, too, Mom. Me, too. I hate it when you go into my closet!" She shouted.

"Oh, for godsakes!" Rosalie shouted back. "Does it really matter? It's not as though I took anything!"

"Yes, it matters!"

Two heads appeared on the other side of the window screen, an elderly couple, Mr. and Mrs. Fleming.

"Everything okay in here?" Mr. Fleming called through the screen.

"Yeah, yeah, we're fine. I was just shouting at my mother," She said.

The two looked at each other, shrugged, and then left.

Rosalie went to the window and watched in silence as the couple walked away, Mr. Fleming pulling his wife's cardigan higher up on her shoulders, a chill having settled in the garden.

"Are they both dying?" Rosalie asked.

"No, just her. She has a few more weeks. He'll die within six months," She said.

"You said he wasn't sick."

"He isn't, but he won't want to live without her after sixty-one years of marriage, and, when you don't want to live, you don't. He'll die after he sees the jonquils come out in April."

"How do you know that?"

"I don't know how I know. I just do."

"Try the dress. The blue one. Blue's always been a good color for you."

She took in a long breath, slowly exhaled. "Why are you doing this, Mother?"

"Because I want you to look your best."

"No, I mean the whole thing. Why have you been going around telling everyone that I'm the Messiah come again, some God of all gods? What exactly are you trying to accomplish?"

"You're special, dear. Look how you knew just now when that poor man was going to die."

"Every mother thinks her child is special. But they don't tell people that they're God."

"Did I say you were God?"

"Yes. Maybe not to me, but I'm probably the only one."

"You arrived from a virgin birth."

"No, I didn't. I arrived from you having sex with some boy at school, and then you and Grandpa and Grandma made up some ridiculous story about you having breathed me into your womb."

"I'm still a virgin," and Rosalie sat back down on the bed.

"Absolutely. You're a virgin and I'm the Messiah and out there in the back of the hospice is the Garden of Eden. Now you have to cut this out, Mom. Really. It's embarrassing."

"You know that you're special. I know that you know it."

"I know I'm not like everyone else. I have, I don't know, some sort of a higher sensibility. I see things, I feel things, that other people don't feel. I have some sort of connection to something higher that other people don't seem to have. In some ways that's good, and in some ways it's a curse, because it separates me from everyone. But it does not make me the Messiah, Mom. It does not."

"What does it make you?"

"Different."

Rosalie looked into Her eyes, sensing what She would say next.

"I don't belong here, Mom. I really don't."

"What does that mean?"

"It means it hurts too much, what I see, what I feel. I want to help people. But they don't really want to listen. They say they do, but they really don't. I don't know why, but they don't," and She sat down on the bed beside Her mother.

"You're wrong," Rosalie said. "People do listen to you."

"Do they?" and She stretched out on the bed, placed Her head on Her mother's lap, and Rosalie began to stroke Her hair. It wasn't clear who was more surprised — Rosalie finding her daughter's head in her lap for the first time in years, or Her, suddenly overcome with a need for maternal affection.

"It's overwhelming, Mom. It truly is. Just plain overwhelming."

"I know, sweetheart. I know. So, why don't you start trying on these nice clothes and then you'll feel a lot better. Afterwards, we'll find some matching heels, and then I'll show you the makeup I bought for you."

She looked up at Her mother and was about to respond when a voice came from the doorway.

"I hope I'm not disturbing you," Theo said.

She turned to see who was standing in the door.

"I'm Theo. Theodore Wainwright. I'm next. But the good news is that I'm also the last," Theo smiled.

"She's very busy right now," Rosalie informed Theo.

"No, I'm not," She said. "Actually, I was just leaving," and She jumped up and started over to Theo.

"What about the clothes?" Rosalie called to Her in great distress.

"You decide," She said. "Let's go, Theo. Tell me what's on your mind."

In truth, Theo wasn't sure what was on his mind. Like all the others, he wanted answers. But his questions were not specific. Why had he been left alone like this? But people die, and couples rarely both die at the same time, unless they're in an accident, so what did he expect Her to say? It's just the way it is. He shared these thoughts with Her.

"Still," She said, as they walked in the garden, "it's very hard, isn't it?"

Theo didn't answer. He looked around at the garden as he walked. The frost had come and frozen the flowers in full bloom. It was a garden of dried flowers. He wondered why they hadn't died, turned brown and black, and fallen to the ground, but they stood there, rigid and radiant, in their frozen state.

"It's not hard," he finally said. "It's impossible, impossible to fill with anything or anyone else," and they walked over to the same bench where She had sat with Pincus, the koi pond in front of them, the water spilling down the rocks, the large golden fish swimming about, making small ripples as they moved.

"For some it's that way," She told Theo. "The lucky ones. The deeper the love, the greater the loneliness. If the loneliness lasts forever, then the love was eternal."

Theo felt a lump in his throat, and he fought the moisture coming to his eyes.

"People think I've lost it," Theo said to Her. "That I've got some sort of dementia. That I'm not all there. But since Bernice passed, I don't much care what I say and to whom. Let's just say that this is now the unedited version of Theodore Wainwright, Jr."

A gust of wind arrived and blew leaves into a whirling cone. It made Theo laugh.

She questioned his laughter with her eyes.

"The leaves remind me of a whirling dervish," he told Her. "I've actually seen them, you know, Whirling Dervishes, the dance troup. A few years ago they arrived from Istanbul and toured America. They had a leader, an older man with a dark beard, wearing one of those fez hats that the Masons wear. He explained it all to us. Their turning is a turning towards the truth. The follower grows through love, deserts his ego, finds the truth, and arrives at the Perfect. Then he returns from his spiritual journey as a man who has reached maturity and a greater perfection, able to love and to be of service to the whole of creation."

Theo laughed again.

"I don't know whether I'll ever find the Perfect, but it's a journey I'd like to take," and Theo stood and started turning in circles, his arms extended.

"I'm a Dervish," he laughed.

She laughed with Theo.

"I have to be going," She said. "I have a patient to see. But you can stay here as long as you like."

"Think I will. Think I will," and Theo went whirling away down a path lined by frozen asters, brilliant pinks and purples, laughing loudly.

Theo's laughter was still resonating in her head when Pincus arrived to pick Her up for their date. Pincus, after some intense negotiation with Doris Pratt's oldest son, Skip, had managed to obtain use of a business suit only one size too big and a Ford pick-up, its door emblazoned with "Skip's Septic Systems: We Pump All Year Long."

"Holy moly," Pincus said when he walked in the room for their date and saw Her. "You look — look —"

"Yeah, I know. Ridiculous. It was my mother's idea. I'll change," She said.

"No, no. I was going to say stunning, gorgeous, beautiful ... Don't change a thing. Please."

"You really think?..." She said, and She looked down at her attire, trying to determine if this could be true.

She wore a white dress with large black orchids on it. The scooped neckline showed off a modest amount of cleavage and was accented by a pearl necklace. Her hair was pinned back on the side with two barrettes, also of pearl. Her face was made-up, but not overly so, and She wore lipstick just a shade down from bright red, which matched her red heels.

"Yes, I really think," Pincus confirmed. "I don't know whether you're the Messiah, or the God of all gods, or whatever, but let me tell you something. If you are, there won't be a nonbeliever left on the face of the earth."

She laughed.

"Beauty is only skin deep," She said, but She couldn't avoid being pleased and was unable to conceal it completely. This evening might not be so bad.

"You're going to turn a few heads tonight," Pincus said and took Her arm.

And She did, starting with the residents in the living room who applauded as She passed through, turning Her face bright pink, and right up to Her walking through the restaurant in downtown Burlington that Pincus had selected, Le Coq d'Or. He had selected this from pictures in a guidebook he found at the Sinclair Inn that showed the restaurant to possess a certain opulence without being overstated, but he had reservations about the name. He knew of an ill-fated opera of the same name that was banned by the Tsar of Russia because the bumbling king in the opera was too close in resemblance to the Tsar, himself. In the opera, an astrologer gives the king a golden cockerel, "Le Coq d'Or," to protect him. Unfortunately, at the end, the king reneges on a promise he made to the astrologer and is pecked to death by Le Coq d'Or. And so, it was with some trepidation that Pincus selected this particular restaurant.

The restaurant appeared as advertised. The tables had white cloths and flickering candles. On the ceiling were large brass chandeliers, their lights enclosed in frosted globes, etched with designs of ivy. The carpet was a deep burgundy with gold fleur-de-lis, and against the wall was an ornate bar with a dark mahogany counter and gleaming glassware.

She turned to Pincus when they entered and smiled with a delight Pincus had not seen from Her.

"A good start," Pincus thought to himself, cupped her elbow in his hand, and gently led her to the table in a corner where the maître d' was pulling out the chair. As she traversed the muted restaurant, patrons took notice, a wave of approving murmurs following Her like a breeze blowing across once-still waters until it reached the shore.

She noticed the reaction, but when She looked out at the restaurant to see what was causing it, all heads instantly turned away from her, as though they were pulled by a string.

The dinner was divided into three acts, seeming to have been constructed by a hardworking, though not especially talented, playwright.

Act I took place from the inspection of the menus, through the declaration of food selections to the waiter (a perfectly cast young man with a thin mustache and slicked-back jet black hair), and ending with the arrival of the appetizers — oysters for Pincus, a salmon terrine for Her.

The dialogue consisted entirely of banalities concerning the items on the menu, the décor of the restaurant, speculation about a large woman at a nearby table who wore a multi-colored dress, adorned with a dozen or more beaded necklaces, and who they decided was a retired opera singer, though neither could name a single opera singer, male or female, living or dead.

Throughout this first act, Pincus did his best to keep the conversation going, and She nodded and smiled and paid rapt attention with wide eyes to whatever Pincus said, Her mother having instructed Her in these fine points of a dinner date:

"You listen, dear, like your life depends on it. You want him to feel like everything he says is of interest to you, that his words are a life-altering event, and that, if you were to choose one last thing before you die, it would be to hear him speak," Rosalie had instructed her daughter. "You say little, smile a lot, and nod until your head feels as though it will drop off your neck. Above all, you must remember that you are in total control. He is trying to impress you, and his entire self-worth depends on how you respond. You hold his life in your hands, dear."

The arrival of the oysters and salmon terrine launched the substance of the evening. A good thing as, historically, Act II has always been the most difficult of the three — the meat of the evening, so to speak, although, on this occasion She had ordered the Dover sole and Pincus the bass.

It began innocently enough with Pincus informing Her that the Ecclesia would be voting to determine whether She was the Messiah and/or the God of all gods, who has come to announce that the Kingdom of God is at hand, that the reign of goodness will now have its turn, people will be fed, the homeless housed, the sick cured, and the children bathed in love.

"They're doing what?" She asked incredulously, dropping her fork on her plate with a loud clang.

"Voting," Pincus repeated.

"And then what?" She asked.

"I'm not sure. I'm not sure that they're sure. I think that they just want some sort of resolution," Pincus conjectured.

"And what happens if they decide I'm not the Messiah? Am I executed?"

"No, if I recall, you only get executed if you *are* the Messiah," Pincus joked.

"It's not funny," She said, forgetting her mother's instructions.

"No, you're right. It isn't funny," Pincus agreed.

"What if they decide that I am the Messiah? Do I get a throne or what?"

"I'm not sure, but I think that they're considering establishing a religion in your name, She-ism I suppose —" Pincus guessed, "— formulating some sort of doctrine — with your consultation, of course, you being, in this instance, God."

"No thanks, Max. True religion comes from the heart, not from a creed."

They stopped speaking while the waiter cleared their dishes and replaced them with Dover sole and bass, poured a bottle of 1973 Laguiche Montrachet, and then backed away from the table as one does when departing from royalty, at which point Pincus and She resumed their dialogue.

"And where do you stand on all this, Max?" She asked.

"I'm not sure," Max confessed.

"Do you believe I'm the Messiah?"

"I'm not sure. I long ago decided to operate on the basis of Pascal's wager. If I believe you are and you are, I'm in good shape. If I believe you are, and you're not, no harm done. But, if I believe you're not, and you are, I could be in for a rough road ahead. So, all things considered, it's two to one in favor of belief."

"That's a cop-out," She informed Her date.

"Yes, but, under the circumstances, a good one," Pincus explained.

"I'm disappointed in you," once again ignoring Her mother's advice.

"Because I'm not unequivocally convinced that you're the Messiah?"

"No, because you've found a way to dodge committing yourself. Who can live like that?"

"Well, you're looking at one person who can. It's not that hard. You should try it."

"What about God?" She inquired.

"I'd think you'd know a lot more about that than I would," Pincus offered.

"Do you believe in God?" She asked.

"I don't not believe in Him."

"You're impossible, Max."

"In my opinion, so is God sometimes, so it all evens out. But I'm willing to be persuaded."

"You don't have to be *persuaded*. Just look inside you. One breath alone permeates the universe — the breath of man is that of God. God dwells in man and man dwells in God and lives by God."

"I'll consider it," Pincus said, and then to try to dissipate any bad feelings, "Truly, I will."

"Look around you, Max. God is everywhere. St. Francis called the sun, moon, stars, water, and fire his brothers. All you have to do is pay attention," She said with mounting passion.

There was a pause, the two concentrating on the food before them as a way of bringing down the temperature of their interchanges. Pincus thought of how to proceed and finally decided to stay on the topic, although he thought it best to approach it from another direction.

"I know you're against organized religion, but it does seem to have, at least for some, for many actually, a comforting place in their lives. Have you ever thought of what kind of religion you might found, if you were of a mind to do so?"

She looked up from Her fish and smiled.

"Yes, I have. It would be a religion based on us all being the children of God, of man as a pilgrim, a wanderer in search of bliss — the craving of heart for heart, of the soul for its perfect mate, man as lover, seeking inward purity and perfection."

She looked up at Pincus to see his reaction, and She was pleased.

"Yes," he said, struck by the simplicity of it all. "That's a religion I could live with."

Both had little to say after that. It seemed that words were unnecessary. From time to time one or the other would make a comment about the food, or the ambience of the restaurant, but otherwise each was content to bask in the silence, to enjoy the connection between them that had suddenly and unexpectedly come to be.

As their dinner plates were being cleared and they were being handed dessert menus, She looked up at Pincus and smiled, a smile Pincus had never seen from Her before.

Pincus felt for the first time that She was seeing him as more than an interesting object, someone to show Her the rudiments of love between the sexes. She was feeling an attraction, Pincus was sure of it, and it made Pincus's heart flame with excitement.

She saw the expression on Pincus's face, reached out, and took his hand.

"This is how it is, isn't it?" She asked.

"Yes, this is how it is," Pincus said.

And the curtain closed on Act II.

Act III, accompanied by crème brûlée and profiteroles, began surprisingly for Pincus.

"Do you think, Max," She said, pouring chocolate syrup over her dessert, "that sex can still be sacred?"

Max's heart raced as he thought of a reply.

"Yes, it definitely can," Pincus finally said. "Might I ask why you're asking," Pincus asked this to lower his blood pressure, but it was unsuccessful.

"You know why I'm asking, Max," She said sweetly.

"I would have thought you weren't interested in such earthly endeavors," Pincus said only half-jokingly.

"It's true. I am interested mainly in the world that exceeds our senses. But I think that pleasure is another way of knowing the world. It's a kind of entrancement, like St. Paul caught up in the third heaven, being ravished out of fleshly feeling, only you need to have the fleshly feeling first to be ravished out of it, and I can't see how you can do that if you haven't had sex."

Pincus had nothing to say, and had he been able to think of something to say, he wouldn't have said it for fear of breaking the spell.

"But I need to tell you something, Max," She continued. "I'm leaving, and where I'm going you can't come with me."

"Where are you going?"

"Into The Singing Machine."

Pincus's body shuddered.

"You can't go in there," he told her. "Nobody can go in there. They're vaporized. They disappear."

"They may disappear, but they're not vaporized. They become part of The Singing Machine."

"How do you know that?"

"I can't tell you how, but from the first time I heard its song, I knew what it was, what it saw, why it sang," She said.

"Which is?"

"It has seen the Absolute. It is the Absolute."

"The absolute what?"

"The uncreated light, Max, the light that bathes the universe. The Singing Machine has seen it, and it sings of it, and it has become it, and now that I have heard it, that is where I have to be. I don't belong here. I belong there. With my Father."

"Your father is in The Singing Machine, too? How did he get in there?"

"He's always been there. He's the Absolute."

"The Absolute is your father?"

"Yes. I have to be in the uncreated light of my Father."

"I don't want to ruin the evening, but this is insane It's total nonsense. It's also not good manners on a date to tell someone that you intend to kill yourself. It changes the mood in a way that can be very difficult to overcome."

"I'm not killing myself, Max. It's transcendence. You should be happy for me."

"Well, I'm not. When is this transcendence going to take place?" he asked.

"Soon," She said, and once again She took his hand. "But before I go I would like it very much if you would make love to me. Would you do that for me?"

And the curtain came down on Act III, but was followed by the Obvious Epilogue.

On the drive home, She seemed to be rather talkative, a way to relieve her nervousness Pincus hypothesized, but not what Pincus needed under the circumstances, as he had much to think about.

Making love to a suicidal woman raised certain issues in the mind of Pincus, not the least of which was that this might not launch a long-term relationship. On the other hand, he also could not entirely dismiss the notion that She might, in fact, be God. Does one turn down God? Can one turn down God, even a self-destructive one? Perhaps, this was all foreordained, and he really had no choice in the matter. In that case, why even bother to consider the issues?

"What was your wife like?" She disrupted Pincus's cogitation.

"This is what you want to know? Now?" Pincus snapped out of it.

"Well, I'm curious. Was she pretty?"

"We're all pretty at the beginning. She was pretty. I was pretty. Group B Streptococcus was pretty. What wasn't pretty? We were in love."

"Did you have great sex?"

"I don't think that D. H. Lawrence would have taken notes, but it seemed to accomplish what we had in mind. Can we change the subject?"

"Did you have sex a lot?"

"We were within the norms. And please don't ask whether I was any good at it, because, since you made your proposal at dinner, it's all I've been thinking about, whether I'm any good at it — still — ever. I feel like I'm back in college, and all I can say is that I've never been one to pray much, but I've been in prayer for the last hour. I'm praying that you are not God, because I know for certain that I could not meet those expectations."

She laughed and slid over in the seat next to Pincus.

"You're wrong, Max. God is merciful. He wouldn't mind if you totally screwed it up, so to speak," and, laughing, She wrapped her arm around his.

They turned into the driveway of the Hospice of Our Lady of Lament.

"Drive down the driveway on the left to the back. There's something I want to show you," She said.

At the end of the driveway was a small cottage, and Pincus pulled the truck up to it, turned off the lights, then turned off the engine.

He sat there in silence for a moment. Pincus turned and looked at Her beside him, then turned back and stared out the window into the darkness.

"Shall we go inside?" She finally asked Pincus.

Pincus sat there, and just when She thought that Pincus would remain in the truck for the remainder of his life, he stirred. His left hand reached for the door handle, turned it, and the door opened. Pincus looked at the open door, surprised that the door had swung open, expecting that it would be locked in place in the same way that he was. Then he found himself getting out of the door of the borrowed septic company truck, drawn by some force beyond his control, slowly closed the truck door, and shuffled off to the front door of the cottage.

"You're doing very well, Max," She said when She joined him at the door.

"Thank you," said Max. "I'm trying."

"I know," She said, and placed Her key in the keyhole to open the door.

"Sometimes, when a resident is at the end, and the family wants to be near, we let them stay here at the cottage," She told him.

"This is for people who are losing their loved ones?" Pincus asked, concerned about the meaning of it all.

"This is where families come to give their love to those they care most about. The grudges and hurts of the past are no longer. There is only love, expressed in the most profound way possible," She reframed the cottage's function and opened the door.

She entered, Pincus right behind her. He looked around the room and was overcome with the feeling that, on entering, he had gone into some sort of trance-like state. He examined the surroundings in an attempt to determine whether he was in a dream. On the walls were paintings of Jesus, Mary, and Joseph, along with a number of saints who Pincus couldn't identify, with the exception of St. Francis, who was sitting on the edge of a fountain, a wall of pink flowers behind him, dozens of small animals — lambs, rabbits, squirrels, raccoons, beavers — all at his feet, staring devotedly up at him as though he had their dinner in his lap, a white dove perched on one shoulder, a second dove in his hand, with whom Francis seemed to be in conversation. In the middle of the room, there was a large bed with a scarlet bedspread and pillows with white satin covers. Over the bed was an exceptionally large crucifix.

"Forget it," Pincus told Her. "I'm not making love to you in the papal apartment. It's not going to happen."

"Can you think of a better place?" She asked, smiling.

"Yes, I can," Pincus answered. "Cadwaller's Can-You-Keep-a-Secret Short-Stay Motel. They've got mirrored ceilings, hot tubs, and a hundred and six porn channels. Or, so they say."

"Sit down, Max," She said.

Max looked around for a chair, but there were none, so, with misgivings, he sat on the very edge of the bed, trying to fight off the feeling that he had somehow been transported to another realm. She sat beside him.

"You can do this, Max," She comforted Pincus.

"Maybe. Maybe I can. Maybe not. It remains to be seen. The question right now is whether I will."

"What seems to be the problem?" She asked with great sincerity.

"This is a classic case of 'be careful what you wish for,'" Pincus explained.

"Why is that?" She asked.

"Because what you get might not be what you imagined. There could be things you haven't considered," Pincus explained.

"Such as?"

"I'm not telling."

"Max?"

"Yes?"

"We have to take off our clothes."

"Why?"

She started to take off Her dress.

"Please don't do that," Pincus said, but before he had finished his sentence, She was in her bra and panties.

"Oh, my God," Pincus said, gasping for breath.

"It remains to be seen," She said.

"There are women who have taken longer to undress when their clothes are on fire," Pincus said.

"Max, do you think you could kiss me?"

"I could certainly try," Pincus announced, his eyes riveted on Her perfect body, and he leaned forward and laid his lips against Hers. He had only intended it to be perfunctory, but poor Pincus was lost. His eyes flooded with tears, and he kissed her gently, once, then twice, and then a third time, each time with mounting passion. She let out a little sigh.

"Yes," She said.

Max kissed Her neck, and then he kissed Her shoulders and arms.

She reached to Pincus and slid off his suit coat, then unbuttoned his shirt. And when she rested Her palms gently on his chest and Pincus felt their warmth, Pincus, as they say, threw in the towel, and he began to make love as he had never made love before, as he never believed that he could make love, all the yearnings of a lifetime fulfilled.

"There is such beauty in the world," Pincus thought, "such terrible beauty."

He cupped his hands on Her cheeks, and he felt Her tears.

"Are you okay?" Pincus asked.

"It's so wonderful," She said. "It's overwhelming."

"Shall I stop?" Pincus asked.

"No, please. Please don't stop."

"Yes," Pincus said. "I won't stop."

And so Pincus made love to Her, reaching a point of ecstasy that brought him out of his body and united him with all that is, and was, and will be. The longing that had possessed him for so long, that had caused him to give up his wife and his profession, was gone and was replaced by something that could never be lost, a sense of majesty and of grace, of something greater than himself. He felt that he had reached a place without place, pure place, a place where only the soul can go. He was floating far beyond space and had the sense that something miraculous was occurring, that Pincus was Her and She was Pincus and there was no separation. They were One.

And then, when all was done, they kissed, and they both wept, clutching each other until they fell asleep in each other's arms.

And that night The Singing Machine sang another tune entirely.

CHAPTER 9

The next morning Pincus awoke to find himself lying next to her fully clothed, as was She. Had none of this happened? Had this night of love-making all been a hallucination, something spiritually induced by Her to produce the same ecstacy, the same intimacy, that love-making provides? Had She brought him to a place to which only saints go, to prove to him that sex was the God-given way for two people to reach oneness, but it did not have to be physical. He wanted to ask Her what had happened, if they had made love or not, but Pincus did not want to know. He wanted to leave it the way it was, the way he would always remember it, and so he said nothing. There was only silence that morning, and a feeling of completion, with one another and with the cosmos. Their silence said that and more.

Pincus had promised to have the septic truck back to Skip no later than 8:00 a.m., and so he headed out as soon as they had awakened. She accompanied Pincus to the truck. She rested Her folded arms on the ledge of the open window, all rosy cheeks and smiles. Pincus placed his hand on top of Her head, and She looked up at him.

"Are you coming with us?" She asked.

"Coming where?" Pincus asked.

"On the hike. I'm hiking Mount Mansfield, remember? All the others are coming. At least I think they are. No, I'm sure they are."

"Now I remember. I'm not sure."

"I hope you do. I'll miss you not being there."

"I'll try," Pincus said, but he wasn't very convincing. He knew that whatever had or had not happened between them would never happen again. Yet, it seemed not to matter, because he woke up feeling as though he now had the entire universe with which to make love. Still, he wasn't sure whether it would now be too painful to be with Her. He was convinced that She would be going into The Singing Machine. He would do everything within his power to prevent it, but he knew it would happen anyway. And She would be gone. One day soon he would never see Her again, but strangely She would still be there. Pincus didn't understand why, but he wondered whether this feeling would grow stronger with each day until She finally departed, and then he could live with it, feeling her presence even as She disappeared.

They kissed through the open window, and Pincus backed out and left, watching Her in the rearview mirror as he drove away. She stood there, lit by the newly risen sun, Her hands clasped behind Her back, Her golden hair blowing in the breeze, getting smaller until Pincus turned the corner and She disappeared entirely, leaving him to wonder whether She had ever been real. Only the sense that he was no longer what he had been when the night began allowed him to accept Her reality.

She appeared at the Sinclair Inn at 10:00 a.m., exactly on schedule, and found the Ecclesia waiting, but in the midst of a heated dispute.

Sister Gloria Gloria had insisted on going with everyone, wheelchair or not, and nobody was able to convince her of the nature of hiking.

"I know full well what a hike is," Sister snapped. "I'm not an idiot."

"It's on foot," Elliott explained.

"No, really," Sister responded.

"How do you propose to go in a wheelchair?" Meyer attempted to clarify the matter.

"I don't propose anything," Sister responded. "Carry me over your shoulder, float me in

the air, but find a way, because, if I don't go, you don't go."

"How is that?" Meyer asked.

"Because, when you return, I will make your lives a living hell. You can take my word on that. Hell hath no fury like a woman scorned, and by the time I'm done with you all, you'll gladly settle for hell," Sister explained.

"Doesn't sound very Christian-like," Florence remarked.

"Well, I'm not asking for your opinion," Sister replied.

"Still," Meyer remarked, "Florence has a point, Sister. Jesus would never have retaliated out of anger."

"Really?" Sister spun around her wheelchair to face Meyer. "Then tell me what you make of 'Hide us from the face of him that sitteth on the throne, and from the wrath of the Lamb. For the great day of his wrath is come; and who shall be able to stand?' Put that in your pipe and smoke it."

"Yes, but," She said from the doorway where She had been taking in the encounter with some amusement, "The Lamb which is in the midst of the throne shall feed them, and shall lead them unto living fountains of waters: and God shall wipe away all tears from their eyes."

"And who asked you?" Sister spun her chair back to face Her.

"I think we should fashion a litter," She said. "The two strongest among us can carry Sister."

Sister did not quite know what to make of this. Her gesture seemed almost too Christian. Sister imagined that, when they reached the summit of Mount Mansfield, someone would invert the litter, and she would go rolling down four thousand feet of rock face, to the sound of cheers of good riddance. Still, she would have to go along with this solution, as there was no alternative, and so she found herself lying on a litter in the bed of the pickup truck from the Hospice of Our Lady of Lament, looking up at the chins of the Ecclesia sitting around the edge of the truck, including Pincus, who had shown up at the last minute.

They disembarked at the visitor center, Elliott on one end of Sister's litter, Sparky on the other. The ridges of the mountain resembled the head of a man, aligned north and south, and each ridge had long ago been designated as such — Forehead, Chin, Adam's Apple, and so on.

"Look," She said as they walked on, "Alpine Azaleas." She pointed to a patch of pink and rose flowers. "They should have died out months ago."

In fact, as they proceeded, they came across more spring flowers – cream-colored Diapensia, and lush purple Lapland Rosebay, delicate tendrils in the midst of each blossom. As they encountered these, the Ecclesia looked suspiciously at Her, wondering whether She was responsible for populating the meadows with spring flowers at the end of October in order to make for a colorful journey.

The group, with Her leading the way, followed the blue trail markers up the steep hill. As they marched on, a mist began to settle on the mountain, enveloping them in a fog and making the giant cobwebs that hung over them glisten.

Soon they entered an area that seemed to them out of a Grimm Brother's fairy tale. The soil was so thin that the trees spread out their roots on top of the boulders in an eerily, almost grotesque, network of interlaced tentacles.

"I thought the purpose of this was to enjoy your company," Sparky remarked, panting in the thin atmosphere.

"You'll enjoy my company when we reach the top," She responded.

"Fat chance we'll ever get to the top," Meyer said, pointing to a crevice that lay ahead. "Is that the only way up?"

"It is," She said, "but I've done it many times. You just have to turn sideways and slide through."

"And what do we do with Sister?" asked Elliott. "Catapult her over it?"

She stopped and studied the situation.

"Well, you can slide the litter through sideways, but, of course, Sister can't be on it," She said.

"And then?" Elliott asked.

"And then you'll have to take Sister's arms, Sparky can take Sister's legs, and slide her through the crack, sideways, as well," She spelled it out.

"Over my dead body," Sister said.

"You can do this," Florence told Sister in soothing tones.

"Shit," said Sister.

Elliott took Sister's head and shoulders, Sparky took her knees and ankles, and ignoring the nonstop stream of admonitions coming from the mouth of the good Sister, fortunately unintelligible because her face was against the rock ledge, Sister was slid through the crevice without mishap, and the Ecclesia proceeded on their way up the mountain, now slowly as the moisture from the mist had made the rock extremely slippery.

When, at long last they neared the top, they heard a honking.

"Is that a car?" Meyer said in a steely voice, dabbing at the blood trickling down his legs from various rock abrasions. "Tell me I didn't just hear a car horn up here at four thousand feet," at which point an SUV rumbled past, kicking up dust. "We could have driven up here? We could have stayed in the truck and driven up here?!"

"It's a toll road," She explained.

"I would have paid," Meyer said. "I would have paid a lot."

"But aren't you glad you're here?" Florence tried to comfort Meyer.

"Not especially," Meyer was not comforted. "I'm particularly not glad that — " but Meyer broke off his sentence, as he saw before and below him the cloud bank that blanketed the Champlain Valley, the peak of Camel's Hump mountain sticking up through the clouds. It took his breath away, and he just stared out at Paradise, dumbstruck.

As Meyer and the others looked, the clouds began to clear, as though brushed aside by a hand, and the sun appeared, turning the valley into an evergreen carpet, Lake Champlain shining on the horizon. They all turned to Her as though She had something to do with this, but She just smiled and sat on a boulder, taking in the view.

Sister Gloria Gloria was removed from her litter and placed on the ground, against a boulder that served as a backrest. She was the first to speak.

"We have some questions for you," Sister informed Her.

There was no immediate response from Her. She continued to stare out at the valley for a few minutes. Then, finally, She spoke.

"Very well," She said. "You may each ask one question. One question per person, so make it a good one."

The Ecclesia looked at each other, shrugged, and then acquiesced, rising and repositioning themselves on the ground before Her.

"Who would like to begin?" She asked.

"I would," Elliot said. "What do you believe in?"

"I believe in all that can warm the heart and the imagination."

"What will I be after death?" asked Theo.

"After death you will be what you were before you were born."

"Does God exist?" asked Meyer.

"One breath alone penetrates the universe. The breath of man is that of God."

"Is there any way to control the universe?" asked Sparky.

"Nature obeys all who believe."

"How should we live?" asked Florence.

"So as not to obstruct the view."

"What is the best way to worship?" asked Sister.

"Any way. True compassion comes from the heart."

She turned to Her mother.

"I have no question," Rosalie said.

"Then you are with God."

"I have a question," said Pincus. "What is the most perfect state on this earth?"

"Union in love. And God is love."

"Are you God?" Pincus asked.

"Sorry, Max, you've already had your question."

That evening The Singing Machine sang throughout the night.

Just before dawn, the Ecclesia found themselves drawn to the machine, still in their bedclothes, robes or blankets wrapped around them in the early morning chill.

Pincus had gone to his window where he saw Her standing before The Singing Machine in the first light of the rising sun, Her face shining like light, Her white dress flapping in the slight wind. She was sublime, Pincus thought, and he believed he understood for the first time the true meaning of sublime. It was greatness added to beauty. And beauty, ah yes beauty, what could this be other than the spiritual making itself known to him sensually, he decided.

Pincus watched as She sang along with The Singing Machine, Her voice, rich with love, coming from a place that was beyond his imagination. As Pincus took all this in, the Ecclesia appeared, one by one, and, finally, Pincus left his window and joined them.

When they were all there, She stopped singing and turned from The Singing Machine, facing the Ecclesia.

"Do you want to know why the machine sings by itself? That's why you've come, isn't it? Shall I tell you?"

No one replied. They simply stood facing Her, holding their breaths.

"It has started singing by itself," She said, "because it wants to be more than it can ever be."

The Singing Machine stopped moving, and then, in the silence, a single note emerged from it like an immense sigh.

PART IX

The Passion

CHAPTER 1

The meeting to determine Her messiahship had been called for 9:00 on the morning after the climb, but it was almost 10:00 before it began. Most of the Ecclesia were so exhausted from the previous day that they overslept, and, as the Sinclair had strict rules about closing and locking the doors to the breakfast room at exactly 9:00, there was an expedition to Joe's Snack Bar for provisions.

"I think," Elliott began the proceedings after the various food orders from Joe's had been distributed and everyone had settled, some still in robes and pajamas, "that we need to establish some sort of criteria for making this determination," and he bit a chunk out of his onion bagel.

"What criteria?" Florence asked, trying to think what these might be.

"I don't know that there are criteria for messiahship," remarked Meyer, sipping a mint latte.

"Well, didn't the last one do, like, miracles and make prophesies?" Sparky tried to contribute. "That could work."

"What miracles have you seen Her do, Sparky?" chided Meyer.

"Well, there's the clouds parting when She got to the top of the mountain and waved her arms. How about that?" said Sparky.

"She didn't wave Her arms for the clouds to part. She sat on Her rock, drinking from her water bottle, while the sun burned the clouds away," Meyer replied.

"Besides, I'm not sure Jesus actually did any miracles," Meyer said as he bit into his ham and egg sandwich. "I know, I know — there's all this business about turning water into wine and the fish and bread, but that's pretty far-fetched. What other miracles were there, really?"

"Jesus answered and said unto them, 'Go and shew John again those things which ye do hear and see: The blind receive their sight, and the lame walk, the lepers are cleansed, and the deaf hear, the dead are raised up, and the poor have the gospel preached to them.'" A voice came from a chair at a desk in the corner of the room in which sat Father Zawistowski, a thin bald man with wisps of white hair sticking out from his temples, thick eyeglasses, wearing clerical garb. The group turned as one to look at him.

"Who are you?" asked Meyer, feeling uncomfortable about what they were doing if a genuine priest was to be in attendance, and deciding that the best defense was a good offense. "This is an important private meeting we're having here. Did anyone invite you?"

"Actually, I did," said Elliott.

This was followed by an immediate uproar.

"Would you like to tell us why you did this?" Meyer asked Elliott.

"I thought it would be good to have someone knowledgeable in Christian doctrine to consult with, if needed," Elliott explained.

There was a shriek from Sister, followed by, "We already *have* someone knowledgeable in Christian doctrine!"

"Who doesn't have a vested interest," Elliott clarified.

"And what, may I ask, is my vested interest?" Sister could barely say the words, her face turning red with choler.

"Well, as I understand it," Elliott said in soft measured tones, "she lived with you, Sister, for several years, so you would not exactly be unbiased."

"She didn't *live* with me." Elliott's tones had not done much to calm the good Sister. "She was one of three hundred and fifteen girls under my care, and that's all."

"Still, I think we all know where you stand on things. You've made that quite clear from the very beginning," Theo tried to help out.

"Oh, really. And I can't change my mind?" Sister retorted.

"You've changed your mind about Her not being the Messiah?" Theo asked with great interest.

"In your dreams," Sister said.

"I can leave, if you wish," Father Zawistowski offered.

"No, I think it would be good if you stayed," Elliott said, and he looked around the room to see whether there were any dissenters other than Sister. As no one spoke up, the matter was settled.

"Very well," Father said. "I would like to point out that, if She is the Messiah and you decide that She is not, there are certain repercussions."

"And what might these be?" Florenceasked.

"*He that is not with me is against me.* Matthew 12:30. As well as, *Whosoever shall deny me before men, him will I also deny before my Father which is in heaven.* Matthew 10:30," Father provided a few notions for the Ecclesia to think over.

There was a silence in the room as the Ecclesia did just that, considering whether they might be getting in over their heads. Finally, Sparky spoke up.

"She would never do that," Sparky came to Her defense.

"Oh, yes she would," replied Rosalie, who'd been taking a back seat, deciding that anything she'd say would only make problems.

"Okay, then, as I said on what seems like yesterday," Elliott said, "we should come up with some criteria to determine if She is truly the Savior returning as prophesied a second time."

"I think you can pretty much discount that," Father said, and, feeling more comfortable about his place in the group, he moved from his chair at the desk to a large armchair next to Elliott. "It's pretty clear that in His first coming, Jesus was the suffering servant. In the second coming, He would be the conquering king, with the armies of heaven at His side. From what I know, this doesn't sound like Her."

The Ecclesia thought this over.

"That's from the Old Testament, right?" Theo asked.

"Yes, it is," Father answered.

"And there were hundreds of years after the Old Testament before Jesus arrived," Theo continued. "So who's to say that during all that time, Jesus hasn't changed his mind, or more likely, God has. God could have thought that He no longer saw a need for a conquering king with armies of heaven at His side. Maybe God thought it might be better to send a woman, balance things out a little. My wife and I wanted to have a girl after our son was born. It didn't work out that way, but it's only natural to want both. And since we're made in God's image, well, why not? Does it feel cold in here? It does to me."

"I'll turn up the heat," Florence said, while the rest cogitated over Theo's commentary.

"I suppose," Father said, "that's always a possibility, although it would be very difficult to know. On the other hand, I'm not sure that whatever everyone here decides will really make any difference. *No man knoweth who the Son is, but the Father; and who the Father is, but the Son.* Matthew 11:27. We can assume the same would apply to the Daughter."

There was a low-level grumbling among the Ecclesia. This was turning out to be far more complicated than any had imagined, and several were now thinking that having Father Zawistowski present might not have been such a good idea after all. They had work to do regarding the Messiah, and if Father kept bringing up Scripture, they were likely to get nowhere at all.

"When you come right down to it," Meyer attempted to move things along, "what do we really know about the Savior from the Bible?"

"We really know —" Sister saw an opportunity to regain some lost ground on the matter of who did and did not know Christian doctrine, "we really know from the Bible that Jesus was a Jew, that he was descended from David, that he was born of a woman, that he lived under the law and preached only to Israel, that he was without sin, that he chose twelve apostles, that he instituted the Eucharist on the night of his betrayal, that he was reviled and crucified, but he rose again on the third day and showed himself to Peter, to the other apostles, and to Paul, and that he now sits at the right hand of God awaiting the great day when he shall come again, and I emphasize *He*, not *She*, shall come again," and Sister nodded her head emphatically, then removed her eyeglasses, puffed into each lens and started to clean them with a hankie, allowing her words to sink in with their proper authority. Then Sister had another thought.

"And while I'm at it, just for the record, we also know that Jesus forbade the least harsh word, prohibited divorce, censured revenge, condemned usury, considered voluptuous desire as criminal as adultery, and insisted upon the universal forgiveness of injuries — according to the Bible."

"Yes," Meyer tried to regain some lost ground, "but what I meant was that Jesus declared himself only to be the Son of Man, so what real proof do we have that Jesus *was* the Son of God?"

A broad smile appeared on the face of Sister and she turned to Father Zawistowski.

"Do you want to take this one, or should I?"

"No, please," Father gestured for her to take the ball and run with it.

"Very well," Sister said. "*And behold there came a voice out of the cloud, which said, 'This is my beloved Son, in whom I am well pleased; hear him.' And when the disciples heard it, they fell on their face, and were sore afraid.* Matthew 3:17."

"A voice came out of a cloud?" Sparky said. "And this means it's God? I don't think so. Any one of us could have shouted out of the clouds on the mountaintop yesterday — 'Hey, you down there, She's my daughter.' Does that make us God?"

"You think you sound like God, Sparky, really?" and Sister broke into laughter.

"I'm not sure we're getting anywhere," said Elliott. "We're here to vote. It's unlikely in my mind that God is going to settle things by speaking to us from a cloud. And it's not really productive to say that since only God can know who is His son or daughter, it's no business of ours. I think that if anyone has anything to say on the matter, he or she should speak, and then we should have the vote."

"I feel that I'm a different person after talking to Her," Florence offered.

"Well, I can't say I'm any different, and I found Her logic to be extremely poor. I was not impressed," Meyer said. "Very faulty reasoning."

"I must say," Elliott entered the conversation, "that I presented her with a perfect opportunity to demonstrate her powers by raising someone from the dead and She refused. I'm going to vote ' no.'"

"I'm not," said Sparky.

The group, all eyes on Sparky, waited for him to say something more.

"I'm just not," said Sparky.

"Well, I think you all know where I stand," said Sister Gloria Gloria. "I would have expected more."

"More what?" asked Theo. "Just because She doesn't agree with you, or isn't flying about with wings on Her shoulders, that doesn't make Her *not* our Savior. She's my savior. She lit me up with love. What else did Christ do, when you think about it? He got people to love him after he was gone, even for people who have never met him, and for two thousand years. I think that's how people are going to feel about Her."

There was a pause as all heads turned to the two people who had not yet spoken — Rosalie and Pincus.

"She's my daughter," was all that Rosalie had to say.

"I'm still undecided," said Pincus.

"You can't abstain, Max" said Elliott. "It's okay for Rosalie, since she's Her mother, and clearly biased, but not you."

"I know," said Pincus.

Elliott turned to Father Zawistowski.

"Do you have anything to add, Father?" Elliott asked.

"As a matter of fact, I do," Father said. "*For many shall come in my name, saying, 'I am Christ,' and 'The time draweth near'; and shall deceive many ... Luke 21:8.*"

There was a long silence, finally broken by Elliott.

"We should vote," Elliott said.

As predicted, Rosalie abstained. Sister, Meyer, and Elliot voted 'no.' Theo, Florence, and Sparky voted 'yes.' And, thus, with a three to three tie, it all came down to Pincus.

So Pincus voted, and, by a vote of four to three, it was determined by the Ecclesia that She was, in fact, their Savior.

CHAPTER 2

It had been raining heavily all afternoon, but the rain had turned to a light drizzle by the time that Pincus found Her at The Singing Machine that night. A bluish light emanated from The Singing Machine and bathed Her in its glow, adding to Her ethereal appearance. To Pincus She seemed almost transparent, and he wondered whether She wasn't slowly beginning to disappear, until She would one night be a vapor, vanishing like the clouds atop Mount Mansfield.

This night She didn't move about The Singing Machine, nor did She sing. She stood in front of it in silence, her tan raincoat clinging to her, her iridescent blue eyes peering out from the hood that covered her head, listening to the song of The Singing Machine, strangely still.

Pincus, wearing a red poncho that Rosalie had selected on their initial shopping expedition, approached Her and stood in the light rain beside Her for a few minutes, saying nothing, listening to the song of The Singing Machine that seemed rather melancholy, perhaps a result of the weather, Pincus thought.

Pincus had been undecided about whether to come at all. He wanted to inform Her about the vote, but he wondered whether this might not be a good idea. He wanted to find some way to persuade Her not to go into The Singing Machine, but was concerned that anything he might say could just push Her further in that direction.

Perhaps, the vote of the Ecclesia would work in his favor. If the Ecclesia were willing to work on Her behalf to spread the word, why not stay and lead them? On the other hand, Her leaving might be the only way to lend credibility to what they preached. What would have happened had there been no crucifixion and no resurrection? Would Jesus have worn out his welcome? And, if She departed in a blaze of glory inside The Singing Machine but didn't resurrect, it might kill the whole thing.

And so, after standing side by side for several minutes in front of The Singing Machine, Pincus spoke.

"When?" he asked Her.

"Not tonight," She answered.

"When?" Pincus repeated.

"Maybe tomorrow night," She said.

A chill went down his spine.

"They voted you their Savior. It was close, 4 to 3, but you won," Pincus tried to put a positive spin on the situation.

"Do I get an official certificate?" She asked. "You know, in case anybody asks if I'm really the Messiah?"

"I'll look into it," Pincus turned to Her and smiled.

"Listen to the song, Max," She responded.

"I don't think it's a song. It's just music. A song has to have words," he remarked, and pulled his hood up on his head, as the rain had become heavier.

"It does have words," She answered. "Someday I'll write them out for you."

"You could tell them to me now. Some day you might not be here."

"Not now. You wouldn't understand them now," and She lifted Her face to the rain and let it splash down her cheeks.

"Is it God singing?" Pincus asked. "Are you hearing God?"

"God is inaccessible," She said. "St. John of the Cross."

"John the apostle said that? Doesn't seem like him."

"It's not. This was another John — one of the thirty-five Doctors of the Church, also one of the greatest poets in the history of Spanish literature. He founded a branch of the Carmelites. There was a fight over his body when he died, so the city of Úbeda got an arm and a leg, and Segovia got the head and the torso. His other leg was stolen when they moved the body through Madrid."

"I'm beginning to see why John might have thought that God was inaccessible," Pincus remarked.

"What he meant, Max, was that, even though the spirit of man is divine, and God is within each of us, we're separated from God by an infinite distance. That's why I have to go," She explained.

"To be with God?"

"To join with the love that is perceived only by the soul and to bathe in its never-changing light," She said.

"Have you thought about resurrection?" Pincus decided this might be an opportune moment to raise the subject. "Aren't you concerned that, if you don't resurrect, you might soon be forgotten?"

"Not really, Max. The whole resurrection business is a total mess. Sometimes you're told that the righteous are to await the resurrection, and then another that they're to be received into Abraham's bosom at the moment of their death, and then another that resurrection is general, and another that it's reserved only for the faithful, and sometimes it supposes a renewed earth and a new Jerusalem, and other times a previous annihilation of the universe. And if nobody can keep it straight, it's highly unlikely in my mind that Jesus ever came back and appeared to anybody at all, because, if it's all so mixed up, what's the point?"

"You don't believe that Christ resurrected? I mean, that is kind of the point, isn't it?" Pincus asked.

"I think Jesus rose into heaven. I'll give you the rolling the tomb's stone away and his not being there, and I won't go into whether one or the other of the apostles might have spirited his corpse away, which I think is a very good word for it. But I do not think, as John has it — and I'm talking now about the first John not the one they chopped up — that after Jesus was crucified, John and his buddies were out fishing one day, and Jesus was standing there on the shore, waving to them and shouting, 'Come have some breakfast with me!' If you're going to come back from the dead, you don't do it to have breakfast with your buddies."

There are some things that are said for which there is no response, and so Pincus said nothing, but just watched the water that pooled on one beam or another of The Singing Machine cascade down as it changed its shape, making it appear to be a waterfall in motion, infused with the blue radiance of its light, its song in harmony with the falling water. Pincus had seen something similar at Versailles one night during his honeymoon with Becki on a glorious night when he thought that his love for her could never be greater and they made love as though there was nothing else that mattered. It filled him now with a sadness that came from a place that he could not identify. He did not miss Becki. He missed that moment when the world seemed perfect, even though what he had now was so much more, and still ...

She saw the way Pincus was looking at Her.

"What?"

"If you stayed, you could be another Moses, another Muhammed. You could continue to share your philosophy with the world."

"Moses and Muhammed were not philosophers. They were men of action. And besides which, philosophy doesn't do it for the multitude. They need sanctity."

"You're not being very helpful," Pincus said in frustration.

"Look, Max. I don't want to be a messiah, or a god of all gods, or a savior, whatever," She said in exasperation.

"That's not the question. The question is whether you are the whatever. It's not something you choose. The Angel Gabriel did not ask Mary how she felt about bearing the Son of God, and she said, "Let me talk to my husband about it and I'll get back to you before Christmas." That's not the way it works. You have a golden opportunity here. All these self-declared apostles are falling all over themselves to be the one most loved by you, even the ones who voted against you, who, I can guarantee you, would throw their mothers off the top of Mount Mansfield if it meant you would embrace them," Pincus pulled out all the stops.

"But why? What could I possibly give them?" She asked.

"Faith," Pincus said. "The godhead has always been an object of devotion and desire. You're surprised? Right now they're all just stumbling about, lost men. And women."

"No, the women are just fine. I'm sure of it. It's the men. They're so pitiable, really — trained to hold in their emotions, disgraced if they cry. No wonder they envy us women our intuition, our harmony. We're closer to heaven. Men are stuck in the mud with their diagrams."

"I'm a man," pointed out Pincus. "I can be as intuitive as any woman, and I have cried, more than once, and without feeling disgraced."

Suddenly Her face lit up.

"Look, Max," She said, pointing to The Singing Machine. "It's forming the shape of the world. There are the continents and there are the oceans."

Max watched as the earth came into being in front of him, the oceans a brilliant blue, water cascading where they lay, the rain making seas of amazing fidelity, and he wondered for just an instant whether he would see the spirit of God moving upon the face of the waters.

"The Babylonians thought the Earth was a great hollow mountain. The Hindus believed that the earth was a giant hemisphere, supported by four elephants standing on the back of a tortoise, and the Greeks thought that the earth was a flat disk floating on water. It took thousands of years before we figured out that it was a globe. Thousands. And now it seems obvious."

"The point being?"

"I wonder whether, when we finally know God's true nature, it will seem obvious, and we'll wonder how we ever could have believed anything else? What do you think?"

"I think you should stay here and not go into the machine," Pincus said. "We had something very special between us the other night."

"Yes, we did," She said, and She reached out Her arms and pulled him to Her, clasping Pincus tightly. It brought tears to the eyes of Pincus.

"You see how I can cry," he said.

CHAPTER 3

After they parted that night, Pincus thought long and hard about his next move and within a few hours, by midnight, he had assembled the Ecclesia for an emergency meeting, all but Rosalie who was with Her.

"This better be important," Sister said to Pincus, and she gestured to Sparky and Elliott to take her from the wheelchair and place her on the sofa.

"She wants to go into The Singing Machine," Pincus announced. "Actually, She's going into The Singing Machine. Tomorrow night maybe."

"Why ever would She want to do that?" Florence asked.

"It's not exactly clear, but She wants to become at one with the Absolute," Pincus explained.

"The absolute what?" asked Sparky.

"There is no what," Pincus responded.

"No what what?" Sparky asked.

"She thinks that by entering The Singing Machine she will be able to penetrate the cloud of unknowing that envelopes the Absolute and hides it from us."

"I'm confused," Sparky said.

"Does She know what will happen if She goes into The Singing Machine?" Florence asked.

"She does," Pincus told her.

"She knows she'll die?" Theo asked.

"She doesn't see it that way," Pincus explained. "She has seen the divine light and She sees this as a kind of transcendence."

"But she'll still die," Theo tried to simplify matters.

"We don't really know that, do we?" Pincus said. "All we know is that whatever goes into The Singing Machine disappears."

"She'll be dead," Theo said. "She'll be dead as a doornail. We can't let that happen."

"Let's not be so hasty here," Meyer said. "I mean, look at us. What have we been doing all these months? Talking about Her. Talking to Her. Waiting to talk to Her. Attempting to be with Her. Dreaming about Her. How long can we continue like this? We can finally get out of this place and go on our way, preaching Her word, being one of the elect, being those few special individuals who walked with Her and knew Her best — if, and only if, we kill Her off."

"You want to kill the Savior?" Sparky asked in horror.

"It's not as though we're breaking new ground," Meyer pointed out.

Sister reached for the knob on her wheelchair to run Meyer down, only to discover to her frustration that she was on the sofa.

"Maybe we should kill you off for having such blasphemous thoughts," Sister said. "The apostles did not kill the Messiah."

"Well, they sure as hell didn't do much to stop it, did they?" Meyer pursued the matter. "How long had Jesus been telling them what was going to happen? Either they were co-conspirators, or they were incredibly stupid."

Sister eyed the ashtray on the table beside her and seriously thought about tossing it at Meyer for such blasphemy, but caught the eye of Pincus, who saw what was on her mind, and Sister just winked at him and smiled.

"What would we preach?" asked Elliot. "I'm not exactly a big fan of Christian doctrine. There're too many rules, easy enough for those few who are already near perfect, but for the rest of us, virtually impossible to follow."

"Well, we could have two sets of rules, if we wanted — one moderately heroic for the common man, and the other exalted in the extreme for the uncommon man," Meyer offered. He liked where this was going.

"Look," Elliott tried to put things back on track. "Our vote aside, do we really know that She's the Messiah? So She goes into The Singing Machine and evaporates. It means nothing if She doesn't declare Herself to be our Savior."

"She doesn't want to be our Savior, or Messiah, or the Mother of all Gods, or anything else," Pincus informed them. "She was quite clear about that to me tonight."

"Well, there you have it," said Florence. "You can't make someone a messiah if she doesn't want to be."

"I don't think we should let Her go into The Singing Machine," Pincus said.

"I agree," said Sparky with great passion. "I think we should destroy The Singing Machine before it's too late."

"That's the most ridiculous thing I've ever heard," said Florence. "If a child is overdependent on his puppy, you don't solve the problem by killing the puppy."

"We're getting off the topic, I think," said Sister. "While I'm no big fan of Her divinity, I do think that we need to save the child from Herself. And if you're all salivating over the prospect of becoming Her apostles, allow me to remind you, first, that it took a hundred years for Christianity to get even the smallest foothold; and, second, Peter was crucified head down in Rome; Andrew was bound to the cross instead of nailed in order to prolong his agony; James the Greater was pierced with a sword by Agrippa; Bartholomew was beaten by rods and then beheaded; Matthew's end is debated — whether he was stoned, burned to death, or simply beheaded, but it wasn't good; Thomas was slashed to pieces with swords by four soldiers; James the Lesser was martyred although no one is sure just how; Simon was crucified; as was Jude in Armenia; Philip did no better; and John alone escaped being killed only because he died of natural causes before they could get to him. So you might want to rethink about our spreading the word. It's not something that seems to have gone all that well."

There was a long silence as the Ecclesia digested Sister's homily.

"Maybe, before we make any definite decision, we should ask Father Zawistowski to have a word with Her," Elliott suggested. "He's pretty persuasive, and he and She have certain things in common that might bridge the gap."

They all agreed that this might be a way to go, although Pincus had reservations about just how much they might have in common.

And so, that next morning She looked up from Her oatmeal and raisins to find the good Father sitting across from Her.

"Good morning," he smiled.

"Morning. Is there something I can do for you, Father?" She asked.

"As a matter of fact there is," Father smiled pleasantly. "I understand that you are about to kill yourself, which is, of course a sin."

"Says who?" and She spooned in another mouthful of oatmeal.

"Jesus."

"Really. Where exactly did he say that?" She asked.

"He didn't exactly say it, but it's certainly implied. And, of course, the sixth commandment forbids killing, and suicide is, of course, a form of killing," Father replied.

"Well, actually, not," and She reached for Her cup of tea and sipped in silence as Father Zawistowski waited for what was to come. "All other acts in the commandments apply to what one does to other people — lying, coveting, stealing, adultery — that's pretty clear, and there's no reason to think that the sixth commandment is any different. So, no, the sixth commandment definitely does not apply to suicide. It applies to killing other people. You want to take another stab at it?"

Father Zawistowski cleared his throat and thought.

"I don't think that there's any doubt that the Lord is against suicide," was all he could finally find to say.

"Well, that brings up an interesting point. Let's talk about that. Since the Bible is pretty much the only place from which we know

God and His word, I find it interesting that in some fourteen-hundred pages, depending on the size of the font, there is not a single mention of suicide, and you certainly have to admit that the Bible doesn't skimp on telling us what we should and should not do. Doesn't it seem a little odd to you that a God who cares about the minutest details, warning people not to wear garments made of both wool and linen — Deuteronomy 22:11 — or not to plant two different kinds of seeds in the same field — Deuteronomy 22:9 — and even demands that a person be stoned to death for collecting wood on the Sabbath — Numbers 15:32-36 — that this God couldn't be bothered to come right out and say that offing oneself is not kosher? So assuming that what is not prohibited is permitted, it would seem to me that suicide is compatible with at least Judaism and Christianity. What do you think, Father?"

Father's mouth hung open in dismay, saying nothing.

"Okay," She continued, "so why might it be that God has nothing to say about suicide? I'll tell you why. Because it's a real problem. He couldn't very much allow that those doing themselves in could still go to heaven or people would be hanging themselves until we ran out of rope. On the other hand, if God said that those who put an end to it all would automatically be condemned to hell, it would not be a nice thing for their grieving families, who already had a whole lot to deal with. So, being a compassionate God, He just kept His mouth shut on the matter, which was a real smart thing to do, I think, because there's really no good way to go here. The long and short of it is, there is no religious prohibition against suicide. Got anything else up your sleeve? I've got ten more minutes before I have to go help Mr. Cabenela die, and, believe me, if he had the strength, he would do himself in quicker than you can say *Pax Vobiscum*."

The Ecclesia were in the living room, reading papers and watching television coverage of the Berlin Wall being dismantled, the residents of East Berlin having decided that the new checkpoints allowing East Berliners to travel unrestricted to West Berlin were not quite as wide as they had in mind.

Father appeared in the doorway and cleared his throat to get the group's attention, then cleared it a second time when that was ineffective, and finally spoke when the second time was no more successful than the first.

"Excuse me? Excuse me," and one by one heads turned to face Father Zawistowski. "I'm sorry to disturb you, but I have an announcement to make."

"In the future, when you need someone to service your pastoral needs, would you be so kind as to find someone else. I ask this because I have reached the conclusion that you are all stark-raving mad. Good day and goodbye," and he turned and left, almost crashing into Rosalie, who was just arriving.

Rosalie stood at the doorway to the living room, looking at the silent Ecclesia, then back at Father Zawistowski departing, and then back at the Ecclesia.

"Would somebody like to tell me what's going on here?" Rosalie asked.

CHAPTER 4

As soon as Rosalie learned what was about to transpire with her daughter, she was on her way to the Hospice of Our Lady of Lament, Pincus at her side.

"I knew something was going on, but She wouldn't tell me what. I was with Her all night. 'Remember when I got the cotton candy stuck in my hair?', 'Remember when we went rowing in Central Park and I fell out of the boat?', 'Remember when they threw us out of church because I kept correcting the sermon of Father Joe, who had his facts so totally wrong?' I felt like I was trapped in a PBS documentary of our lives."

"I think She was saying goodbye," Pincus commented.

"Well, I have news for Her," Rosalie replied, "She can say hello now, because She's not going anywhere."

They trudged on, beneath a slate gray sky, their breaths fogging in the first cold of winter, although it would be a month before winter would officially begin. Vermont knew nothing of solstices. The rain that had been falling the last few days now coated the trees in an icy glaze, the bare branches reaching out like frozen fingers.

"You don't understand, Mother," She said as She removed her washed clothing from the basket on the bed and neatly folded them. "The Singing Machine has shown me the Good, and I see now how far removed from it I am. Listen to The Singing Machine, just listen, and you'll hear the infinite distance between the purity of God and the creature He's created. If I don't leave, if I don't become one with the Absolute, I'll be doomed to remain the imperfect creature I am. I will. Every vice will be reawakened in me, as it was with St. Angela of Foligno. Of course, since Angela prayed to God that her mother, her husband, and all her children would die so she could break free and accomplish her mission, and God did so in a matter of days, her vices may have been a little more extensive than mine."

"If you're telling me that you won't be praying for me to die like that sick woman, Angela, did to her mother, don't expect a pat on the back, dear," Rosalie replied.

"I have to do what I have to do, Mom," She said. "I've reached the third degree of ardent love. There's no turning back."

"You've done what?" Rosalie asked.

"Richard of St. Victor," She explained. "In the third degree, love paralyzes action. Union is the symbol, union with the Absolute, and ecstasy is its expression. The soul no longer thirsts for God, but into God. And this is where I'm going — into God," and She snapped out a pair of jeans, placed them neatly on the bed, and folded them.

"Okay, sweetie, lookie here," Rosalie moved over to the bed, picked up the folded jeans and started to refold them in a manner she thought better. "You can quote saints until there's not a day left on the calendar, but you are not going into that machine. Period. The end."

"I can do what I want, Mother," and She snatched the jeans out of Her mother's hands, and refolded them as She had at first. "I'm an adult, Mother."

"Then act like one," and Rosalie snatched the jeans back off the bed and re-refolded them.

"Maybe I should be going," said Pincus.

"No!" Rosalie and She said simultaneously, the jeans now stretched between them, yanking back and forth.

"Okay," Pincus said meekly, "then I'll stay."

"Mother, let go. Puh-lease. I can fold my own clothes," She said.

"Not from what I'm seeing," said Rosalie, and she gripped the jeans even more tightly.

"Let go, Mom! Max, will you please do something about this?"

Pincus looked at Her, then at Rosalie, then at the jeans stretched tightly between them. He had rarely felt so helpless.

"Like what?" Pincus asked. "Do you want me to fold them? I'm a neutral party."

"No, I don't want you to fold them," She said, Her face turning red from the struggle with Her mother. "I want —"

But She never finished. Her eyes rolled up in Her head, and She fell backwards onto the bed, convulsing spasmodically, a bit of white foam coming from Her mouth.

Pincus looked quickly at his watch, then rushed to the bed, where Rosalie was trying to hold Her down.

"Don't restrain her," Pincus said calmly.

"I can't let Her just go on like this!" Rosalie cried. "What's happening to my baby?! See what this has done to Her?! I can't watch Her like this!"

"Yes, you can," and Pincus rolled Her on Her left side.

"What do I do?" Rosalie watched Her jerk violently on the bed.

"Talk to Her — calmly. Tell her it's going to be okay," Pincus told Rosalie.

"Will it?"

"Yes, it will be," answered Pincus, glancing at his watch. Two minutes had elapsed, and She hadn't stopped. "It will be," Pincus repeated, as much to comfort Rosalie as himself.

"How do you know?" Rosalie asked, trembling herself.

"Because I do. Has She ever had seizures before?"

"Not when She's been with me."

Three minutes. After five minutes, Pincus would start to worry.

"Get a damp washcloth. Not too hot. Not too cold," Pincus told Rosalie, who backed away toward the bathroom, her eyes on Her all the way.

Pincus reached for some tissues and wiped away the saliva from Her mouth.

Four minutes. He could hear the sound of the water in the bathroom. It stopped and Rosalie repapeared.

"Why is She foaming like that?" Rosalie said as she handed Pincus the damp washcloth.

"She's not foaming. It's just saliva. During a seizure you don't swallow," and Pincus began to place the washcloth on Her forehead. Slowly the seizure began to subside.

"Is She on any medication?" Pincus asked Rosalie, who breathed a sigh of relief as she saw the seizure subsiding.

"Not that I know of," Rosalie said.

"I'm not on any medication," She said slowly, Her eyes still partially closed. Then She opened Her eyes and looked up first at Pincus, then Her mother.

"Wow," She said. "That was pretty amazing," and, before anyone could respond, She was asleep.

Pincus and Rosalie looked down at Her lying peacefully on the bed on top of her once-folded clothing.

"I'll refold them for Her once She's awake," Rosalie said.

"Maybe you should let Her do it," Pincus said quietly. "It would be best not to create any tension for a while."

Rosalie nodded, but she wasn't happy about it.

"There is good news," Pincus said. "She's probably not going into The Singing Machine tonight."

The next morning, when She finally awakened, She was brimming with excitement over what She had experienced during the seizure.

"I was St. Martin," She told Pincus. "I saw into eternity, and it was more wonderful than I can describe. Color and sound were the same thing. I heard flowers that sounded and saw notes that shone. The bird's song struck my eyes like a pageant of color and the sky was music. Do you know where I was, Max?"

"In the process of having an epileptic seizure?" Max did not like where this was going.

"I was inside The Singing Machine. That's where I was."

And Pincus knew all was doomed.

Pincus knew this because he looked into Her eyes, watching Her pupils dilate and then constrict, and it all became clear to him. The overwhelming passion, the desire to enter The Singing Machine, this notion that She could become one with the Absolute, the visions of undying light, this was a neurological condition. Her consciousness had reached such a high level that it had leaped over all that held Her bound to this world and it connected Her with another world, a higher plane, what She called the Absolute.

It was this act of consciousness that had dissolved all barriers, that had allowed the Absolute to flow in Her and now She had no choice but to embrace it until She experienced the infinite — and this is what propelled Her toward The Singing Machine each night. God was spread diffusely throughout her brain. She alone had escaped the grid of Her cerebellar map. There was no way back. There would be no cure.

When She had a second seizure and then a third, Pincus had no choice but to take the matter to the Ecclesia, who were not unaware of the situation, and, in fact, very close to sending out the proverbial posse to rein in Pincus, who they considered was responsible for it all.

"Would we be where we are right now," Sparky asked, "if you had kept your hands off Her?"

"Would you like to explain to me how exactly my loving Her has caused her seizures?" Pincus fought back.

"What is Her problem with The Singing Machine?" Sister asked, "Because I, for one, am not prepared to lose our Savior, even though I don't believe that she is our Savior or anything close to it, but majority rules."

"It's complicated," Pincus said. "When I first saw Her before The Singing Machine, She called it Daddy."

"She thinks it's Her father?" asked Meyer. "Surely She can't be serious. It's a machine. It can't have sex and produce a child."

"I wouldn't put anything past it," said Elliot. "I've always had the feeling that it can do whatever the hell it wants, and, if it gets horny, well, watch out."

"Hey," said Rosalie, "I happen to be Her mother, and I can assure you that I did not have sex with that singing scrap pile."

"What are we doing here?" asked Meyer. "Does anybody know?"

"What we're trying to do here, actually, is to keep our Savior from destroying Herself," Florence replied.

"We need to keep Her out of The Singing Machine," Theo joined the conversation. "The last thing we want is for another Savior to die."

"Well," said Elliott, "this may not be as much of a problem as you might think. As Meyer pointed out the last time we met, Saviors have a way of dying, and that's not necessarily a bad thing. It might actually be to our advantage."

"Only if She comes back from the dead," said Florence. "A Savior who just disappears isn't good for much. Without resurrection, She's just another dead person."

"I have an idea," said Sparky, and all eyes turned toward him. "Suppose, just suppose, that She goes into The Singing Machine and doesn't disappear, but thinks She disappeared, and then comes back. Then She's had the best of both worlds, and we've got a resurrected Savior, and off we go to preach Her word."

"What word?" Florence asked.

"We'll come up with something," Meyer said. "Just hear him out."

"How are you going to do that?" asked Pincus.

"Well," said Sparky, "we all know that the only time The Singing Machine is lethal is when it sings on its own. So, just suppose that I rigged it up so it seemed like it was singing on its own, but it really wasn't."

"What's it doing, humming?" asked a skeptical Sister Gloria Gloria.

"I'm playing a recording of when it sang another time, and I can activate its motors so it moves. You wouldn't know the difference to look at it, but it's not singing on its own."

There was a silence as the Ecclesia processed Sparky's plan.

"So," Sparky continued after he felt his words had sunk in, "She hears the machine singing, goes to the machine, goes inside it —"

"And nothing happens. How does that solve anything?" Meyer asked skeptically.

"Nothing happens, but how does She know that? Who knows what it's like to disappear? Maybe you disappear to everyone else, but you can still see yourself. If we're there watching, we tell Her that She disappeared, and then, miraculously, She reappeared. She walks from The Singing Machine resurrected. We tell Her that it must have been God's will, that He wasn't ready to keep Her at this particular moment, and so He sent Her back, reborn."

"Well," mused Theo, "Catholics do have a thing about being reborn."

"This is absolutely absurd," said Sister Gloria Gloria. "You're going to manufacture a resurrected Messiah? I won't allow it."

"Would you rather have Her die, or just spend the rest of Her life miserable?" Rosalie snapped at Sister. "I, for one, think it's a brilliant plan."

"I think that it's a ridiculous idea and the best solution would be just to destroy the damn machine," Pincus announced.

There was an immediate outcry.

"Over my dead body!" Ellott concurred.

"No way anybody is going to destroy our machine! No how!" Sparky cried out.

"Then how is She going to be resurrected?" Theo shouted over the din. "Before we know the meaning of its song?" Theo asked in dismay. "You want to destroy it before then?"

"Okay, okay," Pincus backed down. "Don't destroy it. But what happens if The Singing Machine decides to start singing on its own while you're faking it? That would be a problem."

"The Singing Machine never sings before 10:00 at night, so we'll do this as soon as the sun goes down," said Sparky.

All heads turned to Pincus with the same thought.

"Tell Her that you've thought it over," Sparky said, "and because of Her condition, you think She should go into The Singing Machine after all,"

"Now you want me to encourage Her to go into The Singing Machine?" asked Pincus. "I'm not doing it."

"She'll listen to you," Florence said.

"Don't be so sure," Pincus said.

"She will if you tell Her that you're ready now for Her to go and join Her Daddy, and that's exactly what She'll do if Her mother says the same thing," said Meyer, who was liking this idea more and more. "And we'll also go to Her and tell Her how much we love Her, and it is out of this love that we have all decided to let Her go, and so we've come to say our goodbyes and wish Her a splendid journey."

"Do you think we should have a last supper?" asked Florence. "It's kind of a tradition. I can make a casserole."

"I think we should table that until after we see how Max does," said Elliott. "First things first."

"I won't do this," said Pincus.

"Think, Max," Meyer said, "you'll be the founder of the Church, the one She loved the most."

"No, thank you," said Pincus.

"I think we should feed just enough juice in the machine to knock Her out," Theo offered. "Otherwise She might get suspicious. When She comes to, we'll all fall down on our knees, and shout 'Hallelujah!' and tell Her how She floated in the middle of The Singing Machine like a god, and then just arose and walked out."

"I can't believe that I'm listening to all this crap," said Sister Gloria Gloria. "I'm leaving. You're on your own and good luck, but keep me out of this. Someone help me back into my wheelchair."

"Perhaps, Max should go into the machine with Her?" Meyer proposed, not reacting to Sister's command.

"Don't be ridiculous," Sister said. "And end up with two Christs?

You think people are going to buy a Mr. and Mrs. Messiah?"

"I'm simply not telling Her to go into The Singing Machine," Pincus said emphatically, "and that's final. And, even if I did, which I'm not, I'm certainly not going in there with Her, no matter how foolproof your scheme is."

"Well, like Her mother said," Elliot asked Pincus, "which would you prefer — for Her to die or just be miserable for the rest of Her life?"

"Neither," said Pincus quietly. "Neither."

CHAPTER 5

Pincus stood frozen in the entrance of the Hospice of Our Lady of Lament. Residents ran about, screaming and sobbing. The living room looked like a tornado had hit it, tables upturned, lamps in pieces on the floor, chair cushions scattered everywhere. A woman in her seventies appeared naked, then ran away, as two men in robes were banging the wall.

It had started with Mrs. Cocozza. "I'm dying!" she screamed, as she raced in panic through the hospice. "I'm dying! We're all dying! We're all dying!"

It spread like wildfire among the residents. Soon they were all screaming, "I'm dying! We're all dying!" as though this dark secret had been kept from them, and, perhaps, Pincus thought, in some ways it had. Everything in the hospice had been designed as though nothing ominous faced those living there. All was ordered to forget. But Mrs. Cocozza could not forget, and now neither could anyone else in the facility.

Then, as Pincus watched, She appeared in the living room, where residents were running in circles, screaming. Strangely, She didn't say anything, no words to calm them down, to stop the hysteria, but She just stood there in silence. One by one the residents saw Her, and, to the surprise of Pincus, each stopped their screaming, until all that remained was the prolonged whimper of stifled sobs. She walked to each, standing chairs and tables upright on the way, and She placed Her arm around their shoulders, walking them to chairs, where they sat, taking deep breaths, recovering from the trauma.

She glanced for a second at Pincus, giving no acknowledgement of his presence, and then slowly left the room and walked down the hall. As She walked, the waves of remaining sobs subsided, in the way a tide might come to the shore, erasing the footprints of those who had walked its edge just a few moments before.

When, after a few minutes, She didn't reappear, Pincus walked outside and sat on the steps, wrapping his arms around himself in the cold. Winter had now settled in Vermont for good, or at least for the next six months, and snow flurries drifted down from the sky like an angel brushing dust off its shoulders, Pincus thought as he watched.

Pincus had experienced patients panicked by death before, though never more than one patient at a time, but he found what he had witnessed to be more unsettling than he would have imagined, and he wondered whether the mass hysteria might have had more to do with a sense of the impending death of Her, of the one they loved more than any other, of the one who had brought peace to their lives and comforted their souls. What would happen to them after She was gone? Death had announced itself, not as individual death, but as a universal, undeniable, and spiritual truth.

After some time had passed, Pincus debated whether he should go back inside to find Her, but finally decided that She would come to find him if She wanted. And so Pincus walked to the garden in back with the intention of strolling down the paths to get his thoughts in order.

The garden glistened with its cover of angel dust and looked not unlike the snow globe he once had on his desk. To his surprise, when Pincus reached midway in the frozen garden, he found Her sitting on the bench where they had first talked. She sat there, without a coat, staring ahead.

"Aren't you cold?" he asked Her, but She made no reply, staring ahead as frozen as the garden, so Pincus took off his coat and placed in on Her shoulders. Still silent, She said nothing, but pulled the coat around Herself and wrapped Her arms across Her chest.

They sat in silence, staring at the frozen koi pond. The giant goldfish still swam about beneath the sheet of ice that covered their domain, and Pincus watched them turn circles in and out of each other in an elaborate dance.

"You can't keep going on like this," Pincus said, his heart in his throat. "You must go into The Singing Machine."

She said nothing, staring ahead vacantly. Then in a moment, She spoke.

"That's what you want?" She said, avoiding his eyes. "You're sure?"

"Yes, I'm sure," Pincus lied.

She nodded, and, when She turned to face Pincus, a single tear from each eye made its way down Her cheek, like the Madonna of Syracuse.

"I thought this is what you wanted," Pincus said.

"It is," She said. "But the stronger the pull becomes, the harder it is to leave. No matter how splendid the place I'm going, who would want to leave this?" and She spread out her arms toward the garden glistening before Her.

"You're your own worst enemy, you know that," Pincus said. "By insisting that there's no hell, no heaven, no afterlife, nothing beyond this, by believing that meaning comes only from what we do here, you're making life on earth the be-all and end-all of our existence. It's no wonder you have trouble leaving."

"I never said that this was all there is, Max. The spirit lives on," She said, "and still has the power to influence beyond our death. Its power comes from our good acts and thoughts while we're alive. Evil drains it. Good replenishes and strengthens it. But still, it lives on — and loves on."

Pincus tried to comprehend Her words without success. It made no sense to him that after our life on earth, we could influence anything if there was nothing afterwards. Influence what? And how?

"What if you go into The Singing Machine," Pincus asked, "and you don't disappear, don't transcend anything, don't join with the Absolute — then what?"

"You think I can't be killed?" a smile came to Her face.

"I didn't say that," Pincus responded. "Not exactly."

"I'm not immortal, Max. I can be killed."

A chill went through Pincus's body.

"Will you come with me, Max?" She asked.

"Into The Singing Machine?" and the chill remained.

"No, just to be there. Will you do that for me?" Her eyes searched his.

"You want me to witness your death?"

"It's not a death, Max, and, if it were, the dying want those whom they love to be with them at the end, so I don't see the problem."

"There's no problem, unless you happen to be the person watching the one you love depart. Then there's a problem," Pincus said.

"Then don't come."

"No, I'll be there," and Pincus began to realize that he was no longer thinking of this as a rigged disappearance. He absolutely believed that he would be losing Her, and he wondered how he could stand it.

"So what will you do, Max?" She asked. "Afterwards."

"Mope. A lot," Pincus tried to lighten up the conversation.

She said nothing in reply, just looked deeply into the eyes of Pincus.

"I'll learn to live," Pincus finally said. "Or at least I'll try. With any luck I'll enjoy life in a way I never have before, with my eyes opened, holding on to your memory as a touchstone to move through a new world."

"That's perfect, Max. That's exactly what I would have wanted you to say," and She threw Her arms around Pincus. "Oh, I do love you so, Max."

Pincus wanted to tell Her that this was all a trick to keep Her with him, but the words wouldn't come out. The deception against someone he loved so completely and who loved him in return tore at his heart and could have stopped it entirely were it not that he knew that by doing this, he would not be losing Her.

They sat on the bench in silence, lost in their thoughts, Pincus musing about how bizarre this betrayal was. Is it possible to betray someone into not dying?

At the end, Pincus couldn't stand bearing his guilt. Whether he was deceiving Her for Her own good or not, it didn't matter — deceit is still deceit.

"I have to tell you something," Pincus started to say, but She put Her fingers up to Pincus's lips before he could continue.

"Please don't," She said.

"No, I have to tell you," he said when She took Her fingers from his lips.

She shook Her head.

"I already know, Max. And it's okay. It really is."

Pincus looked at Her. What did She know? That he wasn't telling the truth. That this was all a betrayal? And, if She knew, had She decided to go through with it, anyway? Pincus was about to pursue this when he looked up and saw Sister Gloria Gloria approaching in her wheelchair. She had a large heavy blue wool blanket wrapped about her to ward off the cold. Behind her, guiding the wheelchair, was Meyer Steinmeyer, wearing a giant red down coat, the hood pulled over his head, making him seem like a climber about to conquer Mount Everest.

"We've come to say goodbye," Sister said when she reached the bench where She sat with Pincus.

"And wish you well on your journey," Meyer added, making it sound as though She was taking a cruise to the Bahamas.

"I think I'll be going," Pincus said, giving Her a brief kiss, and then, nodding to Sister and Meyer, Pincus headed down the white path, leaving his coat behind.

"I know we have had our differences," Sister began her farewell, "but I say, let bygones be bygones."

"Water under the bridge," She said, evoking a sigh of relief from

Sister.

"But you have to understand that I had a great deal of responsibility for you girls at the convent, and it was by no means easy. You try handling three hundred and fifteen girls who are being flooded with hormones like an estrogen tsunami, and I'm the only sandbag. Does the Bible have anything to say about sex, other than a lot of begetting? No, it does not. So I'm on my own, doing the best I can under the circumstances. You have to understand that. Catholicism and the sex drive have always been at odds. No amount of praying seems to rein it in, you can take my word for that. You girls rubbed yourselves so much that I would walk into the dormitory at night and think I was in a field of locusts."

Meyer tried to stifle a laugh.

"There's nothing funny about it, Meyer, believe me," Sister sighed. "You just hope that by instilling the fear of God in the girls, they will eventually calm down."

"And love?" She asked.

"Love?" Sister was confused.

"The love of God. Do you think that instilling God's love in the girls might have calmed them down?" She asked.

Sister Gloria Gloria did not reply. A strange feeling swept over her, a feeling that she was truly saying goodbye to Her, that this wasn't a charade after all, and this made her sad, although it was a mystery to her why.

"I have something I've wanted to ask you for some time. May I?" She asked Sister Gloria Gloria.

Sister Gloria Gloria nodded, but she dreaded what was to come.

"Why did you become a sister?" She asked.

"I was called," Sister said, relieved that the query was so easy to answer.

"Called for what?" She asked.

"To serve God," Sister said, and, as she said it, she realized that this was something she had not told herself in a very long time.

"To serve Him how?" She asked.

Sister had to think.

"In whatever way He wishes," Sister finally said.

"And what did He wish for you to do?" She asked.

"You follow a path," Sister explained. "You become a nun, and you learn to pray with your heart, to be a pious person, a good person, and then the Mother Superior gives you a job to do, and I started teaching catechism, and then I became the director of the convent school," but, as she said this, she realized that she might have lost her spiritual compass along the way. Her good works had become a task — educate the girls, control the girls, graduate the girls, all the time keeping the expenses within the budget, a nearly impossible task. She had always assumed that this was doing God's work, that it was for this that He had called Her. The thought that there may have been something else that she had missed had simply never occurred to her. Sister was dumbstruck, horrified, and afraid.

"Why have you done this to me? Do you understand what you've done to me?" Sister said, half to Her and half to herself.

"Yes, I understand," She said, "and I'm certain you'll figure it out. It was so nice of you to come to say goodbye to me. Now if you'll excuse me — " but She never finished Her sentence.

"You can't leave me like this," Sister Gloria Gloria said in a panic.

"No, you can't leave her like this," Meyer seconded.

"Like what?" She asked.

"This," Sister said. "Like this."

"How is Sister to find her way?" Meyer asked.

"Sister will find her way, Meyer. She will have to rely on faith."

"Surely you can't be serious," Meyer responded. "You don't find anything with faith. That's the whole point of faith, to accept something you can't find. Like God."

"Sister doesn't have to find God. God is in her," She said.

"So, I've read," Meyer said.

"Meyer, since this is goodbye, I have something to leave you,"

She said.

"If it's anything like what you've left Sister, thank you very much, but no thank you," Meyer answered.

"I leave you with this," She said, ignoring Meyer's remark. "You have spent your life seeking certainty in an uncertain world. You want to prove things that can never be proven, count things that are uncountable, measure the unmeasurable. But, look into your heart. In moments of deep emotion we plunge deeper into the reality of things than we can ever hope to do in the horns of the most brilliant argument. Ask yourself what has been of value to you? Can you prove love? Can you count the days that make a life worth living? Can you measure friendship and loyalty? Can you solve the origin of faith? Do you truly want your life to be a notebook of numbers and syllogisms?"

Meyer started to tremble as he felt the life he had known slip away.

"Isn't a man measured by how well he has loved?" She continued. "Loving intuition is more fruitful and trustworthy than any proof you will ever develop. When did you last love?" She asked Meyer, who suddenly felt cold and fearfully empty.

"Wait a minute. Am I a spectator?" Sister asked, feeling neglected.

"I was speaking to you both," She said.

Sister looked at Her, her mind in disarray.

"We have to be going, haven't we, Meyer?" Sister said resolutely. But Sister found that she couldn't push the lever on her wheelchair that would initiate her departure. She could only continue to stare at Her. She now knew for certain that she would never see Her again, and Sister's heart filled with a heaviness that she could barely tolerate.

"Will you kiss me farewell?" Sister asked Her quietly.

She stood up, took two small steps to Sister's wheelchair, leaned down and kissed Sister gently on the cheek, and, then with Her fingertip, picked up the tear that was running down Sister's cheek.

"I think I will plant this tear under the snow," She said. "Next year, if you return, it will have become a flower. Which blossom would you like?"

"A rose," Sister said. "Yellow, not red."

She nodded, and placed the tear at the end of Her finger under the snow.

"May I also have a flower?" Meyer asked.

She looked up and saw the tears on Meyer's cheek. She kissed Meyer, as well, and wiped a tear with Her finger.

"And which would you like, Meyer?" She asked.

"A crocus. A saffron crocus," Meyer said.

"I've heard of crocuses, but never saffron ones," Sister said.

"Krokus was changed into a saffron flower by Hermes after the death of his love, the nymph Smilax. I thought it was appropriate," Meyer told Sister, as She placed her finger with the tear under the thin layer of snow.

"Yellow and purple side by side," She said. "It should be quite lovely when they come up in the spring."

And so Sister and Meyer left, feeling a deep sadness, but also, to their surprise, a relief, as though the burdens of a lifetime had been lifted from them.

No sooner had they left than Florence arrived. Florence had spent the afternoon baking a fruitcake, which she presented to Her.

"I had wanted to have a sort of farewell dinner — I was thinking of ribs and chicken and corn on the cob, kind of a barbecue, because that's always so friendly, but there are absolutely no ribs in this town, anywhere, so I made this. It's a lot to eat before you go, and I'm not sure that you can bring a fruitcake to the afterlife, but I didn't really know what else to do," Florence told Her.

"It's lovely, Florence," She told her. "I didn't expect anything, even for you to come, so you being here is all that I could ask for."

Florence smiled. "It is so comforting to think that you will soon be with the angels," she said. "I've always felt a connection with angels, since all angels are women, who I'm sure are treated much better than we women are on earth."

"Actually, not all angels are women," She said. "Maybe not any."

"No, I think you're wrong," Florence said with absolute certainty. "Have you ever seen a male angel? I certainly haven't. I have a collection of angels on my mantel, and they're all, every one of them, female. I don't think I could find a male angel if I wanted one, and I definitely do not."

"The Bible mentions only three angels by name — Michael, Gabriel, and Lucifer — all men, I'm afraid. And the Greek word for angel in the Bible is always masculine. In fact, the word has no feminine form at all. I'm sorry, Florence," She said.

"This is quite disappointing. We women always seem to get the short end of the stick. I was hoping that, at least as angels ..." Florence didn't finish her thought, then continued. "Is there absolutely no way in which we're equal to the men?"

"I'm sorry, Florence," She told her. "There is nothing equal on earth, nor in the heavens. No woman is equal to any man, just as no woman is equal to any woman. We love our children the same, but we don't treat them equally, but for who they are uniquely, just as God loves us all, but doesn't treat us equally. No two stars are the same, and none of us is the same. This doesn't mean that women are not entitled to equal rights. Only that we are not men. But there's compensation, something that eats at the hearts of men. It's something that artists have known since they put paint to board."

"I can't imagine what that would be," Florence said.

"Women own beauty," She said quietly.

Florence looked at Her and smiled. It was something she had always known, though, perhaps, had never thought in words so simple, and she puffed out her chest just a little, proud as a child taking her first steps.

"Florence," She said, changing the conversation, "there's something that I've wanted to tell you. I think you should consider going back to Sparky. I've seen you two together, and there's such tenderness between you. Love is something that grows like a child grows, but it's rooted in caring. The sadness in your heart weighs on me. I know that he's silly and bumbling, but you care for each other so deeply that it would be a pity for it to go to waste."

Florence was speechless. It was something she had long known, and had waited for this moment, the moment when someone would show her how to find her way back.

"You think I should marry him again?" Florence asked.

"I do," She said.

"I thought the Bible says that 'It is better to marry than to burn.' That's not much of an endorsement.

"Actually," She said, "the correct translation is 'It is better to marry than to burn with passion.' So you'll be okay in the face of God," and She gave Florence a smile of great comfort.

There was nothing more to be said, and so they said goodbye and Florence left, passing Theo, who had been standing some distance away, at the entrance to the garden, but now Theo approached Her. He stood, saying nothing, unable to find the words.

"You've come to say goodbye, Theo," She said to help him out. "That's very kind of you."

"Yes," Theo said, "but I don't know if I can. I feel as though I am losing Bernice all over again."

"Perhaps, I will see her where I'm going," She said.

"I thought you've been saying that there's no heaven, no afterlife?" Theo asked.

"It's true. I have said that. But it's more complicated than that, because it involves the eternal life of the soul," She answered.

Theo felt a sudden surge of joy, knowing that his wife might be happy in some better place.

"Is there something you would like me to tell her?" She asked.

Theo's heart skipped a beat. What would he say? She surely knew how much he loved her. And she knew that he carried her memory with him wherever he went, every second of every day.

"Yes, there is something you can tell her," Theo finally said. "My memories of her are embedded in my soul. But not all my memories are pleasant and easy to embrace. There are some things, more than a few, that I regret — words I spoke or failed to speak, actions taken or avoided, silences endured, pain inflicted. I ask myself why I could not have been more loving, more understanding and patient. Tell her I am sorry and ask her if she has forgiven me."

A smile came to Her face and she took Theo's hand in Hers. Then She looked deeply into Theo's eyes, and, at that moment, Theo knew that he was forgiven. Bernice was at peace, and for the first time since she left him, so was he. What is more, Theo knew with a certainty he could never explain that She was, indeed, the Messiah, come at last.

Theo let out a long deep sigh, then looked over at the koi swimming under the thin layer of ice on the pond.

"Did you know that there was a koi fish that lived to 226 years? It died in 1977. I saw a photo of it in *National Geographic*. It was the most brilliant scarlet you can imagine. What would it be like if we lived 226 years? I think it might be exhausting. You'd be babysitting grandchildren until you drop."

She smiled and studied Theo's eyes in the silence that followed. Then She kissed him lightly on the cheek and Theo left, looking back at Her every few steps. In a few minutes, Rosalie appeared and sat beside Her.

"I just hope you know what you're doing," Rosalie said.

"Yes, Mother, I do."

"Well, I don't. Would you like to explain it to me?"

"Not particularly," She said.

"Would you like to tell me why you won't?" Rosalie asked.

"Because you wouldn't understand."

"What is this thing about not understanding? Is this a genetic component of being a daughter? Is there some chromosome that is embossed with the words, 'you wouldn't understand, Mother,' and it's inherited and passed from daughter to daughter?"

"Which means you would have done it as well, Mother."

"Of course, I did it. Just not as often as you, dear. I employed it judiciously for maximum effect, not as a form of punctuation."

"Mother, may I ask you something?"

"You always do."

"Why are you here? Is this just a friendly chat, or is there something specific you wanted to say?"

"You know why I'm here."

"To talk me out of leaving."

"Fat chance of that."

"To say goodbye and wish me well?"

"Just to see you before you go. Is there anything wrong with that?"

"No," She said quietly. "There's nothing wrong with that, except you don't believe I'm going anywhere, do you? So this is confusing to me."

"What I believe is that you will do what you want to do. Come here, dear," and Rosalie pulled her daughter to her. She turned and laid Her head in her mother's lap. Rosalie looked down at her daughter, then out at the snow-dusted garden, and she ran her hand down Her hair.

"Do you think we make a good pieta?" She asked.

"Wasn't he dead when she held him in her lap?"

"Good point, Mother."

Rosalie continued to stroke Her hair, and then placed her hand over her daughter's hand and held it tightly.

"You have not been an easy child. This you know," Rosalie said. "But the struggle has not been without its good moments."

"You think?" She looked up at her mother and smiled.

Rosalie nodded. "I think," she said.

"But, in the end, this was the plan, wasn't it? You knew it would come to this," She said.

"Not specifically, but something like this. Who would have known of The Singing Machine? But once I heard it, it was clear. It would make no difference what I said or did. Not that I wouldn't try, but I might just as well have tried to hold back the sea. Will it be tonight?"

"No, not tonight. I'm too exhausted. Tomorrow."

Rosalie nodded.

"Are you pleased, Mother? You set this all in motion, you know."

"I go back and forth. I would have preferred another group to spread the word other than the fools we found, but so be it."

"Oh, they're not so bad, Mother, and the thing is, their quirks and faults make them relatable. Actually, as silly as they can be at times, I rather like them. I'm not sure I wouldn't have picked them out if I had had the chance. Please think of them that way, okay?"

"It'll be hard, but I'll try."

There was a silence, the only sound being the soft matting of the snow, which had become heavier, falling to the ground with the hush a mother gives her child to comfort her into sleep.

And so it was now. Rosalie began to hum something that she had heard many years ago, when she was a child, something that her own mother had sung to put her to sleep. And, as she sang, Her eyes began to droop and close, and She fell asleep in Her mother's lap, with the falling snow as Her blanket.

While these goodbyes were taking place, Elliott and Sparky were hard at work on faking The Singing Machine. After he left Her, Pincus had to see how things were going, and now he stood watching Sparky and Elliott at work.

"You're absolutely certain that nothing can go wrong?" Pincus asked.

"Nothing we can think of," Elliott answered. "We've got two tape players we're starting at the exact same time, and if one conks out, the second takes over immediately. You'd never know. Sparky just finished testing the mechanics of The Singing Machine, and they're perfect, but we've got an auxiliary motor hooked up just in case. We've got a governor on the electrical charge. It's about half what you get in electroshock treatment — enough to knock her out, but that's about all. If there's anything else that can go wrong, I don't know what it could be."

"What happens when a few hours later The Singing Machine starts singing on its own?" Pincus asked.

"We tell Her it's rejoicing over Her Christhood," Sparky said. "Who's to say it can't sing twice if it wants."

"Suppose She wants to go back in to test our claim?" Pincus still wasn't satisfied.

"I assume," Sparky said, "that by then She'll be as far away as we can get Her in celebration. Besides, while the zap I'm giving Her won't kill her, She's not going to be in any condition to go running anywhere."

"I'm still not sure She's going to believe our story of dying and coming back to life," Pincus pursued the matter.

"She will if you tell her," Elliott said. "She'll believe anything you tell Her."

"I may not be able to tell Her. I don't know how long I can keep lying to Her," Pincus said.

"Well, you'll do it this time if you really care for Her," Sparky said.

Pincus still wasn't satisfied, and he shuffled from foot to foot.

"Okay, look," Elliott finally said. "Unless we blow up The Singing Machine, which is not going to happen, you've got only three choices. One — the next time The Singing Machine sings for real, in She goes and She dies, and I don't think anybody can stop her. Two — She goes in and we play *our* music, and She *doesn't* die. One way She dies, the other way She lives. It's up to you."

"What's the third choice?" Pincus asked.

"When The Singing Machine starts singing for real, you both go in and you both die," Sparky said. "Then you don't have to feel so guilty, if that's what's bothering you."

Afterwards, as Pincus found himself wandering aimlessly down the road, his feet sinking into the rapidly accumulating snow, the crystals melting when they hit his shins and incasing them in ice, he still was not convinced that nothing would go wrong. Fate always had a way of outsmarting the engineers.

And while Pincus was resigning himself to the inevitable, Rosalie and She were encountering a throng of townsfolk at the entrance to the hospice. The crowd had been waiting for some time in the snowy evening for Her to appear so that they could say their farewells — men in plaid wool jackets, women in heavy coats, children in snowsuits, colorful knit caps on their heads.

One by one they approached Her, some with tears, some with smiles, telling Her how She had touched their lives. Families once torn apart appeared together, stronger than before. Young men and women whose lives had been heavy with disappointment were now buoyant with hope. They reminded Her of dinners they had once shared, of how casual encounters had lifted their spirits and sent them in new directions. She did not ask how they had learned She would be leaving, for She knew that there would be no answer. It was something that entered their hearts, from a place unknown to them.

When a young girl of ten, the last in line, was telling Her of learning to play the piano after they had met and how this had transported her to a place that seemed not of this world, The Singing Machine began its song. As the music drifted over the group, they joined hands. An elderly couple reached out and placed their arms around the waists of a middle-aged man with a beard and a woman with long curly hair, and they in turn reached out for those beside them, until all were embracing in a great circle, swaying back and forth to the music. She had been in the center, but now She walked over to two women with whom She had often picnicked on Sunday afternoons. They smiled, made a space for Her, and clasping each one around the waist, She joined the circle, moving to the music with the others.

A heavy-set woman in her fifties with thick glasses and full lips, the town librarian, started to sing to the music of The Singing Machine. She had no idea where she had learned this tune, if she had learned it at all, but the melody came to her out of nowhere, and so she sang with a joy not experienced since she was a child singing to her father, long since departed. One by one, the others joined in the song until they were all singing, arms about each other, shoulder to shoulder. Love, they sang, oh, love.

CHAPTER 6

Pincus wandered most of the night, as did She. Once the townspeople had left, She went from room to room in the hospice, not saying goodbye, as She thought this would be disquieting, especially after what had happened earlier that day, but sharing thoughts, asking about children and grandchildren, husbands and wives, talking but mostly listening. Last memories are always the strongest, and She wanted these to be the best. Then She pulled on Her boots, put on Pincus's coat, as it seemed the right thing to do, and went into the snow.

She walked down the road, kicking through the snow, past Joe's Snack Bar, past the Jericho Center General Store where she could see the hot coals in the wood-burning stove through the stove's iron gate. She stopped to smile at memories and then walked to the bridge over the Browns River, where She stood watching the eddies among the snow-covered rocks, thinking about the summers She had spent on the banks. In the distance was the Old Red Mill with Wilson "Snowflake" Bentley's collection. What fun he would have had tonight, She thought, and She tilted Her head up and stuck out Her tongue, letting the snow fall on it. Then She lay in the snow and made a snow angel, laughing at the irony of it all, fantasizing about whether, when She was gone, children would be making snow-Shes. Then She ran back to the hospice, skipping through the snow, lifting Her face to the sky and letting the snow coat it.

Back in Her room, She packed Her things into boxes, indicating which ones should go to whom, and then took a brief nap.

When morning came, the snow was still falling, though more

lightly. Pincus had collapsed into bed without getting undressed just as the night came to an end and the sky had begun to lighten into gray, not yet day, no longer night.

He had just fallen asleep when he awakened suddenly, aware that something was not right, but unable to get his bearings to determine how long he had been asleep, if at all. Outside the window, the snow was still coming down lightly. At the same time, the sky had taken on a pink hue from the rising sun. At first Pincus started to panic, believing it was sunset, but then, as he watched the sun move above the horizon, he realized it was dawn and he had been asleep only a short while.

Pincus lay in bed listening to the wind blowing through the branches and the song of the winter birds as they awakened to the morning, and then Pincus was gripped by a cold feeling in his gut.

The music was not that of the wind in the trees and birdsong. It was The Singing Machine.

Suddenly, there was the sound of someone running down the hall, and the door to his room flung open.

"The machine is singing!" Sparky cried. "It's singing at dawn! It never sings at dawn! Not ever!"

"It's not your tape?" Pincus asked.

"No!" Sparky tried to catch his breath. "It's singing on its own! At dawn. And She's already there!"

Pincus ran to his window. There She stood in the snow, wearing Pincus's coat, arms wrapped about Herself. She looked up at Pincus and smiled. Then She took off his coat and held it out to him, offering him to come down and fetch it. She wore the white summer dress in which he had first seen Her swaying before The Singing Machine. She appeared as a fairyland creature of the sort found in book illustrations from the last century, Rackham's *Sleeping Beauty*. She dropped his coat on the snow and turned toward The Singing Machine.

Fearing that She would disappear before he arrived, Pincus pulled on his clothes and raced from his room.

"We have to stop Her," Pincus said to Sparky, as he passed him in the hall. "Let's go!"

"No," said Sparky, frozen in fear, "I can't. I can't go."

And so Pincus raced alone down the hall and out of the inn alone.

When he reached the field behind the Sinclair Inn where The Singing Machine sat, there were only light flurries. The sun had finally pulled itself over the white-covered tree tops, bathing The Singing Machine in a shimmering pink light. Pincus stopped when he saw The Singing Machine, its arms covered with snow, reflecting the sun, grander than it had ever been, moving slowly in wondrous configurations, in a dance he imagined mimicked those of the stars. From it came music far more spectacular than anything it had yet produced.

She stood there, Her arms spread, moving with the song, Her face and hair radiant in the light. She had never been more beautiful.

Pincus walked up and stood beside Her.

"I knew you'd come," She said, not looking at Pincus.

"I have to talk to you," Pincus said. "This wasn't supposed to happen this way."

"No, it was, Max. This is exactly how it was supposed to happen."

"I've betrayed you. I told you to go into The Singing Machine only because we had it rigged to make it seem as though it was singing on its own. Then you would live. I never meant for you to go. It was a ruse, a deception."

"It's the only thing you knew how to do. I understand," She said and took a step toward The Singing Machine. Pincus grabbed Her about the waist.

"Please don't," he said. "I'm truly sorry."

"You don't have to apologize, Max. Please let me go."

She turned to Max, kissed him, and then slipped from his grasp.

"Please," Pincus pleaded as he watched Her walk to The Singing Machine.

When She reached The Singing Machine, She turned to Pincus,

and She smiled.

Then She turned back to The Singing Machine and stepped inside. Pincus watched in horror.

She didn't disappear immediately, but stood there, arms bowed over her head, her fingers interlaced, her body sweeping side to side, bathing in the music.

Slowly the outline of her body began to fade, as though dissolving into The Singing Machine.

It was more than Pincus could tolerate. He raced into The Singing Machine, and grabbed Her before She could disappear forever from his life.

"Get out, Max!" She said in anguish.

"I'm not letting go of you! Come back with me!" Pincus cried, but the music of The Singing Machine became louder and drowned his voice.

"You can't come in here, Max!" She cried.

"But I did come in here," Max replied.

"But you can't stay in here! Please get out while you can."

"I'm not disappearing."

"Because I'm not letting you disappear, but I can't last much longer. You have to go, Max. Now. Please. You have to let go of me, Max! Now!"

The urgency in Her voice frightened Pincus, and he took his arms from Her. Instantly, Pincus was expelled from The Singing Machine, as though a gust of wind had caught him and carried him away.

Pincus picked himself up from the ground and stood there, frozen, looking at Her, more radiant than ever. She looked back at Pincus, their eyes locked, and, as She slowly disappeared, Her form nearly transparent, not much more than a wisp of air, She stretched Her arms out toward him, Her strength to reach him gone.

"Life!" She cried out. "More life!"

And then She was gone.

There was only silence, until, suddenly, from behind Pincus there came a wail that shook the earth, the most profound expression of grief that Pincus had ever heard.

"Noooooooooooo!..."

Pincus turned and found the Thaumaturge. He was on his knees, tears streaming down his cheeks. He wore a Hawaiian shirt with coconut-laden palm trees on it, and on his head was a cap with two crossed golf clubs and the words, 'St. Pete Tennis, Swim, and Golf Club.'

As the Thaumaturge's wail subsided, The Singing Machine came back to life, singing a song of such profound grief that all who heard it wept until the sun had climbed to the top of the sky, and some who heard this song find themselves, from time to time, weeping still.

CHAPTER 7

And the Ecclesia came, and when they saw what had been done, they berated Pincus and called him a traitor, and betrayer, the killer of the second true Christ, because they had heard the lament of The Singing Machine, and they knew that their Savior was no longer with them.

One by one, they had arrived, all but Rosalie, who slept, unaware of what had transpired, and, when she finally awakened, she was certain that She had induced a deep sleep in her to spare her the pain.

"I will not believe," Meyer told Pincus, "that She did not know all along that The Singing Machine would sing at dawn, and knowing that, She would not have told you."

"I knew nothing until I woke up this morning and Sparky knocked on my door," Pincus told Meyer, confused about why Meyer, who had been advocating Her death, was now berating him because of it.

"You were the one who told Her to go into The Singing Machine," Elliot said. "This is all your fault, Max."

"You all asked me to tell Her," Pincus snapped back.

"We asked you to tell Her to go into The Singing Machine that had been rigged, not the one that would kill Her!" Elliott returned.

"I'm not sure that She's actually dead," Pincus said, "at least not in the traditional way."

"And what exactly is the nontraditional way of death?" asked Meyer. "I'd like to know. It might come in handy someday."

"Well," Pincus said, "for example, in this particular case there's no body. As a physician I can attest that in all cases of death one encounters a dead body, or at least ashes in the case where death is caused by conflagration."

"I just have to wonder whether this would have happened if She had not been a woman," Florence mumbled, still smarting over her last dialogue with Her. "Women always have a way of being treated as though they're invisible."

"Well," Pincus replied, "first of all, if She hadn't been a woman, She would have been He. And, second, it seems to me that the last time there was a Savior it did happen. He kind of evaporated into thin air. There was no body, at least until he reappeared, at which time he gave no real indication of being dead, or having been dead, at least the way I read it."

"This is blasphemy!" Sister Gloria Gloria shouted at Pincus. "Of course, Jesus was dead. You can't rise from the dead if you're not dead to begin with!"

"I think," said Theo, "that we need to figure out what to do now. There's no use crying over spilt milk. It's water under the bridge. The horse is out of the barn, and we have to move on."

"I could not agree more," Florence said. "There's no sense in our making poor Pincus into some sort of pariah."

"Thank you, Florence," Pincus welcomed the support.

"History will do that without needing our help," Florence continued.

"My suggestion would be that we meet after breakfast to determine our further course," Meyer said. "I'm going into town to get some croissants and brioche. Can I get some for anyone else?"

"They have croissants and brioche at the Jericho General Store?" Pincus asked in surprise.

"They do now," Meyer smiled, not caring to elaborate further.

And, with that, the group made their way back inside the Sinclair Inn, where they found Mrs. Pratt waiting for them. "There will be no breakfast this morning," she said. "We're in mourning, and anyone who gives me any trouble over this will be looking for another place to stay."

The Ecclesia immediately gave their orders to Meyer, and added other items to compensate for what might be a mourning period of indeterminate length.

When they convened after breakfast, there was intense discussion about the next step, although there was a consensus that, through default, they would consider themselves to be the Called and Chosen ones.

"I don't want to cause any more trouble than you believe, incorrectly, that I have caused, but might I ask who exactly has called and chosen you?" Pincus asked.

"Well, you are, in fact, causing trouble. This is no time to split hairs," Elliott replied. "If not us, then who?"

"I don't know who, but in my experience those being called and/or chosen have to be called and/or chosen by *someone*," Pincus responded.

"Max, I'm not sure that this is an appropriate venue for you to be expressing your opinions any longer, considering," Meyer told Pincus.

"Yesterday, you informed me that I was going to be the founder of the church, the one She loved most," Pincus pointed out.

"That was yesterday," Meyer responded. "A lot has happened since then."

"May I at least stay and observe?" Pincus asked.

"If you wish, but I'd ask you to let us do the talking and not stir up anything," Meyer said.

Pincus nodded and settled back in his armchair.

"Now," said Meyer, "I think that there's a clear precedent for saying that our main function as Ecclesia should be to spread the word, Her word."

"And that word would be?" Theo asked.

"Well, clearly," Meyer said, "She has come to tell us how to live together, how to form governments, and to show us the common soul that will unite us in one socialist state," but Meyer noticed that these words, so long ingrained into his being, now had a certain hollowness, as though She had emptied them of their meaning and left him only with a single thought: the eyes of the innocents were upon him and he was one of them.

"She told you that?" Sister Gloria Gloria asked.

"Well," Meyer said, his dogma faltering, "She didn't use those exact words. But it's fair to interpret that from what She did say."

"Namely?" Sister asked.

"Don't put me on the stand, Sister," Meyer answered. "I can't recall word for word."

"I'll take an approximation," Sister said.

"Well," Meyer responded, "it seems to me that She wanted us to experience the kind of love that transcends the universe, the kind that a woman alone can experience when her funklein connects with the cosmos," but for some reason that Meyer couldn't understand, he would have been happy if he never heard the word *funklein* again.

"Did you say that love transcends the universe, Meyer?" Sparky asked. "How can anything transcend the universe? What's it do, fall into a black hole and come out the other end? And what good is love if you have to go through a black hole to find it?"

"This is all a bunch of nonsense," said Elliot, "our trying to figure out why She came and what She wanted us to say when we spread the word. The real question is not why She came, but what we're going to tell everyone about why She came, and that's up to us, and, when you come right down to it, it has absolutely nothing to do with why She actually came, since we're never going to know that without asking Her, which we can't do."

There was silence as the Ecclesia pondered the clear wisdom of Elliot's words.

"Well," said Theo finally, "whatever it is, it better be good, or nobody's going to give a flying fuck, and we're all going to look like idiots, and She's going to be just another small-town mystic who claimed to be the Savior."

"She never claimed to be the Savior," Pincus said, and then slapped his hand over his mouth, realizing he had just violated the terms of his probation. "Sorry. It won't happen again."

"Maybe She never claimed to be our Savior," responded Florence, "but we are claiming it, so we all had better have a darn good story."

"Suppose," said Sparky, "that we say that She created The Singing Machine. I think that makes a terrific story."

"For what purpose?" asked Sister. "The Savior is telling us all to go out and build singing machines? I don't see that inspiring the faithful. It sure wouldn't inspire me."

"It was just an idea," said Sparky quietly.

"Suppose we just told the truth?" Theo asked.

The Ecclesia turned and looked at Theo, convinced that he had descended even deeper into dementia.

"I thought," said Theo, "that since She inspired all of us, she might do the same for others, just as She was."

"She might, Theo," said Meyer, "but the problem here is that we don't actually have Her to inspire others, unless you know something I don't. And I don't think a story about a hospice aide who becomes addicted to a weird machine that makes music and zaps everything that goes into it, and then she jumps into the device and gets zapped, herself, is going to result in a lot of people becoming — what shall we call them — Sheists."

And so it went.

And while the Ecclesia were debating their course as the Called and the Chosen, outside in the newly fallen snow, in front of The Singing Machine, Rosalie knelt beside the Thaumaturge in a vigil of grief.

"I suppose, Daddy," Rosalie said to the Thaumaturge, "this was to be expected."

"I suppose," said the Thaumaturge, tears still on his cheeks.

And when night arrived, the group sat in contemplative silence in the Inn, exhausted from having gotten nowhere.

"The real reason I think She came —" Sparky finally began, but

Elliott interrupted him.

"Sparky, please," Elliott said in frustration. "Haven't you been listening? We're not interested in why She came!"

"But I am," said Sparky. "How come She came? Does *anybody* know?"

There might have been a response had not, at that moment, The Singing Machine began its song.

At this the group arose as one and drifted out the door and around the back of the Sinclair Inn to The Singing Machine, as though they expected to find Her in Her usual place, swaying to the music. But only Rosalie and the Thaumaturge were there, still kneeling in mourning.

The Ecclesia stood before The Singing Machine, enraptured by the music, remembering how She had been when The Singing Machine sang its song. When the music finally came to an end, Sparky turned to Sister.

"I saw Her," Sparky said. "She came back, and She smiled at me."

"Yes," said Sister Gloria Gloria, "I saw Her, also. She told me to keep up my good works."

"I heard Her say that, as well," Meyer Steinmeyer said. "Damn. We should have asked Her what we should say about Her."

One by one the Ecclesia reported on Her having appeared to them. Then they turned to Pincus.

"I got involved in the music," Pincus said. "I must have missed Her."

As the Ecclesia drifted off to the Inn, Florence made a proposal.

"I think that for a while, until we have a clearer picture of things, it would be good if we all stay together."

"I agree," Meyer agreed. "We shouldn't split up. We have work to do."

"Yes," said Elliott. "And I think that we should bring The Singing Machine along with us. It is, after all, in a way, all that remains of Her. And She might reappear from it again."

"What about Pincus?" Sparky asked.

"I'm not sure," Sparky replied. "We should talk about it."

At the end, Pincus was not asked to join them, and he didn't go. The last he saw of the Ecclesia, they were back on the road. Sister, feeling they lacked direction, had rejoined them in her wheelchair, although she had long ago been able to function without it, a secret she kept because she had grown so accustomed to the perks of being an invalid that it would have been inconvenient to give them up. Her role as chief arose not from her handicapped or spiritual status, but was more a function of her still having the portable shrine of the Holy Mother to whom she, and she alone, could obtain navigational guidance.

At the last moment, Rosalie joined the group, having decided to honor the memory of her daughter, as well as being highly suspicious of the intentions of the Ecclesia. Meyer Steinmeyer followed behind Sister, as before, and, finally, as they disappeared down the road, Pincus, from where he sat rocking on the front porch of the Sinclair Inn, could make out Florence Pym, Theo Wainwright, and finally Elliott and Sparky Pym, struggling up the long hill with the giant Singing Machine.

"Well," Pincus said to the Thaumaturge, who rocked in a chair on the front porch beside Pincus, "I can't say that I'm unhappy to see them go."

"Yes. I suppose," said the Thaumaturge, "you feel that you've pretty much made a mess of things."

"Well, I have killed the Savior once again," Pincus noted.

"Not exactly," replied the Thaumaturge, "but close enough so that the distinction is insignificant. Don't let it bother you, though. We pioneers in the spiritual world always have a tough time of it, and She's in good hands now."

Pincus turned to the Thaumaturge.

"Life? More Life?" Pincus asked him.

"Your guess is as good as mine. Still in the final analysis, a richer more satisfying life for us all is the goal of religion. So why not?"

A sudden disquieting thought occurred to Pincus.

"All this — has it been one of your illusions?" Pincus asked.

"It's been the training I promised you. I regret the pain — for both of us. My soul aches at Her departure. But, no pain, no gain. I trust it has not been without its redeeming aspects."

"Does that mean that it all was or was not an illusion?" Pincus asked.

"Let's just say that it was truth rendered expressive," the Thaumaturge informed Pincus.

"Was She God, our Savior, the Messiah, what? Will She come back?" Pincus continued to explore the ramifications.

"No transitory appearance exhausts the divinity. God was revealed before Her. God will be revealed afterwards."

"I don't understand it. What's She accomplished?" Pincus asked.

"We'll have to see," the Thaumaturge answered. "Under the best of circumstances, She will inspire people to love Her after She's gone."

Pincus rocked back and forth in his chair, thinking it over, watching the sun setting before him. He thought he could hear the faint song of The Singing Machine in the distance, but, perhaps, he imagined it.

The Thaumaturge reached in his pocket and handed Pincus an envelope.

"What's this?" Pincus took the envelope in his hand.

"The Synoptics have never been the final word for me, so to speak. For your edification, and so this is not a total waste, I give you the song of The Singing Machine, transcribed into words. The way I look at it, it's not a bad remedy for the weariness of ordinary life, taken from time to time, as needed."

Pincus started to open the envelope, when the Thaumaturge's large hand reached out and stopped him.

"Not now," the Thaumaturge instructed. "In a year or so — after all this has died down. But, for now try this. It's a letter from Her to you. I received it in the mail last week."

Hands trembling, Pincus opened the envelope and read the note inside.

Dear Max,

Out of the deepest love I tell you this. An immense revolution is coming. It will be painful, like the anguish of childbirth, and preceded by dark calamities and strange phenomena. But you must persevere because you will be seeing the birth of the divine spark that is in all of us and that we share with the universe.

At the end of it, we will all be together. And I will see you once again. Truly I will. We will be together once more and forever.

My love, She

The tears that fell down the cheeks of Pincus were not from sadness, but from the most sublime joy.

CHAPTER 8

There are tales and rumors, rumors of tales, and tales of rumors, making it almost impossible to relate with any reliability what transpired next. The only certainty is that Sheism, as it quickly became known, went from a cult to a culture, and spread in a way usually reserved only for pathogens for which no successful treatment has yet been found. Controversy gave way to conviction, and then devotion, and exactly how this all came to pass is as mysterious as Her.

* * * * *

Those who came upon Pantera, aka the Thaumaturge, usually found him in his Hawaiian-print shirt on one or another tee of the Cocopah Arizona Golf Course. When questioned about Her birth, he seemed to vaguely recall an angel descending from heaven and saying something to the effect of "Lo, a virgin shall conceive, and bring forth a daughter, and Her name shall be," but he did not recall the exact name specified by this angel, the precise date, nor whether this was prophesied to be delivered from his own child and resident virgin, Rosalie. As Pantera tells it, there was a heated exchange with the angel in which Pantera informed him in no uncertain terms that there would be hell to pay, so to speak, if anyone, heaven-sent or not, messed with his wife, and, when his daughter shortly thereafter was the one who became with child without the benefit of intercourse, he felt he had prevailed. Questioned about whether the tale of his having had his daughter inhale animalcules to conceive might be true,

Pantera would smile good-naturedly and say, "I suppose that I might have helped the process along a bit, but it was a long time ago, and it's all a little hazy now."

As for whether Pantera, himself, was now a believer of She-ism, one can assume this to be the case from the pendant about his neck. It is identical to those well-known relics to be in the possession of millions of the faithful with small scraps of metal on necklaces or on key chains that they claim to be of the True Machine, suggesting both that The Singing Machine had been destroyed, and, based on the amount of scrap metal resulting from its destruction, that it was once the size of a Nimitz-class aircraft carrier.

*   *   *   *   *

As for the Ecclesia, the following can be reported with varying degrees of certainty:

Sister Gloria Gloria returned to her convent school, expelled all students and converted the property into a conference center where she lectured daily on the teachings of She. Initially, She gave interviews sharing her insights into Her nature, but her fees increased steeply and this ended rather quickly. As for the teachings, themselves, Sister had distilled them to this: "She is, She says, She was." For those wishing to hear more, she offered a retreat that included seven day's lodging, all meals, and a bus trip to the Hospice of Our Lady of Lament where the faithful would have the opportunity to meet for one hour with two terminal patients who had direct contact with Her, if they were still alive.

*   *   *   *   *

Theo Wainwright, by all accounts, became what might colloquially be called a "vagabond." He wandered from town to town, lodging in the homes of those he met along the way and reciting to them in iambic pentameter his tale of She, a recitation he honed as he walked. One example that has survived:

She changed my life in ways that can't be told, and turned my dullest days to purest gold; Her spirit warmed my heart and stilled my soul; Her face sublime, Her body joyous to behold.

As an evangelist, Theo was not always as successful as he would have liked. His preaching universal love and brotherhood at the epicenter of the Rodney King riots that occurred shortly after he arrived in Los Angeles was one example of where he may have fallen short, but the lengthy hospitalization that followed did not deter him in his mission, although his whereabouts thereafter are unknown.

*   *   *   *   *

It is unclear what happened to Meyer Steinmeyer. He left the Ecclesia at the end of the first year and was reported variously to have gone to Moscow, where he taught icon painting at the St. Tikhon's Orthodox Theological Seminary; to Leipzig where he was teaching rudimentary language skills to apes in the Department of Primatology at the Max Planck Institute; and to Gif-sur-Yvette, where he taught messcopic physics at *L'Institut national des sciences et techniques nucléaires*. In all instances, he is said to have slanted his instruction toward establishing a ministry that would spread "the Word of Her," and in all instances he was asked to leave for doing just this, although the faculty was careful not to appear to be anti-She.

The reason given for his dismissal was invariably his claims of being of Russian or German or French nationality, claims that fell apart upon the surfacing of a birth certificate indicating he was born in Baltimore, Maryland of a family that had been in America since the Mayflower landed, Meyer Steinmeyer's birthname being Michael Standish.

*   *   *   *   *

Elliot Pym returned to Jericho, where he established his ministry for Her. The town was in some turmoil as a result of being the place where She lived and ascended to wherever it was that She went. The opinions on this varied from the right hand of God to thin air, not necessarily exclusive, some thought.

The town was now open to pilgrims from 2:00 p.m. to 4:00 p.m. every day but Mondays, a compromise that the town council had reached after their charming village had become overrun with the faithful, terrifying the residents of the Hospice of Our Lady of Lament when strange faces appeared at their windows, hoping to see some indication of where She had dwelled.

In addition, Mrs. Pratt found the pasture behind the Sinclair Inn frequently trampled by the devoted as they searched for signs of The Singing Machine.

Only the proprietors of Joe's Snack Bar and the Jericho Center Country Store seemed to appreciate the influx of religious tourists, but eventually they neared nervous collapse from trying to serve the massive crowds. They realized that they could maintain both the increased revenue and their mental health by opening the town to the faithful for two hours a day, a duration that was more than adequate to wipe them out of virtually everything they had to sell.

"I returned here," Elliot informed all who inquired, "because I found a certain peace of mind in being here. Knowing that I will spend the remainder of my days on earth where She has been has a calming effect on my spirit. Her presence is everywhere. It is here that my soul is immersed in the ocean of Divine Splendor and illuminated by the Sublime Abyss of Unfathomable Wisdom."

Elliot's theology as it related to Her was a simple one. "We do not believe that She has revealed God to us," he preached. "She was never a theologian, nor a philosopher with a more or less well-composed system. To be Her disciple one doesn't need to sign any formulary, or to pronounce any confession of faith. Only one thing is necessary: to be attached to Her, to love Her."

Elliot, like many others, had come to love Her. His heart ached that he could not see Her once again, talk to Her, be in Her company.

"She never argued about God," Elliot preached, "because She felt God directly in Her. It was how it was supposed to be with Christ. Jesus had neither dogma nor system, but simply a fixed personal resolution. It exceeed in intensity every other created will, and even today directs the destinies of humanity. The power of men in association, the Ecclesia, was derived from Jesus. He was full of the idealistic notion that it's the union of love that brings souls together. He declared that whenever men assemble in his name, he will be in their midst. And this is who She was, in all Her being, and this is why I know in my heart that She was our Savior come again.

"Because She showed that the Scriptures are all myth, and not even a very consistent myth, many think that She was against religion, and, especially, against Jesus being our Savior. In fact, it's exactly the opposite."

And it is this, of course, as it is well-known now, that led Elliot Pym to the pronouncement that has brought the masses flocking to Sheism.

"She was the most Christian of us all. She restored the true intention of Christ. She came, not to reject Catholicism or Christianity, but to return to it, to what it was once supposed to be when Jesus walked the Earth."

At this pronouncement, Elliott Pym would pull an index card from his pocket and show it to the listener.

"This is what a so-called true Christian of today must face," he would say.

The card read:

Did I deny or doubt God's existence?
Did I refuse to believe in God's revelation?
Did I believe in horoscopes or dreams?
Did I believe in reincarnation?
Did I presume on God's mercy?
Did I neglect to pray today?
Did I miss mass or a holy day of obligation?
Am I always reverent in the presence of the most Blessed Sacrament?
Have I failed to educate myself on the true teachings of the Church?
Did I fail to contribute to the support of the Church?
Was I the cause of someone leaving the faith?
Did I kill anyone?
Did I entertain impure thoughts or desires?
Did I perform impure acts by myself or with others?

Elliott Pym would take the card back from the not-infrequently trembling hands of the reader and make this observation.

"With a list like this, converting folks from Christianity to Sheism is like taking candy from a baby."

* * * * *

Sparky and Florence, reunited, returned to their inn in Podunk, which now resembled a carnival. Vendors had colorful wagons parked up and down the road leading to the house, selling Philly cheesesteaks from one, sausage subs from another, spun cotton candy from another, fried dough from still another, in what seemed like an endless line of festive fare to serve the needs of the ceaseless onslaught of pilgrims to the Pym's farm.

They came to see the immense mural that Sparky Pym had painted on the side of his barn in an attempt to equal in majesty the Sistine Chapel.

The Singing Machine was painted in its full glory and life-size, as well as the figures of those who peopled the story of Her — all members of the Ecclesia, including Mrs. Rosalie Heiligenschein and Dr. Max Pincus, all with their names written beneath them, giving the impression that they were standing on pedestals, whether or not this was the intent of the artist. The Hospice of Our Lady of Lament floated in the sky amongst puffy clouds, along with the Jericho Center Country Store. Running down one side was the waterfall of Browns River, and surrounding the work and providing a floral border was the garden behind the hospice, including the koi pond in which goldfish stared adoringly up at the figure in the center of the mural — She.

She was dressed in Her cut-off jeans and tight t-shirt and looked not entirely unlike the women one finds draped over red convertibles in sports car ads.

As Florence Pym tells it, getting back with Sparky was, at first, a little strange. But then, to her surprise, she found herself loving Sparky, not for his positive points, but for his defects, and she found this to be a love so much deeper than any other kind.

"We try to make someone perfect," Florence Pym has said, "to be like us, but when we can look at his faults and love these, then that love is so much more powerful. It's not just accepting the ways in which he's imperfect, but actually loving him for them, because that's what makes him human, real, different from anyone else, but even more — they reveal so much about him that's endearing — all those fears he has and the vulnerabilities. You know him better than you ever imagined, and you realize that what you really loved about him was not all those things that you wanted in a man, but the things that drive you nuts. I know it sounds crazy, but it's true."

As for what became of The Singing Machine, Florence had this to say.

"We almost divorced a second time because of that darn thing. When we got back home, Sparky set it out in the field where it had originally been. It didn't sing. It hadn't sung a note since the day after She disappeared in it. But one night I woke up, and Sparky wasn't beside me. I had a feeling what was going on, so I went to the bedroom window, and there he was on his knees in front of The Singing Machine, and I knew what he was thinking. He was thinking of Her. He wanted Her to come back. He was hoping to see Her again.

"I was sitting on the settee in the living room late one night when Sparky walked back in from The Singing Machine, and I said to him, 'Sparky, I just want you to know that I love you for having feelings that are so deep, and for what She means to you.' And there it was. I realized that I was loving Sparky for something he was doing that was driving me completely crazy, because what he was doing was Sparky. And you know what he did?

"Sparky walked right back out the door, and he got a sledge hammer, and he started to destroy The Singing Machine, because he knew that, as long as it was there, he would not be strong enough to resist going to it every night, and he knew that, even though I understood and loved him for it, it hurt me.

"Suddenly, there was a sound from The Singing Machine, like someone wincing in pain, and the more Sparky hit it with his mallet, the more horrible the sounds were that came from it.

I don't know how Sparky continued, but he did, out of his love for me. He must have been in such terrible agony. And then The Singing Machine started to sing. It sang just beautifully, as though The Singing Machine was saying, 'Look what I can do! I'm alive! I'm a beautiful thing!' It sang and it sang and it broke your heart.

"Of course, eventually, when there wasn't much left of The Singing Machine, it stopped, or, at least, it wasn't singing like it had been; there was just this quiet little tune, like it understood and was saying goodbye, like what you sing to put your child to sleep. And then it stopped, and there was only silence. I looked outside and all that was left was this giant pile of scrap metal. It had taken Sparky nine days and he never stopped, and then he came and got me, and he took me by the hand and brought me to what had been The Singing Machine, and he kissed me right there, and we both cried in each other's arms for a very long time."

Pilgrims report that, on hearing Florence tell this tale, they are reduced to such profound sorrow that they fear they may never recover. And, yet, there is a far greater sorrow at the Pym's farm.

On the third floor of their home, in a room with shades drawn, sitting in the darkness on a small wooden chair, is Rosalie. She appears to be twice her age, has lost all color, and her face is expressionless. Day after day she stares vacantly ahead in silence, the way a mother would look after the death of her only child.

"She hasn't talked since we came back here," Mrs. Pym explains. "We've been taking care of her, feeding her, and bathing her, trying to entertain her although nothing interests her. She absolutely won't go out of her room. We think she's had some sort of a breakdown, but we don't know. Maybe she's just grieving.

"When we first left the Sinclair Inn," as Florence tells it, "and word of Her had spread, Rosalie was idolized. People would come up and give her gifts, money, food. They would want to wash her feet, to touch her, to hear a word from her. It never stopped. Everybody wanted her. And Rosalie tried to reciprocate. She wanted to make sure that her daughter's memory was preserved, that She lived on forever in people's hearts. But it became too much.

"The more people clamored for Rosalie, the sadder she became, and then one day, we were all sitting on the side of the road, eating lunch, and a woman arrived with a small boy, maybe four or five, who was covered with thick smelly skin, like scales, and begged for Rosalie to cure him, and Rosalie looked at the pained eyes of the boy and saw in them the hope that his mother had placed there that Rosalie would be able to cure him, that after today his skin would become smooth and pink and smell of soap like other children he saw. Rosalie shook her head, again and again, and then she leaned down and kissed the forehead of the boy, got up, walked away, and she hasn't spoken since. We brought her back here, hoping that after a while she would come out of it, but it hasn't happened.

"We were going to tell her that, as it turned out, the boy was cured — his skin is smooth as silk now — but I thought that might only make things worse. If Rosalie thought it was her daughter working through her, she could miss Her even more. It could be heartbreaking. That's why it's called *misericordia*."

*   *   *   *   *

And finally we come to the illustrious Dr. Pincus. After traveling through every continent except Antarctica, he returned to his apartment in Manhattan, his face brown and wrinkled with suntan, and sporting a large unruly beard that gave him the appearance of a hermit. He hardly ever changed his clothes, wearing an old plaid flannel shirt with the sleeves rolled to the elbows, soiled khakis raggedly cut off at the bottom with tears at the knees and held up with a belt of twine, and on his feet sandals that revealed toenails much in need of trimming.

He had developed a habit of sticking his finger in his ear and shaking it violently, as though to clear water from it. This gesture was a result of a hearing problem that he developed in Papua New Guinea when he was struck by lightning while trying to convert members of the Amungme tribe during their pig and sweet potato ritual.

"I had a basic Papua language book," Dr. Pincus explains, "but there are 841 languages in New Guinea, 11 of which have no known speakers, and I must have used the wrong one, or the wrong words from the right one. You don't think much of all their mumbo-jumbo about the gods being displeased until you tell them something they don't much like and lightning strikes you. Fortunately, they were able to revive me with mud paste and lovi lovi berries."

Sadly, Dr. Pincus appears, perhaps as a result of his many travels, to have lost a few marbles along the way.

When asked whether he now believes that She was, in fact, the Messiah come again, or some sort of god, or the Mother of all Gods, as some now believe, he tends to respond as follows:

"Well, as we all know now, God is entirely a brain phenomenon. Once a certain but unspecified number of constituent neuroanatomical centers exist, and connections have been formed, a consciousness emerges, and this consciousness is God. It's a God without intention, but this God does possess a coherent self, a self that implies a certain order, the same order as that found in the universe, and so it is clear that man is made in God's image, as was She, only on a higher plane.

"This universal consciousness, while it lacks intention, still maintains order and prescribes a limit beyond which it can't act. It can contemplate itself and imagine what might lie beyond itself, but it can't act outside of itself. In this way, it's everything. It's all that exists, but it isn't all that can exist.

"Of course, there is a sadness to all this, and that comes from the problem of self, which is central to the concept of God as consciousness, God as a brain phenomenon, because, if God cannot act upon the environment outside of Himself, He can never have a sense of self. He can never know who He is. God can never even know *that* He is. The sad fact is that only we know that God exists; He does not."

To date, no human has yet understood Dr. Pincus's reasoning. But it does not end here, since the question posed to him was whether he believed that She was the Christ come again.

"Imagine the moment," Pincus says, "when the will of this God, after millennia of silence, of inactivity, of, frankly, impotence, when borne out of sadness, this God, finds Himself able to incorporate Himself into a corporeal being, into man or in this case woman, to walk among us and, at long last, to act on His, in this case Her, consciousness, only to find that Her purity is so corrupted by emotionality and the base human drives that come along with having a body that this God, longing for the bliss of the eternal light from which She came, leaves the earth never to return. Just imagine."

Usually, it is at this point that Dr. Pincus looks up at the listener with reddened and misty eyes.

"I am doing all this out of love. It is my love for Her, what She gave me, what I know She can bring to others, that brings me to act in Her place, and to spread the word, Her word."

And when Dr. Pincus is asked exactly what that word might be, he responds as follows.

"That to know God is to be His son or daughter. That only with the end of selfhood comes the fulfillment of love. That we must all act with our hearts."

On parting, Dr. Pincus tells the visitor, "I started out longing for the love I knew, and I ended up finding the love I never knew."

Then, habitually, he opens a drawer of the table in his hall and presses a scrap of metal into the visitor's hand.

"It's what's left of The Singing Machine. Sparky sent me a shoebox of them. If you place it on the windowsill when you go to bed at night, and you listen carefully, you might hear it sing once more."

Then he kisses the visitor on each cheek, and, as he opens the door, says farewell with these words:

"It's a pity you never met her. A damn pity," and Dr. Pincus wipes his nose with his sleeve and closes the door.

CHAPTER 9

Pincus saved until the very end the envelope given to him by the Thaumaturge on the day of Her disappearance. Inside was the translation of the song of The Singing Machine.

The nurse brought him the envelope and his reading glasses. He was too weak to open it, and so she opened it for him.

"Shall I read it to you, Doctor?" she asked.

Pincus shook his head.

The nurse raised the hospital bed, and then Pincus lifted the note before his eyes and read the few words written on it:

I am the song in the machine.
I am the machine in the song.
I am the machine that sings.
I am man.

Pincus smiled. He knew it would be like this. Man: filled to the brim with wonder, wanting more, always more, a world beyond sense and knowledge, a share of the divine light at the origin of it all, struggling, always struggling, to be more than he is, and singing as he goes.

Pincus looked up at the nurse. It was Her. She had come. She had come as She had promised She would come. They would be together for all time.

She ran Her hand lightly down his cheek.

They kissed.

"My Savior," Pincus said.

She laughed, took his hand, and then She and Pincus floated off together.

ABOUT THE AUTHOR

Born in South Bend, Indiana and raised in Rye, New York, Jeremy Leven was educated at St. John's College in Annapolis, Maryland (Philosophy and other liberal arts), Harvard University (Education and Child Psychology), the University of Connecticut (Neuroscience) and Yale Medical School where he was a fellow in the Yale University Department of Psychiatry's Child Study Center.

He has also been a member of the faculty of Harvard, a Professor of Psychopharmacology, Director of a Mental Health Center, and Director of Drug Treatment and Methadone Programs for Western Massachusetts.

Leven has written two critically-acclaimed novels, published in 17 languages: *Creator* (Coward McCann) and *Satan's Psychotherapy* (Knopf), as well as the screenplays for *The Notebook, Creator, The Legend of Bagger Vance, My Sister's Keeper, Real Steel,* and *Wers Glaubt Wird Selig,* among others. He also directed and wrote *Don Juan DeMarco,* and *Girl On A Bicycle.*

Leven divides his time between homes in Connecticut and Manhattan. His wife of 41 years, the acclaimed psychotherapist Roberta Danza, died in 2017. They have five grown children and four grandchildren.

CPSIA information can be obtained
at www.ICGtesting.com
Printed in the USA
BVHW032016290419
546865BV00001B/2/P